"An atom-blaster is a good weapon,
but it can point both ways."

— *Isaac Asimov*

Also by Scott K Bywater

Genesis Makers
Evolution
Evolution 2
Emissary

Emissary 2

The Sixth Extinction

by

Scott K Bywater

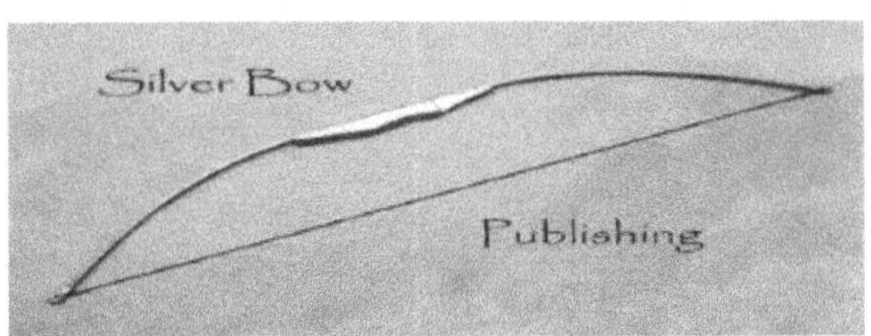

720 Sixth Street, Unit # 5
New Westminster, BC V3L 3C5
CANADA

Title: Emissary 2 – The Sixth Extinction
Author: Scott K. Bywater
Cover Art: by Joshua Nicholas Bywater
Layout and Design: Candice James
Editing: Candice James

ISBN 9781774032572 (softcover)
ISBN 9781774032589 (e-book)
© 2023 Silver Bow Publishing

Library and Archives Canada Cataloguing in Publication

Title: Emissary. 2 : the sixth extinction / by Scott K. Bywater.
Names: Bywater, Scott K., 1962- author.
Identifiers: Canadiana (print) 2023033797X | Canadiana (ebook) 20230437982 | ISBN 9781774032572
   (softcover) | ISBN 9781774032589 (Kindle)
Classification: LCC PR9619.4.B99 E452 2023 | DDC 823/.92—dc23

For the family Bywater
who managed to put up with me
writing at the dining-room table.

*An enormous thank you
to Mary, Josh and Alysha.*

Paragenesis: Mendeleev-3 (M3) mine, Lunar farside

	PRIMARY ORES	**SECONDARY ORES**	
	EARLY	EARLY	LATE
Lead	Galena	Native Lead	Anglesite
Zinc	Sphalerite	Willemite	
Copper	Chalcopyrite	Bornite	Smithsonite
	Tetrahedrite	Tennantite	Azurite
Silver	Acanthite	Native Silver	Dioptase
Bismuth	Bismuthinite	Native Bismuth	Atacamite
		Cornwallite	Mixite
		Olivenite	
		Pseudomalachite	

Contents

Foreword –

Emissary 2 - The Sixth Extinction
"Violence is the last refuge of the incompetent." — *Isaac Asimov*

Mitch and Jessy Taylor are on the Moon, fully suited and collecting mineral specimens, mainly for the Smithsonian in Washington. The oxidised minerals come from an ore deposit in Mendeleev Crater on the *Lunar* Farside and incredibly, they are spectacularly crystallised. It shatters Earthly thinking because it invoked plentiful oxygen, water and pressure on the grey, dead *Moon*...of all places.

Then there is the bizarre object they find sitting within the oxidised zone. God knows how long that had been there. As to how it got there, well, that was a whole other question. Someone or something had clearly placed it there.

As they space hop and time travel through the Cosmos, they are made aware there are only a few truly Earth-like planets in the Universe and they *must* be looked after, no matter what. Enter the Bantha that have taken it upon themselves to be the guardians of those worlds and ensure they are preserved at all costs.

Humanity attempts to achieve the 'no carbon atmosphere' deadline imposed by the Bantha to eliminate carbon energy and implement fusion energy for preservation of planet Earth; but can they?

12

Prologue

Discovery

"Any planet is 'Earth' to those that live on it." *Isaac Asimov*

The rock looked grey and ugly and totally inhospitable from far away. No atmosphere, no life and definitely no hope. Coming closer to its surface it still looked bleak and foreboding. Large and small craters were everywhere, suggestive of a very meagre, protective atmosphere where meteors enjoyed an unimpeded ride. Lava had flowed and dried Eons ago. Grey, greyer and greyest...with a little brown here and there. This was Earth's Moon.

But up close, it was every colour of the rainbow. The rock was truly gorgeous. Colours of yellow and blue dominated, but if you looked close enough, there were reds and greens and oranges all over the place. It was like a subterranean rainbow. The bugs and the minerals especially, shouldn't have been there, if humans were right about their Moon. Yet here they were. The smug inhabitants from the next rock down, were totally wrong. The Moon held surprises even from those who believed they owned it.

Mitch's salt and pepper hair shone in the brilliant light from a distant Sun, despite being hidden behind a visor of chip-proof and vacuum-proof plastic with a thin layer of pure gold to keep ionising particles at bay. Mitch was peering forward, like a statue, surveying the Moon and everything it held.

Jessy gazed at him and thought how good he still looked. He was a God apparently, at least at AASSA and NASA, and he was all hers. Mitch had done just about everything, because unlike most, he wasn't afraid of the vacuum. Respect it, absolutely – fear it, *no*. Bring it on, was his first thought, *if* he believed in it. If he didn't – *forget it*. Not interested. He'd take his suit off and throw it at someone. Mitch was not a shelf stacker at Foodland.

Mitch was rough and tough and obsessed with exploration, wanting to know why it was like it was and how it happened, even though his personal life was fairly much in freefall. Thank fucking God for Jessy, his wife, he often thought. She grounded him when he needed it and pushed him on when he needed it. Jessy was amazing. At least, he thought so. Others thought she was weak and ineffective, held up and backed by Mitch, rather than using the potential she clearly had. But she and Mitch didn't even bother responding to banal insults. It was what it was.

Without her, he was well and truly done for. Mitch had few others that were close - his best friend, Rhys, was dead and the space agency had cut all ties with Rhys's wife which not surprisingly she was very unhappy about. To add to that, his brother and his brother's daughter had been killed in their house by a lunatic who broke in after dark.

Also, his wife's dad had terminal cancer. Apart from that, things were looking great for Mitch. All sunshine and blue skies. *Jesus*, he couldn't believe it sometimes. He'd surely broken a few mirrors. Oh, and he'd been the first human to walk on Mars.

He gazed into space and considered his life as it now was, wondering how many ladders he'd walked under when he was younger. If you took astronautics out of his history, his life would be a complete debacle. Mitch owned a black cat that was in fine health, so it couldn't be that. He definitely hadn't run over it, or even come close to the damn thing. For whatever reason, it refused to come near him, despite a lot of encouragement. It was still running around at home, whining for some poor sod to feed it. But run over it or have it cross his path – *definitely not.* Mitch was very wary of it. And life continued to give him lemons.

1

Oxygen

"Living is a conflict of interest."- *Isaac Asimov*

They were on the farside of the Moon, in M3, specimen hunting in the almost untouched oxidised zone of the orebody. From an economic viewpoint, it was useless to the mine owners, so it was all Mitch's, to do with it as he wished. The mine-owners and NASA were happy to sell it, especially to someone like Mitch. Legally, it belonged wholly and solely to Mitch. Next to them, on the other side of the zone, not far away, was a fully-fledged mining operation that was exploiting a large primary copper, silver-lead and zinc lode, mainly galena, sphalerite and chalcopyrite with some argentite and bornite.

From where Mitch and Jessy were standing, they could see most of the *Jensen-Ortega* (main) headframe and the top of the primary tailings dump. The oxidised fluids formed in a chamber of sorts, sealed off from the thin lunar "atmosphere" that was devoid of everything except some sparse helium and very little pressure indeed.

If it didn't form in a pod, the oxygen and water would have been lost to the surface. A thin layer of KREEP lay over the top of the deposit and held all the oxygen, water and pressure in the chamber. Pressure wasn't lost until the secondary zone was cut and although the Moon's surface was silent as a stone, if it were in a decent atmosphere, it may have made a noise like a deflating balloon.

The primary zone of mineralisation struck downward at 45 degrees and outcropped on the Moon's surface in a spray of altered KREEP that grew into a gossanous hillock on the Moon. A fault had moved almost the entire oxidised zone a few hundred metres to the south, where it was somewhat away from the primary zone of mineralisation. Now, there were two relatively distinct mineral-zones on the Moon – one primary and one secondary, separated by a fault line and a tongue of regular Moon surface. By hand sorting on the primary side, they reached seventy-six percent metal in the primary zone, which was ferried by the Lunar Transide railway complex to the smelter, only a hundred kilometres away, near the Hadrian crater and the Copernican deposit.

NASA had just concluded an investigation into the secondary zone and the presence of oxygen. The occurrence of weathering and erosion in a possibly watery environment was confirmed. *Big fucking surprise.* A report by NASA was forthcoming. The incidence was a first for the Moon and entirely unexpected and stunned the hell out of NASA and the world in general.

The oxidised part of the M3 deposit was quite complex and quite incredible, and totally unexpected. It was basically a conglomerate of deeply weathered manganese oxide, or gossan which was intensely vogued down to the 75-metre level.

On the Moon, you'd expect maybe a smear of azurite or some massive malachite and cerussite but that couldn't be further from the truth. Incredibly, all the secondary fluids were richly oxidised and had crystallised slowly and lavishly.

Within the cavities or vughs, were the lunar secondary minerals, spectacular crystal groups of cerussite, azurite and beautiful mamillary malachite and stunning masses of yellow smithsonite. They were the most incredible specimens ever found, here *or* on Earth. The azurites were even better and bigger than those at Tsumeb in Africa or Bisbee in America. Deep blue and enormous, and amazingly, many were on lunar matrix. As specimens, those from the Moon were unsurpassed.

The characteristic azurite crystals on malachite and then on weathered KREEP were sent to the Smithsonian Institution along with the best libethenites, stolzites, wulfenites and legrandites. They were all extraordinary examples of the species. All came courtesy of Mitch and Jessy. All of them were labelled personally, and they were truly amazing, one-of-a-kind specimens. Museums all over the world were clambering for more, but not necessarily getting any. Demand was higher than high. Supply was very tight indeed.

The most amazing specimen was a large twinned legrandite on a two-foot matrix of weathered KREEP, sprinkled with beautiful, large azurite crystals and all of it covered with a fine druse of libethenite crystals. Bright yellow, coated by deep blue and dark sea green. All crystals were perfect and gem-like, the lustre was mirror-like and unsurpassed. Mitch kept that one for himself – it was a *beauty*.

Both of them made a decent personal income from the specimens, ¾ going to them and a quarter to various charities. Everyone seemed happy with that. The charities on Earth made a killing and were very happy indeed with Taylor Inc.

The best part of the Moon weren't the colours though, or even the crystal size and perfection - they were stunning, make no mistake about it, but these were minor in comparison to the question and the question was, how on Earth do oxidised minerals exist on a world where oxygen and water don't exist, let alone pressure, and according to popular theory that, hasn't existed, in decent quantities since the planetoid formed from the collision of the Mars-sized world with Earth. The Moon didn't have any appreciable atmosphere or pressure, oxygen bearing or not, and never did, and anyone who suggested otherwise was ridiculed and academically neutered and scorned for being foolish in the extreme.

More pressing, however, were the strange goings-on near the base of the oxidised zone. No one could explain that. The presence of oxygen and water was easy in comparison – this, not so much. A bit like the minerals, they definitely had no right being there. This thing -probably even more so. *Much more so.*

An open pit was dug with the mechanical assistance from one of the more friendly M3 techs who "borrowed" an excavator from the mine next-door for the best part of a day. He had control of a machine that was all metal teeth and buckets, and made quick work of the weathered zone, forming benches and paths and everything else that would allow them ease of access. The dump for this pit was full of crystal-bearing rock that was "thrown-out" as gangue.

It was near the base of the hole where things got really interesting. Mitch and Jessy were following a rich lead of lime-green libethenite with unusually large crystals when he broke through into something curiously *disturbing.* "Unexpected" and "troubling" was severely understating it. Mitch stared fixedly at it once it was partly uncovered.

W-What the h-hell is t-that?' Hc blurted, standing up, stumbling backward a few steps and pointing with the blunt end of his rockhammer. '*Holy shit,*' he boomed. He wasn't expecting it.

Jessy was peering intensely at it as well, walking around it, as far as she could go. It was something that was brand new to her – one look was enough to tell her that it definitely didn't belong there. '*What the holy fuck is it, Mitch?*' She said into her mic. Her eyes were huge in the torchlight.

Mitch's voice was crackly through the suit's intercom. '*E-Er...um...I have no idea,*' His bewilderment was written in his stiffly wide eyes. The large crystals of libethenite were forgotten. Mitch saw Jessy's lower lip tremble behind the visor and she held one gloved hand over her stomach, as Mitch met her gaze. What on Earth had they stumbled over?

Jessy stood gawking at it, tilting her head to the side. It had her completely and utterly muddled. It looked very alien. Especially here of all places. Under the ground. What a place to find something like this. Under an oxidised parcel of ore. *How bizarre.* This was way more intriguing than the minerals, and difficult to believe, whatever it was. It looked like something from a different universe.

Very, very odd, Mitch thought, strange, weird, call it what you like, he reckoned. Bottom line - it shouldn't be here, *that much* he knew. Doesn't matter what it was.

'*C-Christ...it's, it's, uh, rippling...moving I-I, um think,*' Jessy stuttered, pointing at the object, trying to move backward but hard up against the rock lentil she couldn't. She peered at the object and the break in the rocks, and what lay below it, pulsing and writhing. It should have been rock-like, more precisely it should have been weathered and oxidised basalt and KREEP, but again, it *wasn't*. There was something peculiar in its place. She tried to study it closely, looking it up and down in the torchlight, not wanting to get too close. Jessy was making all sorts of strange noises. She simply didn't know what it was. Even guessing was hard. There were no parallels in her life she could draw on. She tried to speak but couldn't, all she could do was stare. Jessy tried to work out what it might be – but couldn't. It had no parts she recognised.

'*I can see that it's moving,*' Mitch said loudly and sarcastically, slapping his helmet. '*More like pulsing.*' he added quietly.

Normally Jessy would react savagely if she felt belittled, but there was nothing in her head but fear and intrigue. She was too busy gawking at this thing and wondering about it, to be annoyed by Mitch.

'*But seriously...what the fuck is it? It definitely ain't rock or KREEP,*' Mitch snapped, peering closer by bending down on his haunches and readying his rockhammer. He seemed primed to hit it like a rock and see if the damned thing did anything in response.

'*Der,*' Jessy said, glaring right at him. She knew damn well it wasn't rock, or anything like it. '*Thanks a lot for the insight, Mitch.*' Jessy stood up and stepped back, taking in the entire scene, looking at Mitch sideways.

'*Oh, Christ...whatever Jess...*we should open it up a bit, get a better look at it,' he said, going quiet and staying quiet. Mitch continued to stare at it, seemingly hypnotised by its odd contours and the monochromatic flashing that came from its flat surface, along with the pulsing.

Jessy was still trying to work out what it might be, from its behaviour, but she had nothing. The fact that it was doing *anything* was amazing. It must have been under there for yonks. It was pulsing - that meant it was active. The object had clearly been there for a long time, so doing *anything* was stunning, she supposed. Jessy ignored Mitch and his rants. He could say what he liked, but still, here it was. Buried, but now not buried. It appeared to be tech, of some sort, set in the secondary zone of this deposit. How, why and where? All they had was logic, and they knew how *human* that was. They rightly wondered if it could be relied on in the wider Universe.

'Okay,' he eventually said. 'Rockhammer, right? Dig under it a bit first?' Mitch said with questioning eyes, bending down and peering closer at it. Jessy nodded. The flashing continued. How long had it been doing that for, He wondered? That was the question. All its godforsaken life, or just since they found it. Was it flashing when they found it? Jessy wasn't sure, and nor was he. Had they somehow triggered it into action? What was the true story – did it have sufficient energy to be continuously active?

'Um...yeah, I guess...do the rockhammer thing,' she said tentatively, not really having a clue what they should do next. Mitch wanted to touch it with his rockhammer. She felt like screaming "no" to Mitch but didn't bother. He wouldn't listen to her anyway. He'd just tinker with it more. Mitch was set on auto-pilot, she could see that in his stupid, robotic eyes. He was going to do whatever he needed to do, to find out what this thing was, *his wife be-damned.*

Since returning to Earth, and with the limited integration of four thousand Virijians into a controlled population of people, this was Jessy's first holiday in a long, long time. *And Christ did she need it.* It was Mitch's first holiday, *ever*...at least in recorded history. He was always set to the *'on'* position - brilliant in his field, no one could deny it, but he acted like a fucking robot most of the time. He needed expeditionary stimulation 24/7. Mitch definitely needed to relax. But trouble was, he didn't want to...that's why he loved being an astronaut and pushing things to the limit. It allowed him license to really get down and dirty. Jessy was frequently surprised Mitch was still alive.

The first week of doing very little, they were almost climbing the walls at AASSA, well...he was. They were desperate to escape the boredom, especially Mitch, who was going nuts surrounded by the four walls of the place and doing nothing. Nothing by his standards anyway. They decided to visit and stay for two weeks at the Lunar Sheraton, hoping against hope that it might be a little more interesting, which wouldn't be hard. To say that now was a massive bloody understatement. This thing was *very* interesting.

Actually, Jessy would have been happy just to relax - at home would have been nice. But Mitch made the call, as he usually did. Anyway, she didn't really care, they both wanted *anywhere* but that infernal place called AASSA. Sometimes it was like living with a person who had a battery inserted...somewhere.

The management of the lunar hotel were so happy to have them, they gave it all to them for free - the room, and anything else they sought. The Hotel would make a fortune off the publicity alone. Hundreds, maybe thousands, would follow in Mitch and Jessy's footsteps. Simply because they, *he* was there. When he arrived, they were met with more photographers than a Presidential re-election speech. The hotel drove him from the nearside to the farside by

Roadster, to the M3 deposit, or anywhere he wanted to go for that matter, *chauffeured*. Mitch had never been treated so well. Apparently, this was the life of someone famous.

Mitch and Jessy Taylor were like world royalty. They could stay anywhere and go anywhere...for free apparently. It was amazing. He, *they,* were very popular indeed thanks to Mars. Finally, he seemed to be enjoying himself and kicking back a bit. And now, *this*. It seemed that Mitch attracted strange things, *unique things,* simply by being.

*   *   *

Both of them were standing and gaping at the "thing" they'd unearthed near the base of their mineral dig. Mitch didn't know what to do with it, nor did Jessy. The anomaly just sat there, part of the body of oxidised ore ... for God knows how long.

Looking down, Jessy saw the anomaly encrusted with dirt and crystals of secondary ore, and looking up was the familiar black sky of the Moon. Studded with the brilliance of stars - Arcturus and Alpha Centauri and the variegated colour of gasses and dust and structures known as the Milky Way Galaxy. It was all framed by her helmet.

Mitch dug like a madman, opening up more of the object. The Hotel Manager who drove them personally to and from M3 each day couldn't understand why Mitch and Jessy didn't get someone to dig for them. Afterall, he said animatedly, there'd be a long list of suitors. Everyone would be happy to dig for Mitchell Taylor.

Mitch had told him in no uncertain terms that fossicking for mineral specimens meant getting dirty, it was the only way. *Not* getting some other poor sod to do it for you. *No way.* That was definitely not right, even if it was dressed in a full spacesuit with a chip proof, high tensile visor.

Mitch excavated around what he thought might be the edge but couldn't find one, just more of the same. No edge. It was flat in plan. He was hoping it might be thin, like a plasma TV, but unfortunately it wasn't. In fact, it was as thick as, more like an old fridge. He'd dug and uncovered just shy of three metres by three metres and about two metres in a downward sense. It looked a bit like a black and large, very fat flat screen, buried and set in the orebody with the secondary metal crystals growing around it. There was malachite growing as mamillary masses on its upper surface, near the edge and also down the thing, with dirt and rock, vughs and crystals of copper phosphates and azurite. It seemed this object predated the oxidation event.

Jessy peered at the object with massive eyes, glancing from Mitch to the object, shaking her head. Jessy was further away and able to take a better look at it now.

'*Fuck a duck...,*' she spat, not believing what was happening to them. 'Who would have thought?' Jessy backed away more, shaking her head, pointing at the anomaly briefly with her gloved hand, and vocalised the obvious words into her helmet mic, '*what the hell...is it?*' She whispered harshly, not properly believing what she was gawking at. 'It is a what...a box of sorts...buried, *merged* into the oxidised zone of this, whatever it is,' she said, her face reddening and sweat standing out on her skin as she peered at it and the oxidised minerals that surrounded it. Jessy was completely bamboozled by it. The view was incredible and ridiculous.

'It's part of this zone Mitch, but this *thing* is definitely an add-on...which leads to an obvious conclusion. *Seriously...what fucking next?*' Jessy spat, looking squarely at Mitch, still shaking her head, which in a helmet, was a bit painful because it dug into her neck.

He agreed with his wife. Nothing was more relevant, he reckoned, ogling the crazy looking object. What the hell was it doing *here*, of all places and who or what placed it? Looking at it, he had no answer to "who", "what" or "why". It definitely shouldn't be here, *period*. That's about all he knew. Who or what placed it is extremely intriguing, Mitch thought.

Jessy knew what this thing represented. Both assumed the other knew, which was true, so they didn't bother broaching it out loud. How would the world react? They knew about Virija so the hard work was done. Still, this was so close and very different and more personal in nature. The Fermi Paradox was already gone, now it was shattered and only a memory.

Mitch shook his head and gazed at Jessy in total astonishment, still holding his rockhammer aimlessly. He wondered what sort of handprints...or paw-prints were on its strange black surface. Mitch stood totally still and stared at the object, studying it for a long time and very carefully. It looked like a Plasma TV on top. It was, however, quite thick. Technology? He wondered, it seemed to fit the bill.

They could free it, she supposed, by breaking rock around it. It seemed very wedged in though. The way it looked - it might never come free, no matter how much digging they did – but they'd try.

*   *   *

Jessy looked at her silver Seiko and saw that Jax wasn't due to pick them up for hours. What should they do with this thing? Leave it, in situ or dig it up completely, *if* they could? She peered at Mitch who looked as confused and muddled as she was. What should they do? Both had no idea. They kept staring at it, utterly perplexed. Mitch was gazing with focus, blinking, breathing fast, and could feel the moisture everywhere, as he sweated freely inside his suit. This object had part of him.

After a long time of doing nothing, Mitch was getting fired up, tilting his head, his curiosity with this shiny new object almost ready to explode, his interest in whatever it was, was at maximum. Maybe the object would do something...*eventually*. If they gave it time. He sure hoped so. But maybe he could coax something from it by being proactive.

Jessy felt similar emotions to her first sight of *One's* orb above Titan. *Massive awe and disbelief* – and she remembered it washing through her as she gazed at it. It was like that now. The same thing couldn't be happening again, surely? The *biggest* thing had already been revealed - nothing could be bigger than that. But this object looked like it had something to reveal – it had that odd, exotic look to it. Jessy knew her mind and its convolutions were probably adding that, but still, it looked very strange and out-of-place indeed. She knew it wasn't placed here for no reason. That was a no-brainer.

Mitch watched Jessy carefully and saw her peer down at her own rockhammer and then glance back at the anomaly. Mitch was pretty sure he knew what she was thinking.

'So...,' he stared at Jessy with huge eyes, 'shall I give it a try with my rockhammer?' He, like Jessy, could feel it pulling and dragging at him, so he assumed it might accept an object. If it didn't, nothing lost, he reckoned. Fortune favoured the brave, Mitch thought, if placing your hammer near something could be considered "brave". He chuckled at the prospect. Every time, he looked directly at the surface of the object, he felt goodwill filling his body as if it was telling him that it was benevolent and benign. '*What a crock of shit,*' he mumbled inside his helmet.

But seriously, what was this damn thing doing here, and how long had it been here, and did it explain why the rock above it was so oxidised? Maybe that's why it was in and amongst, *under* actually, the colourful ore. Had oxygen somehow seeped through from the "other side", and if it had, where exactly did it come from? He could sense questions everywhere he looked. Every time, he closed his eyes, there they were – written in bold.

That was the real question though, front and centre - *where* the *fuck* did the object come from and who or what placed it and why? Mitch knew there was water in the form of ice in craters on the Moon and that obviously had oxygen in it, but no way this moon would hang onto it if it sublimated. So, he reckoned that one was ruled out, but he wasn't totally sure. He was no astrophysicist or geologist. Mitch wasn't sure of anything.

An atmosphere containing oxygen and water, or anything really was pretty much a no-go on the gravity-deficient Moon. A nagging voice in the back of his brain kept saying that *anything was possible.* And it *was*, because the zone of secondary minerals, through a geological and geomorphic twist was protected from the thin, pressure-less atmosphere of the Moon.Therefore, in the absence of decent gravity and atmospheric pressure, it seemed unlikely that the Moon ever had oxygen in decent amounts, so perhaps this object *was* the answer in providing the necessary materials. Worry creased the fine lines in his face as he contemplated the scene in front of him. It all seemed very odd and probably dangerous. He started breathing more heavily and ended up gasping as he contemplated actually doing what he was thinking about.

'You may as well do it,' she blurted to Mitch, 'try it, and see what happens.' She watched him closely as he carefully picked up his rockhammer. Jessy moved back a bit as he flashed it around like a fucking sword. '*Jesus Christ*,' she bleated, 'be careful Mitch, please.' She knew he'd do it, with or without her okay.

'*Here we go*...I guess,' he said, glaring at Jessy. He held the rockhammer in front of the anomaly, and nothing happened. The look on his face told the story – total bemusement – he'd convinced himself that the hammer would be pulled in. But there was just the status-quo, and no motion within the object at all. He just crouched there, in front of the object, with his rockhammer hanging in space, doing nothing at all. Mitch felt pretty stupid, having been rejected by the anomaly.

There was no pull from the object at all. It had stopped "sucking" completely. Everything was quite still. The thing had seemingly stopped doing whatever it was doing. There was no flashing or anything – it was just a black surface. It was as if it had "turned off" or gone into "standby" mode. Whatever had happened, it was now completely inactive.

Mitch continued to feel daft. Here he was, dressed in a slimline astrosuit with a backpack and a full helmet and visor, crouched in front of God-knew-what and holding a rockhammer as some sort of "offering". It was all quite bizarre. He looked like a goose. All that inside a farside Moon crater, at the base of some crazy oxidized orebody that, all things considered, shouldn't be there. It was truly insane – the picture was crazy. Mitch felt like he was prostrating in front of the object like a religious fanatic. He stood up in the low gravity and dusted himself off and looked at the anomaly deliberately, totally exasperated.

Mitch decided to really go for it, despite the lack of pull from the object. He stuck the head of the hammer *into* the black surface. As he believed it wasn't a surface, but some sort of a horizon without a definitive hard "surface". Nothing happened as he suspected. He waited and watched. Then a deep, vibrating and pulsing noise started, and the hammer disappeared. *Gone.* Pulled into the maelstrom.

S-Shit...gone?' Jessy said, with slowly widening eyes, staring at the anomaly and then glancing at Mitch's empty gloved hands. Her mouth moved but nothing came out. Finally, she coughed and said, *'W-W-Where?'*

Mitch saw the rockhammer disappear and his eyes widened to hoops. '*Er, well...uh, fucked if I know, it just, er...went,*' he blurted, ogling his own hands, expecting to see a burnt, bloody mess. The rockhammer was fairly ripped from his gloves like someone extremely strong had torn it away, and it presumably went wherever the other end was. That is, the *exit* of this thing. Both of them assumed there was one...but maybe there wasn't. Maybe the rockhammer simply entered this thing and went nowhere.

'*Yikes,*' Jessy trilled, thinking about it. Maybe the hammer was only a few feet away, she thought. Or maybe...

'Could be anywhere, I guess,' Mitch said, staring fixedly at the object, which was, again, totally still and lifeless. *No movement or lights.* His mouth dropped open, wondering who the hell might have put the object here...and more importantly perhaps, *why* it was put here? Who and why, he didn't want much - anything would do really...maybe just the *why* part? It was in an intriguing spot, no one could deny that. Why was it buried? Was it something or part of something that was incredibly dangerous?

Mitch knew he had to tread carefully. Leaving it alone wasn't an option. He *needed* to find out what it was. He knew tinkering with something you don't understand was inherently dangerous and forbidden by AASSA and NASA. *Fuck 'em,* Mitch thought – I'm here, they're not. Ultimately, after reams of approvals, it would come down to someone like him to get down and dirty with it. And here he was – already in place. As far as Mitch was concerned, *it was time saved.* Like Jessy, he felt like he did when *One's* Sphere was seen unexpectantly riding high above Titan, doing not much at all except orbiting – full of information about the solar system and the greater Universe. But giving nothing away. In regard to *One's* Sphere, if it wasn't for the Virijians, humans would have been clueless forever. Decoding the object wasn't an option. It was must.

Mitch was still breathless, rubbing the back of his neck and feeling dizzy, which came and went, and that told him all he needed to know. This anomaly had fully captured his interest and the damn thing baffled him in virtually every way. He wondered if the thing was in part intelligent. Did it know he was gawking at it? Nothing would surprise him. Mitch thought about kicking it or kneeing it, but decided against it. It also scared him. He had to remember - *anything* was possible in the most literal of senses. It could be extremely unsafe to touch it, which terrified him but also intrigued him.

Jessy looked tired or drunk or something - stumbling and then slowly and dustily coming to a halt. Her voice was quaking and hitching. 'S-So...do w-we just wait and h-hope that the r-rockhammer...comes back?' Jessy said, 'or do we wait until Jax comes at 4pm to pick us up?' She was scratching at her cheek and temple, trying to think quickly, but it didn't really work. She could almost hear her brain clunking. Jessy was totally confused about their next step. She ping-ponged her gaze from the object to Mitch. This was his domain but she didn't like his expression. His entire face had blanched and his eyes were as wide as they would go. Mitch's level of intrigue and interest was well above ten. That meant trouble for all of them, she was sure.

In actuality, right now, Mitch wasn't sure what he should do either. He tried to think of something to say to Jessy but struggled with that too. He could only think of inanities and platitudes. He knew she hated those. Mitch clawed at his chin and really thought about the object, tilting his head to the side and pursing his lips, thinking hard, inside his helmet and visor. He'd thought of *One* and the Virijians and dismissed both out of hand. It wasn't them, he decided. They didn't work on such obscure scales, he was sure.

Mitch said, 'What do you think we should do?' He knew what had to happen. At least he thought he did. Definitive thinking was hard under these circumstances. He thought he should include Jessy on their way forward. She'd like that, even if she had nothing to add.

At that moment, amid a huge amount of vibration and dust, as though it emanated from the core of the Moon, the rockhammer returned as though spat from the anomaly, doing a couple of cartwheels in the dirt and coming to a halt on the rocks turned green by veins of malachite and libethenite.

'*Fuck me*,' Mitch exclaimed, peering at the rockhammer now sitting in the dirt on top of the mineralisation. '*Holy shit*,' he added, into his mic, surprised by its sudden return.

Jessy stared at the hammer while Mitch slowly walked up to it, her head flinching back a bit as she shook her helmet to get hair out of her eyes. She thought the hammer would eventually come back but that didn't reduce the shock, especially with earthquake-style vibration and a storm of dust accompanying it. Then *bang*, it was back. At no time did she lose eye-contact with the hammer. Jessy looked at it sideways. It looked strange and very different indeed.

'Is that my hammer?' Mitch queried, gawking at the handle. It appeared ridiculously old and worn.

'It looks, uh...very different indeed,' Jessy said, trying to scrutinise it from a distance. She didn't approach it and acted as though it might bite.

Mitch picked it up without a second look and surveyed its severely weathered handle, squinting at it through his visor. *'Jesus Christ,'* he barked. It looked ancient.

Where in God's name had this thing been? His mouth fell open as he looked carefully at it. It looked like an old explorer's hammer, like Robert Scott's from Antarctica maybe. The strange thing was, it was almost brand-new when it went in, but now it looked as old as ....well, just as old as. Where had the fucker been and better still, who or what had used it? He wondered what finger...or paw or *whatever* prints were now on it. Mitch continued to swear under his breath which Jessy heard perfectly through her helmet.

'Uh, yeah, it's different alright,' Mitch said, regaining his composure a little, 'this thing was pretty new when it went in, and *not so now.*' He mumbled something under his breath again, glancing over at Jessy grinning. 'It's the reverse of you, looking younger every year, this thing looks a hundred years old,' he said, chuckling a bit. The horror of it hadn't dawned on him yet.

Jessy surveyed him carefully, feeling very anxious, and despite the potential peril of their situation, here he was chuckling like a bozo. Live and learn, she supposed.

'You are so full of it, Mitch, I don't even know where to start or even if I want to,' she said, really meaning it, eyeing the reflection off the object's semi-lustrous surface. That thing had inhaled the hammer with nary a sideways glance. Jessy glared at Mitch and swallowed hard, tapping her foot, freeing dust from the lunar surface.

'II think we should focus on the hammer, not on you, or on what rubbish you might say,' Jessy eyed him with a focussed gaze, mouth opening and closing with something approaching scepticism, and hoping the next words out of his mouth weren't about him.

'You might be right,' he said distractedly, peering at the aged rockhammer and its split wooden handle and heavily rusted head. Wherever it went, it went from new to old...*very old apparently.*'

Did that happen on the way there or on the way back, or both, she wondered? Her head was spinning. Mitch was similarly curious and totally without any answers. Everything in front of them was a mystery.

Mitch glared at his hammer sideways. 'Where have you been, you little fucker?' Mitch whispered, staring at the rockhammer blankly, walking slowly up to it in the low gravity. 'There are two options, I suppose, Jessy. The first is to send a *Go-Pro* through, the second is, one of us goes through. We're suited up so we're good to go I suppose.' Mitch turned around and gazed at the object. 'We, um...don't have a Go-Pro...so that's out.'

Silence pervaded the dig as they took stock of the object and where they were and what Mitch had said. Jessy thought about it and didn't like it, not one bit. She shook her head furiously. Mitch was clearly thinking about it very seriously. His brow was furrowing and he gave Jessy a curt nod, still thinking deeply. His mind was already made up.

I-I...*shit Mitch*, I hadn't thought that far ahead,' Jessy mumbled. 'I don't think either of us should go. It could end in vacuum you know...*space*.' She yelled the last word. Her face was drained of blood and her breathing was bursting in and out. Her heart started jackhammering in her throat. 'No way it's going to be one of us, remember what happened to the hammer?' She uttered loudly, glancing at Mitch gravely. Daring him to say it. And get his head bitten off if he said the wrong thing.

Jessy reckoned Mitch was a fucking lunatic, totally obsessed by the *need. The obsession*. Well, she wouldn't accept it, but it would do no good. He would still do whatever he wanted; she was dealing with Mitchell Taylor. She could feel the anger and the heat rising inside her suit. He'd put his entire life at risk, his son Josh and her, his wife – *everything*, just to feed this...*obsession* of his. There was way more to life than exploration – and she'd told Mitch as much a thousand times. And it all made zero difference. He was as bad now as ever. Probably worse.

'If not us...who?' Mitch said softly, reading her mood. Jessy was tapping her foot lightly, almost ready to rumble, almost ready to detonate. Mitch had to tread very carefully - he could see that. Jessy was ready to let fly. One wrong word and it'd be on. By "wrong word", he meant anything to do with hopping into the anomaly – like his hammer. He wouldn't give up though. Somehow, he wanted Jessy's approval. He'd go without it if he had to, but he'd prefer her blessing or at least her understanding.

We have to go, there's no one else, what are we gonna do, throw Jax in unsuited when he arrives to pick us up?' He said, staring accusingly at Jessy.

'Don't be ridiculous...'

'There you go then,' Mitch interrupted, 'I go, and come back, richer in knowledge about where this thing goes. It goes *somewhere*. Remember, water and oxygen came though, so...that's good, right?' Mitch felt his confidence growing. He ran his hand across his suited chest and smoothed it down, as he waited for Jessy to respond. He smiled feebly at his wife.

'Maybe,' Jessy said quickly and quietly. 'That's only a tenuous theory...or maybe, Mitch, it's a one-way ticket to hell. Perhaps it connects with a deep *fucking* ocean.' She turned around to front the rock face, clenching her toes, thinking how irrational and gung-ho he was at times. Jessy knew what was going to happen. And she didn't like it at all. It just showed the depth of his obsession and what was most important to him. She'd been married long enough to see their future. It wouldn't matter much what she said, or what she did, he would listen carefully and make all the right noises, then take no notice of what she was saying at all. The bastard would completely do his own thing. Mitch would do whatever he thought was best for Earth and best for Mitch. That was the Mitchell Taylor way. He was a former test pilot after all. His family was a distant priority for him, and that really pissed Jessy off. Josh didn't deserve it.

'Do you remember your stupid hammer, Mitch? The state of it when it returned?' She glared at him best as she could through a visor, in a last-ditch effort to make him see sense. 'The entire hammer was as good as a Goddamned *fossil*.' Jessy spat.

'*Jesus, thanks for the rev-up,*' he said, giving a shocked, deeply pained look, reckoning she was at least half right. His confidence was waning. Anywhere literally meant *anywhere*. Surprisingly though, he felt okay about it. Being a former test pilot, he was conditioned and comfortable with risks. Jessy wasn't. Especially with a little boy who was highly dependent on his parents.

Mitch felt sure going "in" would lead him somewhere safe. Somewhere with hard ground, pressure and an atmosphere he could breathe and would keep him snug and protected. When he wasn't looking at it, he felt less certain. In fact, he was terrified. But peering directly at it, he felt good, it appeared benign and altruistic. But was it really? Was his confidence and acceptance of it misdirected? He wondered, gazing at it. That was foremost in his mind.

He needed to comprehend the risks – entering the damn thing could kill him instantly if it led somewhere unfriendly to humans. Mitch needed to do this thing with full understanding of the possible consequences. If he did, he knew it'd be the first time he'd done that. Forget the test pilot crap, he thought. That was all macho bullshit. Personal risks were always as scary as hell.

'There's me and Josh to think about,' Jessy said, getting hotter and hotter, as she considered it, knowing full well he'd do what he wanted anyway. But she put it out there to see what came back. She'd tried it before and it hadn't worked. She'd gotten zero "family-matters" back.

'You think I don't know the risks? *Jesus...of course I do,*' Mitch shrilled. 'The point is, if I don't go and go now, the jugheads at USPA will get involved, because they pretty much own the Moon, right? And then there's NASA. The approvals will be never-ending and it will go on forever. I'm a former test pilot, I was the first on Mars, and I don't need to remind you about CX-1. I'm suited up and ready to go Jess. Right *now*. And the approval would eventually be forthcoming from New York and Washington for me to go, but it'll take time. I'm the obvious choice...*and* I'm here. Look at me Jess.' Mitch held his arms out and looked down at his suit, and then glanced at Jessy, smiling widely.

'Oh...you're *here* allright Mitch...*whatever*,' Jessy snapped, playing the only card she could think of that had a chance of influencing Mitch. The pity card. 'Me and Josh'll be fine,' she said. Her jaw tight as a drum as she looked down, trying to reign in the frustration she was feeling with her husband. Jessy surveyed him closely and didn't need to wonder long if her strategy had worked.

'Okay, good...I, uh...think,' Mitch whispered, not totally sure if Jessy was serious or not. 'I will go and hopefully come back armed with information,' he said, smiling hopefully at Jessy, one that wasn't returned. Jessy didn't feel well at all. She knew what was in front of her. Jessy could feel the moisture of cold sweat under her eyes.

She was suddenly cold all over and almost fainted at the mosaic of ghastly thoughts that were grinding through her mind. Jessy dug fingernails into her thighs until it hurt, which brought her back to some fragile semblance of reality that didn't last very long. *Shit*, so much for that avenue, Jessy thought, but she was hardly surprised with Mitch, annoyed – yes, *shocked* – no. She was used to his reckless and selfish behaviour. If that stemmed from being a test-pilot, he could have it. It was bullshit. Very stressful and potentially destructive to families.

He took his age-worn rockhammer and chipped away enough of the rock overhang to ensure there was sufficient room for him to get to the object. It was still a tad tight for his dimensions. He had four hours and 45 minutes of air left so he was going okay. Sweat beaded his forehead inside the helmet and his arms ached from the rocks he'd pounded. The sweat on his forehead wasn't from exertion though.

He peered over at Jessy who was making her way slowly toward him. It was time to go. He felt the rush of discovery envelop him. And the terror of abject failure. Mitch was petrified about dying, but more scared about somehow disappointing Jessy. He thought she was somehow urging him on with her combative behaviour.

'*Okay hero, go your hardest,*' she said, finding it difficult to take his decision seriously. 'W-What if you don't come back?' Jessy whined and stuttered, 'what do I do if, after ten minutes, if there's nothing?' She'd gone from confident and deriding to an emotional wreck inside a couple of seconds. Jessy wore an expression he hadn't seen before. It was soft and emotional but a hint of anger danced in her eyes. She couldn't wait to hear his answer. He was being Mitch the narcissist. Big time. And she never liked that.

'It wouldn't be here if it went somewhere lethal. I truly believe that' Mitch pursed his lips in thought narrowing his eyes. He was trying to convince Jessy and himself too. 'This zone of altered ore needs water and oxygen which was partly due to a meteorite but not all of this, *no fucking way,*' Mitch exclaimed, 'it needed a long-term supply of air and pressure, which presumably it had with this thing. It came from somewhere that was or is *alive* with oxygen.'

'We don't know anything about it,' Jessy said. 'It's not venting any EMAR at the moment so w...'

Mitch spoke over top of her, a big mistake. If he was trying to piss Jessy off – job well done. He continued to talk over her, 'an object has to be shown to the anomaly first, to elicit some sort of response, like the hammer,' he said, holding both thumbs up to Jessy, after he'd just talked loudly over her objections and treated them like they didn't matter a dram. He looked and sounded like a complete idiot with his thumbs in the air and a forced smile on his face. She felt like walking up and punching him but managed to abstain.

What an absolute goose, she thought, staring right at him. Jessy contemplated his glorious history and continued to peer at him, wondering what was wrong with him now. Why doesn't he show some of that glory to her? Would this be his final act of stupidity, or would it be another notch in his NASA belt. No doubt he hoped so, but she wasn't so sure. In fact, she had massive reserves. Despite her irritation with him, Jessy hoped with all her might it would be fine. She had little doubt he would give it a good go. The odds of dying had to be high though. Jessy really didn't understand why he was going through with it. The idiot had so much to live for. His days of "testing things" was over.

His breath came in quick shallow gasps as he ogled the pulsing anomaly. He sure as hell hoped that it worked as he thought it would. Of course, and that was his biggest worry, he could age severely while he was in there, alive or not, wherever *there* was. Theoretically, he might arrive back nearly dead of old age, or be exactly the same. '*Fuck me,*' he whispered to himself. '*I need to do this,*' he steeled himself, breathing and whispering forcefully. Mitch knew what he had to do. This was surely the ultimate in exploration. Mitch needed to get this over with. Mitch needed to prove it to himself – he needed to prove that he still had it.

'I'll see you when I get back, okay?' He knew he had to do this, it was his destiny, he could *feel* it bubbling and fizzing, urging him on. He could feel a strong, almost fierce calling. Still, it was difficult. When it came down to it, he was terrified of this odd object. But there was somehow a higher calling. It beckoned silently to him, just by him gawking at the damned thing.

*   *   *

Mitch recognised it for what it was – the need, the absolute compulsion to *explore*. He'd had it since he was a boy. It was a fully-fledged *obsession*. He could do nothing about it. And quite frankly didn't want to. He enjoyed taking risks, exploring for the greater good. He needed to show the world that Mitch Taylor still had it. So far it had served him well. The fact that the anomaly pulled at him and invited him in when he looked at it, didn't help either. He was fully, *entirely* under its spell.

Jessy swallowed, nervously holding her breath, staring as if she was in a trance or a spell. She was resigned to him going now. He'd made up his mind. In this state-of mind, Jessy knew that words of caution, no matter how well intentioned or how loud were nothing more than whispers in a windstorm. 'Bye Mitch, see you in a few minutes, *right*?' Jessy shrilled. She was terrified.

He lined himself up with the anomaly sat flat at the base of the pit. They were totally alone at 11.30 AM Farside Time, the sky was black, and star-filled, the dusty lunar landscape quite bright with the huge Sun at about three-quarter height. To Mitch, everything seemed ready. All that was left was him and it.

Mitch sat on the anomaly until a vibration commenced and the lunar dust started rising. It stopped after about ten seconds.

Then with his heart beating like a drum in his throat, Mitch very slowly disappeared and the vibration stopped at the same time, replaced by supreme stillness. The lunar talcum slowly sank to the ground Jessy walked slowly up to the object and sat on her haunches in her full suit and surveyed the object very closely. It looked exactly the same as before, even though it had taken Mitch. She was convinced it wouldn't work, despite the rockhammer – *boy, was she wrong*. It took Mitch, lock, stock and barrel, as soon as he sat on it.

'Come back to me Mitch.' Her voice was shaking and her heart was racing inside her suit. She struggled to believe he'd actually done it and done it so quickly. Maybe she should've tried to stop him with more vigour, but then she realized what a hopeless task it would've been after he'd made his stupid mind up. It would've been a total and utter waste of energy. Mitch would've pushed her away and gone anyway. He saw it as *his* job to tie down exactly what the damn thing was. In this scenario, where it was a choice between exploration or testing something truly intriguing, he was the very embodiment of "impossible to deal with", she thought, shaking her head, angry that he was actually gone. She wondered where that left her and Josh.

The real question was ... where in God's name had he gone, and what the hell was he facing now, she wondered. What sort of environment was Mitch in? Jessy squeezed her eyes shut and whimpered something incomprehensible to herself. She stamped her foot on the ground in annoyance, resulting in a cloud of dust enveloping her that gradually fell back to the ground.

2

Habitable

"Nothing has to be true, but everything has to sound true."
— *Isaac Asimov*

Mitch looked himself up and down. Everything seemed to be in the right place. He was right - he knew he'd be right - he was *alive* and had a hard surface under him. Thinking of Jessy, he grinned and chuckled. 'I fucking well told her so,' he said curtly to no one, still laughing evilly to himself. Mitch was pleased to be where he was.

But where the hell was, he – what place was this? It had to be an asteroid or more than likely a planet, didn't it? Mitch asked himself hopefully, pushing back against a mostly dirt wall. The wall he was pushing into seemed to be made of rock and dirt, it was certainly hard. He knew he wasn't where he used to be, that much was obvious. He'd clearly shifted. And importantly, he seemed to be safe and he felt okay, which was critical. But where had he been sent and he wondered if this was where his rockhammer went?

Mitch settled down and eyed his surrounds for the first time, it looked like he was in a cave of sorts, the anomaly, pretty much a copy of the one he'd just used, was set in the wall behind him, which he'd simply fallen out of. Onto the dirt, in an untidy heap. Mitch was surprised to just shift and then effectively fall out of an object that was set in a wall. That was an odd setup. This place had Earth-like gravity, so it must be a planet, he supposed.

Mitch was just happy that he appeared on solid ground and not in space somewhere. If it turned out to be an asteroid, that'd be okay. Anything remotely solid was a good result, but an asteroid probably wouldn't have this gravity.

He drew his legs in and stood up in his suit, suddenly realising he had no recollection of either travelling through the anomaly or ending up on the ground. Standing up tentatively, in what felt pretty much like Earth, he rubbed his chin, having no idea how it all happened. It was reasonable to assume; that it was instant transmission, as unlikely as that was. Mitch asked himself again *what* he'd expected? Essentially, he got what he asked for. He had his feet on solid ground. Mitch had a strong feeling that he'd end up somewhere "safe". Now, he just needed to work out where the hell he'd gone.

The wall directly behind him had a passage that narrowed alarmingly, to nothing, not far behind him. It seemed to end in a rocky, dusty wall, with a small, shallow depression in it. He'd prefer not to go in that direction – it looked like a fairly solid wall. Instead, ahead of him was a large cave opening that seemed to lead outside, onto a reasonably flat area, that appeared well lit, seeming like the middle of the day in the mid latitudes. It was a no-brainer which direction to go. He wondered if he was still in the Milky Way Galaxy.

Mitch felt sure he'd find more answers in the direction of the light which was streaming in. Fully suited, breathing oxygen from his fan-driven backpack and hearing only the staccato rasp of his own breathing, he ambled slowly to the entrance of the cave, expecting anything and everything, then moved onto a ledge that gave him a fabulous panorama of his new home. It was definitely a *rocky planet*, as he thought.

'*Jesus, holy fuck*,' he spat into his visor, as he ogled the odd landscape. Looking out, he was bemused and muddled, scrutinising the view, not of green plants, but of black or dark grey foliage and two very close, reddish stars that were quite dim. The sight was absolutely incredible. This definitely wasn't Earth, in fact, it was *nothing* like it...apart from the gravity.

Amazingly, the sky here was coloured bright purple because of the scattering of compounds in the atmosphere by the severely reddened light from the two relatively close stars. *Wallah, a purple sky.* With his eyes closed, he felt like he might still be on Earth, but with eyes open, one look put paid to that idea. Mitch was unquestionably elsewhere. The view was quite incredible. Very, very, different from Earth. It looked alien indeed and Mitch quickly realised he'd been sent out of the solar system. Probably *way* out. The whole lot was very different from Earth, down to the colour of the foliage, and the sky. The fact that there was foliage at all meant there was land-life and active evolution, and to Earth, that meant the Fermi Paradox was definitely no longer a paradox. Mitch and others already knew that, with the Virijians and with the events that he'd been privy to. It was clear to him that where suitable conditions existed - life would find a way.

Mitch thought about getting back to the Moon and instantly felt hot and started sweating, *panic-stricken*, running back to the anomaly to make sure it would still activate. He thought it would activate on demand, whenever he needed it to. He was wrong. Deep down he knew it'd be a problem, clearly it wasn't meant to be a "*whenever gateway*".

'*Fuck, shit...why won't this piece-of-shit turn on*,' Mitch screamed at the object, flicking his head and helmet so his hair exited his eyes, peering hatefully at the anomaly. It still refused to turn on, despite multiple attempts to sit on the stupid thing. He returned to the ledge and sat down roughly in the dirt, annoyed and totally muddled. What to do he wondered? He *had* to return, or Jessy would be a write-off for the rest of eternity.

If and when he did finally return, she would kill him, he was sure of that, if nothing else. Mitch pictured her angry, nasty face yelling all sorts of insults. He couldn't wait to return to that. Mitch peered outward and pondered what planet he might be on and where that planet might be located. The question of why and how, was way too hard...maybe he'd contemplate that later. Perhaps when it was dark. *If it got dark*, which he thought it would, based on the position of the suns in the sky and the vegetation. Of course, their position in the sky could be orbital inclination, or maybe this world was even tidally locked? Time would tell. Right now, he knew fuck all. This place was a total unknown.

He didn't know if this planet rotated. It might be he was in the eyeball of what was an icy planet. Time may well be a *place* on this world if it was tidally locked by the dual stars. They seemed close enough. So, it might be like the Moon, with the same face always fronting the red suns. It hadn't gotten darker which wasn't surprising, but the suns, both of them, had gotten slightly lower in the sky, which wasn't definitive, but suggested it wasn't an eyeball planet. Anyway, he was here, that was the reality. The details were just icing.

But the only means of returning to Earth had seemingly been withdrawn. The damned object wouldn't turn on, so he was stuck here it seemed. At least until he got it going again. So, he guessed he should explore the place a bit, there was little else to do. Explore, and of course think about Jessy, and Josh. Mitch *had* to find a way back to her. If there was a way here, there'd hopefully be a way back, he thought, hopefully. What a load of nonsensical crap, he reckoned after the idea crystalised between his ears. Whomever placed the object on the Moon may have made it for one-way travel only. Mitch reviled the thought and tried not to entertain it. Positive thinking, in these situations, was critical – he was told that by several MD's, it was the chink in his armour. He was way too pragmatic and too much of a realist.

Mitch looked out at the dark landscape and questioned whether he needed a pressure suit and helmet at all. He was also wondering what might be out there. Maybe nothing. Was there mobile animal life to go along with the strange, coloured vegetation – and would they hurt him? Mitch looked up and hoped to God there was an active and effective magnetosphere on this world to stand in the way of charged particles. Or he could be dead quickly, and unpleasantly. It was clear that they were very close to the small, reddish stars. He had little doubt they'd give off a number of ionising nasties.

Mitch felt reasonably sure he wouldn't be offered this chance just to die ugly not long after he arrived. Besides, this planet must have a decent atmosphere to sustain all that vegetation, so a magnetosphere probably did protect this planet – or the atmosphere would have been blown into space by these close red stars. That wasn't anywhere near definitive – there were no facts to back it up - it's just how he felt.

Mitch jumped onto his haunches, stood up and ambled slowly down the rocky hill toward the dark vegetation thick on the plain below. All his fears were flashing through his mind, mainly, he was concerned that there was something to be feared in there...something with sharp teeth and claws that would see him as "food." The whole ecosystem scenario came back at him. He was fundamentally a meat-bag, ripe for the picking by all and sundry.

From where he was, the forest or whatever it was, looked totally amorphous...but that was probably his eyes. Mitch could see fine up close, but further away his vision was shit. He refused to even contemplate glasses or contacts, not because of ego, he said. So much bullshit, Jessy thought, he was damn near blind without his glasses. He just refused to accept it.

All things being equal, the vegetation should have been green, but it wasn't, it was virtually black, and it was everywhere. It was a thick forest, but very dark in colour. Mitch was sure he could see anthracitic tree-like things in there. Clearly, evolution, was in synch with the starlight being received from the two dim looking stars. The vegetation wanted to get as much energy as it could from the severely reddened and depleted light. And the chlorophyll or maybe retinol or whatever substituted for it, was very dark, apparently getting energy from all colours of light, leaving only the very dark "colours" to be reflected. Mitch was stunned by the view but it made sense. Afterall, the small, red stars were very different to the Sun, certainly in terms of the EMAR they produced.

He walked over black grass, deeply rooted in dark loamy soil which gradually transitioned into full-blown forest. From here he reckoned it looked like pretty typical sub-tropical rainforest, just a very different colour.

He'd tried the object three times without it "turning on", so he guessed it wasn't going to activate. It was time to see if there was anything on this world that could help him. *Food,* he reckoned, for a start. Then water and shelter. He also needed to be wary of other possibly mobile members of the environment. From the outside, he would say no, they don't exist, but, well...who knew? He needed to get a lot closer to have an informed guess. At the moment, it was just unfounded wishful thinking. There was no sound apart from a bit of "swooshing", he could hear through his sound grills. There was no movement on the ground, only in the upper parts of the trees. Wind, he thought.

Mitch had broad strands of a bamboo-like growth in either hand. It was sharp at the top and would act as a weapon, should he need it. They were pretty pathetic really, but they provided some semblance of security as he entered the truly unknown. He really hoped he didn't need them, because, as a weapon, they sucked. But really, the lack of sound in the forest meant nothing. There could be all sorts in there, and he knew it. Predators made it their business to be quiet. Mitch could restate all that test pilot crap in his head, but that's all it was...*crap.* He was terrified.

If there was a largish predator in there that happened to be hungry, he was in serious trouble indeed. Being a test pilot or *whatever* wouldn't save him. Mitch realised there'd be no defending against a killer that was serious, in its own backyard. He'd be screwed. He could wave the bamboo around and even use it in a stabbing motion, but that was very unlikely to save him.

After all the thinking he did, Mitch decided that he would have to put a toe-in to find out. If he didn't get eaten or trampled or somehow killed, he guessed he was right. If he was wrong, it could be very unpleasant indeed.

He had now been out of touch with those on the Moon for thirty minutes. They, and by they - he meant *Jessy,* would be beside herself. She'd be inconsolable at this point, he knew. *Jessy better be,* he thought with a tight smile, gazing around tensely. She'd be ready to throw something at him.

He entered the shrubbery of the forest and immediately heard sound everywhere, through the sound grills of his spacesuit – muffled trilling, chirping, squeaking and buzzing, the sounds of a forest back home. Apart from the dark colour, it was all Earth. It was lush tertiary forest - there were thick, intergrown, leathery vines hanging everywhere as were palms and ferns, some towering with flowing vine tendrils wrapped around, searching for places to climb. There were things that looked like lianas growing all over the place, on the ground and climbing everything with tendrils growing on every surface. Stranglers and root climbers were everywhere with huge flower-like things that were deep black and lustrous and probably parasitic, growing off palms that grew in every spot imaginable. Trees that were short and branchless and presumably dead were almost fully covered by dusty vines and were everywhere. Some had fallen over, heavy with vines. Long vines grew upward from black pods, forming pseudo telegraph wires through the jungle made of vines and leaves.

Strange, dark flowers drooping with heavy insides, were everywhere on the tree-things and on the ground. The most bizarre residents of the forest he could see were massively tall things that reminded him of tall, skinny trees. But these things were on huge dark stilts that arrowed into the soil and had few branches. If they weren't "walking trees", well, they sure looked like it. The tall, thin "trees" looked ready to blast off. Everything he could see was black or dark grey, very unusual, almost affronting to the human eye.

Like home, there were leaves, logs and pieces of plants and trees everywhere underfoot. Clearly, he was tromping through a complex and elaborate ecosystem, and he knew what that probably meant for him.

It was warmish and humid outside – his thermometer reading was splashed in green in the top part of his visor. It was 28 degrees outside with humidity of 75% – warm and humid in anyone's book. There were enormous "walkers" wound with dark vines and peppered with small mushrooms which also grew on the ground by themselves, in groups of almost round large growths, which looked like groups of giant Chuba-chup lollypops.

Everywhere, growing and rising through the top of the canopy, and growing almost sideways from the ground were dark, almost branchless trees. Mitch's eyes were huge as he scrutinised the scene carefully and listened intently. There were bohemian things that looked like Barber-poles, red and black stripes, that grew straight up in groups.

Mitch could already see wiggly things under his feet. But it wasn't the small things that concerned him. He'd already seen a line of large ant-like insects ascending the trees in a few places. They looked like black ants with overly large pincers. He'd also seen largish webs between plants but nothing else. Something spiderish must have spun them though.

Ahead of him was more of the same - thick and crooked and very dark tree-things, with long "walking" buttresses between which carbon-grey tangles of brush and ferns grew, and he could hear what sounded like a waterfall and river in the distance somewhere.

Mitch could hear a sound like faraway water hitting something hard from a height, like rocks. It must have been a few kilometres away though. Hiding behind a tree-thing and peering through a gap between the roots, he spied a relatively large eight-legged *something* that looked a bit like a black lobster with an exoskeleton, thin spindly legs, two prominent black eyes and two heavily articulated thin arms with crab-like pincers which it was using to efficiently catch smaller animals that looked like prairie dogs with six legs and lots of feely things all over its body, including some that were quite thick.

The Sextapod lobsters with their many legs were surprisingly quick and agile, dashing one way then the other - picking the prairie dogs up with seeming ease from the lower branches and the ground using the thicker feely things which acted like arms and fingers. Overall, it was dark and creepy in the forest, knowing those lobster-things were running around, everywhere it seemed. Mitch saw one race up a tree but that's all he saw. He assumed it didn't go up there for nothing but he lost it in the darkness.

There were vines higher up, and a lot of them had trailing black moss which also grew on the north sides of the trees. And they were black as well as regular white mushrooms everywhere, growing on the trees and on the ground. White looked extremely out of place here, and it begged the question of how the colour happened? It was only fungus, he supposed. The forest was lush and alive, and dark, although the starlight did reach the ground in a lot of places. It still seemed incredibly out of place - the whole lot of it. A black forest indeed, even if it *was* logical – it looked amazing to the human eye.

Mitch felt and heard a thumping sound and vibration come through the forest. He also saw green insects walk over the ground in single file, doing the same over bluish mushrooms that grew in a clump near the trees which appeared Earth-like except they had more branches and the branches themselves seemed to have thick branches.

Mitch again watched a trail of what looked like large blue ants with overly large pincers that wound from the ground up the trunk of a tree until he lost sight of them. The thumping was way louder now and Mitch could feel whatever it was, get closer through the souls of his feet. Whatever this thing was, it was *big*...big enough to make the ground shake. Mitch gawked in the direction of the noise waiting for something to materialise from the thick vegetation close to him.

A large group of something loud and noisy went by overhead, distracting him, but all he could see were small arms and long, skinny legs. Mind you, Mitch was hiding behind a large thatch of palm-like plants and couldn't see a lot in any direction, including up. So, he wasn't surprised that his vision was severely limited. He was waiting for the *whatevers* to pass him by. Once the noise retreated a bit, he extricated himself from his hiding place, first making sure it was safe to move.

He chastised himself for expecting anything to behave like an Earth animal. The animals could swing one legged through the trees as far as he knew. This was an *exo-forest*, he had to keep reminding himself of that. Literally *anything* was possible, he thought grimly, subject to the nebulous laws of evolution of course.

He didn't have to wait long. It was bigger than an elephant with monstrous tusk-like extrusions, probably coming from its mouth, although he wasn't positioned to see its head. He stood on the other side of a large thatch of palm-like things and watched, surreptitiously, staying as small as possible.

Mitch really didn't see much at all but he strained to see what he could without giving himself away. Even if it wasn't a meat-eater, this thing was huge. Mitch was sure, being trampled or impaled on one of those tusks was on offer. Mitch was barely breathing, trying not to move, variously sweating and shivering. This crazy, dim place was as frightening as hell.

His plan was to initially and briefly look deeper into the forest and then retry the anomaly. See if the damn thing allowed him finally to re-join Jessy. She must be beside herself by now. He could imagine her face. It wasn't pretty.

So, Mitch pushed further into the unknown. *Everything* he looked at was dark. To Mitch, it seemed like he was walking through a dark room with a dim light that flicked on every now and then.

He continued to be happy, *ecstatic* really, that he was on solid ground. Quite easily, he could be floating through space with no hope of return to Jessy. Although the alien object remained dead, he reckoned there was a chance of it reactivating. Why it was in stasis, he had no idea, but he remained hopeful. A positive state-of-mind was critical to any mission, especially this one. What he was slightly less positive about was this planet's wildlife. If there was something huge with monstrous tusks, there was probably something smaller, faster and more agile that wanted to eat him. This place could be way more of a nightmare than he already knew.

There was still a deep, loud thumping in the distance. Also, in the distance were very tall mushrooms with huge tree-like trunks of pure fungus holding them up, or so it seemed. They were supporting huge cylindrical domes, at least twenty feet off the ground and gigantic in diameter, with a network of fungus that held the dome structure in place.

It was clear that a beautifully synched ecosystem was established in this place. It was equally clear that it rained a lot around here. It looked, to him, like tropical rainforest...apart from the colour, and a few other things. It looked almost like Earth. That meant there was probably a river or waterway nearby. He'd already heard a waterfall and it was humid. There were purple clouds in the atmosphere with decent vertical development. That meant rain, and soon.

Mitch moved slowly and tentatively off the fairly sharp line formed by the grass and the beginning of the jungle undergrowth. Incredibly, he could hear a panicked sound wafting from somewhere in the jungle. Someone or something was yelling loudly and incomprehensibly.

It sounded like...no it couldn't be, surely. Mitch's head moved   around wildly inside his helmet, ending in the direction of the unexpected noise. Moving slowly between trees, he tried not to squash small mushrooms that vented black spores or something into the air when he trod on them.

Something ahead was moving around manically, yelling loudly, sounding panicked and frightened. Mitch walked closer, around a nest of trees over a some kelpy looking black stuff that grew straight from the ground.

'*Jesus Christ*,' he huffed to himself, hauling himself over the top of a steeply bent black-grey tree that had probably been pushed down when young. Finally, he saw what was making all the fuss. It was *Jessy*, as he suspected. She was caught in some sort of wettish sand or dirt, stuck up to her chest with her arms swinging around madly, searching for something to grab. Her legs were probably doing the same inside the mix of water and black dirt.

She was doing quite the opposite of what you should do when caught in quicksand on Earth, although certainly it was the most natural thing to do. She locked panicky eyes onto Mitch and half-smiled as she moved manically, her arms immediately moving in his direction, her eyes saying, "*save me now*".

'*Save me Mitch,*' she cried as soon as she saw him.

Mitch grabbed a vine and pulled it hard and it came free. Mitch tossed it to her. Jessy grabbed for it but missed. '*Grab it,*' he barked.

She was buried in the sand up to her neck now. '*Grab the fucking vine Jess,*' he bellowed at her and rotated the vine so it was right by her. He could see it was her last chance and opened his eyes as wide as they would go. Jessy forced her hand up through the sand and grasped the black climber. Mitch pulled the vine gently, not knowing its snapping point, to hopefully overcome the suction of this unknown alien sand. Thank God, it acted like regular sand. Mitch pulled Jessy free, on her side and then her stomach. She was lying in the dirt and the dark vegetation, huffing and puffing, gasping for breath and trembling. She came within a hair of death in the watery alien sand.

'*Jesus...shit,* how did you get *here?*' He knew the answer but peered at the black sand, wondering, then back at Jessy, eyes widening again, sweating like a dog, puffing loudly, waiting impatiently to hear her story through his puffing. Hurry up, he felt like saying, as she hoisted herself into a sitting position, sweating and hot, and looked directly at Mitch.

He was also huffing and puffing mightily, glad he was alive. Glad *she* was alive. It could've so easily been different for both of them.

'*Fuck me, where were you?*' She yelled at Mitch. 'You were gone almost an hour for Christ's sake.' Remember "*ten fucking minutes*". Jessy stared at him with wide eyes, clearly on the verge of losing it, still breathless, sweating and looking around wildly. She was hot, sweating profusely, shaking her head.

'It didn't damn well work,' Mitch snapped, 'I tried to come back, but couldn't...*the Goddamn thing didn't let me*, it wouldn't *fucking turn on,*' he yelled in frustration, spitting and searching for something to punch.

Jessy gawked at him and realised it was not at him her anger should be directed. It was as if she'd been pricked by a needle and deflated. Her anger disappeared. Replaced by thanks. Thanks for not being dead or floating in space. Her *or* him. Jessy suddenly looked ready to cry. Her anger turned to sadness and gratitude.

'You were gone well over half an hour,' she said softly and I couldn't wait any longer...I just couldn't. She swallowed the sob that rose in her throat. Her shoulders heaved and she shook a bit. Jessy peered at Mitch with huge, wet eyes and palpable sadness. Jessy just stood there, gazing sadly and for a long time at Mitch, wiping at her nose with a tissue from her pocket.

Eventually, she spoke, sobbing through the terror, 'so-I went through the-object out of desperation, fully expecting to die, probably badly, and eventually, I was spat out here.' Her shoulders shook again, and her voice cracked, and again, she looked like she might cry, thinking she'd lost her family for good. Jessy still looked ready to cry, but it didn't hold Mitch back.

Here?' Mitch whined, 'where is *here*, because I sure as hell didn't see you go past *me*.' She started shaking her head well before Mitch had finished.

'Not where *you* ended up, you goose, I came out *there*,' she said, pointing with a gloved finger over his right shoulder, up near a tree on the beginning of the uplands. Mitch turned around and studied the area carefully. He scratched his chin. Now, he was really confused. He came out there, but she came out up there. *Huh*?

He pointed an index finger, 'up there?' He asked. 'It's the same as the anomaly on the Moon, right? She nodded agreement. 'Er, um...another one I mean. So, there's at least two on this world that are connected to the object-thingy on the Moon?'

'Yep,' she confirmed. 'Quite similar really. Identical probably.'

'So, there's more than one of those things on this rock...er, where...exactly?' Mitch glanced left and right, acting like he didn't know where they were. He knew where one was. The other – *dunno*.

'All I know is there's one of these things about two hundred metres up that hill,' she said, staring at the spot where it lay. 'Others, if they exist, I have no idea about but it makes me feel this planet or place must be important.' Jessy said, feeling hot and thoroughly confused and bewildered, a state-of-mind she'd had since she'd spied the object on the Moon. Confusion seemed to be a constant mind-set, she thought. Confusion and serious disorientation. She'd felt "tilted" ever since she saw it. Jessy groaned, touching her face and feeling moisture, which she quickly wiped off. Jessy felt like telling Mitch to fuck off but thought better of it. She hated being treated like a child.

'I agree, but why the hell is this planet *so* important?' Mitch said, shaking his head and looking around, eyeing the strange vegetation, which smothered his forward horizon. 'Maybe there's a lot more to this place...a civilization perhaps, just not right here. I mean, imagine if we were sent to Earth, but landed in Africa, in the Congo River Basin – you wouldn't think our planet was a host to intelligence at all. But it is – *just not there*. Anyway, we're here, so I guess we need to suck it up...right?'

'Yeah, I suppose,' she said slowly,' glancing down and flattening out a crease on her suit. 'Um...do we need this get-up on Mitch, and the oxygen to breathe, the manufacturer's say they're designed for maximum comfort...what a load of crap that is. Comfort compared to what?'

'There's carbon-based life out there and it's obviously respiring...it's *alive*,' Jessy said, sweating into her ventilation garment.

Mitch looked around and surveyed the whole area, taking in the vegetation, the gravity, and the cloud formations. They should fill the atmosphere with oxygen if chemical processes were the same or similar to Earth. Jessy and Mitch knew it was a mighty big "if". It was all guesswork, horribly qualitative, he knew, but it was all he had.

'I'll, uh...try it first, and assuming all is fine, you follow, how's that sound? 'I'm sure it'll be fine; the plants seem to like-it. Mitch's voice caught on the last word in particular. He knew what a risk this was.

'If the air's no good, close your visor and re-pressurise straight away,' she said emphatically. Jessy reckoned he'd be without air for a minute maximum - if the air was no good. It didn't stop her from feeling a little terrified though. The atmosphere might be poisonous, although that was very unlikely indeed. If Mitch turned frog-green she reckoned, it'd be obvious to all. Jessy chastised herself. *Positive thoughts please*, she screamed to herself.

All the vegetation was apparently breathing the air. Mitch looked out and saw the health of the forest, everything suggested it should be okay...*forget* about the colour. But what if the foliage breathed something very different and *didn't* respire oxygen...what then? Then, well...we re-group. That's all he could think of. Re-group...It mightn't be like Earth and they knew it.

All Mitch had in his suit was a chromatograph that was programmed to detect certain "techno-signatures", not the components of the atmosphere unfortunately, which would have been so useful. Mitch turned the device on by pressing a raised button near the base of his helmet. The unit fed its output into a detector that interpreted what it found. The result would flash in front of him, on the visor. From what he could see, it was scanning. Soon it would be reading and then *wallah* there would be the answer. Right in front of him.

Incredibly, the device read phosphine PH_3 and choro-fluorocarbons $CCl2F2$ as trace atmospheric elements. The former suggested life but it wasn't definitive. It could come from volcanic eruptions or the ageing of dead vegetation in swamps or the like. And this place definitely had vegetation. CFC's though, and the latter were absolutely definitive of mobile intelligence.

They do not occur naturally and only come about if they are manufactured by industry, perhaps refrigeration. CFCs very strongly suggested, in fact, proved, mobile intelligence. Something was very clearly on this planet with them. Hardly surprising given the existence of the shift, but it was good to know. Things seemed to be finally falling into place for them.

*   *   *

Mitch hit the button nearest his face and waited the ten seconds to feel the click against his skin. It meant that the visor was unlocked and could now be opened manually. He'd already shut off his own oxygen which flowed internally within the suit. The fan was off. He pushed the visor up and felt the vibrance of the atmosphere on the skin of his face.

Mitch took a sip of the air around him and it seemed fine so he breathed deeply and exhaled – it too felt fine. The atmosphere was thick and vital and full of oxygen and pressure as he *hoped*, and probably nitrogen as well, but he really didn't know. What he did know was that it felt and tasted pretty much like Earth. It was really good to breathe unimpeded.

He told Jessy about the techno-signature and her reaction was to nod knowingly and grin. She knew there had to be a civilisation here – now she knew it beyond any reasonable doubt. Jessy kept staring at Mitch with satisfied contentment, still nodding.

Humidity and warmth bathed his face, and the atmosphere seemed eminently breathable. Not surprising, given the health and vibrancy of the forest, but not guaranteed either. He remembered *anything was possible* when you weren't on or near Earth. Mitch felt good though, there was no dizziness or anything adverse at all...yet.

Jessy was studying Mitch closely, hoping to God he didn't gag or otherwise cough, start to foam at the mouth, and die in front of her. So far it was looking very good. He looked like he was tolerating the air well.

'No problems,' he said, breathing deeply while strolling around slowly. 'It tastes good, a bit chocolatey actually.' Mitch breathed deeply again, grinning widely at Jessy.

'Great...that's good Mr Comedian,' '*thank Christ,*' she thought, ogling Mitch direct in the eye and grinning. 'At least one thing's gone in our favour. The vegetation sort of gave it away, but it's good to see it works like it does on Earth.' Mitch nodded and agreed with his own sentiment. He hadn't forgotten the techno-signature, *CFC's*, it was still top of his mind - he thought they might see a "person" anytime. Again, Mitch compared it to Earth where natives inhabited the jungle and in canoes on waterways. Was it the same here, he wondered?

It was warm and humid, as expected. Mitch rapidly disrobed and encouraged Jessy to similarly exit her pressurised suit. '*Thank fuck,*' he said, forcefully under his breath, mirroring Jessy's earlier comment. It really felt good to have the environment suit and skull cap off. Slimline and efficient it might have been, but it still felt like it weighed a fucking ton.

Jessy freed herself from her helmet and the pressure-suit with a minimum of fuss. With the suit off, it was like Earth, and quite warm, similar to

Jamaica back home, where she'd recently holidayed. Blinking, then focussing her gaze back on Mitch, she was amused at his clumsy efforts to disrobe.

'Yep, it's great,' she said, 'breathing is just like it is at home.'

Both of them removed their pressure suits, not only leaving them sweating in the warm, humid atmosphere but each of them only had their thin white undergarments on. Almost ready for the beach - apart from the fact they would look like people from a generation or two before.

'It *is* quite the look, thank you,' Mitch responded lightly. He gawked at Jessy and glanced down at himself, she looked very athletic and well defined in her outfit, despite never doing any gym work at all. "Good genes", she would often say. Jessy was probably right. He was quite sure he looked fat and old and totally out of place with her.

Anyway, he thought, it was what it was. Most older people would look out of place with her, he supposed. Mitch tore his gaze back to the dark jungle. He wasn't sure what looked more enticing. The jungle or Jessy.

He didn't like the way he looked, and glanced again at Jessy. There was no assurance coming from that direction. 'Er...um...perhaps we should poke around and then try your anomaly again. Either that or just try for home straight away?' Mitch clearly didn't want to make the decision by himself. Or at all. He was out of ideas and uncertain, pulling at his ear and thinking hard.

'Sounds good to me, the first one I mean.' Jessy was combing her hair with her fingers, also looking very ill-at-ease. She was worried about something different. Visions of something rearing up at them from the darkness was high in her mind. She hadn't forgotten about the techno-signature.

Those things Mitch told her about, what did he call them...Sextapods. *Holy shit*, Jessy thought to herself, they could be anywhere. And they were definitely predators. She knew sharks ate small fish as well as larger on Earth. Maybe these Sextapods did the same thing. Ate whatever they could find – big or small. She smartly decided to keep that one to herself.

'Ooookaaay, let's go then,' Mitch said, seeing Jessy fall into line behind him as he started to walk. As soon as they touched foot inside the jungle, they heard the disturbing noise of wildlife. It was everywhere, the loudest was a hooting sound that was made by something high up in the trees. It sounded like a bird...maybe an owl, but here, it could be literally *anything*.

The creatures didn't fly or even have wings, but had the bodies of birds. There was one on the ground, totally still. It had eyes that darted everywhere, a bill, and crimson feathers. It looked and acted like a chicken but presumably lived at least some of its life in the trees by running up them with clawed feet. The creature came down to feed on something in the soil. It didn't look dissimilar to a bird, but had no wings. It was ultra-quick and very nervous. It moved like lightning when disturbed.

There was a lot of them up there if the noise was any guide. Jessy was tentative, almost frozen to the spot behind him, studying the crazy wingless birds that blocked the ground in front of them. One of them scooted up a tree-thing and was gone, off to join its hooting mates further up. It seemed incredibly quick and agile, although very, very edgy.

One of the sextapod's came ambling their way and all the "flightless bird" creatures shot up the tree like buckshot to get away from it. Its arms caught one of the pseudo-chickens before it could get away, stuffing it into a loose flap of skin, presumably a mouth on top of its head. It looked vaguely like an Esky he had at home, with the lid being the mouth. It seemed very dumb and did things for necessity by instinct. It also didn't seem to be scared of humans at all and didn't pay them any attention which troubled Jessy for some reason. Not from what it might do, but what it might mean for life on this planet.

Mitch suddenly understood why the almost-chickens lived in the trees when they didn't have wings. Clearly, it was to avoid predators, which might have included several, he thought, not just the "eskies. He believed there were many other dangerous creatures they hadn't laid eyes on yet.

Whatever they did, they knew they had to remain vigilant. Sextapods they could probably handle, but others, like that one with huge tusks, or the ones that thumped through the forest and made the ground shake, Mitch wasn't so sure about it. Could they handle a predatory rhino – it would be difficult to say – probably not. They sounded, and the few they saw, appeared extremely dangerous, potentially they were *killers*. Impaled on an alien tusk wasn't the way he wanted to go. Mitch wondered where the civilisation was.

Jessy and Mitch, could again hear something large and heavy tromping through the jungle, feeling its footfalls, the thunderous vibrations and the noise getting louder, and then gradually receding, vibrating less as it presumably left the area. Jessy swivelled her head to follow the noise, her owlish eyes seeing nothing apart from the swaying black jungle. She stared at Mitch uncomprehendingly. Get used to it, he thought, quite seriously, gazing back at Jessy. The forest was probably teeming with creatures like that.

Neither had to say it. Both of them wanted out. Screw the black jungle and the likely civilisation. As intriguing as they were, they wanted back to the anomaly and then back to the Moon, that was the plan. The occupants of the jungle would eventually kill them, they both felt sure. The intelligent creatures, the industry and the civilisation that created the CFC's, would unfortunately, have to wait. Mitch, in particular, wasn't happy with that. They had just confirmed that a civilisation was in residence on this planet, but before meeting them, back they had to go. If possible. But they simply had to. Marrying risk and reward told them that it was required to avoid disaster.

Would the anomaly work though? That was the question they had to confront and it was top of mind for both of them. Mitch kept replaying the tricky nature of the one in his cave, in his head. Over and over and over. He was sick to death of it. Hopefully, the other machine wasn't as temperamental. *Not as fucking painful.* Mitch knew that Jessy wanted home desperately.

She couldn't help but wonder and worry. What if they went somewhere else, into the vacuum of space say? She knew *what* then, and it wasn't good. Jessy knew Mitch was worried too - he just didn't show it like Jessy did. He managed to keep a lot of himself hidden. She had little doubt that NASA had taught him that. Everything she felt was written on her face and in her movements. Jessy was an open book, easy reading if you cared to look.

'Let's go then,' Mitch blurted, more as a suggestion than anything else. Jessy was ready to run for the horizon if her expression and body language were any guide. She was terrified of this black place.

Mitch wouldn't mind staying awhile to get a look at the night sky if there was night on this planet. Find out, if he could, where the hell they were, or as best as he could. Were they still in the Milky Way Galaxy? Who the hell knew, there were no guarantees that anything in their new sky would look familiar, but if it did, he could hopefully narrow down their location.

Retracing their steps, they both paced up the ledge and stepped inside the mouth of the cave. Mitch deliberately made as much noise as he could. Jessy stared curiously at Mitch as he jumped up and down several times, stirring up some red dust. It was a cave after all – he didn't want any surprises inside. From where they were they could just see the dark surface. Just as it was left. Nothing had changed.

*   *   *

It was now dusk - dark enough so they could see some of the night sky. And what a night sky it was. Turns out, the dark they were in right now, was as dark as it got around here. One of the suns stayed not far under the horizon all night. Mitch reckoned it was probably like the period of "darkness" during the winter months at the poles of Earth. Twilight at best. It certainly wasn't what we on Earth would term "night". It was a bit like early dawn on Earth.

From what they could see, this world was much nearer to a galactic centre than Earth was, and hopefully it was *their* own galactic centre, although it probably didn't matter much. But still, "home" had a whole lot of inertia. The Milky Way Galaxy was home. "Close" was relative. The word "close" meant "near" but tens of thousands of light years away, even though it was still inside the Milky Way, wasn't "near" home using any logic you like. So, what galaxy they were in, was probably irrelevant. "Close" didn't matter a dram. Even one light-year was a long, long way.

In the sky, the stars that were there were mainly small and blue but *all* were quite tightly packed, and literally everywhere. It almost looked like they were touching, but Jessy knew it only looked that way. Parallax was a bitch. Mitch hoped this planet had a powerful magnetosphere or they were cooked. The fact that there were likely "others" on this rock gave him self-assurance.

If they were near *our* galactic centre, as they hoped, there should be an abundance of large red stars, more than a few of which should be bloated Wolf-Rayet types. But they could see none of those, just a sky full to bursting with younger main-sequence stars. There were some older, larger and redder stars, but they seemed vastly outnumbered by younger ones.

Space looked alien whatever way you looked at it. Very different to what they were used to. Normally Sirius or Canopus were centre-stage in the night sky – not so, here. So, she reasoned, they were elsewhere, not in our galactic centre, and she shared her views with Mitch. Jessy looked from the sky and turned her head toward Mitch, 'we're not in our Galaxy, you know.'

'You don't fucking say!' He goaded. 'Thanks a lot…I already worked that one out, But the most important question is…where the hell are we? It sure looks like a close-galactic centre, being so crowded with stars and all – and I'll bet that cloudy, bright gas formation up there is hiding a super-massive black hole of God knows what size.'

Mitch told her the sky was sort of like Earth's, but everything about the galaxy was magnified, because they were closer to its centre. That made sense to Jessy. Anything that suggested "home" was closer was fine by her.

*   *   *

'*Jesus…sssshhh,*' Mitch whispered forcefully, holding an arm up, gawking at the entrance to the cave. Jessy took a quick glance at the same spot, fully expecting some inconceivable form to be standing or stooping there. She drew away from the noise and was now hard up against a rocky cave wall.

'I don't…like caves,' Jessy whispered to herself, expecting no one to hear. Mitch did. Soundwaves echoed and were magnified.

'This thing might be our saviour,' Mitch responded, 'we know what's in this one. Well, we know most of it.' Mitch realised *anything* could be inside. Making noise to scare things worked with Earth animals, here – who knew?

Thankfully, the footfalls they could still hear were declining in volume, presumably meaning it or they were moving away. By the strength of the footfalls though, and the vibration - whatever made them was bigger than big. Scavenger, herbivore or predator? It might have been a combination of two or all three. Its behaviour might be unlike *anything* they'd seen before. Of course, it could be very familiar as well. Basically, it was a big, and a fat unknown. Everything was up for grabs in this place and both of them knew it.

Then he glimpsed it, from behind the trees, there were two of them and they were slowly wandering into the deeper jungle. From the edge of the cave, they could see the source of the noise - they weren't quite as big as they thought, but they were big enough to be a real problem. They had a huge funnel like mouth ringed by several rows of teeth. These things were undoubtedly predators and were probably hungry – predators were always hungry. Thankfully, for Mitch and Jessy, they were going in the opposite direction now.

They had four legs and a horse like body but the rear legs seemed overly stocky and as far as they could see, the feet on the ends of the short legs looked large and basically sans toes as they would define them. The four eyes on the head seemed very odd indeed, they appeared to look in different directions at the same time, and were juxtaposed over and under each other near the top of the head. The creatures blinked rapidly and seemed very nervous, despite their size, yet they moved slowly and heavily, looking at the forest behind them, to the side and in front of them.

Mitch and Jessy couldn't garner any more detail because the creatures were now moving away from them. The Pièce de résistance of these animals were the tusks, at least two metres long, and jet black and God knows what they were for, fighting with others of the species, Mitch hoped. Or maybe it was how they killed their prey. They looked horrifically sharp. Impaling things seemed to be an obvious use.

'*Jesus, thank God they're not...um, angry,*' Mitch heaved, peering nervously at them. He took a loud breath and peered upward in the semi-dark, and after ten or so seconds of deep thought, he pointed.

'*Shit...we are near our galactic centre,* I can see Alpha A and B, Eta, the Mag Clouds, Sirius, Canopus, but...uh, they look a *lot of* d-different from here. We're *in* the Milky Way, but much closer to the bulge, not on an arm...like Earth is. *Holy shit,*' Mitch exclaimed, surprised he could make some sense from the crowded "night" sky. So much for the theory that life can't exist close to the centre of the Galaxy. It was clearly wrong. Perspective...parallax, Mitch reckoned, depends what angle you're looking from. Everything looked different from here. *Boy, did things look different,* Mitch thought to himself in astonishment, as he scanned the crazy sky. Different, but the same stuff, he thought soothingly.

*   *   *

'Time- to see if this fucker finally works...er, I'll try first...right?' Mitch said tentatively. It hadn't worked before - but maybe this time, *finally* - we *are* in a completely different spot.' He held his breath and crossed fingers hoping to Christ this one functioned and that he ended up somewhere familiar or safe.

'Um...yeah...given that there's no room to go together, -okay,' Jessy said cautiously and nervously, 'you, uh...go first Mitch.' Jessy was more than happy to go second. She really didn't want to go at all. But there was little choice. It was go - or stay in this place *alone*. She wanted to stay here even less than Mitch did. So, the answer was clear.

'Get suited up,' he said seriously, working on himself and seeing Jessy going hell for leather in the corner of his eye. He wouldn't do anything until she was fully suited and ready for vacuum. She already had the ventilation garment and the skull cap on and the pressure suit and helmet didn't take long. Soon enough, they were both suited and ready to go. Mitch eyed her up and down. Everything was in order.

'I hope we *both* end up in Mendeleev where we started,' she mewed, as Mitch aligned himself with the anomaly. He eyed her very carefully. She did the same with him. They were both terrified for themselves and terrified for their partner.

After about twenty seconds, just when both thought it wasn't going to work, Mitch descended into the anomaly and disappeared piece-by-piece. There was no pain or anything approaching it, despite the rather slow dissolution. Quickly enough, he was gone. The object was empty again. It had done its work.

Despite her trying over and over, it stayed off and Jessy could only remain on its harsh glassy surface - going nowhere at all. She reckoned she would need to backtrack to the other anomaly that spat *her* out. And then hopefully get some action.

Backtrack she did, and Jessy ended up sitting on her anomaly about ten minutes later. Here we go again, Jessy thought. '*Shit*,' she said to herself. The same question she'd asked herself so many times, came yet again - where the fuck was she going to end up? What was she doing? *She didn't want to stay here alone*, was her answer, screamed inside her head. If she did go, Jessy prayed all her bits and pieces would be put back together right, if dissolution and reformation was indeed how it worked. If that didn't happen, well, who knew how the damn thing did it?

'Okay, you fucker, let me in.' She was, by now, truly scared shitless. Jessy thought of Mitch and after about ten seconds she too descended into the object and was gone, piece-by-piece. Soon enough, she was entirely gone from the cave and the Universe.

*   *   *

Mitch looked around wildly after he ascended from the machine. He was still breathing inside his helmet and suit and he was back on the Moon, atop the anomaly. He realised he'd made it to firm ground.

The first emotion was relief and a slow smile crossed his face as he realised all was well. He quickly dragged himself off the object with shaking hands to allow Jessy to egress. Both fingers on each hand remained firmly crossed in the hope she'd emerge unscathed.

He waited, and then waited some more. This time, Jessy didn't come back when she was expected. Mitch tried to think of something else but couldn't...that's all he had. She wasn't here – and should be. '*Where the hell are you?*' Mitch moaned to no-one but himself, for the umpteenth time. His legs were stiff, and his pulse raced making him lightheaded. He was terrified for Jessy because if she didn't come now, she probably wouldn't come, *ever*.

All of a sudden, the vibration started, and it felt like something extremely deep and heavy, allowing apparently, Jessy to ascend and appear on top of the object, helmet and suit, *everything*, apparently intact and accounted for. A quick once over by Jessy made sure everything was where it was supposed to be. And it was. Ten fingers, two arms and two legs, plus she felt fine, breathing, thinking, respiring like a creature does. Whomever put her together had clearly done a good job.

'Not bad for a few million light years,' she said, grinning and puffing at the same time. He was stoked to see her in front of him, but unhappy that she took so bloody long to arrive. "What happened to *right behind me?*"

'I, uh...came as quickly as I could,' she blurted, peering down and not recalling a thing about how she got back. It must have been extremely quick.

From where she was sitting, Jessy could see Mitch with azurite, malachite and stolzite, and a little yellow wulfenite amid the vugs and crevices of the weathered and oxidised KREEP and gossan.

The view, though dim, was still quite incredible. *Whew*, she thought, sweating like she'd just done a vigorous workout. She let out a huge lungful of breath into her helmet.

50

3

Goodbye

"Intelligence is an accident of evolution, and is not necessarily an advantage."
- — *Isaac Asimov*

The huge asteroid was on its own hyperbolic orbit with an eccentricity of slightly more than one, meaning it had the momentum to only be a sightseer to our solar system. It was a quick hello and an even quicker goodbye – it came from The Altar constellation.

The rock would have left above the plain of the planets near Neptune if the Moon didn't get in its way. Earth knew it was going to miss, and at worst provide them with a pretty fireworks show on the Moon and then in the upper atmosphere of Earth. But it was worse than Earth thought, by a large margin.

The asteroid was 500 metres through the middle and composed almost entirely of iron and nickel, and would hit between the Copernicus crater and the Apollo 14 descent stage, in a massive detonation of KREEP and basalt that would thrust billions of tonnes of material beyond lunar orbit and into space, much of it to burn up in Earth's upper atmosphere, and offer the people of Earth their promised fireworks show. The rest formed a torus of matter behind the Moon, much like a trailing tail. From the Earth, when the Sun was just right, it was a truly gorgeous sight.

Apart from a sizeable Moonquake, the farside of the Moon was impacted little. The nearside was impacted a lot, because the Moon had an atmosphere like a creampuff, so the rock easily penetrated to the ground.

The asteroid had struck the Moon and kicked up millions of tonnes of rock and dirt and dug a huge new crater near the existing crater of Copernicus.

The orbital momentum of the Moon around Earth was overwhelmed. That meant the orbit of this almost-world around Earth had shifted substantially.

Mitch and Jessy were back on the Moon, having shifted to and from the exo-planet, courtesy of the alien shift which with a touch of Hiesesenburg, entanglement, De sitter space and nonlocality sent them and brought them back. Why this planet was connected to the lunar surface, they still had no idea, despite visiting it. Mitch knew there had to be a good reason for it, they just didn't find it. Presumably they wanted to make contact with Earth. The reason for it being placed there, was eating away at both Mitch and Jessy.

*   *   *

So...w-what do we do now?' Jessy eyed Mitch squarely, 'text Jax, go home like, normal. Pretend nothing happened...that all is in order?'

'Yep, apart from the pretend bit I reckon, full disclosure I think would be way better.' Mitch scratched his helmeted head. That'd be the best for everyone, he thought.

'I'll text Jax then,' Jessy said, grabbing her phone from her pocket, slowly. In the Moon's weak gravity,' she knew if she dropped the phone it would continue in whatever direction her scrabbling fingers pushed it, a *lot* further than Earth's gravity would allow, where the phone would simply hit the ground and the glass probably break. Jessy realised she might never see it again, which would never do. That phone was her life. It contained information, photos and videos that were totally irreplaceable. Her entire younger life was contained within in it. To lose it would be heartbreaking.

She proceeded to message Jax which wasn't easy with vacuum gloves on. Slow and careful won the race on the Moon, she knew. In space or on the Moon, everything took way longer to execute.

Mitch pushed the specimen bags in the pneumatic tyred trolley, while Jessy followed him up the few large steps to the surface level. Her phone vibrated in the Velcro'd pocket and she very carefully retrieved it to read the text which she assumed was from Jax.

'*Whaa...*,' she uttered loudly, taking a step back, peering at her phone like its writing had just changed into a different language, or hieroglyphics, or something entirely foreign. '*What the fuck does that mean?*' She all but dropped her phone, but thankfully had an iron-grip on it. Jessy flinched and shook her head as she read the ridiculous message again. She glanced at Mitch disbelievingly and then back at her phone, eyebrows riding high, eyes bulging. What on Earth did that crap mean?

YOU DIED NEARLY 20 YEARS AGO. PLS RING ME?

She showed Mitch, and he did a double take. '*What the fuck?*' He stared at Jessy and every now and then glanced at the phone, hands on hips. 'What does he mean "You *Died*"? Has he totally fucking lost it?' Mitch whispered emphatically. *Crazy fuck*, he thought angrily. '*What is he talking about?*' Poor old Jax, something has really got him going. 'Been dead for twenty years indeed, *yeah right*, hang-on, I'll take my pulse, make sure I'm okay. He had his gloved hand hard on his wrist. '*Yep, I'm alive alright.*' Mitch shook his head and snorted his disbelief, smiling widely, thinking Jax has really lost it.

Mitch thought about it more and thought about Jax long and hard, staring blankly at Jessy, suddenly falling headlong into confusion and horror. Did he mean that Josh was suddenly *27*? Little Joshy, the toys, the Mario-kart bed, *no way*. It was insane just to contemplate it.

He also had a suspicion of what he might be talking about. It's not possible though, he reckoned grimly, but he knew it probably was, 's-surely...it's n-not p-possible,' he moaned in a strange pitch. Mitch covered his mouth with his palm, his body hot, his brain in overdrive as he thought about time dilation. Mitch also thought about Murphy's law, then instantly discarded it. It can't be real, he yelled at himself.

'Surely, he's lost the plot. Has J-Jax gotten sick...*where is he for God's sake?*' Mitch said, taking a step back, wobbling, almost falling and nearly fainting. He scrunched his toes together inside his boots. Get it together, he commanded himself. 'By the sound of it, Jax wasn't even on the Moon.' Mitch said tentatively, still thinking about Josh. Had he gone home without them? That only added to the intrigue. Jessy worried that Jax was really medically sick.

'*Fuck*,' Mitch yelled, thinking about it. '*Fuck, shit,*' he repeated, louder. He started to sound a bit like a madman. Jessy eyed him carefully - she was now worried about Mitch as well. It was unlike him to swear so loudly and with so much raw anger. To outwardly mean it!

Jessy rang Jax's phone number by linking her phone to her helmet-comms and indeed he was at work with AASSA on Earth doing fuck-knows-what. There was an odd delay that was longer than usual, which put her off even more. It was a fine and sunny day on Earth on Thursday, July 23, 2047 Twenty years after they left the Moon! The worst possible news was true.

It *was* nearly twenty years into the future. They were on the Moon alone. The most astonishing thing of all was actually true. Jax was fine, and he was correct, they had come back, essentially forward in time. Earth and all that rode her, had aged twenty years, but they had not. They had been elsewhere, and were subject to the vagaries of time on the way there or back or probably both. Then they were just plonked back here, without knowing why they went forward such an ironic amount of time. They understood time dilation, but the amount of time they jumped seemed rather suspicious. Was it simply on a whim...Jessy seriously doubted it. There had to be some intelligence involved, some *knowing*. it seemed to be too much of a coincidence to be believed. Mitch knew extreme gravity was the reason why – but twenty years...*please.*

Her first thought, if it was somehow true, which now seemed likely, was Joshy. He was now 27 with his parent's dead for twenty long years. They'd left him with his godmother for two weeks while Mitch and her had holidayed on the Moon. Two weeks had somehow turned into twenty very long *years*. Jessy was too dazed and shocked to cry. It was way too much to believe. Her son, all his formative years...*gone.*

Dead...the word really didn't equate to anything real or tangible for her. Jessy terminated the call and dropped her phone after saying to herself she wouldn't. It landed, wrong side up, dropping slowly in the reduced gravity.

'*Twenty fucking years,*' she said, almost in a trance. She found it hard to ascribe much value to what she just said. Jessy was still standing, but nearly mentally unconscious. If there was ever a reason to faint, this was it. She stared at Mitch and said nothing for quite a while.

'*Holy shit Mitch*, he went to our *fucking funeral*, after we were pronounced legally dead. Josh spoke at our funeral Mitch...poor kid. *Jesus*, what a fucking nightmare for him.' Mitch nodded distantly, not really believing this could be happening.

Again, she stared at Mitch and said nothing, then opening her eyes as wide as they would go. '*Josh, 27...it's not possible. No way.*' Jessy couldn't and wouldn't believe it, shaking her head, but it seemed to be true. Everything pointed to it being true. *Impossible* to believe. It couldn't be, surely.

'Mitch, no...it can't be' Jessy whimpered. But she knew. Josh indeed was 27 years old. The truly incredible seemed to be true. They had been declared dead by petition with no bodies or contemporary death certificates to prove they were in fact dead.

Jessy kept asking, '*how?*' But she knew that somehow, the shifts had impelled not only a spatial dislocation, but a temporal one as well. Jessy knew Einsteinian space could work like that. Where the fuck had they been for all that time though? That was the question. *Nowhere* was the answer. For them, it was all normal, they didn't know any different. The time they missed on Earth simply didn't exist for them.

Mitch goggled at her, saying nothing for a long time. Time was extremely relative, that they both knew. One of the spatial shifts, he and Jessy took, clearly invoked a time shift or slippage or *something* which equated to about twenty years. They went forward almost two decades. Which felt like nothing to them. They should be pleased it was only twenty years, Mitch supposed. It all sounded very unlikely indeed, but Mitch reckoned it had happened to them. It sounded impossible but travelling through time was specifically allowed by Einstein's theory of relativity. Even aeroplanes have an effect on time, although miniscule. The faster you went, the slower "time" went until it ultimately stopped at light speed.

Jessy had explained it in a fair bit of gobbledygook detail. What was *truly* incredible was that Jax had the same phone number, after all that time. Normally, younger people's, phone numbers were changed all the time.

It was one thing to be physically able to time-travel, but it was another to actually get it done. For time-travel - we simply don't know how it works, but clearly somebody or something does, or maybe the dilation was just a fluke. The question remained though – who or what had impelled the translocation? Was it just how the shift was, or was there some intelligence involved, that directed the period of the move? Long story short – why 20 years, it seemed a might odd?

'Ring Jax back, ask him how in God's name it all happened?' Mitch said, with an unfocussed gaze. 'He'll have no idea of course, but make sure they know it was nothing to do with us. And then ring Emma, see about Josh. This'll really blow her mind, not to mention Josh,' he said, grinning and then peering soberly at Jessy. '*Holy shit*, everyone will be floored – totally bloody floored. Back from the dead – something that doesn't happen every day.'

Neither him nor her could really believe what was happening to them or *had* happened to them. Mitch was speechless as he contemplated it, taking shaky breaths, his hands all over his face, thinking of poor Josh and the hell he must have been through over the past decades. Both his parents dead and Joshy alone with no parents, was perhaps his biggest nightmare. Hopefully, Jessy's friend and Josh's godmother, Emma had looked after him well.

Most believed time travel was impossible - both of them now knew it wasn't. What the hell would Josh think. *Jesus Christ, fuck*, Every time Mitch considered it - a new horror came to mind. Poor kid. He was sure it would have given him PTSD or chronic anxiety, panic disorder or something similar...maybe everything combined.

*   *   *

Josh was aware that his mum would speak to him soon. From where, he worried, her tomb, or coffin maybe? Josh grinned tightly. Where the hell *would* she call from? He was really, truly worried about speaking to her. It'd been so fucking long - he didn't know her at all – so much had happened to him. Josh knew he was no longer the youngster he was when she last saw him. He wondered about her too, twenty years was a long time, he reckoned while pulling a strand of hair so hard, it made his eyes fill with tears.

The whole thing was too ridiculous for words. He was stunned and dazzled, overwhelmed and dumbfounded, happy and confused, terrified and gladdened by their return. Really, he wasn't sure how to feel, there so many emotions. When he first found out - when he knew for *sure*, he collapsed in a heap – unconscious. *Enough said.* Anyway, he had a lot of work to do.

Jessy and Mitch both reckoned getting Earth in the picture as soon as possible was the right thing to do. They'd ring Joshy again and attempt contact when direct line of sight comms was possible. Then they could hopefully have a decent conversation and answer some of his questions, hopefully in some depth. *Like where the hell mum and dad had been for the last twenty years.* Her mind spun and twisted, thinking about the questions he'd probably ask her. She put herself in his situation, and her mind went for it again. It was a truly ridiculous situation for such a young man to have to deal with.

Direct line of sight contact would be much better than relying on a scratchy, unstable line facilitated by the ageing *Eaglehawk* satellite. That was worse than a piece-of-shit now and more often than not, didn't work, or at best offered static filled comms full of complete dropouts.

There were several Roadster's left at Mendeleev when everyone left, which was surprising because they could be dismantled and flatpacked home pretty easily, but she guessed they weren't much good or worth much on Earth.

Subject to various tests by Mitch, they'd use one of these to travel to a spot west of Babcock's Crater. From there they would phone Josh for an almost real-time conversation. Anyway, that was the plan they had. And it sounded okay. As long as the phone towers were still intact which they currently didn't know but they'd soon find out.

Mitch and Jessy made their way slowly to Mendeleev Base, which was brought to the Moon in a number of small boxes and basically just inflated, and then stabilised with a heap of metal rods, including an airlock that didn't look too good, but actually worked pretty well, they were told.

Seeing that all the lights were out in the base and it was mostly deflated, it looked dead and deserted. It was depressingly dark, but with no one there to look after it or really need it, the need to light it up or oxygenate it, was absent. The structure was impregnated with woven Kevlar to protect insiders from micro meteorites, ionising radiation and cosmic rays.

Also, for the latter two they had an Electrostatic Shield system which acted as a magnetosphere for their location, basically four large electrically charged spheres atop large masts that deflected solar wind and ionising radiation like Earth's magnetosphere does. The lack of power meant that was off too. So, at the moment, they were open to whatever came at them from space and the Sun, small meteorites, cosmic rays and the like. Thankfully, their suits also did that for them.

She knew the Electrostatic thing worked in the lab, turning a potential killing field, if a large sunspot happened along, to a walk in the park, as long as you stayed within the pseudo-square confines covered by the machines. Of course, if it was off like now, it was useless.

'Just as I thought,' Jessy said, 'the door is unlocked and there is zero oxygen or pressure inside.' Totally empty, she thought to herself, gawking at its collapsed contours.

'Let me check the Enabling Repository inside and I'll report,' Mitch squawked, walking slowly away, taking very short steps, straightening out the front part of his pressure suit as he walked along the dusty lunar surface. H smiled. For him, it was good to be back in space.

*   *   *

Little Joshy was an adult, it was impossible to reconcile, she thought, and ridiculous to try and get used to, at least in the short term. Jessy - immediately chastised herself for using that word. Nothing was *impossible* out here. She could swear by that from previous voyages of ridiculous discovery that rendered the word obsolete...and effectively meaningless.

They'd missed out on so much at home. All the birthdays and Christmases...*gone*. Josh had negotiated his teen years without his mum and dad and become a fully-fledged man. The mental image was almost too much. From a child's clothes to a suit, in a few days. She felt like crying or stamping her feet or screaming...perhaps all of them. It couldn't be true, but she knew it was, and that was the worst part of it. There was absolutely nothing she could do about it now. What was, *was* ... and was now irretrievable.

And when she saw him, when she actually laid her peepers on him, it would become completely true. He would be a man. A grown-up person. The last time she remembered Josh, he was a young boy, still fascinated by boy-things. *But now...Jesus, shit*, she supposed time travel was like that. To see him as a man though, it was genuinely ridiculous to contemplate.

Jessy cleared her mind as far as she could then went looking for the oxygen generating plant and in a short time, found it. As she thought, it was cycled off. Almost all the oxygen held by the Moon was in its regolith, as *moon-dust*, and with a bit of electrolysis, out it came in enormous quantities. The metal obtained by the process was very valuable too. So, extracting oxygen for their use was useful on two fronts.

Jessy had already powered the huge machine up which also included turning on its own buried power supply and starting the thermal engine. Enormous solar panels and lithium-sulphur batteries that created electricity in the first place were part of the "magnetosphere" set up. Jessy made sure that the panels were all exposed and plugged in, and the external doors were closed and secured. It was a huge piece of machinery and was already going about its job of noisily putting a breathable ether and pressure inside the small base for them. Windows and the sides of the structure were snapping into place as the inflation continued. The Electrostatic system would turn on once the pressure increased, she hoped. If it didn't, she'd do it manually.

It would be good not to have to wear a pressure suit and helmet inside, they were a pain in the arse, although an absolute necessity a lot of times. Especially, *obviously*, when outside, she thought, gawking through the plastic window at the vacuum beyond.

Mitch had found what he was looking for. Each breathing unit when fully filled would be good for about fifteen hours. Getting to where they wanted to be should take about twenty-four hours, as long as they averaged around forty-five k's an hour. It was a fair speed but the "Ash" road built by the mining company was good quality. So...he had vehicular support, battery power, breathing units and access to unlimited bottles of oxygen. Mitch was pretty much set to go.

*   *   *

'Piece of piss,' Mitch said, glancing at the Roadster. 'We'll make it easily,' he said, grinning slightly and peeping cheekily at Jessy.

'We'll see,' Jessy said, thinking he has no idea. When it came to driving, the man was a boob. Although that was back home in a petrol driven car. Here, as an astronaut, he should be okay, shouldn't he? Jessy wasn't convinced about his questionable driving skills.

Fully charged, the Roadster would get them to their immediate destination, but they would have to fit one of the other Primaries on it to get back to the base.

With twenty-seven oxygen breathers on board, they were good to go. Ready to eyeball Earth and speak to it directly - a direct line to Earth was their goal. Little did they know that certain things had changed. The changes wouldn't make anything impossible, but it would make everything a bit more difficult.

4

Starman

"I do not fear computers. I fear the lack of them." - — *Isaac Asimov*

They were just over a thousand k's from being in line of sight with Earth. Mendeleev Base was now empty again and the primary orebody at Mendeleev only a memory, as were the techs and grunts who operated the base and mined the ore, which was now completely gone, at least at the percentage of metal the owners wanted. All that was left was a labyrinth of backfilled tunnels.

The only thing that remained at Mendeleev was the slightly depleted oxidised zone of colorful minerals which were still everywhere. It remained a massive source of fascination for Mitch especially. And a financial source that they could both share. Elsewhere on the Moon there was only the NASA research base-camp near the Shackleton crater at the lunar south pole.

They'd started up the electricity and O_2 generator in Mendeleev base, located a Roadster, charged it and taken a spare battery. They'd also grabbed twenty-seven O_2 breathers - all the car could carry. Life-essentials were also taken care of, food and fluid in the form of chocolate snacks and water bottles were everywhere in the back seat of the car, along with bottles of oxygen. Diet and teeth be-damned! So much for low-carb eating, Jessy thought. Now was not the time to worry about kilojoules or teeth.

They could see brighter sunshine ahead, the beginning of the nearside that faced Earth and got the reflection from its parent planet as well as the Sun. They drove into semi-illuminated sky, it was gorgeous. It's not that they hadn't seen the Sun before on the Moon, it was just so good to see the other side of the Moon again. And the vehicle had performed on point for all those kilometres. Things were finally looking good.

'Mitch,' Jessy glanced at him, 'um...where is *Earth*? Jessy clearing her throat, gaped and pointed straight ahead where the planet should have been. Now it was only space and the odd hydrogen spiral.

'It's...it's, ah...*not there*,' Mitch whispered forcefully, looking for it all over the sky, confirming the glaringly obvious, spinning around to Jessy, mind blank, staring at her unfocussed. What the hell was going on? This had instantly become very confusing. As if we haven't seen and been through enough, *everything* was turning to shit, Mitch shrilled to himself, gazing grimly into the distance, resolving what he thought was Earth. It was so fucking far in the distance...it had clearly changed from a close relationship with Earth to a rather distant, loose one.

Instead of a huge shining half-sphere it was reduced to a rather small, unimpressive blue coin in the distance. The Moon was far less imposing on its larger kin and was no doubt less of a vista for those on Earth. Somehow, the Moon was now in deep orbit.

Holy shit,' Mitch screamed.

Jessy peered at empty space. First, the Titan thing and *One*...then Josh, and now this. So close to one another. *Christ...fuck*, she thought, none of this *was happening, could be happening,* she screamed silently to herself, staring at a smallish Earth and shaking her head at the new planetary positions. All of it was genuinely beyond belief. She felt tilted somehow. Jessy shook her head to try and right herself.

'*Okay,*' she said firmly and straightened out a bulge in her suit. 'Earth's...er, s-sort of left us, so...what do we do now?' Jessy kicked a small rock in front of her and a sluice of dust, dirt and rocks were sent flying in slow motion in that direction, gradually falling to the ground.

'*Christ knows,*' Mitch said, slowly bending down on his haunches and picking up a handful of Moon dust and letting it run slowly between his fingers. 'There's nothing we can do. Just get used to it,' he supposed.
Fatigue was overwhelming him and he knew Jessy would be feeling the same. She could barely walk a straight line, the poor bugger. Mitch stood tall and ambled slowly toward the Roadster, signalling Jessy to follow with his hand. His mind was doing backflips. Where the fuck was Earth...like, what had pushed it so deep? And when did it happen?

Did the Earth or did the Moon move – or both? Anyone's guess, he reckoned, he wasn't sure what would be a tell-sign for that. A large, brand-new crater probably. He believed it wasn't Earth that had moved. The little he knew of orbital mechanics - he was pretty sure it was something that happened to the Moon. It was only hanging onto Earth's gravity well by a thread. Just a medium-sized hit in the right place would send it deeper, or perhaps away for good, never to return. If something big had hit Earth or the Moon, people at AASSA would know in detail.

*   *   *

Mitch set his suit-alarm to wake him. He was due for an O_2 change in nine hours. He saw Jessy doing a similar thing, so, he didn't need to remind her. Mitch got in the unpressurised Roadster and pushed the seat back, reclining almost fully until it hit the backseat. He was asleep almost immediately. Jessy followed close behind. She too, was asleep very quickly. It had been an inordinately busy day with driving and the like and both of them were heavily fatigued.

*   *   *

Mitch woke abruptly and thought foggily, the Earth is almost without its satellite...the tilt of the planet would no longer be as stable, the tides would be smaller, the sodium tail gone, the weather would be wilder, days would be a tad shorter and eclipses as they used to be, would just be a memory. He thought of all this while he was waking up in the front seat of the Roadster. But life would go on. Earth would continue to survive and thrive. The Moon was so deep that it would have little more gravitational influence on Earth than the Sun.

Mitch and Jessy made their way back to the star-pocked view of the "nearside" which was darker than it had been previously, without the reflected light from Earth. "Earthshine" was fairly much gone.

'Is that Earth?' Jessy asked, pointing upward, pretty much straight up. A small bluish disc dominated space in the direction of her hand. The "new" Earth. A much more distant blueness, almost three times as far away.

'How far away is it...do you think?' Jessy said, blinking manically at it, trying desperately to focus. It sure looked a long way away.

'A million k's at least I reckon,' he was sure...'wonder what happened to push us there, to a new orbit?'

Jessy looked at Mitch with an unfocussed gaze, 'a big lunar asteroid strike maybe?'

'I wonder.' Mitch said, thinking hard. He stared fixedly at the pale blue dot, and then glanced at Jessy and moaned softly. His question about Earth was more rhetorical than anything else.

With all the early warning systems in place and all the NASA and ESA telescopes looking out for the planet, Jessy felt quite comfortable that it was not the case. Not so, for the Moon though. It was unpopulated and lacked the technology looking out for it and it was wide open to all manner of cosmic threats.

'Will my phone work if I call Josh?' Jessy asked. She held her breath and tensed her toes.

'Nokia and Vodaphone have cell towers here, so if they're okay, then yes - there will be some extra delay, but the signal should get there, assuming the towers are still standing,' which he assumed they were. He turned around and realised he was too far away to see the towers from here. If they were there, they were well below the lunar horizon.

'Just keep it light,' he said firmly, 'and keep it about him,' Mitch looked at Jessy closely, making sure she got what he was saying. Jessy hardly needed Mitch's advice to be a parent to a youngster, even under these ridiculous circumstances.

She didn't even know what Josh did at AASSA. Jessy would try and coax that answer from him. Be the inquiring mother, she thought. He might be intensely sensitive - she'd try and keep that a priority in her mind. Jessy bit her lips and tried to smooth her suit with her hand. She was petrified about ringing her own son. Jessy put herself in his position and that made things even worse.

'Remember, he's only young,' Mitch said, eyeballing Jessy closely. Don't fuck it up, he was really saying.

Jessy plugged her phone into the mic extension cord, an RCA connection that fed directly into her own helmet mic. So, she could speak from the normal position and talk to her phone.

'Okay, here goes,' she said, eyeing the phone nervously and crossing fingers on the other hand. Who the hell did Mitch think she was, Jessy asked herself, glaring at him with narrowed eyes. 'Hello, er, Cass, um...there will be a lot of delay...and echoing, um...apologies for that, she said.

'It's Jessica Taylor here, after Josh, if he's there.' She could tell she sounded like a bloody robot. Her heart was hammering as the phone rang at his desk. Cass didn't say a word, she knew Jessica would ring for Josh, she'd been told and initially thought it was a horrible joke. When she found out it was true, she flat out fainted on the floor.

Jessy was thinking on the fact a week ago, he was so small for God's sakes. Josh was her brave little boy. Little Joshy. At *work,* in a suit, it was almost too much to conceive or believe. She felt dizzy and definitely off her game. Her whole world had just imploded into a black hole from which there was no prospect of escape.

'Hello,' Josh said. It was a deep male voice - way too deep...from someone all grown up. The whole exercise was breathtaking, not to mention, bat-shit crazy. 'It's...it's your mum here Josh, your dad and I are both on the Moon...we um...uh, went inside this object for what was only a few hours for us, but when we came back out, well...' Jessy felt dizzier as she laid out the stupid story, short as it was. It sounded like the biggest load of crap imaginable. 'Nearly twenty years had passed on the outside, just like *that.*' She stared at her phone fixedly, waiting for her boy to speak. Poor kid, she wasn't sure what he was supposed to say – talk about colossal pressure. Jessy waited and tasted the sourness of stomach acid, pushing the phone connection further in and hearing the crackling.

'By the way hon, there will be a delay of a few seconds for anything you or I say.' Jessy was still waiting for Josh to respond. Jessy knew it was a whole lot to digest. He knew about it but she was sure it completely blew his mind. To finally speak together after he went to his parents' funeral, probably blew it again. They were lucky he wasn't restrained in a facility for the permanently insane after hearing and reading about them. Mitch and Jessy should really count their blessings. God knows what drugs he was prescribed. All because of us and our tinkerings with time.

The last thing he probably wanted or needed was a phone call from dear old dead mum, even though he was already aware of their miraculous return, he would still be completely gobsmacked and utterly confused. And totally taken aback that they had the balls to ring him at work.

For them it was a lot simpler than it seemed. Josh spoke on his phone with his free hand shielding the words from others in the office who crowded around his workstation. He fairly spat at his phone. 'You were *supposed* to be dead, I even went to your funeral, there was a flag and all that nationalistic crap,' he whispered vehemently, seemingly annoyed that she had dared to ring him, made worse because he was at work.

'Anyway, when do we get to meet, er...you and, um...dad?' She realised by the way he spoke - he was deeply sarcastic like his father. Jessy couldn't help it - she felt a bit of pride. Like father, like son, she reckoned.

But she hadn't expected the level of angst in his voice. Although, who could blame him? Twenty years of never knowing us, imagining us, missing us - then there was hearing about us daily, what we'd done, the statues, bridges, buildings and of course AASSA, now known as the Mitchell Taylor Space Centre. All of it was right in his face. Poor kid, she thought - *poor fucking kid*, she silently repeated, having to continually live all that. Imagine driving past it every day. PTSD, obsessive-compulsive anxiety, panic, agoraphobia – it'd be lucky if he didn't have them all, rolled into one massive fucking disorder.

'We can meet as soon as we're picked up and ferried to Earth,' Jessy said, glancing at her phone. 'They can follow the GPS in my phone. Were probably the only one's still up here.'

'I'll pass that on,' Josh said coldly.

'By the way Josh, what do you do with AASSA?

'Analyst,' Josh said, and then voiced something unintelligible to someone near him. 'I need to go,' he said and terminated the connection to his mum. Jessy removed the RCA plug and pocketed her phone.

'Well, there you go Mitch,' Jessy said, 'he hates us.' She looked at her phone and thought about his curt responses. Jessy glanced at Mitch, fumbling her phone, eventually grabbing it in the almost absent gravity, saving it from a slow freefall to the lunar surface. Jessy felt like crying. Her eyes were full of tears and a thin rope of them made their way down her cheeks.

'It's not like that,' Mitch replied. 'We'll just have to explain it to him, make him understand that we didn't leave by intention. He's just overwhelmed right now.'

You got in the damn thing "by intention",' she said, staring at Mitch accusingly.

'I got in the damn thing to see what it was and where it went, *not* just because I *wanted to.* Who the hell could have predicted its time-effect,' he said forcefully? 'I didn't, you didn't, but in retrospect, we probably should have...after all, we went very quickly to wherever we ended up.'

He was seething at the suggestion of her assigning blame, mainly because he knew it *might* be true. Maybe he did enter the object because he wanted to. Who fucking knew? It was exploration for exploration's sake, wasn't it? That's what astronauts were supposed to do. He wondered if maybe he was wrong. Second-guessing was also a strong part of his makeup.

'*Whatever* Mitch,' Jessy said, looking flustered. 'We need to get back to Earth right? So, we...'

'Hang on Jess, you don't believe me? I totally want to tell you that I entered only to...'

'Wait.' Jessy yelled, cutting Mitch off, 'we need to know when the spacecraft is coming, so we can make sure we've got enough life-support.' Her cheeks were bright crimson. 'We *need* to know, so we can forward plan, simple as that.' She said anxiously, with hands on her hips. 'Not endlessly discuss your justifications and pretexts to entering that thing.' Jessy was talking angrily with bulging eyes and flaring nostrils, that not even the helmet could hide, not happy with Mitch at all.

She reckoned his reasoning was just so much bullshit. He had tunnel-vision obsession and was so ego-driven, it was ridiculous. Mitch made a great astronaut but as a husband and father, she wasn't quite as sure. In fact, in her eyes, he wasn't worth jack squat as that.

*   *   *

She phoned Josh again to ensure NASA were coming, and to catch up with her son again. Couldn't be as bad as last time, she hoped. Cass took the call and heard the extended silence and knew it was delay caused by distance, and diverted the phone call to Josh straight away, rather than intervene.

Josh took the call and only waited a few seconds for Jessy's voice. 'NASA want to assist – they are going to send a Lunar Express to get you and dad, it'll be there in thirty-three hours,' he said with authority. 'Starting in one point five hours when it'll take-off from Florida. The *Lunar* will do an Earth-loop first to assist with acceleration and then onto yourselves at the Moon.

'No problems getting the craft?' Jessy asked, thinking he must have had all sorts, organising the craft for them. Even with private venturers into space, vehicles capable of moving humans and obtaining orbit were still hellishly difficult to acquire. Sean had told her frequently what a pain in the arse NASA were to deal with. Everything had to be in triplicate and signed off by everyone right up to a doubly difficult POTUS for off-scheduled craft.

'When I told them it was for you, it was basically "how far", even POTUS, so none of it was any real problem. Getting a craft, or lift-off, no probs, or anything else really. Amazing how fast things happen when both parties agree so quick. Even NASA were fine, despite the, ah...issues with the Moon. Remarkable what happens when you drop the name of Mitch Taylor.'

'What do you mean "issues with the Moon"?' Jessy asked. It was obviously deeper but...what else?

'It's now in a very deep orbit, more than a million k's from Earth,' he said clearly. The Moon's orbital-period is still the same at just over twenty-nine days, it's still tidally locked, it just goes faster around the Earth to get it done...there's the same symmetry.'

'One more decent strike and it'll be gone for good, I guess,' she said, with a growing smile. 'It was an impact on the Moon, right?

Josh said yes and asked his mum if she was actually listening to him, to which she answered, "of course she was". 'Welcome home,' he said warmly and then disconnected. A man of few words,' Jessy said, grinning faintly and eyeing Mitch knowingly.

'That's our son, Jess,' Mitch said, grinning affectionately and shaking his head, having listened in to the entire conversation remotely through his helmet.

Soooooo, we've got a day and a half to wait until they arrive.' Mitch said, wondering what the hell they were going to do for that long. We've got plenty of oxygen, food, water and the like. It's the minds we have to keep busy, somehow, Mitch thought, *humming* inside his helmet, glancing at Jessy and raising his eyebrows.

'I don't think so Mitch, we're not just-married,' Jessy said, smiling and gently shaking her helmeted head. 'Besides, that won't waste much time.' She wore a huge smile. 'Think of something else.' She knew the statement was steeply rhetorical because they were both fully suited and the vehicle unpressurised. Game over Mitch, she thought, putting a finger near her mouth on the visor and giggling.

*   *   *

Having observed Earth and the Moon for a few hours, Mitch wondered why the Moon shifted. It was a complete mystery so far, although he had ideas...presumably, from what Josh had said, which wasn't much, Earth didn't know either, apart from a large meteor or asteroid.

It was believed to be large enough to shift the Moon's orbit but not large enough to send the Moon packing for good. Further studies were required around seismic resonances.

*   *   *

It started as a dim light in space which slowly got brighter and they could see it moving against the background of stars. They could see the lights of the craft at the limit of their vision. It looked like the atmospheric descent of a small meteor.

It began as a moving single light in space and rapidly got bigger. Then it pivoted in space and ignited its MPS with its RCS still operating to turn it and bring it in, rear fins first. The craft landed almost perfectly, straight down, throwing the fine lunar talcum high into the anaemic atmosphere. It came down like the old lunar modules from the Apollo era, although with this one there was a lot more balance involved.

Mitch and Jessy ambled slowly toward the rocket sitting not far away on the Smyth Mare. Most of the dust kicked up by the new arrival was still floating in the weak atmosphere, and some escaped the gravity well of the Moon and headed into space. The engines were now powering down, the vessel having landed and the pilots waiting impatiently for Mitch and Jessy to clamber aboard amid the descending dust.

Climbing the ladder, they folded themselves into two of the vacant seats, watching the clouds of dust slowly descend past the starboard window. Jessy grinned firstly at the 2IC, the co-pilot and then the pilot, who both nodded back. She sat down next to Mitch and strapped in army style. The pilot nodded in return, but that was all the acknowledgement they received. They were right behind the pilot and could see every move he and the co-pilot made. He spoke to his buddy throughout take-off as they shared and confirmed various data related to the spaceplane.

Then they eventually took off and they barely noticed it - in a very short spray of lunar dust and dirt and an equally short countdown. Mitch remembered taking off from Kazakhstan on Earth. It was a nightmare of noise, pain and *hoping* the rocket would stay whole amid massive rattling and vibrating, while it pierced the Earth's atmosphere. This, in comparison, was so easy. Gravity was like that.

Mitch and Jessy both felt the gees as they were forced back slightly into their seats, again nothing like in Russia, but it was good because the momentum meant they were going home. Even though *home* might not be as close as it used to be.

'Can you hear me, okay?' Mitch asked, staring at Jessy.

'Of course,' Jessy replied, why wouldn't I?' She bugged her eyes out as though he was asking her something very unnecessary. Jessy looked down and made sure the mic was where it was supposed to be.

'Well, I didn't mean it like that. Anyway, it doesn't matter.' He glanced at her, 'We're alone what I mean, and the answer is yes, right?'

'Again, of *course*. Why are you being so weird?'

'I'm not trying to be. Just wanna make sure we can speak alone. I know, *I know*...of course we can.' They were almost helmet to helmet, speaking through their personal comms system.

'I want to talk about *One*,' Mitch whispered, feeling OMS kick in to transfer them to an Earth bearing course.

'Go ahead,' Jessy said, pretty sure she knew what he was going to say.

'Well, er...okay, with the shift of twenty years and taking the relativistic impact of the Virijian ship into account, they're due in a couple of weeks. Zamindar confirmed it. All we need to do is to recover the Sphere, right?'

Jessy pulled back from Mitch and grimaced, with widening eyes. '*Jesus*, are you serious...*all* we need to do? And, how the hell do we do that?' She said, shaking her head and looking closely at Mitch in wide-eyed astonishment. Seriously, she thought, what a bonehead. That was a *major* undertaking - surely, he got that? It wasn't like swooping down and picking it up with your teeth. Mitch was such a tool sometimes.

'Has to be a commercial chopper, but that trip's got to be ten thousand k's,' Mitch said, doubting whether they had the technology to deal with it. He seriously doubted whether they could go that far in a chopper, unless they re-fuelled half-way, which obviously could be done, but they'd prefer not to, given the cargo being carried and the likely occupants of the craft.

'I'm wondering whether we should bother getting the Sphere at all,' Mitch said, clearly still thinking it through. What if they've evolved into, er...silicon...er, you know, into robots? He peered directly at her. 'They might decide to erase us, with only disdain for our humanity, total and utter indifference, as though we're no more than a virus. Their whole outlook may have changed. In spite of all the work they did in getting us going, they might be completely different now...have a completely different way of thinking and operating.' Mitch grimaced and looked away. They were an old species so he didn't think that would happen, based on nothing more than their age. Jessy nodded and seemed to believe it though.

'*Shit*...I hadn't thought of that,' Jessy finally squawked, wondering what in God's name they could look like and think like...now. But seriously, she hadn't considered that they could be robots or even something else similar. '*Shit*,' she repeated, pondering way too deeply. She wondered what else she hadn't considered, feeling her entire body covered in a sheen of ice-cold moisture. Ironically, she felt super-warm...everywhere.

Too late to worry about that now, they invited themselves a long time ago. Be pretty dumb to change our mind so late. Despite many apocalyptic scenarios filling her mind, it was what it was. Jessy acknowledged that it may have been the wrong decision, but so too was saying "no" now. So, they had to ride with it. We needed to welcome them to our shores.

One had created everything around her - Jessy knew that much as truth. *Everything* owed its existence to *One*. But that didn't mean they were the same beings now. Although twenty years for them was probably the same as the twenty years for her and Mitch had elapsed like nothing at all. It passed like a virtual finger-snap.

That meant whatever they thought then, was probably how they thought today. Jessy realised there was a hell of a lot of "maybes" involved in her thought process – and that in itself was a major worry. They'd just have to wait and see. *It would be what it would be,* a thought process that was anything but comforting.

The humans needed the Sphere because that's how we were supposed to meet - it would be a massive sign of rudeness if they were to leave it where it was. As far as she was concerned, the Sphere needed to be in front of them. Even though she wasn't looking forward to the meeting - that was how *they* were supposed to enter this world according to their own statements.

Jessy eyed Mitch steadily, her eyes were swollen and full of broken red capillaries. She looked haunted and weird. 'We'll have to take the chance,' Jessy whispered, 'we can't back out now.' *As if,* she reckoned.

'I haven't told anyone they're coming,' Jessy said.

'I only told Ben,' Mitch said, staring fixedly forward. I know Sean did the same as I did. He told Ben about it in super detail. That's it. Ben hasn't spilled the beans to anyone apart from POTUS. If he did, they would have put him in a padded cell with all the chemical comforts. We'll get Ben and Sean as well as the Virijians to meet us at AASSA, *then* we get the Sphere. *One* are so utterly prevailing, it is hardly smart to say no, you're *not* allowed to visit. If they want to visit, best to say, come right in. Because they'll come anyway.' Mitch said forcefully.

He was actually shit-scared about the meeting, but tried hard not to show it. Mitch ran his hand through his hair again and again. It all seemed way too soon. The twenty years they'd skipped went like a blink of the eye. He felt like running or vomiting.

*   *   *

The craft they were in, pivoted and staged a controlled landing, rear fins first, at the Lunar Centre AASSA in bulls-eye Australia. Mitch and Jessy felt the violent bump which meant, they assumed, that they'd returned to Earth and landed safely. It was a flawless computer-driven landing in arid, central Australia.

Sean and Ben watched, spellbound as the vessel turned downward and landed slowly from space. The manoeuvre wasn't regulation for them, so it was heart-in-mouth stuff, until the vehicle made it onto the pad. Landing vertically onto land was pretty new, for Sean and Ben it was brand new – they'd never seen it before. SpaceX had made it routine.

Sean imagined Mitch on Mars ambling across Chryse Planitia like an apparition. He hadn't clapped eyes on him for decades, which apparently for them was only days. It was all so crazy. Time itself was crazy, easy to manipulate if you knew how. But it was very fundamental to us humans, he reckoned, smirking to himself.

He saw Mitch and the others go through the open door of the tarmac area and into AASSA proper. He and Jessy looked so bloody young, which he reckoned they probably were, Afterall, they'd effectively dodged twenty years.

'We should go and welcome 'em back to AASSA I suppose,' Sean said.

'Yep, I reckon.' Ben agreed, and started walking forward.

'*Not every day we get to meet a dead man,*' Sean said, chortling briefly turning his face toward the ceiling and then grimacing. '*God Almighty,*' he wheezed, looking around and not really seeing anything, but admitting to himself, he was as nervous as hell. He didn't think he'd ever be meeting Mitch

69

Taylor again. It felt like a crazy, insane dream. Back from the dead – *who would have thought*?

Both Sean and Ben walked down the almost empty slope that led to the main Customs area on the ground floor. Jessy and Mitch had just departed their vessel and walked into the airport, with each of them holding their own helmet and pressure gowns. Mitch and Jessy saw the two of them less than a hundred metres away. Jessy waved to Sean as soon as she saw him.

Ben and Sean, even though they'd only been apart for a short while from Mitch and Jessy's perspective, still looked like familiar old friends, especially Sean, with whom they'd shared so much. Ben and Sean hadn't seen either of them for over twenty years, and he was quite certain they were both in the cemetery. Who could forget the funerals? And now, here they were. It was ridiculous, but if you drilled down bit, so was time itself.

All that was missing from the picture was Rhys, Mitch thought, swallowing heavily, remembering his face, especially the crease in his cheek when he smiled. It was really hard to believe he had been dead for over twenty years. And unfortunately, he really was dead. *Burnt and gone.*

Scared out of her wits, Jessy approached tentatively, as did Sean.

'Hello,' She said sternly, to Sean whose face predictably crumbled and he whispered brokenly, 'come here you.' Sean and Jessy embraced and both unsurprisingly, cried all over each other. Mitch shook Sean's hand firmly and slapped him on the back, exchanging wry grins.

Sean was now seventy-four years old and apart from greyer hair and a few more wrinkles, looked exactly the same. It was old weather-beaten Sean. Mitch and Jessy looked, at first sight, like his son and daughter.

'What about Zamindar and Char?' Jessy said, peering at the group a little unsure. Surely, they were needed more than ever right now.

'Er...they're in transit from Gaia and due to arrive in about two days,' Ben said. 'And we have a pretty much brand-new, long-range Apache Helicopter coming from NASA. I need to give them a reason why you need such a craft as soon as we can. If it wasn't for you and your name, they would've said no, outright. Luckily, I know the Administrator quite well,' Ben said with a gleam in his eye. 'The name *Mitch Taylor* didn't hurt either. They've heard of you *alright*. Paul nearly fell over himself agreeing to it as long as Mitch was involved and would sign for it.'

'Well, that's nice to hear...remember *One*, that's what the chopper's for...to pick up the Sphere. It's the twenty-year anniversary on Wednesday, next week Sean,' Mitch gawked at Sean, swallowing hard and blinking overly fast.

'Yeah, I know,' Sean said. 'Ben reminded me. It's been a long, *long* time since that event ... *for us a-anyway*.' He didn't know where to look, and ended up staring at the ground. He acted like a nervous kitten, straightening his shirt with a hand.

'Very long time,' Ben agreed, but we should get the Virijians to retrieve it, save time.'

Mitch scowled at Ben who immediately wondered what he'd said wrong. '*That is such bullshit,*' Mitch said angrily, glowering at Ben, who reared away from Mitch, 'we can't leave it all for the Virijians to do, *One's* was an invitation to us – to *humanity, not to the Virijians.*' Mitch clenched his jaw and peered angrily at Ben. 'Therefore, it's up to *us* to do the grunt-work, *not* the Virijians.' He grimaced and glared at Sean and then Ben. They made no eye contact with Mitch and both looked down at the floor. As usual, he was right. To both of them, he seemed far more intimidating and serious than he had before. Ben looked at Mitch and couldn't help wondering what that alien shift had done to him.

'*Jesus Christ,*' Mitch said, clenching his jaw again, and staring skyward, 'how far away is that Goddamn chopper?'

'About four hours,' Sean said, peering at Ben, who nodded, 'Relax Mitch, it'll be here soon.'

'*Really*?' He said irritably, and continued to look skyward impatiently. '*Shit,* that long,' he said, and followed with various grunts and indistinct mutters of displeasure. He focussed into the distance but predicably, saw nothing. Must be still on its way, he knew.

*   *   *

The Tshuapa River was slightly south of the bigger Lopori River and was tropical in every sense of the word. It flowed west to the town of Mabdanka where it merged with the mighty Congo River. None of the Lomami who lived there knew it was home to an object engineered in a different universe. None would even know what that meant. The people of the Congo had no idea the jungle was home to anything but trees, vines, nuts and water. And that was to their betterment.

The Sphere had woken after years of inactivity but outwardly it looked no different. After millions of years orbiting Titan in the freezing cold of the vacuum, time wasn't noticed or was of the slightest significance to the object. It passed through amhibolites and pyroxene-rich rocks as easily as neutrinos go through an iron block, ending up on the surface of the deeply weathered granite, *waiting*. In reality, it wasn't on the surface of anything, it was stationery relative to the partly liquid core of the planet. The object looked like it was sitting on granite, but it only looked that way. It was actually in a stationery orbit above the core. It did in reverse what Char had done twenty years ago. It was waiting for its role in the apparent *Protocol* between the two races.

Around them was a dense jungle with a huge canopy more than a hundred feet off the ground, stuffed full of all manner of animals, some nice, some very nasty indeed. The whole thing was home to huge trees, fungi, plants, animals and water. More than three hundred centimetres of rain hit this area each year and the Tshuapa River was full to the brim as it meandered its way toward the much larger Congo River.

The Sphere just sat there on the weathered granite below ground while life went on around it, birds chirped and tweeted, monkeys screamed and chattered, and water burbled and gurgled. The Sphere just ... 'was'.

*   *   *

The chopper lowered the specially modified Sproule Net toward the banks of the Tshuapa River and the Sphere. It had been raining all morning – heavy. Typical of this place in the wet season. Rain, then more rain. And after that, rain. Very, very tropical.

They had travelled from Australia to hopefully collect the Sphere and return it to AASSA to facilitate the arrival of *One*. It was time to *tell* the world...and watch it destroy almost every fundamental theory about humanity. Still, truth was truth. If it *was* truth of course - it was still hard to believe, but it seemed to add up to something that made you giddy and off-balance.

They were all worried about how humanity generally would acclimatise to the news of *One*, the grand cosmic designers. They were so advanced - it was impossible to get your head around their true abilities. They had such cognitive oneness that they were truly the magicians Arthur C Clarke spoke of. A created Universe had been theorised many times, a lot saying the odds of it being true was not zero, but no one sane and not a religious zealot, believed that the Universe was unnatural.

But in fact, yes, it was. It was created by advanced aliens from a different universe, who wanted a playground for their technology and desires. This most unlikely and fantastical scenario was actually true. It was thoroughly unbelievable, but it was true. And Earth would soon know. They could make up their own minds. Many wouldn't believe. Being cynical about new things was part of the human condition.

Again, whatever had happened, had happened. Mitch wondered what Josh would make of it, let alone the rest of the world. That there was a maker, a cosmic producer, a civilisation that was so advanced and lived for so long that engineering an entire universe was within their technological grasp.

All this stuff made your brain and your head spin. The human brain didn't have enough connections to properly deal with such a stunning concept. Everything and everybody apparently, owed their existence to them. *One* was Nature. *God*, if you will. And Jessy, and he and others were supposed to meet them, and complete some so-called *one-contact protocol* which was supposed to allow humanity to integrate the information successfully. There was only one issue to be concerned with – *nobody outside of AASSA knew about them yet.*

If Mitch and Jessy hadn't "gone away" for twenty years, Earth would already know, but they didn't, and as a result of their "trip", humanity didn't have a clue. But now, the planet would finally know the truth.

The Fermi Paradox and the great silence would be the first thing to go, followed by most of philosophy. Jessy could imagine the unrest it would cause. There'd be riots and uprisings on the streets - some would believe, some wouldn't. Humanity would find severe negatives in such a bold declaration.

There'd be riots worldwide. From Spain to Lebanon, China, the US – you name a place and it would be bursting with unrest. A lot of the population would be on the streets. Because suddenly, severe unknowns and strangeness would be introduced to daily life. By quantifying reality, *One* had ironically made everything in the Universe different.

Mitch kept saying it was all too ridiculous for words. There was one thing they did know - Mitch was right. They would meet them, incorporate the meeting into history, and move on with their civilisation - that was the plan. The only problem with that - the plan was so much bullshit, Jessy was sure. Meeting them would be so incredible, and it would stay with them forever. *That*, she was sure about.

*   *   *

Mitch sent the net down exactly as he was shown, and the expert NASA had found from Kilimanjaro Search and Rescue helped strap the Sphere in. It was strangely light, and that surprised no one, except the African who strapped it on. He lifted it up and put it in easily. It was as light as a soap bubble apparently. By the size of his smile and the brightness of his teeth, he was pretty pleased with himself. The Sphere now resided in the cargo hold of the chopper. It was humanity's object again.

They left immediately, the pilot getting light on the skids and slowly rising in the air, and then all the blades were pitched forward, and with the engine screaming, they started toward their destination at the AASSA base.

The Sphere itself was unpacked near the main runway by Mitch who did it easily. It *was* relatively light, albeit awkward for him because of its shape and size. The chopper leapt away from the space centre in a spray of golden dust and was into the sky and soon became a dot in the distance and then was gone. It was going back to NASA from whence it came.

All that needed to happen was for Josh to arrive, hopefully followed by the Virijians...and then there would be a formal briefing of everyone on *the List*. Those that had been chosen to be present when *One* appeared. Mitch thought of Galileo, Newton, Hawking and Carl Sagan, and a hundred others, and reckoned they all deserved to be here way more than him. Mitch and Jessy were introducing *One* and shattering the Fermi Paradox on one hand and trying to give it some perspective on the other. And didn't expect to be successful in the least. But, he guessed, he was in the right place at the right time. Lucky me, he thought curiously, scratching his jaw. Strange thing is, he didn't feel lucky at all. Mitch felt, well...unlucky.

Josh was due for arrival on a Gulfstream G550 in about three hours' time. AASSA had very kindly chartered it from U-jet and all they were waiting on was its arrival, at 4.25 P.M. local time. This added to Mitch's anxiety. The whole thing made him feel bilious.

Meeting his own boy shouldn't have such an effect on him, yet after so many years, it did. Hardly surprising, he reckoned, given that he'd apparently *died*, and the pending visit of *One*. The term "it's all happening" didn't do this time in his life justice.

*   *   *

Josh was back in AASSA territory, again. He knew this place so well. This time though, it was very different, indeed. Josh was supposed to be on holiday in Sydney but he was called back to South Australia almost immediately. To meet with dear old dad, he was told. Plus, a surprise, apparently. Whatever the hell that meant? His dad had been presumed dead for the best part of twenty years – that was a fair surprise in itself! Surely that was enough of a surprise.

Mitch peered at his son closely as he walked across the tarmac as a complete stranger. Josh could have been anyone. He looked nothing like the six-year-old that he'd left. Josh was just starting "big school" when they left him. Now, he was all grown up and in his prime.

He would've been proud of his boy, no matter what, but he reckoned Josh was a mirror image of him in his mid-twenties. Good looking, tall, athletic, closely shaven and a short haircut. Josh was every inch of Mitch at the same age. Mitch thrust his chest out as he watched Josh make his way toward the terminal.

He stared at him as he went through Customs and approached them. It was going to be like meeting your younger self. Mitch braced himself for an onslaught of very strange, *weird,* emotions. He tried not to feel them by pressing his toes deeply into his shoes and clenching his legs.

Holy shit, here we go, he thought, seeing Josh approach. Mitch felt like smiling and crying at the same time. Jessy, was rubbing the back of her neck, taking short, mincing steps, and struggling with the same emotions. She wasn't sure what to do or how to feel. There was a gamut of uneasy emotions warring inside her as she gazed at her son. Jessy stared at his face closely, searching for bits she remembered, of which there were many.

'Hello Joshy,' Mitch whispered hoarsely, he like Jessy, watched Josh's face and his eyes carefully. Mitch's stony veneer was cracking. This is the same kid that was fascinated with his toys and Mario just a short while before, from their perspective. Josh would play with his toys for hours in his tree-house. No doubt, he wouldn't give a toss about them now. He had more pressing "man" issues to deal with. Mitch knew the sorts of things that would be high in his mind now, and it wouldn't be toys.

Looking at Josh, it was incredible and impossible, and emotional beyond words. They looked at each other, studying each closely. Josh rubbed the stubble on his chin, still peering closely at his father. If Josh had similar feelings to him, Mitch wouldn't be surprised.

D-Dad?' Josh said. 'You sure as shit look like me,' Josh said. They stood still and ramrod straight, only a few metres apart. Silence pervaded the two as they sized each other up, like two roosters. Josh walked up to Mitch and they both hugged tightly, father and son lost in time but now reunited. They held each other at arm's-length and hugged deeply again. Mitch slapped him on the back as he hugged him tight. Jessy cried, tears streaming from her eyes as she watched the two embrace. By the time he got to her, she was a soaked basket-case, ready to collapse to the ground.

From counting on the wall to a fully-fledged adult, who the fuck would have thought, *instantly.* One minute, a boy, the next, a man. For Mitch and Jessy, anyway. The shock was electrifying and profound.

Josh hadn't seen his brothers or Alysha for years. He knew his other family members were all in the United States, but doing what, he had no idea. They never caught up - which was sad, although he knew Mitch had plans to find them all and meet. Hopefully it would go better than his last phone call with them which was nothing short of horrible and very short.

For whatever reason, they didn't want to know him. That was sad too, *family,* he reckoned. You can't choose 'em. It is what it is. It can get pretty ugly at times. *C'est la vie,* he thought.

5

NASA

**"A pawn is the most important piece on the chessboard—to a pawn."
— *Isaac Asimov***

Zamindar and Charijiok would now arrive by Ajiron at 3.30p.m. EST. At that point there would be less than an hour until the twenty-year timeframe, as best as they could agree on, ticked over. Hopefully, they would appear at the beginning of the twentieth year – but who really knew? It could just as easily be at the goddamn end.

Nobody really had any idea at all, it was all guesswork, or it was based on our own logic. There was that old chestnut again. Was our logic, logical in a wider sense? Of course, we thought so. We would have to run with it because it's all we had. In our minds, twenty years, occurred at the beginning, not the end of the year. Time would tell if even that stood up.

It would be more likely at the beginning of the year but maybe that wouldn't be the case. Just because it made sense to us, it meant nothing when dealing with them. And with One, they probably didn't come any more alien than that. Which probably meant thinking very differently indeed.

The most pressing and serious question was – *why* did Jessy and Mitch time shift twenty years, the exact time, give or take, before *One* arrived? The coincidence was way too much for Mitch to accept. Occam's Razor wasn't meant to be stretched so thin. Surely, it couldn't be an accident, could it? As far as he was concerned, *One* refused *not* to have him and Jessy here. That was sort of an answer, as contrived as it was.

So...that was his view and he acknowledged it could be wrong, but he stuck to it anyway. Besides, he couldn't think of anything else. As far as he was concerned, mere coincidence wasn't a realistic option, Mitch thought, gazing at the sky, waiting impatiently for the Virijians to arrive.

*   *   *

The Ajiron descended straight down and kissed the Earth about two hundred metres from the Sphere. A cloud of reddish dust was blown up as the

Ajiron itself, came silently to rest on the ground. Zamindar and Char were inside, and visible from the outside. Like two huge puppets piloting the craft.

Mitch felt like waving, followed up by vigorous hand-shaking, but didn't do either, knowing the disinterested response he'd get back, despite the fact that they hadn't seen him or Jessy for twenty years. To the Virijians - it wouldn't matter. Inanities and pleasantries weren't for them. Mitch knew them well.

Mitch, Jessy and the two Virijians were expected to brief NASA this afternoon and then they would tell the world. They weren't particularly happy with the short lead-in time, but that was literally their own problem to deal with. There were bigger things to be concerned with and they'd seen how fucked up it can all get when things are supposed to be kept on the down low – but *aren't*. This would at least obviate that problem, he believed. By making a single address to the media. Then, the world would make of it what they would.

Of course, most would initially say *bullshit* but hopefully over time, the source of the data, together with their own explanations and rebuttals, would eventually, perhaps gain general agreement among most of the population of Earth. Still, some would never believe. They had to accept that there was a certain percentage of people who could *never* be persuaded.

They hadn't seen the Virijians for twenty years or at least the Virijians hadn't seen them for that period, but as was expected, all Mitch and Jessy got from them was indifference despite giving them an effusive greeting. That was the human way. And they got the Virijian way in return.

No wonder they'd lived so long as a species, Mitch thought. They never got emotional - if coming back from the dead after two decades didn't affect you just a little bit, it's unlikely that anything would. They were genuinely robotic in the way they acted and reacted.

They all stepped into the Ajiron and sat down behind the pilot seats. Destination was NASA HQ, Washington D.C., Columbia, in North America. Zamindar and Char looked precisely the same as they both remembered. And they were exactly as indifferent, Jessy thought, and as ugly as ever, although both, especially Zamindar, had the appearance of a reliable, trustworthy friend. Both the Virijians stared forward and by the look of their cranial knots, were chatting feverishly to each other. Exchanging flight information hopefully. No doubt it was that and perhaps a little bit more.

*   *   *

Mitch walked in, as head of their group, and saw all the NASA heavyweights seated around a huge oak table which had five spare seats near its head. Mitch and Jessy walked into the room and made eye contact with as many suits as they could and all of them nodded and smiled back. James Walker continued to look down as they walked past, he was the head of USPA and an Executive Director here at NASA.

Seniors from all G20 Governments were present, waiting anxiously to ferry details back to their respective nations. Also, there were several members of NASA's agencies at Toulouse, Stennis, Capetown and Ningpo. The Director of the Astrophysical Council was there, as were four members from the NSA and SSEC. George Jerome was present from CNN. Paul Black from the UN. And two members of the Presidential Committee from the Whitehouse.

'As if the Moon wasn't enough,' George fumed, flicking his pen from hand to hand, eager for the meeting to start. The sooner it starts, the sooner it finishes was his general philosophy with meetings. The title of this debrief was intriguing though, but then so were most, just to get bums on seats. This one was compulsory and looking at the addressee list, its intrigue level went up a notch or two. It went from probably boring to possibly compelling.

There was also the Assistant Secretary of Defense and chiefs from the National Science Foundation, the Science Advisory Committee, The National Security Council and six of the eminent dozen, Earth's cognitive front-line for anything interstellar that required real brain power to be applied. They were different faces and different names but most of them were from the same agencies as his previous meeting with Brian Gates about CX-1. Brian was dead, poor old sod, but Mitch reckoned he would have added as much value as this lot put together.

He surveyed the faces of those present and had to physically hold himself back from shaking his head and grunting in disbelief. He knew he shouldn't be so judgemental, but such was life, he thought, trying not to grin. Many were looking down at their phones and the remainder looked as though they had just gotten a shocking diagnosis from their doctor. Mitch could see that his work was well and truly in front of him.

Unfortunately, he would be doing most of the talking. Who he was addressing looked and sounded like a complete rabble, even if on paper, they weren't. They were the highest representatives from NASA and the Government to be assembled in one place since Oumuamua appeared in the solar system.

Mitch stood up and coughed loudly, more to get their attention than anything else. They were talking and doing anything other than paying attention. All eyes were now on him. That was good and he should be used to it, he supposed, but he wasn't even close to feeling at ease. Talking to this mob was the last thing he felt like doing, mainly because Mitch knew they didn't like him. Many of them actively disliked him. Some of them outright hated him.

C'est La Vie, he thought. *Fuck 'em*, he spat silently. He knew there was nothing he could do about it.

'Uh...for those who don't know me, I'm Mitch Taylor, Head, er,' he glanced down at Jessy and shrugged his shoulders, 'former Head of AASSA.' He held in "first man on Mars", but he was sure they knew it, apparently it really pissed Americans off, so he didn't say it. He didn't want to irritate 'em so early, Staring at the table in front of him,brim full of fuckers, Mitch thought from his experience most of these Government types were insufferable. He peered at the faces around the table and grinned mischievously. He was sure this wasn't going to go well. He knew what they were like – especially as a group.

Mitch hadn't written anything down or gotten anything straight in his mind. He felt sure he could wing it. After all, he'd been front and centre when the object was found and when it revealed its detail to the Virijians. He felt reasonably confident he could convey a decent overview.

Now, peering at the seriously unfriendly faces, he wasn't sure it was such a great idea. He was sure they were just waiting for him to fall flat on his arse. His confidence had evaporated into the ether somewhere between his chair and the mic.

'Are, um...we ready...sound level, okay?' He got the thumbs-up at the back to suggest it was okay. Apart from that, there was little response from anyone, and he wondered if they were fully awake and focussed. Most of them looked half asleep. This'll wake them up, he thought evilly.

'Okay, we detected something with no light curve orbiting Titan when we were on the way back from engaging CX-1.' Mitch thought he may as well get straight into it, rip the Band-Aid off in one motion as it were. He gazed around the table, they generally looked extremely bored. He felt like clapping his hands to wake them up. Or yelling, "*hey.*" He didn't do either, but he sure as shit felt like it. There was some movement and talk, but generally, it was pretty quiet. Mitch got straight down to it.

'Turns out, it was an object, a sphere actually, orbiting Titan, made by a race of beings twenty *billion* years old.' Saying it out loud made it sound nuts...the product of a very deluded mind. There was commotion in the rooms now, it sounded a bit like a jeering football crowd, George was yelling "*listen*" over and over, Mitch soon felt like the single umpire, alone and helpless against a crowd that was coming over the fence and there was no security to hold them back. It seemed like everyone was yelling at him at the same time. None of them, apart from maybe George, was on his side, it seemed. It was rapidly getting very ugly and very loud indeed.

Jessy was sure this was how the population generally would behave if the information was released in one tranche, without explanation. *Panic*. Born of complete confusion. That's how *she* felt when she first had it laid at her feet by the Virijians. Why wouldn't the greater population feel the same way? Totally and *utterly* muddled.

Zamindar stood quickly, he could tell the meeting was getting out of control. '*Please listen*,' he boomed, 'if there are any inconsistencies, I will tell you,' he toned loudly to all of them, including Mitch and Jessy. Mitch peered at Zamindar and thought, great - *no pressure* - he hoped like hell his memory stood up. Maybe he should've written something down, made sure he remembered it all. All the detail.

Now that he had their attention, or more accurately, because it was silent, he dove back in. Mitch considered deferring to Zamindar to speak about the Sphere, but in the end he didn't. He'd do it himself. Why? He reckoned he could remember fine by himself. And it was his responsibility. The object was left for *us*, afterall. For *humanity*.

'These beings that designated themselves with the number *One*, claim that they, through their munificence with genetics, transformed the early Ape life into intelligence.' Mitch looked around, all the suits were quiet and staring at him, waiting for more. Zamindar was watching him and listening closely and importantly, was silent.

'*One* say that they created humans, from what would have been a permanent sensory backwater. From a creature with Ape like instinct to a creature that was conscious and self-aware.' The eyes nearest to him gaped disbelievingly and those eyes were mirrored all around the room and in Zoom. All of them found it difficult to believe. They all gawked at each other, waiting for someone to say something. Zamindar's silence was deafening. His eyes said it all.

'What about *evolution.*' Neil from the NSA said loudly, 'I'd always heard that *it* was the reason.' Everyone nodded at Neil, then looked at Mitch, demanding a response. Mitch visibly swallowed and hand-combed his hair. Mitch was already at the mic.

'No...I mean evolution still occurred. It's still an accurate theory, it just didn't lead to us, *homo*, splitting off from Apes and becoming truly intelligent and self-aware. They went to great pains to explain that intelligence wouldn't have appeared on Earth without them. Without their help.'

Everyone understood the implications of that statement. *One* wee mum and dad. All the suits looked like they'd been hit by shovels.'

Zamindar gazed directly at Mitch, as did Jessy. It was time for the big one. If they found that hard to believe, which clearly, they did, try this on for size, Jessy thought. Zamindar looked like he was urging Mitch on with his eyes, but he was probably making that one up in his mind, he wasn't sure.

Jessy stared wordlessly at Mitch, her heart pounding. She knew what he was about to broach. It was *the* most momentous and glorious thing. And the most difficult part to get your head around. She was sure most of them wouldn't understand, either the concept or its implications.

Mitch took in a few deep breaths before he continued. 'They claim to have created the Universe.' He was pretty sure that'd get 'em. Mitch eyed the Secretary of Defence squarely. Take that, he thought, raising his eyebrows and staring at him like a mad bull, red in the face. The General was staring flat-eyed at him and looked completely frozen. His mind was actually racing – he was bewildered and muddled, unable to process Mitch's statement at all. '*W-W-Whhhat?*' he moaned

A lot of them threw their hands in the air. All were staring straight ahead. It was too much to accept for most. There was one question that was repeated and came through the vociferous rabble. *How?*

Well...the answer to that was fuck knows. None of them, not even Zamindar, knew the real answer to that one. He knew what they'd have to do, but actually doing it remained an utter mystery.

'They do not discuss any technical details.' Mitch said. Many were shaking their heads, rolling their eyes or smirking, sceptical about their claims. Mitch continued, 'They bent space using a monopole and it inflated into what we have today. Of course, the energies have to be manicured very delicately. *Anyway*...It's pure Cosmogenesis...they are *everything* to us, Mother, Father, you name it...t-they're *it*. They obviously exist in a completely different universe. The concept of a multiverse, as it turns out, is quite accurate.' Mitch watched Zamindar and noticed his silence.

'But, where, who...*why?*' Peter Tracy from the SSEC spluttered, Peter ground his jaw and opened and closed his mouth, but no further sounds were heard, none that were intelligible anyway. The rest of the heavyweights appeared shocked and looked pale, with expressions like they'd been struck by hard implements. To hear what they just heard was difficult, upsetting, and extremely confusing and disconcerting.

No one spoke for a long time – silence descended on the room like a heavy shawl. No-one knew where to look, or what to say. Even Zamindar had nothing to tone, which was probably good. It meant that Mitch had conveyed it correctly. If he hadn't, Zamindar would have had no problem contradicting him or standing over him and completely re-issuing his sentences. He watched James Wallen, Director of the Astrophysical Council, continue to shake his head and roll his eyes. Clearly, he was still sceptical about the claims. Wallen. found it all quite implausible. 'It's one thing to know how to do it...and another actually doing it. Do these *"whatevers"* expect us to believe they've actually done it? I mean created the Universe? That's a very, *very* big place - *come on Mitch for God's sake*.' He stared at him and he was clearly waiting for Mitch to laugh or to retract the claims. Nothing came. James was left hanging with his thoughts laid out or all to see. Looking rapidly left and right, no one was able or wanting to engage with him. He was on his own to question what Mitch and effectively, Zamindar had told him. Zamindar simply glared at him wondering why this time-waster had bothered to speak at all.

Jessy's blood was boiling as she gazed at the pompous goose called James. Mitch could see he was pressing her buttons in the worst way possible. Having her walk up to him, and punch him square in the face, and telling him to "shut it" would be a bad look. But that's where it was rapidly heading. Mitch realised he needed to be put in his place, without inflaming others.

'James,' Mitch began, 'this isn't a Q and A session, it's us telling you what we found out there near Titan, and what it told us, via the un-encryption by the Virijians.' He spoke slowly and emphasised every word. Jeff Rahman began to rise. Zamindar turned his bearish head toward Jeff and toned.

We simply conveyed what was written, no more, no less Mr. Rahman.'

'I'm not suggesting you lied,' Jeff gasped, feeling the weight of Zamindar's ponderous stare. 'Maybe you just read it wrong,' he looked at the ground, wishing he hadn't said anything. '*Jesus*...those eyes,' Jeff thought, focussing on the floor. He suddenly felt very hot.

'*Stop*,' Zamindar thundered, speaking to everyone, 'It is as stated.' Char peered at him. There was no more toning. Everyone around the table was quiet. There seemed to be no more questions. Or none they had the nerve to bring up in the presence of the Virijians. Everyone was unnaturally quiet. It was a table of Politicians and it was quiet. *Amazing*. Perhaps Zamindar should come in when Congress was debating a bill, Mitch thought, grinning.

Eventually, after a long period of silence, someone did speak. It was Jack Abrams from NASA. 'So, you want humanity to meet the makers of the Universe? What the hell do -they look like? 'What do they want from us?' He glanced from person to person. 'They're fair questions, aren't they?' Jack was a painfully thin man who acted like a nervous bird - fidgety, uneasy and frightened, his thin, white hands were shaking before they were pocketed, and his eyes bounced from one person to another. He licked his lips constantly.

"Your guess is as good as mine Jack, who knows? They probably want nothing. They said it's their 'single contact protocol' that they also say has been successful. Apparently, such knowledge in the absence of being able to discuss it, has led to the death of some civilizations. Apparently, some have been unravelled, whatever that means.' Mitch sighed.

'Unravelled?' Jim whispered forcefully. *Shit*, he thought. Noise levels in the room were approaching an intensity that was similar to a jackhammer. Silence had definitely left the building for parts unknown.

'*Jesus...listen,*' Mitch screamed to the lot of them. They might have been successful in their own fields on Earth, but here in crazy town, these people were way out of their depth. They were simply politicians for God's sake. Their reactions were more like your run-of-the-mill people, Mitch reckoned. And it wasn't good. Predictable perhaps, but definitely not good. Looking at them, he was reminded of infants who couldn't get their own way. Outbursts weren't far away. He'd try and soothe them but only so far. After that, they were on their own. God only knows what would happen then. It could turn into a real circus,

Mitch spoke to Jim and whoever else may possibly be listening to him, "Unravelled" could mean many things - successful in extending *species life*, we think. The lives of their children as it were.' Everything sounded very different when spoken out loud, he reckoned. 'Life extension to the human *species*, I think *One* meant.'

'Does that include how to overcome global warming, giving us new technologies perhaps or does it mean literally extending our individual and collective lives, genetically or robotically.' Jim asked.

Mitch hadn't thought of it that way, it was a bit left-field...he scratched his chin. '*Hmmm*...I've got no idea. It's a good question. Um...Zamindar?'

'I believe they were referring to strengthening the civilisation's hold mentally, but the statement is open to interpretation,' Zamindar conceded, staring directly at Jim, then glancing at Mitch as if to confirm it.

Toby Jonas from the USPA spoke to Mitch and Jessy. 'Who will be at the front line when *One* arrive? Er...whenever that might be,' he added, trailing off as he peered around the table.

Mitch stared at Peter. He should know, probably does fucking know. at. 'The eminent dozen and six others, also Jessy, myself and the two Virijians.

The Assistant Secretary of Defence, General Peter Drummond, looked serious and spoke as though he had a mouthful of gravel. 'AASAA has a direct line to the NSA?

'Correct Sir,' Mitch said, a little confused as to what the question might be, and where it was headed.

'Okay then, so what war-footing are we on?' The General's eyes bored into him, waiting for an answer.

'Same as yesterday I suppose,' Mitch said, butting into the conversation, immediately cottoning-on to where this line of questioning was going. He would be better referring that to one of his minions.

'Well…what if an army of them pour out, armed to the fucking hilt.' He glared straight at Mitch, both eyebrows as high as they could go. His eyebrows were mostly hidden under his tangled grey fringe.

'Why General,' Mitch peered straight at him, 'if that happens, then we are thoroughly fucked, 'if they can create a universe then surely, they could weaponise their technology. You can have a war footing of anything General, and it wouldn't matter a dram. 'Being prepared is fine, but our capability in space is zero…theirs would be, er, well…infinite. They are billions of years older than us, and exponentially…way out of sight, wiser in tech - they clearly have command of forces we could only dream about. If they want Earth, then it would already be theirs. Let's face it, they wouldn't wait twenty years to do it. 'But we don't think it'll be anything like that. In any event, we have no defence, so we just turn up and hope for the best.' He looked at the General and smiled.

'Hope for the best,' he snorted, 'it'll be the first time in history we've done it this way, but considering the circumstances, what choice is there I suppose?' He looked totally defeated as he looked down at his shoes. Peter Drummond hated the outcome, but there was no alternative. The situation was exclusively a once-only offer. He felt like throwing his peaked cap on the ground and jumping all over it. He felt totally useless. And he hated that.

Mitch was still standing, gawking at the crowd of dignitaries seated around the mighty oak table at NASA. He saw slack jaws and open mouths and sweat coated foreheads, eyes were wide, some bugged out like strange insects or deep-sea fish, totally gobsmacked to know they were here only at the behest of *One*. Via their genetic tinkering. To know they made the Universe literally from nothing was mind-shattering. To think everything they believed in was wrong. *And now they were here to visit*. That really finished it off nicely.

Mitch walked backward, then forward, and looked squarely down the table at the central camera. There was also a camera behind him that looked straight down the room. He appeared very serious, looking down and then directly at each of them.

'Gentlemen…no doubt, their tech, should they choose to show it, would be like magic to us. Their weapons of offense or defense will be the same. All of you must realize there's no fighting them, there's only making friends with them. So, they don't want to get rid of us, which for them would be so easy.' Mitch made a failed attempt to smile at his audience. Eventually, he gave a tense nod and waited for the avalanche of questions.

'What happens when this hits the media?' Everyone turned to look at George from CNN. He didn't really look like he wanted to talk. He actually felt like hiding under the table. After seeing all the eyes on him, he looked terrified, George was all eyes. Normally, he was calm and eminently self-assured. Not now though. He was the reverse of that. What Mitch had said, and intimated, bit deeply. George immediately thought about the church...what of religion...the bible? He had no immediate answer. He just knew they were in a lot of trouble. 'Er...well,' George continued, '*shit*,' he said, as he stood up. 'It'll be the s-same with the general population as it's been on us, they'll be totally gobsmacked, scared, unsure of the future, unsure of its effect on everyday life...it'll be all of those things and probably more, other stuff that we haven't even considered yet. There will likely be panic on the streets, more crime, depending on what happens tomorrow. It could be better or could be worse...much *fucking* worse.' George had mental images he could've done without. Visions of police shooting people, tear-gas, armed mobs and massive riots on the streets.

Zayne Doyle, the Head of USPA said, 'George and Mitch need to give POTUS a full briefing right away,' he glanced at Mitch and almost growled. 'And he will be required by legislation to give it to the community – the *entire* community, because it *will* affect them. He already knows about *One*, but he'll be floored by the detail – the whole lot sounds like a fucking fairy story.' His mouth snapped shut and it stayed shut. He had nothing more to say.

Mitch knew POTUS already had a reasonable understanding of what was going on. He'd been briefed by Ben from AASSA some time ago but had said nothing to anyone, although pages were added to a certain book. And then it was locked up again. POTUS didn't say anything to anyone about it. He couldn't be relied on for much, but for maintaining privacy of the information, apparently, he *could* be relied on.

'So, AASSA can expect a crowd when they arrive.' Jessy stated.

'Standing room only,' Mitch said, 'at least for the initial bit, depending on when they arrive of course. Officials only, per the invite list. The public themselves will be stopped at the gate and the fence surrounding the place. We'll all be advised of the details of the meeting later.'

'*If* they arrive,' George said gruffly, peering heavenward and shaking his head. He doubted they'd turn up, certainly when they were supposed to. With that, George and Mitch together with Jessy and the rest of the new arrivals, including Zamindar and Char, got up and left the room. Mitch and Jessy with George headed for the White House for formal discussions on *One* with POTUS. They were expected in the Oval Office in one hour. And they needed to be early, apparently.

*   *   *

The three of them had shown their I.D. and passed through a metal detector and submitted to a pat down and were ready to meet POTUS in the

Oval Office. They'd been escorted to their current seating outside the Oval Office by the Secretary of State. John MacAfee who was very polite if not a tad unfriendly. He was more like a robot than a real person. He even walked stiffly. If he spoke in beeps and dings, Jessy wouldn't have been surprised at all.

Although POTUS was a total buffoon, with a major case of self-importance and a global-warming sceptic, his station demanded respect, even if he didn't. And so it was that they were escorted into his office and offered three seats near old Resolute, occupied by the President. They stood, and in turn, shook his firm paw and re-took their seats.

'So, I hear that you've got quite the afternoon planned?' POTUS sat down behind his desk, making various groaning noises and other unidentifiable sounds as he sat down.

'Well yes sir, quite the day, making contact with *One*, whom I believe you are a little familiar with already so Ben tells me,' Mitch said, his face glistening with sweat. Journeying to Mars, meeting ETs for the first time was one thing, but venturing to the White House was a totally unfamiliar and unpleasant experience, well and truly beyond his pay-grade, not to mention his experience, *period*. Meeting POTUS had a dreamy, ethereal quality to it, even if he himself was an idiot.

'Ben...yeah, yep...pretty familiar by words, not personal experience of course. If this goes well, I'll, I, er...I m-mean *we'll* be re-elected. I'm talking about the GOPs obviously.' The President looked a bit sheepish but still puffed his already ample chest out. Stroking his ego, or at least not deflating it, was a good idea, no matter what was at stake. It got a lot more done.

Mitch watched POTUS, thinking should I, or shouldn't I. The conversation was sort of paused so he went for it. He gave him a spiel about climate-change and he saw his lips tighten. By the time he got to "tipping point" his lips were almost puckering, which either meant he was bored and annoyed or excited about what Mitch was saying. The only time he got excited was when GOP numbers were increasing. That only left the former.

'It will go well Mitch, won't it?' The President asked, more as a demand than a question. He knew his chances of re-election hung at least partially on what happened at AASSA. The President was a bloated fool, but as POTUS, his view was to be valued.

They recounted what they knew about *One* to POTUS who seemed to know most of it anyway. They were essentially God. Agreement was total on that score. He knew they were advanced as they come, and they could destroy Earth with a flick of their finger if they desired. He knew what they'd done for humanity and why they were here.

'Good luck tomorrow, make it work Mitch,' the President's eyes bored into him. POTUS didn't want to rock the boat, by having him and his entourage turn up to greet them. That was a mighty good strategy. An unusually good strategy. They all agreed with it unconditionally and nodded to him firmly.

'Yes Sir.' He wasn't sure what else to say. Mitch reckoned he should've said, "it'll be what it'll be". That was far more appropriate.

They were then moved out of the room by the Secretary of State who held his arm out fully erect in the direction of the door. They were escorted to the front gates and then it was up to them to make it to the airport. They filed out of the presidential shuttle at the gate and jumped in a Washington cab and wondered if the meeting ever took place. It had that dreamlike feeling to it. Mitch wondered if it would have put them out, to drive them to the airport. In importance, he felt about one rung above a vagrant.

Did POTUS really comprehend who and what they were meeting with? Mitch doubted it. He probably thought they were more Democrats to defeat.0 POTUS seemed to know what they were talking about though, but he had probably received a high-level briefing from one of his many reports. That was probably who Ben spoke to, he thought.

POTUS was probably none the wiser about detail, as usual. Unless what Mitch and others had heard about him was wrong, he only knew the bullet-points. That was probably good. The less he knew might be to their betterment. He was supposed to enlighten him in detail about *One*. Mitch didn't and wouldn't – he reckoned a high-level overview was all POTUS could handle. His minions like General Drummond or James Wallan could give him what he needed. If they couldn't, that was their problem. He honestly didn't care.

6

One

"The true delight is in the finding out rather than in the knowing."
—*Isaac Asimov*

No one was sure if or when they would arrive or whether any noise or anything else would accompany the increase in mass the Sphere would undergo. This apparently would give them access to our Universe. Or was it their universe? They occupied a different universe altogether

They created our Universe from scratch, all the quasars, all the stars, all the dark matter, dark energy...everything, so it worked together, like a very, carefully manicured pie. And it evolved the right way, so life was afforded the potential it needed.

The most important thing was, what the hell would they look like? What would they be like? It was a very banal fear which probably painted humans for what they were – a very juvenile species. Still, it was front and centre in their minds. It wasn't a matter of not thinking about it – the brain just did it for you. Jessy's fear became more and more real as they moved toward the twenty years ticking over.

They might conceivably be electromagnetic radiation or some other "natural" phenomenon, like integrated sets of information. They could literally be anything, the net thrown could be much wider than humans assume a "natural" being could be. He reviled that word because it honestly meant nothing. "Natural" had no meaning when it came to One. They were nature. One might have eventually all graduated to a massless form of life, to facilitate the never-die civilisation...total immortality. Natural meant made by One, he had to remember that, so did they all, Virijians included. They made Earth.

His heart pumped hard and judging by her eyes, Jessy was having similar internal agitation. Incredible as it might seem – soon, they would meet them. 'Remember,' Mitch said, 'they're essentially God.'

It felt so soon for Mitch and Jessy, too soon, so incredibly long for Sean. Were humans even close to be ready for a meeting? Who fucking knew, He just wasn't sure. The whole of AASSA was now closed. Armed guards were stationed at the front doors and the front gates. No one could get in or out. It was just them, waiting for *One* to arrive. The time had come. The Sphere was in front of them...waiting to complete its primary purpose. Jessy and Mitch were ready to explode. They could both feel their hearts beating hard in their throats. *What were they going to confront?* It was them, at the front of everyone. And that was part of the problem. Mitch and Jessy looked round and felt quite inadequate at the head of humanity. It made sense though – they were the ones who made contact with their Sphere.

Sean, Mitch and Jessy were seated with the Eminent Dozen, Paul Black from the United Nations, and Government types, including George, James, Peter Drummond and the two Virijians, plus two others he'd never seen before. Specialists no doubt. Unnecessary security possibly. If they were needed, it was truly goodnight. They'd have no hope at all. Security against them...*good luck*. They were waiting for the twentieth anniversary of their meeting with the Sphere to tick over. Twenty years since they saw it riding high above Titan. It seemed like only yesterday to Mitch as it was literally only a few days ago.

He looked back and conceded it was a strange sight indeed, almost twenty people, seated around and gawking at a dull, grey sphere about two metres in diameter. In the background was Australia, and in the foreground were runways, hills, AASSA, golden sandy plains, craggy vegetation and above them, brilliant blue sky. Everything seemed ready for this meeting. All they needed was *One*, the timing of which, no-one really understood.

Mitch looked closely at the Sphere in front of them, it appeared brand new, despite its seemingly long and perilous adventure around Titan.

There was only a few seconds to go until twenty years ticked over. Millions of years in space orbiting Titan, and years underground in Africa, and it looked virtually brand-new. There were no blemishes or any signs of degradation. Many of those present wondered what in God's name it was made of. Most settled on it being made from some strange alien alloy. *Der.*

He was waiting for what might happen when its mass magnified. Mitch realised that compressed matter did strange things to the ether. Still, he covered his eyes with a hand and counted to ten. '4, 3, 2, 1,' Mitch whispered, gawking at his phone. 'That's it, twenty years.' He glanced around and looked back at the Sphere. There was no movement at all...anywhere. Everyone watched the Sphere closely. It just sat there. There was no suggestion that anything was different. Everything looked as it had.

'*Fuck*,' Mitch whispered under his breath - maybe they *had* got this thing all wrong, which had just *really* dawned on him. 'We could be here for a very, very long time,' he said, looking at all the people around him. 'They mightn't come 'till later in the year.' If *ever*, he thought again, casting doubt on the timeline they'd all thought was correct. He let out a deep breath that sounded like a deflating balloon. As much as he didn't want to admit it, he was glad they hadn't turned up. Everyone glanced around at everyone else, not sure what to do, given that the twenty years had officially ticked over, and they remained alone. Mitch tried to be disappointed but found it hard to do.

Still, time went on and nothing happened. Jessy wondered what would happen if they had to wait hours, days...months. What if they meant *approximately* twenty years? Or in the twentieth year? God knows how long they might have to wait. Her glances around the seated dignitaries continued. She tried her best not to appear nervous but was sure that's how she looked.

Zamindar stood to his full seven feet. He'd heard quite enough. '*They said exactly twenty years,*' he boomed to them all. There was no ambiguity, *One* said twenty, and I believe that is what they meant. By twenty they truly meant twenty.'

Okaaay, Mitch thought slowly. 'Twenty means twenty,' he repeated in a whisper. Well, where the fuck are they then? He thought, gawking at the Sphere. That answers that question, quite unambiguously, Jessy thought.

She heard a deep noise and immediately gaped back at the Sphere but it was just Sean humming some inane tune. 'Sssshhh,' she said to Sean, forcefully. He stopped humming mid-tune and looked dutifully chastened. Poor old bugger had lost himself in the vagaries of old age.

After more time elapsed, it seemed to finally happen. The Sphere, quite suddenly, split in half, a line dividing the two hemispheres where there wasn't one before. It slid slowly open, the two hemispheres coming apart by widening and forging a V, at the same time, giving off a large amount of gas. Same as the first time they found it. The gas emanated from inside it somewhere. Now it formed a cloud obscuring the Sphere for a short while, then forming a cloud above it. Then it was pretty much absorbed by the air and gone.

Jessy was terrified...she might be about to come face to face with an entity that was way more powerful than Biblical renditions of the strength of God. The Biblical God did not possess the strength and the knowledge to create universes. This one did. Her heart felt like it was in her mouth Jessy was still totally and utterly blown away by the thought of *One*. Meeting them, was very nearly too much for her. She felt dizzy and started wobbling in her seat until she grabbed the side of her chair and steadied herself. Jessy straightened herself up and braced every muscle she could and thought about something else. She sat down, looked at and thought about clouds - it helped a little bit.

The Sphere continued to sit before them, the gas dissipating into the ether. It was splayed and ready for something to crawl out, Jessy thought, gawking at the Sphere and shivering in the enervating afternoon heat of the Australian outback, which was a strange place in itself. Something extraordinary was about to happen, Jessy felt sure. She looked at the sky and the Australian wilderness, the stunted shrubs and the sand everywhere. This was some of the oldest landscape on the planet, measured in billions of years, but it had never been witness to anything like this. Jessy held both sides of her chair tightly, to remain upright, and fight the dizziness and light headedness.

Maybe they'd already come out, and were just floating around, unseen. She kept telling herself to lose all preconceptions of form, but she was really struggling to do it. What if they were made totally from EMAR...what then...would we even see them? There was only a small part of the spectrum that was visible. They would have to be able to make themselves seen and or heard, or why bother coming? Perhaps their single contact scenario had altered or changed in format. Maybe they no longer used the Sphere to move. Who fucking knew? Jessy thought nervously, conceding that humanity knew less than zero about them. The Sphere was probably in orbit a long, long time. Despite its updates, a lot may have changed in that time. *One* now, probably weren't the same as *One* then. Jessy wasn't sure what twenty years meant to them – she assumed not much, but what if it meant a lot?

Jessy wasn't sure of anything, and struggled just to breathe. *Calm down*, she implored herself, holding her toes tight inside her shoes, breathing slowly and steadily and tapping a fist gently against her lips. Blinking slowly and deliberately, she felt like running, but it was too late for anything like that. Anyway, she was now frozen to her chair and couldn't move. She just sat and watched. She supposed that was better than feeling like running.

Something was happening inside the Sphere, there was clearly movement and noise, but *what* was it? It was a brand-new noise to Jessy. She had never heard it, on Earth or in space. A deep, growling sound was followed by distinct pulsing, a beating sound like a heart. The Sphere blinked out totally for a second, disappearing then returning. It was slightly closer to them than before. It reverted to deep, guttural pulsing. It sounded like it came from deep within the Earth, not unlike the deep vibration associated with an earthquake.

All of them gaped at the Sphere with massive and timid eyes. It was definitely doing something significant. Would *they* emerge from this thing? Paul Pattinson from NASA had legged it, this stuff was apparently well above him, beyond his pay-grade and knowledge and everything else, he said, at least that's what he was yelling when he left. The whole thing clearly scared him half to death. Poor fellow was white as he breathed violently and jumped and flinched at the tiniest sound. He was wound tighter than a drum. Most of them felt like following him, but didn't. Like Jessy, they realised it was too late to do anything. They were all here until this thing was resolved, one way or the other.

Surely Paul realized the place was locked down. No in or out.

*   *   *

It half-crawled and half-walked out of the Sphere into the light and heat of the AASSA base. It first looked at the gathered crowd and then turned a full half-circle to look at the landscape around AASSA. Jessy reared back in her chair visibly paled, her lower lip dropping and trembling. She could see this thing for what it was. It seemed to be looking around, turning its body without moving its legs. There was no doubt about it, *One* were tangible blood and flesh creatures, at least that's how it seemed, so far. Everyone was riveted to their seats, eyes owl-like, gawking at this thing not far away, which had come to visit.

The thing held its arm up toward the sky. It started raining, then it stopped – then it started again and stopped again. A tornado started to form, and before anyone panicked in earnest, it went away. It put its arm down. Normal weather continued. Apparently, it was a show of power. *Magic*, if you will. The thing gave a small, shy smile.

Jessy was stunned like she'd hit her head on something unyielding like a steel block. Her dream came thundering to mind. *Surely not*, she thought. It was too absurd for words. Jessy watched the creature move, presumably gawking at everyone. It was a real being – it had skin and presumably muscle, bone and blood, and everything else that makes a real being *real*.

Mitch, too, was stunned. This was an omega, maybe Kardashev 5 or 6 species as we would define it. It was a man though, undeniably a *Homo Sapien*, at least from the outside. A lightly tanned Anglo-Saxon. It can't be, *One* cannot be human, can they? Mitch thought, freezing mid-movement as he gawked at it. Another similar man appeared from the Sphere. Now there were two of *One*. Weren't humans a species from Earth?

Jessy related it to her dream while on the Virijian craft, and was dazzled, she was correct, *somehow* - they looked like us. *One* were man. *Humanity*. At least they looked like us, on the outside, she thought. How could a dream be right, well, of course, it could in theory, but they looked *exactly* like her dream. Orgel's Second Rule was well established on Earth, but here...*now*?

'We are pleased to meet you all.' He looked at them all, with very Earthly green eyes. 'My name is Quan, this is Quin,' he said in very Earthly, un-accented English. Our design merges with yours, these are environment-suits grown from your DNA, it contains nucleotides, RNA primer and DNA polymerase, just like you,' he raised his arm toward Quin. 'We both have very similar but not identical suits grown from human DNA.' Mitch and Josh stared at each other wide-eyed and trance-like. Jessy gaped at *One*, studying both of them closely, seeing how thoroughly seamless they were. '*Amazing*, she said. *Fucking amazing.*'

They could pass for humans anywhere. Yet they *weren't* humans, apparently. Mitch was staring blankly with his mouth open. Quan's voice was English, but there was little doubt he would be able to speak other Earthly languages as well. And God knows how many exo-languages as well. This "man" was very old, no doubt and could probably take any form he desired. The fact that he looked like a human meant nothing.

Quan had a wide silver colored ring on his second finger. He pointed it at Anzac Hill. Seconds later there was an explosion or implosion of green and red. A lightning bolt of colour leapt from the hill and went straight up into the stratosphere. 'Fusion fire,' Quan said dramatically. 'I could have demonstrated a nuclear explosion, but that would have been very unwise. It could also have been gravity waves, an aurora, an FRB, a GRB, or a plasma jet, but again they would have been too impactful.'

'Another demo I guess...like m-magic,' Mitch said after putting his tongue back in his mouth. Everyone was gawking at Anzac Hill and glancing pensively at Quan, whose arms were now limp at his sides. He raised his arm again and went to touch his ring. The demo hadn't finished yet. He still wanted to establish his superiority apparently.

Quan vanished and reappeared three metres away. Then he vanished again and reappeared back where he started from. He had stopped and started time, apparently. At least, that's what he said. It was seamless if that was the case. The huge eyes of the viewers said it all. Their respect and fear for this being was at maximum. The natives were enthralled.

Then Quan removed the ring from his finger and gave it a distinct tweak. All the chairs lifted a centimetre off the ground. Everyone assembled was totally weightless for a short time. Then the chairs hit the ground almost as one, in a group thump.

General Drummond pulled his peaked hat down tighter and spun his head in every direction, and generally looked bewildered and bamboozled. 'The boys at NASA would be beside themselves if they saw that...any of that.' He said, looking pale and hawkish. The spectators gasped and "oohed" as they felt gravity give way but were now silent...and a bit overwhelmed. Without impacting the atmosphere or the air-pressure, Quan had turned gravity off in this area momentarily.

Mitch was uber-impressed by the show and looked at both of them, taking it all in, contemplating what *One might* have been. Certainly, the show itself was absolutely incredible, and it wasn't just magic, because that was just an illusion and make believe. This was as real as it got.

They were here on Earth, so they looked like us. The ultimate in effective communication techniques, he reckoned. Look like us, speak like us.

Zamindar toned to Quan. Mitch thought he could see curiosity in the Virijians eyes as he toned, but he doubted it. If he did, it'd be the first time he'd ever shown anything apart from robotic expressions. So, he didn't think so. He watched the Virijian closely to confirm his suspicions. He supposed it would be a good time to do it. Maybe, the Virijians only showed emotion to races superior to them. Selective emotion as it were. Afterall, the Virijians could potentially learn a lot from *One*. Still, Mitch doubted it was true.

Mitch wanted to ask one of the bigger questions, but he knew he had no breath and no voice. His breath was stuck in his throat and he could feel his heart pounding. Fingers seemed to tighten around his throat to the point where he struggled to breathe at all.

Mitch coughed piercingly, and sucked in a deep breath, punctuated by several gasps. 'What are you really, *physically* I mean?' Mitch said rather bluntly, glancing at Jessy, then back at Quan. 'You said that...,' Mitch looked at Quan's body quickly, 'it was an "environment suit"...so what is your real form?' Mitch sucked in air from the corners of his mouth as he waited for a response. Mitch suddenly wondered if maybe he'd overstepped the mark. He was about to backtrack a bit when Quan started talking and broke the uncomfortable silence which had descended into painful stillness – it was just Quan looking at the AASSA base and a number of breathless humans. Quan suddenly came to life as though he'd just been plugged into an energy source.

Quan fairly blurted, 'like Quin, I am normally part of what you term dark matter.' There was a collective intake of breath as the words were spoken. 'We, or should I say, some of us, are uploaded into nanotechnology that only interacts with mass and everything else only extremely rarely. Our population in nanotechnology is indistinguishable from Dark Matter.'

'*You must be fucking joking,*' General Drummond said, taking off his peaked cap and running his hand through his thinning grey hair. '*Shit,*' he said in complete exasperation. 'He speaks in fucking riddles too,' the General replaced his cap and realised Quan could hear him. Not that it mattered much. He made sure his cap was pulled down tight. 'Dark Matter indeed,' he grumbled. General Drummond had barely heard of it.

'Just listen General, he's making perfect sense,' Mitch said. The General was variously grimacing and frowning, trying to make some meaning out of it. Mitch could see the poor sod trying to hide his inner misery with a probing stare. He was such a dinosaur of a long-gone cold war. Drummond was totally unsuited to this type of encounter. Still, here the poor prick was, trying to come to terms with the incomprehensible, and doing a piss-poor job of it. He was much better suited to directing a battlefield.

Quan was very active, moving his muscular arms until they finished on his hips. 'Much of the influence from what you term dark matter is from other universes, but about a third of it is a real gravity-heavy particle. Once you get larger colliders, you will discover the sterile particle. A million of my race - along with Quin and myself, were transcribed into the quantum realm. We were encoded into dark matter, becoming immune to supernovae and gamma ray bursts in the process - only responding to gravity and pretty much remaining indistinguishable from the rest of space, so detection is very unlikely, probably impossible. This is very important to my race.'

'So what we think is physics, what we naturally assume are particles like the Higgs boson and WIMP's...is...um, actually *you*? Mitch struggled to believe that anyone, irrespective of age, could do that. It sounded insane. Mapping, scanning, saving, emulating, uploading...and how is it that "you" go with it, along with all your memories and personal bits and pieces. Sounded next to impossible to Mitch. To capture the "you" part was next to impossible...wasn't it?

'Partly correct,' Quan said, peering at Quin. 'Life is not just in the equations - life *is* the equations. Some of the subatomic particles are alive. It's just scanning, imaging and emulation and then after working through a few ethical and political considerations, *wallah*, you are there. You and I don't have to be made from atoms and molcculcs that make things like bodies "work",' he walked back two steps and then continued to talk to those assembled, like a congressman hell bent on getting his point across. Everyone wondered and worried what that point might be though. Jessy was still on edge and a bit breathless from the explosions and the loss of gravity especially.

'It does initially, seem impossible of course, but then it can be a cloud of anything like nano machines, forming a host into which something alive can be uploaded. And we as a species are then fairly much indistinguishable from the normal background of space, and are fully immortal, again, of great importance to my race.'

'*Christ Almighty,*' Mitch whispered hoarsely, this is all gobbledegook, isn't it? Was dark matter somehow alive? No wonder we haven't found the stupid particle, if *One* considered it difficult to detect, what hope did we have...seriously? He pondered what sort of tech would upload biochemicals and photo-chemicals to particles we can only sense through gravity very rarely?

It was all Double-Dutch to Mitch. He couldn't even imagine what manner of technology was involved with it. He wondered how the best AI programmer would view it. Probably as so-much mumbo jumbo as well.

They all gaped at Quan and studied his every move as closely as they could, although he looked so much like an ordinary man in ordinary work-a-day clothes, with jeans and an untucked white T-shirt. He or it or whatever, also had a short beard in an extraordinary mirror of a male human being, straight from any walk of life.

Jessy followed him closely and stared fixedly at Quan, concurring that he looked and moved like any male homo sapien. And Quin was dressed the same way and moved the same way. They were actually attractive males, she thought. Just external "environment-suits" apparently.

He was sure they'd pass any test there was, as Quan had said, even DNA and RNA was at their base, and all the other stuff that went with it. *One* for all intents and purposes, *were human*. He knew it was probably only skin deep but it seemed so real. He had to keep reminding himself, they were *not* human. They simply wanted to make us feel comfortable by appearing to look like us. And they did it very well.

Quan looked directly at Mitch with bright green eyes and could tell he was intrigued with *One's* own condition. 'You *will* find dark matter and dark energy, do not worry, it is simply a matter of energy on your part. Keep looking at Higgs – that's your key.' Quan laid his green eyes over everyone. 'Some of it will be us,' Quan smirked at the group.

'It is pleasing to see that you have grown into truly intelligent people, I have seen some of your scientific and medical achievements, your art and architecture Quan said, eyeing Jessy, having already scanned her entire body, including every organ.

It was spoken by humanity's creator, so she wasn't sure how they should feel. *Thanks*, I guess, she said to herself. How the *fuck* did they "see" these things. Presumably, they made themselves invisible somehow. Mind you, "dressed" as they were they blended in nicely. They looked exactly like we did.

Jessy felt "natural" enough, which in a sense she guessed they all did, all the humans that is. She wouldn't presume to make a judgement about *One*. But without their input, we wouldn't have split off from Apes apparently and become our own species. We'd probably still be walking with four knuckles on the ground, doing Ape-things. We'd still be grunting like Apes did today. All the miraculous and fabulous inventions of humanity – *forget it*. If the species didn't rise, nor would any of its achievements, and there was a long list of them.

'We worked on your species for an unusually long time, we had to do our work because life in this Universe had turned out to be exclusively microbial only,' Quan said. 'And so, where it was multi-cellular, we went to work to ensure intelligence arose.' Quan nodded crisply at all of them. 'And now we are face to face, he said, peering straight ahead with his bright eyes. Now, his eyes didn't match his body, or something. Quan didn't look quite right. He was asymmetric. Maybe it was time to go or perhaps something else was wrong.

Jim Vincent was head of USPA, and found it all quite implausible and profoundly overwhelming and bewildering. He expected no less, waiting for them to arrive, but still it felt awfully like a fairy story. He'd read some left-field ideas on advanced life, but this was left-field of even that. These guys were super advanced but it wasn't Dyson spheres and antigravity guns they were confronting; this mob was further along than being massless. They blended with space and particles. They took the meaning of "advanced" to a new level.

Jim said, speaking slowly with spirited eyes and a mesmerised gaze, 'they've uploaded themselves into *physics* for Christ's sakes. The Universe, in part, was impelled, literally driven, by their existence. How in God's name could they do that, he asked?' He continued to ask *how?* Over and over and over. He couldn't even guess how. It was obviously do-able, but seemed genuinely impossible. Their understanding of the Universe must be absurdly accurate. It reminded him of a quote by an old astronomer he couldn't extract from the depths of his mind. But, anyway, it was related to standing on the shoulders of others, from a tech viewpoint. *One* were so old that the view from other's shoulders in their race must have been insanely panoramic.

'Just relax Jim, we are here, you are here, that's all you need to know, same for all of you here today,' Quan said calmly, moving his arms like a human. Jim wondered how this thing knew his name, but it was a minor detail in the scheme of things. *Dark matter*, he hadn't forgotten. Jim was stiff, sitting in his seat like a robot, totally unable to move. Perhaps Mitch gave them my name, he thought. The poor guy forgot he was wearing a nametag.

The rest of them just stared at Quan, terrified and welded to their seats, wondering what the hell they should do...or say. Whatever they said would help to paint us as the childish species we were. Of that, all of them were very sure indeed. Silence was best from humans, Mitch reckoned. Especially from the General. The man was a fool.

'You are a very special race, but to be clear we are *surprised* you are still here. Surprised in a very good way,' Quan said, gazing at all of them, and around, looking at the landscape and the sky. 'You are the only ape-extracted intelligence that hasn't destroyed itself with nuclear weapons. Of course, that could still happen, but you are the only ones who have gotten this far. We hope there will be others, as species age. So, yes, you are very special indeed.'

'So, what sort of species have you *made* intelligent...like us?' Mitch raked his hand through his hair as he waited for the response he assumed would blow his mind. Quan seemed like he was thinking about it, but he probably wasn't. Quan performed what looked like a 360 and ended up facing them again after turning through a full circle, now gawking at them all with his bright green eyes.

'This Universe was made mainly to encourage creatures that exchange oxygen and carbon dioxide, meaning intelligence is primarily bipedal, with two arms, two to seven fingers, an opposable digit, and is human-like, *humanoid*. Of course, there are exceptions, the Universe is a very big place, but most of the species are this way.'

'So...you didn't interfere with *all* life?' Mitch asked, holding his breath. This was truly a wonder-world, right here, right now. Quan physically winced at the word "interfere" suggesting they didn't see it like that.

'No.' Quan replied loudly, clearly not wanting to discuss it further.

Mitch stared at Quan, his answer hanging in the air, answered but unanswered. The issue of "why" was implied but not touched by Quan.

Zamindar and Char seemed to be studying him carefully, but they might have been conversing, certainly both had their cranial flesh moving, so they were either talking together or conversing with Quan.

Suddenly, there was an explosion of voice from Quan. He seemed happy to be asked and sounded almost boastful. He'd decided now to speak. 'Some of them are similar to your animals here on Earth, others you will not be familiar with. Most of them are similar to your lizards although they are bipedal and have arms, generally with three or four fingers and a thumb. Similar to upright dinosaurs. Some are like your crows with legs and arms and no wings, land octopi with hard legs and arms, while a few are bipedal elephants with two arms and two sturdy legs. There are a few others, but that covers close to all of them that are like you. Seventy percent of them, before they destroyed themselves, were similar to you – derived from a hairy ape."

Since you put it like that, Jessy thought, not sure if she should be offended or not. Derived from a hairy ape indeed. Jessy had her arms firmly crossed over her chest and her lips pressed firmly together. She felt like flipping the bird to Quan. 'Hairy ape,' she kept repeating indignantly. '*Indeed*,' she repeated, glaring at Mitch.

Mitch not only knew what he wanted to say, he *felt* the questions he had, the most important one was irritating his throat, annoying his vocal folds with unwanted pressure. It was fairly bursting out but he tried to keep it in. It had to be answered or he'd go stark raving mad. He'd ask it and see what happened. Nothing might be the result, but at least he'd have asked. He could then put his mind at rest. At least until he got the answer – if he got an answer.

Mitch started, 'Do y-you know why Jessy and I went forward twenty years, using that, er...Lunar object?' Mitch's eyes were gawking downward as he spoke, wondering if the question should be asked at all, but his head was angled upward and he ended up with his eyes plastered directly on Quan. He waited rigidly for the answer...this would take it even further toward absurdity if the answer was as they both expected. That *One* were involved somehow.

Quan gazed at Mitch quizzically. 'We didn't want this to proceed without you, afterall, we were coming for you...and of course the rest of humanity. So, we limited the time shift you had tangled yourself in. Otherwise, you would have shifted quite randomly on the return trip, from tens to thousands to millions of your years.'

'So, *you* placed the shifts?' Mitch asked, hoping like hell he hadn't gone too far in asking the question. Mitch knew they weren't here to answer questions about the shift. If they weren't answered, so be it.

'We did not put them there, the intelligence on the planet you visited did,' Quan said quite sternly. They wanted to make contact with Earth, it seems - when it was worth it. Not until you found the shifts and used them yourself.'

Mitch was stunned. He and Jessy could've come back to Earth a million years in the future...if he did, *Jesus Christ*, what would he have seen? Humans would have gone, he assumed. Would we have returned to an empty world or a world populated with a different intelligence...or maybe humans would have been super-advanced. Any of those outcomes would have been drop-dead unpleasant. I guess the rockhammer should have been a good indication of what might happen. His mind was spinning and contorting, thinking about what *could* have been. And what wasn't...thankfully.

Quan squared himself with those in front of him. He nodded at Quin and turned back to front the bevy of human heavyweights that sat before him, all of them looking terrified. Nothing much had changed for them. They watched in horror and flinched at the creature's every move, knowing his capabilities. If they can summon weather on demand, and everything else, creating catastrophe would be easy for them.

Mitch and Jessy recoiled at singing birds - they were steeply on edge - like everyone else. *One* had them seriously concerned. Their capabilities were fairly much unlimited – their mind-set was completely unknown.

Quan moved closer to the assembled gathering. Presumably to make an important point. Quan spoke loudly and clearly. 'You are killing your planet,' he said with an alarmingly aggressive and very sincere tone. It seemed that Quan chose his words and his tone carefully, looking deliberately at each of those assembled before, during and after he spoke. Quan was making a very serious point indeed, that needed to be understood by this audience. Quan went on, deep lines on his face suggested he was mightily concerned.

'Eighty percent of most countries in your world discharge sewerage directly into rivers, seas and near the coast. Waste from industry is similarly discharged. Most importantly, greenhouse gas levels are rising as are sea levels, and ice flow zones are reducing in critical zones.'

Quan stopped talking, kept walking and peered at all of them, and smiled. None were expecting that. It seemed totally out of place, given what he'd said. Nearly every human felt their heart rate rise. Not because of what he said, because everyone here already knew it, but by the source of the information. They simply weren't expecting it from him.

'Temperatures are increasing globally, because of humanity. It is already killing your people, your vegetation and animals. I realise most of you accept that humanity and its civilisation has created a problem, but someone needs to do something about it. *Now.*' He paused again, to great effect.

'You have twenty years to fix it, otherwise the greenhouse runaway will have started. And then it is very hard, if not impossible, for you to reel it in. There is a great deal of talk about mitigation and reduction of carbon, there is a Union of Concerned Scientists looking at it, but the problem is this - your issue is global, but your world is broken into small countries, each with its own self-serving leader who is beholden to its people. There has been an effort made, but it is *insufficient* to meet the problems of your planet's atmosphere.'

Quan seemed to be getting worked up, or perhaps he was trying to act like a human, either way, he was a very compelling speaker indeed. 'There needs to be *one individual* or group that is empowered by global resolution to make decisions. Countries are too self-interested to do it. But do this, or you will all die. Your species will become extinct.' His words were very powerful and rang in their ears like a threat of Armageddon from the Old Testament.'

Quan stopped speaking, to allow them to absorb the message of irrevocability, if it continued. There was nothing new in all this, it was just the sheer strength and nature of the orator. It was simply where the message was coming from. For Mitch, and hopefully for everyone it was the ultimate proof that unavoidable Armageddon was approaching unless something concrete was done about it *right now.* When the creator of the Universe tells you climate change is a problem, action needs to be taken. *Pronto.*

'*Jesus holy fuck*,' Jessy whispered to Mitch, 'We knew it was a problem, but not like this. Who do we send this message to?' she said louder, to include Quan and the rest of them. They were all looking at each other, pain and discomfort carved in deep, ugly lines on all the faces. Mitch was frowning with a shiver of apprehension. This thing was our problem...and it was out of control.

'Will *you* help us?' Mitch asked, from the first line of seats. Mitch looked directly at Quan who seemed to have kind eyes. He realised they needed a lot of help. They, *humans*, were doing a piss-poor job of it so far. If someone didn't help them, they were done. Help was needed desperately from a third party.

'*No,*' Quan said firmly, this is something you have to do. We are at the limit of what we are able to do to assist. For you to endure as a species, it is critical that you learn to live in harmony with your world. It is vital that your species learn this lesson. So, it is over to humanity.' Quan gawked at the seated mob and smiled again. 'Your achievements to date are exceptional, but you risk being a flash-in-the-pan species if you don't solve this.'

'Sounds like the fucking Virijians,' Mitch whispered to Jessy. "Over" is about right, Mitch thought, with an ironic snuffle.

Quan hadn't finished with humankind yet. 'Your situation with atmospheric change is akin to setting off your global stores of nukes at one time.' Quan said. 'Your planet will be destroyed as a life-giver. Time is truly ticking,' Quan said firmly. 'You must endeavour to live cooperatively with your planet. Time is not over, but it is *right now* that real action needs to be taken.'

'*For fuck's sake...we get it...but who the hell do we tell?*' Jessy said to Mitch, who ... the world, the UN, POTUS, that Earth is on a path to destruction?' Some of the UN were here but they were no help at all. Jessy would make sure the GA knew of this and ensure the International Court of Justice knew all about Quan. All of them, and every other Government around the world knew about climate change, so it'd be wasted oxygen – they'd heard it every day. "Oh, the world is gonna end unless we change things". All of them had heard it so many times before it had lost its zing. So far, the message hadn't hit home. Every country had tried a bit, but only where it didn't interfere with the economy.

'So far,' Mitch said glumly, 'all the talk about looming apocalypse has caused is "targets". He shook his head. 'It ain't enough - we need a total, legislated shut down of everything atmosphere-affecting. Burning *anything* must stop. But that of course interferes with the economy and the fucking budget. Mitch felt like pulling all his hair out. It'd be like burning the budget or dropping it in acid. The world won't go for it. Mitch clenched his jaw to cracking point – we had two competing issues coming at each other head on. It was climate change versus the economy and there would be no winner.

Josh looked at Mitch as though he'd been struck by lightning. 'Pigs might fly too.' He said loudly, other things came flying out of his mouth too, but they were incomprehensible. Safe to say he wasn't happy with stupid "targets" being the reaction from world governments. Climate change had to be "balanced" with the budget. That was old thinking that would ultimately lead to the death of Earth as a life-giver.

'
Maybe, coming from Quan, even though he wouldn't be doing the oration, the words were *his* and he came, not just from a different planet, but from a different fucking *universe*, so that could make the difference. *Should.* And there was a lot of world government and officialdom here. If it didn't make

the difference, nothing would. Mitch pulled at his hair, beyond frustration. He threw his arms in the air and glanced at a poker-faced Zamindar. Mitch couldn't help grinning. The situation with Earth's climate-change was truly a hopeless joke. The planet had the ability to mitigate the problem, almost to zero, but didn't want to because of the side-effects.

On the one hand we had a dying planet and on the other was the economy, budget and day-to-day living of an intelligent species. They bumped heads all over the place. Bringing a sustainable planet and a functioning economy together in a healthy relationship was the biggest challenge the globe had ever faced. It was one that hadn't yet been solved by humans.

Quan said global warming was very real. Most already knew that, but governments refused to change by the amount needed to really make a difference. Money and economics was way too important in the bigger scheme of things to priorotise the environment above it. Ridiculous but true.

The world needed to wake up to itself. Leaving it to someone else to do, simply wouldn't do the job. And the targets set by global accords were bullshit, everybody in the know knew as much. Targets were profoundly influenced by economic factors. Way, *way* too much. We needed to save the world, *period.* A healthy economy might save a government, but not the planet. Mitch recognised climate-change for what it was. *A potential civilisation killer.* He knew that. And with the Universe mainly microbial, it couldn't be allowed to happen. We were too rare to be lost to climate-change.

The mix of economic and carbon targets was the wrong fit for Earth. It was way wide of the mark if the goal was to maintain Earth as a living, breathing system, where floods, wildfires and droughts were seen only rarely. Mitch peered directly at Quan, lifting his chin and holding his chest out.

'It's been said before, and it has had little impact. If it doesn't work now, *nothing* will work.' Mitch stopped talking and breathed deeply, wrinkling his nose, and lowering his eyes at the same time. He tried to be confident but really struggled, knowing how deeply coal burning was set into humanity's global economy - and way of life. It was part of the human psyche.

Mitch thought about it and looked angry, to say the least, if smoke came out of his ears, Jessy wouldn't have been surprised. His mouth was tight and grim as he spoke, 'If I hear, *"meeting our targets"* as though climate-change was cured, *one more fucking time*, I'll scream and I won't stop screaming until someone slaps me hard and then sutures my mouth shut. You are so right, we need *one* person or group to speak for the globe, empowered to the teeth. Voted by the people to make decisions in the *planet's* interest. Not in line with economic factors or some fucking budget, but as the *highest* priority,' Mitch boomed, happy to get the words out in the right order. He was huffing and puffing, almost hyperventilating at the crazy thoughts in his head. He was convinced, and always had been, that the planet needed one independent person or group. Not a fucking government with all their vested interests, Mitch was totally convinced that this was the *only* way to go.

'If we rely on individual countries to do the job, we are well and truly fucked,' Mitch said. 'They all have their own agendas, and their targets are a joke and *way* too heavily influenced by economic factors. It's understandable, but *seriously*, if we rely on those, all hope is lost. We need to change, fundamentally, as a planet. Otherwise, it'll take two hundred years, which we don't have.'

'So...work and earn no money and generate no greenhouse gas, you mean...employment beyond money? Good luck with that nonsense,' Jessy looked at him as though he'd grown a third leg. Mitch looked straight back at her, deadpan.

'Yep,' Mitch said, quite seriously, 'beyond money...but how we do it,' he hit himself on the forehead and shook his head, *'fuck knows?* But if we don't, we're *gone* as a species, so we better find out how to do it, and make it work. It'll be hard, close to impossible, but it's gotta be done. Gotta means *gotta*. If we want to keep existing as a species, that is. Or we could just roll everything up and be done with it.'

Mitch gazed at Jessy with a ghost of a grin, still shaking his head. He said it but didn't think they could do it. It was truly a fool's errand. The question of "how" was high in his mind. He knew with this world as it was, there was no hope of that happening *ever*.

Jessy stared at Mitch in horror, scratching her jaw. Combing her hair with her hand, Jessy kept staring, slack-jawed and blinking fast, contemplating how screwed they really were. Work for no money, *yeah right*. There was no way the world would agree to it. No fucking way. The people would have to be told. *Threatened* with the law. Beaten over the head with the truth and educated. Whatever the answer, they had to make it happen or they were done.

Somehow, industry, houses, cars and planes had to stop using coal-based electricity or oil or fuel, whose production and burning pumped carbon and oxides into the atmosphere. Simple really. *Not.* Cut emissions to zero, no problem, right? But it somehow had to happen. Or they were all genuinely done for. The planet, like the human species, would be dead if they didn't. That was something humanity couldn't tolerate...surely?

Quan and Quin had gone. They had left Earth to itself, so it could form part of their research presumably. *One* had seen Earth again and said what they wanted to say and observed what they wanted to observe. The Sphere once again had made itself whole, like they first saw it orbiting Titan. Now, humans could do what they liked with it, *finally* - it had served its primary purpose so Mitch and Jessy didn't really care what became of it. The Smithsonian could have it and put it on display. The first alien device used on Mankind's planet.

Jessy looked at Mitch hopefully, raising her eyebrows and diving straight into a conversation. 'Uh, maybe we should try and make some form of contact with the race that placed the lunar portals, she said, now that we know for sure who made them and put them there and why. They want to meet us...maybe help us.

'What about Josh?' Mitch said, a little flabbergasted by the question. He'd also thought about it but hadn't got near asking the question. He also realised they only had one chance to go and it would mean leaving Josh, Earth and the Moon *again*, Mitch took a deep breath and looked pensively at his wife. He sort of agreed with Jessy because that society had shown so much interest in them as a species. By leaving the connection for humans to find in the first place was evidence of that. If it wasn't subject to dip slip movement along the lunar fault-line, it would've been found ages ago, and probably be seen from Earth or identified from lunar orbit. It would have stuck out like the proverbial. Jessy and Mitch both wanted to use the shift for the sheer science, philosophy and wonder it offered. Before it was used by people with a militarised or just wrong agenda. Both wanted to get there first and make contact with this civilisation. They had discussed it in detail and it turned out, she was as bad as he was. Jessy was obsessed by this world – it was all she could think about.

They had one chance, and she wanted to take it. There was one thing that held them back though. And it wasn't climate-change on Earth. The UN would be the arbiter of that – now it was to be expedited above her pay-grade. She and Mitch would watch it closely though and get involved if they were needed.

He and Jessy had just made a decent re-connection with Josh. His brothers and sister refused to have anything to do with either us or Josh. Not that he blamed them, it wasn't their own call to make. One day they might want to reach out, who knew? That made it even more important that they maintain their close connection with Josh.

Jessy had already thought long and hard about Josh. If she asked him to go with his mum and dad, would he feel obligated to come with? That's not how she or Mitch wanted it - Jessy didn't want it to be an obligation thing. Plus, he'd be something else to worry deeply about.

'Ring Josh, tell him what we're doing, why and where we're planning on going,' Jessy said, smiling briefly, ping ponging her gaze between Mitch and the floor, rubbing the back of her neck. It suggested that she didn't entirely agree with what she was saying – she was unsure. Actually, she was completely flummoxed.

'Josh has his own life now,' Mitch whispered to Jessy. Like his brothers and sister. 'We can't impose on him, right?'

'So...*ring him*, tell him what we're planning, see what you get back,' she said with a trembling mouth. She agreed with Mitch, he should be set free, especially now, but he deserved to at least know what they were doing or planning. Like it or not, *and he probably didn't*, but they were part of his life now and he deserved to know.

Jessy realised it'd be up to her to telephone Josh. Mitch would never do it. He'd picked up the baton as "good-time dad" perfectly.

*   *   *

'Hello Josh,' it's your mum here...er, how are you?' Jessy darted her gaze between the floor and the phone. If this call went well, she'd be stunned. '*Jesus mum, I'm at work*,' Josh whispered forcefully. All those who worked at AASSA had been relocated temporarily to the fourth floor of a building in Adelaide. Josh hated it. Noisy, too many people, dirty, you name it, it was awful, for someone from the country. He liked and was used to the open spaces of the outback. Easy driving, much fewer people, nicer people that actually took the time to say "hello" and that's the way he liked it. This city stuff – he found it hard to believe so many people chose to live here.

I know, I er...called you there,' Jessy said with the slightest hint of sarcasm.

Um yeah, right, well...what's happening where you are?' Josh asked gruffly. He felt off-balance, trying to talk to his mum with so many of his cohorts within earshot and he knew a lot were listening.

'Me and your dad are going back to the lunar farside.' Jessy gulped and silence descended on both ends of the phone. 'Er...to try and make contact with the species that lives on the planet, that the gateway leads to. They showed so much interest in us, they clearly seek contact. And we refuse to let NASA turn it into a spectacle, or the military to take over. So, we don't tell anyone and do it on the down-low.' She paused in case he wanted to interject. He didn't so she continued. 'It's where we spent twenty years Josh – which for us was so brief.' Josh understood, but that didn't mean he truly got their motive for leaving again. Or agreed in the least with their decision to go. If there was a problem with time the first time, why wouldn't it happen a second time? *Seriously*? Wasn't it obvious?

'Um,' Josh spoke softly, 'you shouldn't um...go,' he said, sitting on his chair and fingering his necklace, holding the side of the chair in a death-grip. He knew very well what happened the last time. He didn't want the same thing happening again. *Lost in time, is definitely a once-only.* If the same thing happened again, he'd be fucking middle-aged. All the shit he had to put up with the first time. It was horrible, and he didn't want it repeating. *Anything but that.* 'Mum, don't go, you don't want the shit that happened the first time repeating.'

Well, it's a nice sentiment, but we are going Joshy.' Jessy paused and tried to regroup. 'We have nothing else to do...and you know your dad – he's not one to hang around. You do remember that?' Josh answered in the affirmative. His dad had been discovery-crazy all Josh's life, or at least that part he remembered. Jessy continued, 'We need to find out why they placed the shifts and see where evolution is at on their world, and avoid the rest of the world turning it into a parade.'

She stopped to make sure he was still listening. Josh confirmed he was still there. Jessy knew travelling at or near the speed of light did strange things to time. It either ticked slower, or didn't tick at all. Despite the fact that *One* probably saved them from coming back in the 10,000's the first time, Jessy still wanted to go. Scratch that, she *had* to go.

Jessy glanced at her phone and spoke. 'Given the nature of the shifts they placed, they must be significantly ahead of us. Maybe they can give us some idea how to overcome global warming,' she said upbeat, throwing it in at the last second because she thought Josh would like it. Jessy stopped talking and could hear quick, shallow breathing on the other end of the phone.

'Come with us Joshy,' Jessy deliberately breathed slowly and her tone became much softer and more motherly. Jessy had no intention of saying it, in fact quite the opposite, but she blurted it out anyway, it came out of its own accord. The-old-loose-cannon strikes again, she couldn't help herself. It had her feeling like she was balancing one-legged on the spot - waiting for a reply from Josh.

She wondered what the fuck was wrong with her. The poor kid needed to be left alone – not hassled to within an inch of his life by his mother. *He was 28 for God's sake...not eight!*

Er...ah, I can't mum...it's...um, too short notice, but, um...*good luck okay.* Don't go um, dying or travelling through time...*okay.*'

'Of course, we'll try not to Joshy, it is short notice, but, oh well, thanks Josh.' She waited a bit, then disconnected.

'*Shit*,' Josh whispered, '*Fuck, fuck, shit,* he swore to no one inside his work-station. That didn't go too well *at all*, he thought. He should've said, "Oh, you caught me off guard, sorry". Instead, he fumbled and scrambled, said "no" and then hung up. Josh was sure he must have sounded like a complete knob. *Damn it*, he thought again, thinking about his mum and all the good times he must have had when he was younger – he'd seen the photos of birthdays and the like. Certainly, a lot had happened when he was little, but all that seemed irrelevant now.

Goddamnit, Josh yelled to himself, surprise had gotten him once again. Once more, if only he'd thought more deeply before he spoke, he'd be a *hell* of a lot better off.

*   *   *

Jessy, Mitch, Zamindar and Char were at Boca Chica in Southern Texas, waiting to board SpaceX's Musk3000 flight to its newish facility near the Sheraton Hotel on Mare Tranquilitatus on nearside Luna. It was a weekly service to the Moon, but now it had further to go to get there and the cost of a ticket had unfortunately gone north. It was a direct service and bypassed the *Alpha* space station, operated by NASA that orbited the Moon as a way-station.

Moon itself now orbited Earth a bit more than a million kilometres from Earth. About three times further away than it used to be in a reasonably stable, now resonant orbit with parent planet Earth. It remained tidally locked, which surprised many of the "scientific establishment" on Earth, but there you are. Like many other things in space, Occam's razor doesn't always hold true.

From Tranquilitatus, they would catch the Lunar Transide railway to Mendeleev and use a Roadster to take them the rest of the way to the mine and the object. In the meantime, they waited inside the spaceport terminal which, apart from them, was empty of people. Zamindar and Char were reading up about the SpaceX Spaceplane that would take them there. They would normally do the same distance in a minute or so. Here, it would take close to a full day to journey there on much slower Earth tech.

The Non-Disclosure Agreement signed by their and our United Nations barred the sharing of any technology or sociology or anything really, between humans and Virijians. Zamindar and Char demanded it, to keep the peace on their home planets. There were some on the Virijian worlds that didn't trust the human world at all. They thought we would pose a risk to them if they shared their tech with us. Not now perhaps, but in the future sometime. And maybe they were right. Who knew? Theoretically, we could use it directly against them, or reverse engineer the tech and come up with who knows how many weapons of destruction, and in both cases, *overnight*, become a very potent enemy. That was the fear anyway.

Mitch and Jessy had already witnessed what the Virijians could do to someone they thought posed a risk to their planets. So, Mitch and Jessy didn't push it. They were pretty desperate to remain in the Virijians' good books. Avoiding their fury was a good idea for anybody.

Jessy watched Mitch as he focussed on someone in the distance who was approaching. He was the only other in the building, so he stuck out like the proverbial, despite still being rather blurry. Mitch peered and gave a crisp nod, a small grin giving way to a full-blown smile. Jessy felt warmth spreading through her entire body as she watched the person approach.

'Hello dad, mum, guys, what's up? Josh said, peering at all of them, smiling widely at Mitch and Jessy.

'I thought you couldn't make it, honey?' Jessy said, smiling broadly. She wore an irresistibly devastating smile as she looked at her son.

'Didn't want you to make any, er...rash decisions, you know, disappear for twenty years, things like that.' Josh said, raising his eyebrows at Mitch and nodding firmly, smirking very slightly.

Mitch glanced at Josh, then Jessy and couldn't help but take the comment personally. 'That was nothing *we* did...' Mitch felt the pressure from Jessy's eyes, they were bulging and pained and said, "shut up you idiot". We don't want a re-run of all that, is all.

Jessy embraced Josh and held him tight. She didn't give a stuff who did what, at least he was here now. 'Are you coming with us, or did you come here to see us off? Jessy asked, chewing her cheek, waiting for his response with gritted teeth. Mitch looked at Jessy grimly not believing his wife would put him on the spot like that. Josh wrinkled his nose and ping ponged his gaze between the two of them, not having a clue what to say. Good work Jessy, Mitch thought.

She hoped for the best, but expected the worst. Looking at Josh, she could tell he was nervous, despite his overt bravado. He was taking short, jerky movements and pacing, clear tell-signs that she recognised from his younger days. She giggled to herself very quietly, noting that it had stayed with him.

'Josh...it's okay. Don't worry about what...' Mitch was cut of mid-sentence by Josh.

'I'm, coming with...if there's room,' Josh said, offering a half smile, glancing tentatively at Mitch. 'Someone's got to stop you from making dumb decisions. Besides I hate what I'm doing with AASSA. *Analyst my arse,*' he said with feeling, smiling and closing his eyes, rubbing them with the heels of his hands. 'I've had quite enough *of that place.* 'He took his mother's hand and was quiet.

Jessy felt so happy she was at bursting point, feeling warm and tingly, head to toe, very happy that her son was coming with and doubly nervous about what was in front of them, thinking, this object better play ball.

'So, a babysitter, right?' Mitch said sarcastically, grinning at his son.

'Correct,' Josh replied, grinning back, 'a babysitter.' He peered at Mitch. 'You need one...*big time.*' Mitch broke into a sneeze of laughter. He was also very nervous about the future with his son in tow.

Boarding the spaceplane, it was like any regular commercial airliner. But technically it was very different indeed. It had two airbreathing engines and a third rocket engine filled to the brim with liquid hydrogen that would cut the plane free of Earth and send it on to the corridor to land on Luna. The vehicle had room for fifteen souls. The Musk Spaceplanes were fucking amazing.

As they took off for the Moon, they had a last look at AASSA and its small buildings and sprawling contours and of course the desert beyond which essentially went all the way to the horizon. The Moon was in the upper left corner of the rear window. Only a small but still prominent dot now. It was so far away, although very close in cosmic terms. So, it was sand, snakes and tumble weeds below, clouds, space and the Moon above.

*   *   *

The five of them were dressed in white helmets with their fixed lights and light blue pressure suits and a backpack. The most eye-catching thing Jessy saw was the greenness of the mamillary malachite exposed at the base of the pit. There were glints of light flashing from all over the southern part of the cut as they made their way toward the base. They were the oxidised crystals of the upper secondary zone, lateral to the economic primary zone of mineralisation that was mined out some time ago. The oxidised ore belonged wholly and solely to Mitchell Taylor.

The image of Zamindar and Char on the Moon, albeit behind visors, was strange because Jessy knew who and what they were, but to the mainstream, it just looked like two very tall, massive astronauts, going about their business on the Moon.

Jessy saw the object in the bottom of the pit and headed down to it, followed by the entire group, ambling along the downward trending, dusty road, their footfalls throwing up grey talcum until it was all over their feet and legs, then the rest of it fell slowly to the ground in the weak acceleration, owing to very low gravity on the relatively small mass Moon.

Her heartbeat harder and faster on first sight of the object. She now understood its potential not only for spatial displacement but for temporal displacement. Jessy knew exactly what it was now, it was a gateway – to an exo-planet that had shown a lot of interest in Earth. Why it didn't just contact us direct, they didn't know...but realised there had to be a very good reason.

The destination they sought was a planet. They thought they knew where it went, but how could they know for sure? The prize-wheel came anxiously to mind. And what of its temporal potential...they couldn't possibly know that for sure, either. All they could do was either use it, or don't. That's it. And their son was coming with which made the decision to go, easier, sort of. They knew it shouldn't, but it did. The decision should stand by itself, but in this case, it didn't. They needed Josh with them. But that meant he had to use the shift as well. That was the troubling part.

Maybe the object led to the planet like *One* said, like it did last time, maybe it didn't. Perhaps its destination *was* like the prize wheel, totally and utterly random, maybe it was dependent on how heavy the traveller was. Who knows, it might be based on anything...or nothing, even something that appeared to us as totally whimsical.

It was apparently left by the intelligence that lived on that planet – so that was a huge positive in its favour. Presumably, they wanted to meet us. Jessy felt comfortable going if that was the reason. And that reason was the most likely by far. Still, her anxiety levels were sky high. The fact that they could have contacted us direct also played on her mind. *Afterall, they were as close as the Moon.* Had she made the right decision? Who would go first...or last? She had a dry mouth and some of her muscles were twitching and quivering involuntarily. That was a really odd, disconcerting sensation. Jessy was frankly scared out of her mind, rubbing the back of her neck through the suit and breathing in raspy gasps. She despised making decisions for a group. As a manager she made a great team member. As a mother she wasn't sure.

'Me first,' Mitch said, swallowing heavily and almost gagging, already guessing it would be him anyway, so he may as well seem keen. It might help the others. He refused to think about or mention the time element. Josh was with them so it took a bit of pressure off. Or put more on...he wasn't sure. Whatever happened to us, would probably happen to him as well. He *had* to go though. So did Jessy. If Josh chose to accompany them, so be it.

I'll go, and...' Mitch opened and then closed his mouth, saying nothing else, doing nothing but grinding his teeth. 'Then I'll come back to confirm all is okay to go,' he whispered, trying to hide the fact that he was still grinding his teeth. They could tell he didn't want to do it, by the grim, forbidding expression on his face, and the hard swallow. If he didn't want to go, then why agree to do it in the first place, and then volunteer to go first? *Obsession, duty* and *responsibility* were the obvious answers. In that order. But he wasn't all that keen to go *and* come back straight away. Fair enough, she reckoned, but Jessy also knew it had to be done to prove the trip was okay. Better Mitch than someone else, she supposed. At least he was used to it.

Mitch crouched on the object and peered at them quizzically as if what he was doing was a walk in the park. He pretended to yawn. He also noticed how sticky it was on the surface, not sure what that meant. Mitch was inwardly terrified of this thing. No-one, least of all him, knew how it worked, only that it did, which hardly put his mind at rest. Maybe it wouldn't work. Coming back to find skeletons didn't make a pleasing image either. '*No,*' he whispered to himself. He tried to escape the thoughts he had and focussed on his wife.

Eventually, Mitch started melting through the sticky anomaly, until he was gone. After five minutes of waiting, glancing eyes, uncomfortable silence, and a lot of *hmmppphing* and other anomalous noises, Mitch returned, doing pretty much the reverse of what he did before. Importantly, there seemed to be no time delay in him returning.

He effectively came straight back. Everything looked good. Both Josh and Jessy nearly collapsed with shock when he returned but eventually got themselves together enough to slowly smile when they realised his test had been successful. Zamindar and Char were their normal vanilla selves throughout. They were solemn when he left and solemn when he returned.

After a minute or so his thumping heart and rib-stretching breathing returned to normal, Mitch felt like he could talk and make some sense. 'Um, ah...it was fine, *fine*...I ended up where I did before, ah...er,' he still gasped for breath, shivering quite violently, 'near the mouth of a cave on the side of a hill which seemed to lead down to a valley of dark foliage.' He sucked in a deep breath and shook his head.

'What planet is it...well...I just don't know? I actually don't have a bloody clue. No idea what it is or where it is,' he said, appearing relieved that he was back in their timeline and clearly anxious about what lay in front of him and them. At least the object acted like they hoped it would.

'Well, I suppose it's about my time, Jessy said with a half-hearted shrug, getting to her feet. 'I'll follow Mitch, then Josh and lastly will be Zamindar and Char.' They all nodded and understood. All of them felt slightly better, having a plan of sorts to help them move forward. Everyone was on their feet now, readying themselves for movement toward the object.

Mitch sat back on the shift and disappeared once again. In turn, one after the other, they all disappeared from the Moon and were unknowingly dispatched from the Galaxy inside an artificial Einstein-Rosen Bridge, a tunnel through spacetime and a hell of a lot of matter. They weren't de-materialized and rebuilt as Mitch and Jessy thought. It was just an instantaneous bridge to another place.

*   *   *

All of them were delivered, one by one, to the new planet. Where it was, no one knew. They'd need to see a night sky to hopefully determine where in the hell It was – Zamindar would know straight away, he didn't need a night sky to help him know where they were. The Virijian had an inbuilt 3D GPS or something similar.

First, Mitch ascended, then Jessy and Josh, then the two Virijians. They were all there, as a group, breathing heavily with their artificial supplies of oxygen filling their suits.

Josh had convinced himself that he'd end up in orbit somewhere, doomed to expire on some unknown alien stellar wind. He was truly stunned to find his way to the desired end-point. Hard ground. Mitch had a dry mouth and felt weak, he thought he might topple after he stood up. The fact that he'd done it twice helped little. Using the object was still a huge mental battle.

Looking around, Jessy felt that the atmosphere was eminently breathable. They were *invited* here afterall. An intelligent oxygen-breathing civilization and forest lived here. She tried it first by turning off her personal supply of oxygen, and then sipped it by first pressing the release-button on her visor and pushing it up a centimetre. Then off everything came off, leaving her dressed only in thin pants and a tee-shirt.

The atmosphere was thick and warm and inviting. She looked quite incredible, without the helmet and the suit. As soon as everyone saw her take a few decent breaths and enjoy it, they all removed their helmets and took several deep breaths of the beautiful air around them. They literally couldn't wait to get the heavy and cumbersome units off. The manufacturers said they were slimline and provided flexibility. What a load of crap.

Mitch stood up and looked around the cave, studying it in more detail than before. He smelled mould and dampness and saw that it was made largely from a greyish, very hard, fine-grained rock, probably volcanic, not that it meant much. Vesicular and bubbles came to mind. And dykes. The cave led to a wide mouth and a vegetated valley beyond. It was covered with grey to black vegetation, same as last time. All of them were standing, seemingly waiting for directions. Mitch was the boss, apparently. No one had anointed him so, but still he'd ascended to the role nicely. He reckoned the Virijians were boss, if only by their first-rate intuition and general intelligence.

'What do you want from this world?' Zamindar toned, looking directly at Mitch. He clearly wanted and expected an answer. Mitch didn't answer and only shook his head, thinking it should be drop-dead obvious. Maybe it *was* to humans. He had to stop taking things for granted, he saw that. 'Stop using human logic, forthwith,' he said loudly to himself. Obviously, it wasn't logical to everyone. Especially not to the Virijians. Logic was very relative, apparently.

'Er, um...well,' he was taken off guard by the Virijian. The question was unexpected. He thought their plan was understood by all. 'We want to make contact with the intelligence that *One* told us were the makers of these shifts,' Mitch said, 'hopefully we'll see how they overcame their own global warming.' Assuming they had, Mitch chastened himself silently. He honestly had no idea what the status of their "civilization" was. He was entirely in the dark about them. He just hoped they weren't warlike and wanted to kill them, which he admitted was ridiculous but possible. Mitch had no idea about their mind-set. They could be anything.

'Assuming they have defeated climate change,' Josh said the words that Mitch was thinking. Maybe they're drowning in carbon like us.

'Yes, *assuming* they have,' Mitch said, taken aback by Josh. 'The fact that the air looks clear from here, means nothing. Think of Earth. As soon as you leave a city, it's clear. But there is a lot of carbon being produced by humans. *A lot.* I mean...people will soon be suffocating in the streets. Wildfires will destroy *countries*, and others will be lost under metres of water, then, there's hurricane strength winds and endless rain...all caused by greenhouse gas...carbon and the like. And the fact that...'

'Soapbox, right?' Josh whispered, looking at Jessy and grinning. He didn't look at Mitch who was about to tee-off on global warming. That's what Josh reckoned was the problem, there was way too much lip-service about climate-change, and not enough meaningful action.

'One of many,' Jessy whispered, goggling her eyes and peering at Mitch, hoping against hope that he'd shut up, or run out of air...soon.

'Time to leave,' Zamindar toned, walking to the mouth of the cave. At this point, human daydreams interested him zero.

'Yep,' Mitch agreed, joining him, as did everyone else. As a group, they left the cave and began to walk down the scarp to the valley below. It was crowded with tangled grey and black jungle, and it was warm and quite steamy, not to mention, dark. It felt like rain was imminent but there were few clouds in the sky which was a vivid purple colour, due to scattering and absorption of certain molecules, the planet received from its small reddish stars. The vivid purple sky and lighter purple clouds, Mitch knew were also due to the chemical makeup of the atmosphere and probably the planet itself. Whether it was good news or bad for them, he wasn't sure. They were on the lookout for anything that suggested "civilisation". Mitch reckoned a sign with "Civilization This Way" would have helped, or a used Coke bottle. He almost laughed out loud at the prospect of either.

They kept one eye on the horizon, when they could see it, which was almost never. Everything ahead of them, or anywhere they looked really, appeared bohemian in the extreme. Darkness and deep greyness was all they could see, and it was extremely off-putting to the human eye. All things being equal, it should have been deep green, but there was none of that, anywhere. It was like walking sideways, or doing something very unnatural indeed. Nothing seemed quite right. Josh guessed he'd eventually get used to it. He had to remember he was on a planet with an ecosystem that was in synch with completely different conditions to Earth.

Mitch couldn't help wondering *where* they were. All of them shared the same thoughts. They could be a long, long way from any civilisation – but that didn't make sense. They surely wouldn't put the shifts in the middle of a jungle, would they? With hundreds, or even thousands of kilometres to travel? Mitch doubted it, but again, that was *human* thinking. Surely, they were on the fringe of a "jungle".

That brought them back to a little chestnut, that was actually a coconut-sized paradox involving human logic. In a broader sense, how logical was it really? In other words, was human logic, *logical* in the wider sense of the universe. Mitch knew it was a circular argument and it wasn't just a slam-dunk at all. Was logic relative or absolute? That was the question that couldn't be answered. Even Zamindar couldn't answer that one.

Josh walked to the edge of the jungle where it stretched upward to the cusp on the highlands. It looked like they were on the edge of a group of parallel mountains.

'What direction should we go in?' Josh asked, wrinkling his nose and staring at Mitch, hearing and feeling a strong warm breeze. Apart from the colour of most everything, it felt like Earth. Josh reckoned Mitch should make the decision about what to do next. They looked to Mitch, waiting for directions.

'Gee...let me think,' he said sarcastically, 'er, wait...go as straight as you can,' he didn't say "of course" but he thought about saying it, 'straight until we can't go straight anymore,' Mitch finished on. That seemed logical enough, he teased himself silently.

'*Jesus, okay,*' Josh exclaimed. Walking between two large jet-black trees and over a thick fern covered root, he walked and jumped around a large weeping fern that was dark grey in colour and then stopped dead in his tracks. Everyone else was right behind him and froze. Then they followed his movement and hunkered down with him, hiding from "something" behind a huge grey fern with large and intricate leaves. Incredibly, the leaves were dark grey as well as huge.

'*What do you see?*' Mitch whispered forcefully to Josh. He could see him staring at something and followed Josh's finger which was pointing slightly to the right of straight ahead. The structure in front of him looked homely and familiar. Josh's breath came in quick, shallow gasps. He found it hard to believe he was face-to-face with something as mundane and prosaic as a fence.

It was a high, solid looking fence that seemed to be made from metal, or at least some sort of metal-*like* alloy, and it appeared to enclose where they were, certainly if it kept going. And it was right in front of them, and presumably on either side of them as well. Encircled by a barrier, he wasn't sure if that was good or bad. But it wasn't surprising - the fact that it was there was logical.

'On Earth this fence would be made mainly from wood and wire, here, it looked quite solid, and made of God knows what sort of metal,' Josh whispered to whoever was listening. He peered at the fence and went closer and inspected it close-up, or as close as he could go and still focus, thinking how out of place the thing looked. There didn't appear to be any paint or even a coating on it, although it appeared wet.

Zamindar looked at Mitch closely after he watched him inspect the fence. The big Virijian clearly had something to say. 'It is composed of rare-earth's, mainly yttrium and erbium metal. This planet is rich with them in huge deposits of almost pure xenotime.' Mitch stared at him and then at the fence.

'Well...there you go then, not something I would have guessed.' Mitch said. He looked at the fence in a new light.

They made their way toward it, over the fungus laden soil, between trees and skirted around massive black palms and huge dark and white mushrooms with fat treelike trunks. There were also less familiar grey shrubs and spongey blue ground to be crossed before they would get to the fence, hopefully as a group. Off to their left was a watery, swampy area with black groups of sword-shaped leaves rising from the ground all over the place.

They could all see something small crawling over the leaves, and something small taking flight to land on other leaves. They were all too small to visualise individually. Insects or similar presumably. Life definitely. They had long translucent wings, but that's all they could tell from this distance. The fence or barricade or whatever it was, was about seven feet tall, looked super-slippery, had a sheen to it and appeared wet, but probably wasn't. Mitch was going to say "oiled" but that was ridiculous. Why would you oil a fence?

By the look of what appeared to be its binary stars, it was about noon if it were back on Earth but Mitch wasn't sure, these stars went across the sky at 45 degrees. God only knew how long a day was on this planet. By their appearance, both stars were reddish and probably relatively small compared to the Sun. Mitch plugged that time in on his watch and told Zamindar, he'd note the time when it got dark, if it got dark, which he assumed it would at some point. There was that Earthly "logic" or "prejudice" again.

With a single timing, they wouldn't be able to tell what this planet was doing, rather, they would have to guess by the amount of daylight there was and where the suns were in the sky. It was likely that without a substantial satellite, they had no stable seasons at all. It was certainly warm enough to be summer, but the warmth might be due to other factors.

So, when they boiled all their knowledge down, they knew fuck all about this rock...seasons, day and night, and what exactly was in the atmosphere of this planet, apart from best-guesses. And they would have to check on the suns to see how fast or even *if* the planet was turning on its axis - or whether it was tidally locked and maybe even an eyeball planet. If it was the latter, given the vegetation, we must be right in the sweet spot, the eyeball, with most of the rest of the planet made of glaciers, or similar. Mitch was sure the suns had moved in the sky but he wasn't absolutely sure. That was the problem with this place – there were few definitives.

Zamindar told them that the planet was 1.2 times the size of Earth and that it did rotate, at about 40 degrees every twenty hours. Josh stared at him, dumbfounded, as did Jessy and Mitch. But no one bothered to ask him *how* he knew. He just did. He was Zamindar, so no one questioned him. Anything scientific – he seemed to know the answer.

Every hundred, maybe a hundred and fifty metres on the fence there was a small seemingly wooden, house. The wood if that's what it was, was in asymmetric planks that left gaps or holes in the structure. Presumably, it was made from the stuff of the trees. It was also a slightly different colour from wood on Earth, but that could have been the color of the treatment used.

Mitch could see movement inside, through the gaps, but not individuals. There was definitely something moving inside though – it was silhouetted by light streaming in. He squinted at the trees in the background like Mr. Magoo. Mitch made no reference to his piss-poor eyesight at a distance. He looked and watched as if he could actually see some detail, which he couldn't. His eyesight at a distance was terrible.

Mitch heard something really odd. It sounded like a...he didn't know how to describe it. It was a whirring, humming, thumping sound like nothing he'd heard on Earth. To the point where he didn't have a word to describe it. Mitch stood stock still and stared at the spot he thought the noise came from and saw nothing. It was probably a creature, but he had no idea what might have made the noise. Maybe the sound of wings moving rapidly or a mating or warning call from some creature, but probably something completely different.

*   *   *

Zamindar stood tall behind a dark tree and watched the movement in the hut get more spirited, and then swivelled his eyes to Mitch. Zamindar was going to leave it to Mitch, but it was obvious that he needed help. Mitch was essentially blind at a distance, and Zamindar knew it.

Zamindar toned to Mitch and Josh, 'sentries are stationed in each hut. This world has been waiting for you to arrive for a long time. These creatures are security for the fence.' It was all "der" stuff for Zamindar. The humans were dumbfounded and bewildered and watched the huts closely.

'Waiting for *them* – amazing, Mitch thought.

Char was focussing on the small hut that was right behind him, while everyone else watched the house to the right. His dual hearts pumped his nickel-blood a little harder as he watched the shadows start to solidify. From side on, he could see a pendulous head, and probably long, thin legs. Large eyes and two arms with a vaguely human physique completing the picture. Skin seemed to be grey to very light brown.

Jessy watched Char turn around as she was observing the "huts", under his shoulder. She was stunned by the creature's appearance, as it ambled forward, presumably on its rounds around his/her or its part of the fence. From their position, it was difficult to tell, but she could see it had green eyes, a slipstreamed nose, and four fingers, one probably a thumb. She couldn't tell from here, but they looked to be on the end of very long and thin, almost skeletal arms. The creature looked familiar but she couldn't place it. She'd seen something similar somewhere – it licked its lips in a familiar way but she couldn't place it. Incredibly, Jessy thought she'd seen something like it before. Now, watching it move forward, she felt more certain than ever.

Zamindar toned, 'Up there,' he used his left hand to point, 'is a lizard, warm-blooded, quite intelligent, significantly more than humans.'

'Er...thanks,' she said quietly, also realising that the Virijians were facts first, the rest a lot later, if ever. Feelings absolutely weren't factored in. It made Jessy instantly wonder, what they did for fun. She gazed at Zamindar and couldn't imagine him doing anything for fun only. Jessy couldn't help but smile and giggle as she imagined the Virijians playing golf or some inane board game. *No way*. The thought of them at Disney World, completed the ridiculous picture, turning her smile into a face-splitter. *No way* was her considered conclusion again. They were always as serious as.

Zamindar didn't respond to sarcasm, recognising the comments for what they were. He did sometimes respond to genuine requests for information, like this time, 'it is essentially an evolved dinosaur. Substantially older than humans as a species.'

'*Shit,*' she blurted, thinking about it. 'So, they are like the dino's back home, that would have evolved if that k/t meteor hadn't hit?'

'That wasn't the only reason they went extinct…but sort of, yes, although they are far more technically evolved here than they would have been on Earth. Had they not been by devastated by the asteroid, they would have hit an evolutionary brick wall in another thousand years or so. Morphologically, we are not sure. Likely, the same, Zamindar said, sounding very serious indeed.

The creature up ahead was dressed in blue coveralls that seemed to be standard dress if the other two creatures were any guide. They had emerged from the other hut's further along the wall, taking a cursory look at the fence. All of them were walking along their section of the barrier, paying superficial attention to what might be inside. They'd been doing the same for a long, long time. After doing the same thing, day after day, and getting no result, they must've been very bored with it. Any thinking creature would be.

Protection and detection was their game. And they were very serious about it. But the daily repetition without real result had to take a toll surely. Jessy was sure they couldn't concentrate every second of every day. Although this was a completely new species so she guessed anything was possible. Maybe concentration and single-mindedness was their thing…who knew?

Zamindar had been silently conversing with Char for several minutes, trying to determine why they didn't just make contact with humans, rather than by placing a remote object on the Moon. They could have easily done so, being so very close. The objects must have been put there at least a century ago, or it would've been detected by electronic eyes looking permanently skyward and the satellites that scour the entire Moonscape. Jessy was thinking the same thing…*why*? They'd travelled so far, by God knows what source, and didn't even leave a "sorry I missed you" card. Well, they did leave something but it ended up being buried and moved by a fault and proved very difficult to find indeed.

It made perfect sense to Zamindar, humanity would be hardly worth contacting before they had spaceflight and some consuming capability. Perhaps they knew the species was intelligent but pre-space-able, so they left a portal that was only a short distance away from Earth, in space. So, again, it was a timer. They were gazumped by a fault line that effectively hid the anomaly, but humanity eventually found it. By "humanity", it was Mitch and Jessy that finally uncovered it. Fluke it may have been, but still, it was them that discovered it, all through their love of mineral collecting. How bizarre.

Mitch rubbed his forehead "They must have been patrolling this area for a very long time. Or maybe they'd done calculations to determine the earliest point we could get to the Moon and commence mining operations, assuming we ever did of course. Maybe the object wasn't buried when they left it, so it was probably just a matter of mapping the Moon.

'But what if we never got to the Moon?' Jessy said. 'Would they have come looking? 'It was only an accident that we found it.'

'I doubt they would have ever come looking,' Char toned, 'unless the shift was used, they would assume you were not worth interacting with,' the huge Virijian said. 'Otherwise, they would not have left the object. We are still surprised that they have the technology to build these objects. They must have several physical prodigies amongst their population. To manipulate cosmic strings, dark energy, magnetism and move wormholes takes some skill - more than a species their age should have.'

'So, what do we do now?' Josh asked, looking at the strange creatures ahead of him. They were talking together, he thought, watching the one who was doing the talking, as its mouth moved and its tongue worked overtime.

'You rush them and make a citizen's arrest,' Mitch said, chuckling, centimetres from his son's nose. He thought he was quite the comedian. Josh ignored him. He was just being himself – a sarcastic, arsehole.

Zamindar ignored both of them, and was about to tone, Mitch could tell by the static between his ears. The Virijian was peering right at him, 'we should walk up slowly to that one with our hands in the air,' he pointed at the nearest creature with his middle arm, 'and tell it how we got here, although it'll probably already know...it's pretty obvious I guess.'

Char toned, 'I agree. Do it carefully, and as Zamindar has suggested. At all times we remain subservient. That should do it,' Char reckoned.

Jessy nodded, 'yep, make sure they don't panic, maybe put our arms up *and* your hands, they can't get that gesture wrong.'

Mitch nodded at Jessy. 'Yeah,' he said, immediately thinking of Sean Monterrosa in California. He remembered this guy was trying to surrender to Police, but he was shot dead anyway. There was more to it, he reckoned, at least he hoped so. He hoped like hell they wouldn't be shot dead. Put your hands up and survive, Mitch was fairly sure that's how it would work.

'All right then, a decision's been made,' Josh said. 'Let's go.' He gawked at his mum and dad. Neither engendered much confidence, as they gazed at each other with sweaty foreheads, generally looking and feeling terrified. Josh had the feeling that *anything* could be coming straight at them. These lizard-people couldn't be expected to behave like humans or follow what we referred to as human "logic" or norms. They may behave totally differently to expectation. *Careful,* was the only way forward. Surely, holding your hands up would convey the right "acquiescence" message, wouldn't it?

With that, everyone stood up slowly, and walked to the opening in the fence that was enclosed by a gate of sorts, or something that presumably swung back or otherwise opened. Josh gave it the smallest of pushes as a tentative first step and it opened, not by swinging back as they expected, but by retracting downward into its own sheath. *Go figure,* he thought. Rare-Earth fence – he hadn't forgotten. No-one expected that, except maybe Zamindar. He seemed to have an exceptional handle on the potentials of evolution. A well-developed sixth sense perhaps.

Stretching their arms out and up, the Virijians held their outer two arms up, and they were mirrored by the humans as they walked around the mouth of the opening, ensuring that their arms and hands were held straight up as far as possible and their phones were safely stowed in their pockets. They were terrified and felt ridiculous with their arms in the air, as if they were about to surrender to the law.

They were satisfied not to be shot straight away. All of them could see the indigenous creature not far ahead. From the rear, they could make out thin legs and a tall frame with greyish-green, gnarly hands covered with thin hair or fuzzy fur. He was absolutely no "looker" by Earth standards, he was the stuff of nightmares. But he may have been attractive on this place.

Josh clapped to gain his attention. The creature turned on a Dime, like it was waiting for them, which, in a sense they supposed it was. It, looked at them, widened his green eyes to the point where they were huge, and started jabbering in a strange language that sounded like utter gobbledegook. To say it was excited was a massive understatement.

The creature stumbled backward several steps and started wobbling, after looking at Char and Zamindar especially, then spoke to someone remotely after touching something on his bulging, hairy wrist. More of the jabber ensued. Mitch could hear clicks and a sort of whistling sound it made, seemingly with the back of its throat. It was the way this creature communicated, language presumably. It sounded like a cross between a chicken and a blackbird. He also made a low-pitched sound by banging his lower arm, near his wrist. Overall, it sounded and looked very strange indeed. Mitch immediately wondered if it was widely used or not, it looked overtly difficult, a bit like an odd Eastern ritual. But what did he know? The indigenous life might, *probably did* find it second nature.

Mitch held one hand up and stood in its path. Presumably, this creature had just spoken to a superior, somewhere. The creature gaped at them, two different species of intelligent beings, in fact there were three, brought together under the most extraordinary set of circumstances. Mitch could see the lizard species had large, green-centred eyes and short fur over the head and probably down its entire body, as far as he could see, beneath the uniform, *probably*. He was definitely a lizard, of sorts. Movement and the angular shape of the tongue and eyes with slit-shaped pupils sort of confirmed it. The grey scaly skin beneath the hair made it definitive. To Mitch that's definitely what it was. It even had a flap of skin near its neck that they hadn't identified from further away. Mitch wondered if that was a frill of some sort.

It peered at them like someone was shining a light into its eyes. The creature took a few deep breaths and visibly swallowed. Its eyes closed and then re-opened rapidly, sideways to the way it worked for humans. It's pupils sort of blinked sideways as well, independent of the eyes as a whole.

'Welcome to Jarith,' the creature said quickly in Mandarin. It may as well have been alien. It was a total nonsense to most of them, although "Jarith" was clear enough. They looked at each other. Mitch shook his head. It was no surprise they didn't understand what it said.

'Sounds vaguely familiar,' Josh said, taken aback. He glanced at Mitch who nodded. Still, he couldn't understand it though, but he'd heard it before. That in itself was incredible. It was vaguely familiar. These creatures were clearly schooled in what we understand as language.

'Welcome to Jarith,' the creature said in pretty good, unusually accented English. Sort of like a high latitude's inflection on Earth. They all understood. It made sense - Jessy reckoned. It was just very high pitched - it was probably these creatures' physiology combined with nerves. It sounded like it had taken a good swig of helium.

The creatures knew where we were from, and thereby knew the languages most likely...she guessed. So, all guards were schooled in them, she guessed again. English and Mandarin. That seemed logical enough. Bully for them, Mitch thought, *human logic* actually stood up. They also knew Hindi, Spanish, Russian and French.

'Thanks,' Mitch returned. He wasn't sure what else to say. Clearly, none of them were keen on talking. Just looking and assessing closely. Josh and Jessy gawked at the creature, along with Mitch. She expected to be put under lock and key, or handcuffed or similar, at least at first.

So, Jessy was relieved she was still free to move around. Hopefully, it would stay that way. The Virijians carefully assessed the behaviour of both groups, ping-ponging their gaze between the Jarithian and the humans.
Mitch and Jessy peered, with naked curiosity at whatever it was. Was it male or female, they both wondered, or was that distinction moot? Based on

employment and the way it looked and carried itself, it was male – but was that simply Earthly bias.

The Virijians were looking backwards, and seemed disinterested in what was in front of them, something else had their attention. A noise started emanating from somewhere over the forest. Whatever it was, was coming in to land, a craft, a bit like a chopper but not a chopper. Certainly, it sounded sort of like one, just quieter. The air was being hit by something, it sounded like a rotorcraft of some kind, but it was very quiet, whatever it was. It was pure white and they could see it, approaching above the trees, quite slowly. It was a craft and presumably, it was coming for them. The similarity to Earth tech was astounding.

Jessy watched it move across the trees, then it came to a complete halt and started to descend to the ground using some manner of VTOL engine or engines which were now making a lot of noise as they presumably fought with the gravity on this world. With widening eyes and a slackening mouth, Jessy watched the vehicle as it landed on its wheels and powered down. There were only two aboard, and spare seats were at the back that were seemingly for them. What was this vehicle, it had wheels and wings and blades – so was it a hybrid method of transportation? It was too big to be called a flying car, Jessy thought, too odd to be called a plane or a helicopter. Definitely not a chopper, she reckoned, there were no blades, but something sounded like it was chopping the air. The blades could be folded up and hidden when not in use. She didn't watch close enough to know if this is what happened.

Hopping in the ship after being hustled toward it by their new friends, they sat in the chairs which were all soft and appeared to have nothing they would term hard at all, including the legs of the chairs, or whatever they were sitting on, which were short and cylindrical. Soft to the touch without anything added to it, like a linen cushion. Despite being a naked chair and looking like metal, no part of it was hard, but seemingly, supportive enough and sturdy enough to hold her and everyone else up. What it was made of was a question that filled both of them like air in a balloon.

Looking at their reptile suitors, they noticed that they'd all turned their scaly heads, and apart from the pilot, were all focussed on them. Thankfully, the pilot seemed to be watching the instruments and where they were going. They were the centre of the Jarithians attention, inspecting the humans every move. Which seemed fair enough – they'd waited *so* long for us to arrive.

Mitch felt compelled to say something. No one else was saying a thing and it was getting a little uncomfortable – the Jarithians were content just to watch the new arrivals. 'Er, um...thank you for picking us up.' How fucking eloquent, he though after he'd said it. Great first words.

'You are welcome,' the pilot said in stilted, unaccented, but high-pitched English. They continued to observe the humans closely. All the Jarithians remained focussed, eyeing the nearest human meticulously, assessing their entire body, from top to bottom. They showed no embarrassment in doing so and chillingly, licked their lips while doing it.

Looking beyond the craft, through what he assumed was vacuum-proof glass of some sort, he saw a city and surrounds of relative sameness, the houses around the buildings of the city looked like fish-scales and the buildings were shaped like pentagons, a few were trapeziums, all were a darkish colour and all quite low in profile. Visual consistency was clearly a thing. It was very different from Earth. On Earth, it was inconsistency that ruled. Here, it was the exact opposite, assuming this was a normal Jarithian suburb.

It was toward one of the larger pentagons they appeared to be headed. The flying-machine they were in, arrowed that way. It was fascinating to finally spy some of their architecture. Unlike Earth, which had a hodgepodge of all shapes, there was a tectonism to all the buildings they could see.

Gratified that he and Jessy knew where they were headed, he leant back against the strange seats and surveyed what the pilot was flying through. It was completely dark now and a small and angular moon was shining to the left of their path of travel, moving noticeably. The dual stars had both set and were gone below the horizon, replaced by a very alien sky filled with very unfamiliar stars and constellations.

Jessy reckoned the galaxy in the northern part of their night sky, almost side-on and small, was the Milky Way Galaxy, and if it was, it put them a *long* way from home – probably millions of light years. If the planet they were standing on was in the Andromeda Galaxy, the view would be like this. They slowed down and seemed almost to stop in mid-air, Mitch grabbed Jessy, and both felt their stomachs drop as they descended vertically to a soft landing, near a pentagonal structure. They'd VTOL'd to the steps of an alien building.

The pilot and co-pilot exited first, directing them to come in through the same doorway, the door sliding back after some unknown stimulation by the pilot. Mitch was pretty sure it opened on its own - he wasn't entirely sure though – but it opened widely. The whole side of the vehicle opened – for back and front seat exit and entry. They all departed the vehicle and stood on, as they realised, a soft but strangely firm surface - it seemed very counter-intuitive. It was a hard surface when you walked on it but soft if you jumped up and down. The maroon substance or colouring underfoot was everywhere, extending from the Vase-like buildings to the roads and to the houses.

Everything looked brand new – there wasn't a mark on anything, including the roads. Everything looked polished. It wasn't just new-looking, it appeared as though everything had been shone up. The gleam on everything was amazing. The road if that's what it was and the buildings and houses seemed to form a "oneness", composed of a very fine-grained, lustrous maroon coloured substance that was literally everywhere. Everything within sight appeared to be made of it. Mitch felt the stirrings of deep obsession. He had to know what it was – because it seemed to be at the base of their infrastructural technology. Was it nanotechnology, he wondered?

Mitch also wondered, was the extreme cleanliness and the complete absence of rubbish for *them*, as visitors, or was this how it was normally? They hardly had the time to clean up. He reckoned it had to be the latter, but time would tell, he supposed. If they saw the greater area, that would tell the more complete story, he thought. Must be for us, was his final conclusion. You didn't wait for someone for so long without some degree of pride in your planet.

Mitch spied a number of pentagonal buildings that were made from small cubes with a large porthole covered with glass or some other clear substance in each, and stacked on top of each other. Were these things hotels or houses, or something else? The two creatures started to walk ahead and they flourished an arm for them to follow, which they did. Pentagonal structures were everywhere, on both sides and ahead.

Jessy wondered where all of "them" were. So far, they hadn't seen anyone – even from a height, they were absent. There were roadways and areas between structures that, using Earth norms, should have been populated – but it was all empty. Then, there was the rural part of the planet, which they hadn't seen. Surely, there were beings, vehicles and domiciles there. Maybe there had been a demand made for everyone to stay home. Here, it might work, but on Earth it quite simply wouldn't work. There were way too many free thinkers and sticky-beaks.

They continued to sit in a large grey room with no furniture in it which led to a door, and Jessy was sure everything in it was made entirely of the same softish material – Mitch wondered if it was soft to avoid injury, certainly it made sense with the road and the flying thing. Here, he wasn't so sure. He didn't feel like asking questions of them yet. His head was full of them though. Mitch felt sure Zamindar would know, he'd ask him later. He guessed it wasn't a priority to anyone, even if he thought it was.

'*Ooookaaaay,* what now?' Mitch said, after a long silence. The room was pin-drop quiet. You could easily hear a closed-mouth question. Or a muted grunt. You would be able to hear most anything. Mitch could hear nothing. No sound at all. Not inside or outside.

'I think they're trying to put us at ease, believe it or not, hence the table and the near empty room,' Zamindar toned. Mitch reckoned they were doing a piss-poor job of that. The Virijian continued. 'Their own personal items have been removed as far as they could, on short notice. They have been waiting for you for a long time,' the Virijian continued to tone. 'I have scanned the pilot and it seems that they have been waiting for a century of your years for you to make the voyage. They preferred that contact was made here, rather than them just turning up at Earth uninvited. They knew that your species would not react well to a surprise visit from space.

Mitch thought about it and quickly concurred. He stared at Jessy in silent horror. '*Got that right,*' Mitch said, nodding his head and opening his eyes wide. '*Jesus,* can you imagine if it happened,' he moaned. *Holy fuck,* he thought, imagining a ship landing on the White House lawn, totally unannounced. The DoD would use it as target practice.

'Yep.' Josh said, agreeing wholeheartedly with his dad. '*Shit,* that would've created quite the scene.' *Pande-fucking-monium,* he was sure. Josh thought about them landing at Time Square in New York or Tiananmen Square in Beijing. What a head fuck that would have been.

'*Yes, oh Christ yeah,*' Jessy whined, 'imagine the panic if they'd just tuned up, unexpected,' Jessy said horrified, 'it'd be truly chaos...at least half the population would be in an awful state. Under their bed scared.'

'But,' Zamindar continued, 'they would have done so in another century if you had not turned up, so it is a good thing that we are here. We have avoided all that. By the way, the object was supposed to be a lot easier to find, but you know all that.'

'Why have they just left us here?' Josh asked, gazing at the walls and the two doors that were firmly closed. 'They brought us in here and then immediately all left. Doesn't that seem strange?' Josh frowned at his dad and rubbed his chin.

'They haven't left, they're coming back,' Mitch said, 'through that door,' he pointed toward it, 'make no mistake,' Mitch said, expecting an avalanche of creatures to come through at any time. 'They'll be back,' he confirmed, giving Jessy a nod. Mitch was certain.

Mitch wondered if he should tell their new friends about *One.* Maybe they already knew. Maybe, like the Virijians, their system wasn't gifted a Sphere. Should he tell them, the Virijians would say no and start spouting their *greater minds* crap. Mitch would think about it. He wouldn't be told what to do. That made him wonder for the first time why *One* told humans at all? Was boasting behind it or was it simply for the conveyance of accurate information? Mitch was highly cynical about *One's* motivations, but that may have just been the human mind - always viewing the worst for a certain behaviour. It's rarely benevolence, right? Before he could think further, something ahead of him changed substantially. The door in the wall vanished – it didn't open or slide anywhere – it just disappeared. Clearly, this race had a granular understanding of quantum physics.

A single creature with a very long and pronounced neck, walked slowly through a large, smooth hole in the wall dressed in a distinctive and very different dark brown, with a fitted top and pants that moved better than nylon. Whatever it was, was *very* well fitted. The creature was slim and carried itself like a royal entity. Folding its legs up, it sat down slowly in front of them and eyed them closely.

It glanced down, almost shyly. Then looked up with large, green-centred eyes, gazing at all of them, speaking lightly and quickly. 'I am the leader of this world and I speak for the planet.' He studied each of them carefully, one by one, including the Virijians, and he took his time on each. 'You can call me Rinmal.' He resumed his downward stare. He definitely had the air of royalty, even though his kind "used" to be lizards. *WTF*, Josh thought.

Josh gazed at Rinmal who was flicking his forked tongue forward, quickly and repeatedly, and then gazing at the rest of the group. Mitch wondered if their tongue was used for smelling like Earthly lizards do. Hardly a regal thing to do, he reckoned.

Looking at the humans, they appeared like sideshow clowns with their mouths open. God only knows what the Jarithians thought of them. 'Why are we here?' Mitch whispered hoarsely, still staring at Rinmal. It remained uncomfortably quiet in the room and every word or movement made an echo. Mitch glanced at Jessy, wondering if he'd get any response from Rinmal.

'We didn't bring you here, you came to this galaxy of your own volition,' Rinmal said in perfect English, deep and without accent. It was like listening to one of the royals on Earth, but free of the posh accent. 'All we did,' Rinmal said, 'was leave the means to get here without travelling in flat space.' He glanced around the room, seemingly surprised that those from Earth were finally here.

Zamindar and Char already knew, they had scanned the Jarithian in full and knew everything about him, and now knew everything he did in his recent lifetime. What he knew, *they* knew as well.

Rinmal gave them some background to humanity as far as they were concerned. 'A rotating black hole with an Einstein-Rosen bridge at its core with no time offset gave them access to a patch of space not far from our Kuiper Belt. Earth gave off so much electromagnetic radiation, and was located almost straight away. Mitch was sure with all the EMAR it emitted, that the planet would be lit up like a fucking Christmas tree.

'But there was war happening across your world,' Rinmal said. 'Your race was pre-nuclear so we made the decision ultimately to leave a remote envoy. We believed that contact would be more appropriate when war was over and we hoped, the acquisition of nuclear technology had occurred. These were all wishes you understand, and it is remarkable that they've come to actually be a reality.'

Fuck me, Jessy thought, bringing a shaky hand to her forehead. Earth stuck out like the proverbial sore thumb, hardly surprising they wanted to make contact. The techno-signatures must have been overwhelming.

'So, you now tick all the boxes,' Rinmal said, 'we genuinely welcome you to our home planet.' Rinmal smiled generously at all of them, looking deeply into each's eyes. Apparently, he really believed what he was saying. At least that's the feeling he emanated.

'We came here for a reason,' Mitch said, becoming less nervous and more serious as he spoke. He was about to ask him what the Virijians had already said no to, because of the NDA they each signed, substantiating that the Virijians wouldn't reveal their technology to the humans, or anyone else. The reason for the question was obvious.

The Virijians had promised, by executing an NDA with their President, that they wouldn't pass on anything that by itself or in conjunction with something else, would manifestly change our behaviour on Earth or in space. The Virijians bent the agreement but never broke it. They were very clear in its application. Peace on the Virijian worlds was of critical importance. Keeping the Virijian rebels happy was paramount to obtaining peace.

They respected the NDA at all times, ensuring amity was maintained within their empire. So far it had worked. But they had to continue to keep it high in their mind. The Virijians never forgot it and always operated within it. The only thing he ever got from Zamindar is that he and his people used four dimensional computers and he said that without meaning too. It meant less than zero to Mitch. Zamindar refused to elaborate on it and no doubt would deny ever saying it. 4D computers were double-dutch to humans.

Josh glanced at Rinmal and then at Mitch and Jessy. He felt like he had to say something...no one else was. The Virijians weren't saying or toning anything, just sitting there like two huge puppets. The time was right, Josh thought.

Josh glanced around the room. 'You've obviously overcome global w-warming,' Josh said, quieter than he'd hoped. He wasn't entirely sure how to say it, but thankfully, Mitch was nodding at him, urging him on, and looking to stand up. 'We are killing our planet,' Josh said dramatically, and louder, standing up to his full height, positioning himself next to Mitch, 'mainly by pumping carbon dioxide into the atmosphere. Sea-levels are rising, as are the number of extreme weather events - wildfires and of course, floods and high temperatures, oh, and glaciers are receding in the north and south.'

'Basically...as a species, we're a fuck-up,' Josh rubbed his hand over his face, thinking deeper. 'We know what the problem is, we just refuse to fix it properly,' he continued. 'We'll go part way, but when it comes down to it, the economy *always* wins. We'd rather kill ourselves and all the animals and everything else, rather than solve the problem properly, apparently. The trouble is, climate change is way too implied, a lot of people simply don't believe it, or don't believe it *enough* to prioritise it and fix it. If it was more quantitative, we'd do whatever we needed to do to save the planet. If we were directly poisoning the surface of the globe such that crops failed to grow, humanity would fall over itself in doing what it had to, so that the masses were fed. After a few moments of silence, Josh cleared his throat and continued on, 'Unfortunately, it's not that clear with climate-change, but what is crystal clear is that dealing with it impacts the economies of all sorts of countries. To fix it we need to cease burning fossil fuels – coal and oil – *period*. And replace it with something else. So...you see our problem. Economy always wins and that stance will kill us and everything else.' Josh stared unwaveringly at Rinmal then glanced at his dad.

Harsh, but true, Mitch thought, having listened to Josh. Money might have made the world go around, but it was the main reason that carbon and other greenhouse gasses were killing the planet. Take it out of the picture and the issues would be solved. Small task indeed.

'We all understand the problems,' Josh said loudly, 'but humanity is at a dead loss as to how we can fix the problem for good, apart from setting useless targets for carbon production, and the use of a little wind, green hydrogen and solar energy which will never be enough for humanity's needs. The planet needs to *stop* burning fossil fuels to obtain energy and stop burning oil to feed cars and planes. *Stop fucking burning - period.* There are reduction targets and everyone knows about it, and talks about it, but it's all hot wind and *bullshit*.' Josh was getting fired up by his own voice and the frustration associated with seeing the problem *and* the answer. And that the human species would go extinct by 3050 because of it.

Mitch looked at Josh and smiled, nodding at him and telling him quietly that he'd take over. Josh was too fired up to continue – Jessy saw him spitting when he spoke. It was time to stop. 'Sit down Joshy, leave the rest to dad.' For Josh, regurgitating the problems of climate-change was doing him no good at all. Josh drew in a hissing breath and tried to relax and breathe normally.

'By the time it's remedied, the planet will be gone,' Mitch said seriously, impassioned by Josh's words. '*We need your help*.' He said loudly. All the humans nodded in Rinmal's direction.

'*We do.*' Josh said in absolute agreement, nodding like a madman. 'We need a lot of help to find our way,' Josh implored, staring at Rinmal in frightened desperation. Otherwise, our planet is gone.'

'Follow me,' Rinmal said, as he unwound his legs and got to his feet, walking quickly toward the door. All the humans got up from their chairs and followed him quickly in single file. 'I have something to show you,' Rinmal said. They went with the two at the door who had been spoken to by Rinmal and who were now gesticulating to them, returning to the flying machine and buckling up for take-off. The buckle itself was soft and pliable, and the rest was fabric not unlike Earth. Made sense, Mitch thought, less injuries he supposed. Everything was soft, including the buckles.

Zamindar had once told him that the softness of the interior of any vehicle that flew or went at speed *anywhere* was a reasonable measure of how advanced a species was. Now, he truly understood what he meant.

Mitch gazed upward and saw the sky through something that looked like glass - it was filled with stars, to make a beautiful, alien, twilight sky. There were none of the regulation stars in the sky, Sirius and Canopus weren't there and there were none of the nebulas or constellations. There was a galactic centre but it looked very disorganized and nothing like the Milky Way. He got a look at the ground when they levelled off in the craft, it was so much like Earth, far from how this place looked in the daytime.

There were the lights of intelligence everywhere. He guessed lights here looked like lights on Earth. Lights were lights, he supposed. Still, it was an amazing sight, even though it wasn't completely dark.

'We are going to look at our *saviour*,' Rinmal said, holding his chest and having a gleam in his eye. He gawked at the rest of them and, apart from the Virijians, all of them were definitely grinning a bit. The Jarithian was definitely showing a positive emotion.

'And I believe it can be your saviour as well.' Rinmal said, watching all the humans closely. They were approaching a similar shaped vase-like structure that was lower and much longer than the building in which they met all the Jarithians. This place was very different for a good reason.

They landed just outside the structure, although there was ample room on the roof to land such a craft. Maybe it wasn't strong enough, who knew why they didn't take advantage of the extra room? They all pondered the same question as they VTOL'd to a soft landing in front of it. Rinmal had certainly filled them with intrigue, but this place was also somewhat foreboding. And what the hell did he mean by "saviour"?

Following a Jarithian, who flourished an arm for them to follow, they moved through two sets of soft, grey and brown material that appeared in front of them, which was a peculiar but easy thing to do, they entered a very large room with fifty or so machines that were close to spherical and each about the size of a suitcase sitting on the "polished" maroon floor.

'These objects are fusion reactors,' Rinmal said with the sweep of an arm. 'They power half the planet, and the energy they provide produces zero carbon or other greenhouse chemicals,' he paused and peered at Mitch deliberately. 'They do not affect the atmosphere of our world in any way. Fusion energy saved this world, and it can save yours. Clean, safe and unlimited energy can be drawn from simple chemical reactions if you have the technology and the required mechanical engineering skill to produce them.'

All the humans were thunderstruck, Josh, because he didn't know a damn thing about fusion, until Jessy filled him in with the important details. Josh had heard of it afterall, it was the same as the Sun, but he was definitely not anywhere near an expert. Mitch and Jessy were stunned because they'd never seen fusion reactors so unbelievably small. The reactors he knew were the Tokamak, M.I.T. and ITER that were huge, bigger than a *fucking* international airliner and all of them failed to produce more energy than was pumped into the damned things. On Earth, fusion energy was no more than a dream. One that was always in the future somewhere…but strangely never seemed to get any closer, despite improvements in technology. The potential it held for clean, unlimited energy was underlined by the massive investment they received – tens of billions of dollars.

After eyeing their small, working machines, Mitch said, 'Earth has a few reactors, but they are huge, you've reduced them to…*to this?*' Josh said, his arms hanging limp at his sides. He walked up and peered at one of them, the machine didn't even feel warm at close quarters. If it was connected to something, which he assumed it must be, it was on the underside, out of view. Or it somehow worked on something akin to WI-FI.

Josh was dazzled by what he was seeing. How on Earth would we replicate what they'd done here, we simply didn't have the know-how, let alone the engineering abilities. Unless they were talking about teaching us…*he hoped* that's what Rinmal was suggesting. 'Are you saying that you will teach us the detail and componentry of constructing these things?'

'It's the only way,' Rinmal said. 'If you wish to leave carbon behind you, it is the only realistic option. Solar and other "natural" energies will not do the job for Earth.' He shook his head at green hydrogen and solar. 'Your civilization requires too-much energy for that.'

'You will borrow two of our people who are schooled in making these reactors. Humanity can do it,' Rinmal said. 'With the knowledge and the teaching, it can be done. Obviously, it won't be easy.'

'*Jesus,*' Josh said gruffly, 'we'd be like children learning from our masters,' he took a deep breath, curling his hands into fists – 'maybe that's how it had to be, learn, and hopefully *live* as a species. It'd be like Jesus teaching his bloody disciples.'

'If it has to be, it has to be,' Mitch said, staring at Rinmal. Mitch then stared at Josh with eyebrows disappearing behind his fringe, repeating Rinmal's sentiment incredulously, '*he got that right.*'

'It'll be massively hard if not impossible, and that's not related to building the fusion reactors.' Mitch knew how deeply rooted fossil fuels were on Earth. 'Earth is in love with fossil fuels – coal is a huge part of the economy and it feeds all manner of ancillary industries across the globe.'

'Thank you fucking Plato,' Josh quipped, grinning at his dad, he already knew all that crap. Josh didn't need it thrust down his throat.

Mitch knew that electricity was right there to be generated from fusion energy and had been since the Universe began. One look at the night sky and stars was enough. Everywhere in space, hydrogen was being fused into helium. Once $E=MC^2$ became a thing on Earth, humans knew it could run literally everything, electricity for homes and businesses, and charging the batteries for electric cars, trains, trams and electric aircraft. Goodbye carbon, hello healthy, renormalising atmosphere and world, as long as it wasn't *too late* for all that to happen.

But he knew, as they all did, that technology and engineering was only part of the problem. The other part was way more difficult and intricate than even producing the energy.

7

Anomaly

"The easiest way to solve a problem is to deny it exists." —*Isaac Asimov*

It was now time to leave the new planet. Coming with were two of the indigenous lifeforms, Cranreb and Davtep, who would demonstrate and instruct those back on Earth, how to construct a small nuclear fusion reactor. They were designated as the holders of the tech and the engineering know-how. Lunar-sourced Helium-3 and deuterium would be fuel for the new reactors. And copious amounts of clean energy would be the result.

With Cranreb and Davtep's help, they were fairly certain it would allow the humans to produce clean, safe and unlimited energy from the strong nuclear force. Using power from seawater, they'd produce and then yield "waste" in the form of balloon-ready helium. Fancy, learning the key to climate change from a lizard species. *Such was life,* Mitch reckoned. He was secretly excited and terrified to see how Earth's population reacted to it. He knew there would be horrendous times ahead. They buckled up and took to the sky with thousands of other craft this time. Whatever ban on movement that had existed, was now gone; the sky and ground were teeming with life. *Other life.*

Sky-rules must have existed, but up there, they were entirely anathema to Mitch, the vehicles were sort of all going in the right direction, but equally they were going everywhere at different heights. Movement in 3D was very problematic indeed. No-one seemed to crash though, so whatever systems they had, crash-avoidance software, rules and so forth, seemed to work well, even though there was a crush of vehicles.

The vehicles near them, seemed way too close for air travel, but that was probably just the human experience. Most looked nothing like cars back home, but he wouldn't be surprised if there were wheels hidden somewhere inside. Not surprisingly, the design of these vehicles was alien. The flying machines were mostly rectangle-shaped in plan with the edges shaved off, rounded and quite slip-streamed. It was probable that they were used for land *and* air transport. But he didn't know – he hadn't seen one land and then drive. The vehicles on the ground, apart from having wheels, looked very similar to the ones in the air, but there were no definitives here. A*nything* was possible.

Josh saw the fence disappear under him as they flew onward - now he knew where they were. They were alone in the sky. Presumably, you needed special clearance to fly over the fenced area, which only *they had* apparently. The crush of craft stopped before the fence-line as though it was identified by the vehicles AI as a "no-go area"– which it probably was.

Making their way downward, they made contact with the ground with very little noise and nary a bump. The doors slid back automatically on both sides. Josh jumped out, followed by the other humans, and eventually the pilot, once he was satisfied that all was in order. He watched the humans and Virijians closely, presumably, to make sure they alighted from the craft safely. On the other side of the craft, the rest of them exited, apart from the co-pilot, if that's what he was, who stayed aboard. Jessy eyed them all and tried to grin which was only brief if it was there at all. She made another brave attempt to smile but her facial tics were enough to give away her anxiety - she was clearly terrified of what was around her or what was in front of her.

Jessy was pretty sure she knew what the next step was, and she didn't like it one bit. She hid behind Mitch as he started walking, staying in lock-step with him. Jessy didn't want to see a thing, and didn't, apart from the back of Mitch's back. Everything else was hidden from her. That's how she planned it, and how she wanted it. See nothing, know nothing...hopefully do nothing.

Both of them suited up while Cranreb and Davtep put their own blue suits on which protected them from vacuum and temperature. Mitch and Jessy put their own cooling undergarments on first.

The others' suits were very slimline and the helmet was essentially the same with two small built in oxygen cannisters. Mitch and Jessy had lights attached to their helmets, they didn't. Behind the visors the Jarithians looked genuinely alien. From a distance though, Davtep and Cranreb looked like any two astronauts...as long as you didn't look too closely. The humans looked extremely bulky in comparison, with their cumbersome pressure suits, helmets, lights, backpacks and everything that went with it.

'Let's go,' Mitch said, hitting Josh and Jessy lightly on the shoulders and nodding at the two Jarithians who nodded stiffly back. Mitch felt more confident with the shift now that he met with the Jarithians and was assured there was no time shift invoked by the shift. Mind you, they were unable to explain how they lost twenty years, which was disconcerting.

He was told this time, there would most certainly not be a problem with time displacement. This was purely a spatial shift, Rinmal said. That was good enough for Mitch but he knew a spatial shift by its very essence, played around with time. "*Only* a spatial shift" didn't make a lot of sense. But he went with it. Speed of travel impacts time and it would only be through a complex series of moves within the shift that its impact on time is negated. Jessy was still horrendously nervous – she didn't trust anyone, – just because they said so.

The proof was in the eating. And they'd eaten from this trough previously and been stung badly.

Mitch began feeling hot and started sweating. He hoped like hell the Jarithians had gotten the time-cancelling equations correct. If he went back to Earth and Sean was dead of old age, they would pay somehow.

Nodding wasn't a natural movement for the Jarithians. Clearly, they weren't used to doing it. It all looked quite robotic, probably meaning they were only mimicking the emotion they'd seen the human's exhibit.

All of them walked up the gradual slope to the cave entrance.

'Okaaay...'Mitch said, 'we're first, so it's humans, Virijians, then Jarithians.' Mitch peered at each of them as he spoke. He thought to himself. Three species from three different worlds. It was fucking incredible. All of them were focussed on saving Earth and saving humanity from themselves. But what if they we're too late? What if it was too late for the planet? Mitch couldn't help but think...what did they do then?

What if the slippery slope was now vertical and Earth's climate would rise up and kill the human species, even if they stopped producing greenhouse gasses right now. Mitch shook his head as hard as he could. He struggled to stop the thought process. One of them dominated all others – *what if they were too late*? Well, they were fucked, that's what. They needed a new planet. *Period*. And that wasn't going to happen.

They all took turns to use the shift and they continued until the cave was totally empty of any bio-chemistry whatsoever. It was just a cave now, free of any life at all. Just dirt and rocks were left. And some alien materials deeper within. Rinmal had made his way back to a ferrier-vehicle some time before.

*   *   *

Having shifted, Mitch and Josh saw something they didn't expect to see. They appeared from nothing and were both staring at the back of a humanoid structure of some sort. A head, two arms and two legs, etched in golden metal, bronze presumably, but it might have been anything suitably bright. It was actually made from copper and there was some green oxidation on the left foot. In Mitch's field of view was only Josh. Jessy; the Virijians and the Jarithians were all elsewhere, on the Moon hopefully.

Josh got to his feet dusted himself off, looking himself up and down, breathing heavily. '*Thank Christ*,' he whispered breathlessly, looking sideways at the new planet he and his dad found themselves on. 'What the *holy fuck* is *this* place?' He could see it was hard ground under him which was really good. Josh rubbed a suited forearm across his face to get rid of the sweat and the dust, and turned his head in every direction, searching for anything familiar, which he couldn't find. He was stoked to be on solid ground though – 'but seriously,' he said, pointing with a gloved hand, 'what the hell is *that*...I mean, we should be on the *fucking Moon*.' Josh shook his head, pissed that they were here, by themselves apparently. And Jessy was nowhere to be seen.

He glanced around, nothing made sense, he could see Mitch, but no one else. They should all be here by now. Clearly, everyone else went somewhere else...to the Moon presumably, where they should be. Mitch refused to consider any other less agreeable option. He stared at the statue and perused it closely. *WTF*, was high in his mind.

At least they were on a hard surface, he thought, a solid surface, and not lost somewhere, floating in the blackness, he thought very seriously. Josh had convinced himself that's where he'd end up. It was a very welcome surprise when it didn't happen. But he was now facing a statue, *it had to be a joke.* It couldn't be real. It was sure like a fucking joke, that was supposed to be funny, but wasn't.

'It's you...it's, it's...*fucking you*. What the hell are you doing on...on, *there*?' Josh pointed with his gloved finger. 'Something definitely ain't right with this place,' Josh boomed, 'something's very wrong here,' he said, gaping at the rest of the place. He looked at the sky...the clouds. '*This 'ain't Earth...that's for sure,*' Josh said loudly. Mitch could tell, the boy was on the cusp of losing it. He talked tough – but his grip on what was real was loosening, he could see that, and hear it in his voice. Mitch knew he would have to watch him closely. What they were doing was ridiculously difficult for a civilian with zero experience. He knew about and had been educated in "expect anything" by NASA – Josh hadn't been.

That said, Mitch was really struggling with it all. Mitch was silent, walking around the statue, almost choking, breathing in the impossible, with a head-full of questions and several expletives about "why". To say he was flabbergasted was severely under-playing it. Mitch blinked at it rapidly, totally taken aback. Josh gawked at it front on, speechless. He glanced from the statue to Mitch, unable to say anything apart from uttering a muffled sigh.

Josh eventually found his voice, 'Nc. I have a look at it.' He stared long and hard at it, 'Nice pose.' He gazed at Mitch, hoisting both eyebrows as high as they'd go. 'Who the hell are *you?*' Josh asked his dad curiously, looking at Mitch full in the eye for a moment.

'It looks like you *now*...um, that is...same age.' Josh rubbed his chin, thinking deeply about his father. Out of the corner of his eye, he could still see the statue gleaming in the sunlight. Something was very wrong with all this, he thought.

Indeed, it was Mitchell Taylor in a very serious pose indeed, looking ready for battle or something. But looking from the side of the statue, Mitch seemed a little different – his eyebrows were slightly raised...weren't they? Now, he wasn't sure. He walked around to the front again and his expression remained the same as the first time he saw it, thank God.

Underneath was a dusty plaque that had Mitch's full name and underneath, some indecipherable symbols that were written in a bizarre language, that didn't mean shit to him.

'*Fuck me*,' Josh rasped again, 'a statue of you.' He couldn't get passed it, and felt like laughing, despite the chilling circumstances. He was such a tool, Josh thought – his dad was standing with his back to the statue. He could deny its existence as much as he liked. Josh had seen it – and he knew.

He was joined by Mitch and they both stared at it together, wondering what in God's name it meant? What had he done for a planet he knew nothing about? Was it yet to happen and if so, how would that work? He didn't see any sense in it. I suppose you can go forward in time, near anything is possible.

Mitch was blinking like a mad-man and biting his lip, thinking about time-travel. No reasonable explanation apart from extreme mass and its effect on time came to his mind. Mitch was totally stumped and looked like it - clearing his throat as he opened and closed his mouth without speaking.

'*Good God*,' Mitch eventually blurted, having looked longer and more closely at the statue. 'What a waste of whatever it's made from,' he said, knocking on it and getting little in return. Whatever it was made from, didn't echo. It didn't respond at all in an audio sense.

Mitch peered around and saw that they were surrounded by a few decimated buildings with rubbish and broken stuff everywhere, behind, and to each side and in front. A bit of the top-most rubbish was discharge from something biological and the rest was broken, crushed, busted and smashed *things*, including hard stuff that seemed mostly to be a bluish-grey colour and seemed to act as concrete for whatever this place used to be.

Josh identified glass, metals, and something like plastic, but it was very thin and had holes in it, as though it was in the final stages of decomposition. He identified other stuff that was probably electronic in nature. It was all crushed so it was hard to work out what it used to be. Josh recognized tiny transistors, pronged devices and rectangular objects that probably charged the things. Transistors were small and appeared in small, thin, round machines that were crushed or broken; a few had straps attached to them, like a watch. Were these their version of mobile phones strapped to wrists? It would seem anything bigger than a few centimetres was crushed and shattered. There were also clearish broken glass-like fragments, green blocks and strips of a metal-like substance that were, presumably, used in the local building process. Interestingly, they were all heavily rounded. Dirt and copious amounts of dust covered everything. It was difficult to tell what it used to be, destruction was so total – a suburb of dwellings, if that's what was here, reduced to nothing more than a bit of rubble and dust.

The blue stuff appeared to hold all the buildings and everything else together, like concrete. It definitely wasn't cement though – it was very fine grained and in fact looked a lot like broken blue quartz. It had blocks and metal sticking to it and through it, on occasion. Everything in sight was destroyed. The whole area they were walking through, painted a picture of catastrophic destruction. It looked almost perfectly post-apocalyptic.

Mitch wondered what the *fuck* had happened here, with the question of why they were on this planet never being far away. He wondered why they'd been split up...was it by chance, or deliberate. The latter made him feel uneasy. Because that likely meant an intelligent hand was involved, the nature of which they could only guess at. Mitch wondered if his fate was already written.

Something had happened here which totally devastated the landscape. Nothing was intact or left standing. Whatever it used to be, was strewn everywhere. Mitch reckoned they could see what looked like a gargantuan rubbish tip back on Earth. There could see no life anywhere. Presumably, everything alive had been killed by whatever did this damage. He'd check the CLH to make sure there was no residual radioactivity, and to see what was in the atmosphere. This place had been decimated by something – and if Mitch had to guess, it looked like nukes had hit it. It looked entirely ruined although there was no fire damage he could see, which was odd. Mitch was curious as to how it all happened. The CLH would help a lot. If radiation was high, they needed to get the hell out of here, underground maybe. Mitch doubted they'd be sent somewhere dangerous. Why - he didn't know? He could well be totally wrong, and he knew it.

It was interesting that the statue itself was still standing, amid all the destruction and demolition. It was also interesting that they had materialized at the foot of the statue without an obvious Jarithian shift underneath them. They'd just gone through the shift on Jarith and appeared there, wherever *there* was. And there was no physical shift. That begged the obvious question, that, despite the devastating goings on with the planet, a shift was somehow still in place. Everything about this place, devastation aside, was *interesting*.

'Okay statue-man, what now?' Josh said, half grinning at his dad. He couldn't and probably wouldn't ever get it out of his mind. His father, a statue on Earth...okay, they could pick worse people, but on an alien planet, it made little to no sense. To Josh, he was just dad, no matter where he was or how he was depicted. His dad's idea of a parallel universe or a multiverse was nuts, but it also answered the question. .

But seriously,– a statue; they must have had a decent reason or reasons for doing it. Statues aren't done for nothing. Mitch mused about the planet, eyeing the statue suspiciously, which made him look like a grand explorer from yesteryear. 'But, what the hell did I do for them?' He eyed Josh who shook his head and grinned wryly.

'Yeah, well, we can't answer *that*, but we can ask where we are...and probably more importantly, what the hell happened to this place?' Josh kicked a small piece of plaster-like material aside.

Mitch reckoned this place used to be near a city. The whole area in front of them and behind them was full of shattered pieces of buildings, large and small, interior and exterior. Plus, some biological waste from something alive that probably survived the extermination. There was dust and dirt everywhere, blanketing the broken and shattered remnants. Whatever had been done to this place, happened a while go.

Mitch wondered what Jessy was thinking in his and Josh's absence. That he was lost *again*...probably in time, similar to what had happened previously. She'd be thinking about the end of her world, he was sure of that, if nothing else. It'd be all death and destruction. That'd be pure-Jessy.

'Where are they all?' By "they" Josh meant whoever had built the structures, or whoever lived in them, before they were devastated. He peered around – 'there's gotta be something around here,' he whined, surveying the dumps of broken materials closely. He'd seen the biological waste. It was strong evidence that something was still alive. 'But where were the dead people?' Josh looked up at Mitch, posing the question.

'They're all dead and decayed,' Mitch responded, also peering around and seeing nothing alive, or even dead. He was surprised too, that there wasn't at least some evidence of those killed by the catastrophe that had clearly impacted this whole area.

Had there been a general announcement to flee? If there had been, then - where were the victors? Were they on their way here maybe – if they were, from where are they coming? The questions were endless. The answers, zero. They still had no idea about anything. Wouldn't the victors have started returning by now? Both of them gawked around and could see nothing but rubbish and relics.

'Where are the goddamn skeletons then?' Josh said, sighing heavily, surveying the area in front of him more closely. '*Uh-Oh,*' he whispered, spying white bones in the distance. There was a set of bones off to his left. '*Jesus*

Christ,' he spat, looking grimly at a skeletal nightmare. He peered closer, '*Chhhhrrrist,*' Josh spat. '*What the hell is that*?'

Josh looked down and grimaced. It definitely wasn't human. '*Oh shit.*' Two legs and two arms was a terrific start, but the skull was something else entirely. There were two large, acutely slanted cavities for eyes and an odd flange that extended around the entire skull between its nose and mouth, with a horn-like excrescence on the point of the head. Additionally, there were only ten pairs of ribs. These things were similar, but very different from humans. Especially the skull and upper torso. It seemed like they'd been dead for a long time, if Earthly rates of decomposition were standard through the Universe which Mitch reckoned, maybe they were but maybe they weren't.

'What about the statue, was it *definitely of me?*' Mitch asked, peering back to whence they came. The further he got from it, the less likely it seemed.

'Oh, it was definitely you. Trust me.' Joshn stared at Mitch and smiled widely. 'I feel like bowing, or prostrating, kneeling or doing *something,*' Josh said, still grinning at his dad and talking mockingly. He still found it very hard to believe. Even Earth didn't have his statue yet. He guessed that was something you did when the person was dead. Was that an unwritten law? He wasn't sure but it sounded about right.

'Bowing will definitely not be necessary.' Mitch was certain he'd never been to this planet before, wherever the hell it was. He didn't even know where it was. Maybe it was in another universe, and it was a different "him", or he did it in the future, meaning time displacement again.

Josh looked at Mitch, smiling drolly at him. 'You do realise that you and Jessy were the first to meet the Virijians and then there's *One* and oh, don't forget Mars, Josh trumpeted. The real question is – how did they find out about it all? And the best one of all - why did they care so much?'

Mitch scratched his chin and thought about it, 'we do transmit into space. I suppose, they could know I went to Mars. But for everything else, um...that would mean they're somehow monitoring us, because sure as hell this planet built the statue some time ago.' No way it's that...*no way*. Mitch kept thinking and came up with nothing.

'Wish I could read the plaque on the statue...*how the fuck does getting to Mars effect this planet*?' Mitch said, pondering deeply and coming up with squat. Unless it was purely the space-flight thing. He genuinely had nothing to explain what seemed like a bad joke. A statue...on another planet, *come on.*

'It doesn't explain it, not directly, but maybe they really appreciated what you achieved in space.'

'Okay, fair enough,' Mitch said. 'You can never have too many admirers, right?' He'd given up trying to make sense of the statue.

'I still don't understand how they know so much about me,' Mitch said, leaning forward and feeling a tingle at the base of his spine.

'Jesus...are you kidding me, you've heard of a fucking gift-horse, right? Well, just accept that a planet-load of beings appreciated what you did in space, and leave it at that.' He really didn't want to insult him, but he was making it really hard not to. '*Move on*', Josh said acidly.

They turned 180 degrees and walked down what looked like a road made of stuff that was also the same bluey-grey colour that they saw associated with the destroyed buildings. They hadn't seen anything they would term alive...or even dead, apart from one skeleton, anywhere. But he and Josh remained frosty just in case they met something. Coming face-to-face with something indigenous and angry, wasn't likely to end happily. They were waiting for something to move amid the rubbish, but so far, they hadn't seen a thing. Maybe whatever it was, slept during the daytime. Everything they'd seen was just broken and very dead building components and one odd skeleton.

Mitch had noticed his knees getting progressively sorer as he walked, which was odd. They were now so sore, he had real trouble walking on them. His elbows weren't too good either, but at this stage, it was mainly his knees. He searched for a reason and could only find one. Mitch in a self-diagnosis decided that he had decompression sickness, "the bends" from this damned spacesuit and the nitrogen rich air it brought with it. He changed the mix on his backpack to pure oxygen – which would flush the nitrogen bubbles from his system...hopefully. If he was too far gone, he would need a decompression chamber. If he needed it and didn't get it – he was *fucked*. And he knew with absolute authority that there wasn't one on this damned planet.

Thankfully after two hours he was feeling better. Nitrogen bubbles had certainly lodged in his knees and elbows and probably every other joint too. The oxygen-only "diet" helped him reabsorb the nitrogen, allowing Mitch to walk on his legs like a "twenty-year-old". He didn't want to jinx himself, but he felt really good. His knees were entirely back to normal, as were his elbows.

Mitch, newly animated, ripped the Velcro open on one of his waist-pockets and retrieved the pesky CLH, the compact laser heterodyne - that was designed to give an unambiguous list of atmosphere components and the levels of dangerous ionising radiation. The gravity felt Earthlike but, what the hell was actually in the atmosphere - he was keen to know. The device was designed with just that in mind. Mitch had quite enough of this bulky and heavy spacesuit, despite what the makers said.

He switched the CLH on and checked the settings. The receptor was exposed to the air for a few seconds and then the protector put back on. The result was pretty much as they expected.

Nitrogen 80%
Oxygen 18%
Neon   1%
Carbon Dioxide 0.5%
Ionising Radiation 3.88 mSv
Atmospheric Pressure 1001.13 Mb

Apart from the neon and slightly higher background radiation, it was pure Earth. Pressure was good and there was no residual radiation to be concerned with, which, gazing at the destruction, he thought there might be. Clearly, it wasn't nukes that had caused the damage.

Mitch pressed the button on his helmet and heard the beep after ten seconds, and pushed his visor up slightly to allow a sip, knowing the atmosphere was very breathable. He followed with the rest of his suit and the cooling vest and skull-cap. It all came off.

Josh did the same with his suit. Both of them were quickly free of their spacesuits and helmets and could move freely again. Josh swung his arms from side to side and raised them above his head in delight. He was happy to be free of the constricting, tight and heavy garment.

'Whoever built those things,' Josh pointed to the rubble and outlined buildings with his fingers as he spoke. 'They all must have died in a war of sorts,' He was making all sorts of odd noises as he walked...cogitating about their new environment, head moving in all directions, 'but there is almost no radiation,' he repeated.

Mitch couldn't work it out – all this destruction and so little radiation. Mitch reckoned the damage didn't look like it stemmed from regular munitions...so, what was the answer? Mitch was also thinking, looking at Josh derisively, *thanks, Mr. Einstein,* he was about to tell him to shut it, when something ran from the ruins and nearly scared him to death. It was the size of a small dog, black, and had lots of legs, noticeable when it scurried across a clearing some distance in front of them. He definitely wasn't expecting it, it was the first thing they'd seen that moved. The first sign of life from a clearly devastated world. Mitch saw blackness, legs, legs and *more legs.* That's all he could tell. It was so quick.

An animal, he reckoned, scared by our footfalls and rustling though the rubbish, like a dog or the like, Mitch assumed. But it looked unlike a dog. The thing had way too many scurrying legs; it looked more like a very large cockroach as it scurried through the rubble like a rifle shot.

Mitch wondered again about Jessy, what the hell must she be thinking? That he and Josh were gone - *forever,* lost somewhere in the wrinkles of spacetime. Gone for all time? She might well be right. Why did we come here and they went somewhere else? That question had no answer and it was driving Mitch mad, Mitch assumed Jessy had gone to the Moon where *they* should have gone, but he really didn't know – all he knew was, she wasn't with him on this world. Such were the nature of these shifts, he reckoned, they'd hook onto odd things at odd times. Which meant "exits" could be many and varied, despite the best intentions of the builders. Well, *whatever*, he thought, having no real idea of how they worked – apart from a good helping of entanglement and probably Heisenberg's uncertainty principle. And plenty of finger crossing that they'd go somewhere safe.

Mitch glanced at Josh who was peering down at the ground, kicking at something small and sighing heavily. They both wanted home with equal ferocity. Home meant the Moon.

We should keep moving,' Mitch said, open mouthed, struggling to speak, he was thinking about the past so hard.

'Why should we bother?' Josh said, staring at his dad full in the eyes. 'There's just more of the same out there,' he said, lifting his eyes and nodding his head toward the nothingness. 'Why do we need to keep moving - all we're gonna see is more of this. Hardly worth seeing...I wouldn't think.'   His motivation to walk was nearing zero. Josh was still scared of what they might find. He'd be more than happy to stay where they were.

'*Why?*' Mitch spat. '*Fucked if I know*...because it feels right...okay?' Mitch said angrily to his son. 'It's probably the only thing we can do,' He peered at Josh and shrugged his shoulders. 'Apart from rolling up the footpath and giving up completely, er...we need to know *why* we were sent *here* of all places. If we don't keep going, then I don't know what to do.' Mitch had never been so unsure in his life. *Stop, go*, who knew what do? He had no idea. He gasped fearsomely, sick of everyplace and everyone.

Previously, he'd always had a goal but now with his son in tow, apart from keeping Josh alive and maintaining his own life, he had nothing. He laughed shrilly to himself about keeping Josh alive, he had fuck-all control over his own life let alone Josh's. Were they just sent here randomly, or was there actually a reason? If there was a reason, what was it? So...onward it was. Until they knew different.

'Maybe we came here randomly or by mistake or chance or something, totally beyond our, anyone's control,' Josh said. All that did was cost oxygen.

'Well, if that is the case then we are truly fucked. But if we did come for a reason, then we better get about finding it.' Mitch walked ahead, surveying the destruction closely. He turned and raised his eyes at Josh as he went by, pushing him slightly.

'*Whatever,*' Josh grunted and walked slowly behind Mitch now, looking slowly side to side. '*Come on, let's go then,*' alluding to their lack of pace and direction.

They started walking and kept walking, *where*, they had little idea. But they kept going. Kicking at small stuff in their way, until they heard a loud noise. They heard it and literally stopped on a dime. It was a loud scratching sound that came and went. Apart from the wind, it was quite prominent.

Mitch held his arm up and placed fingers on the other hand against his lips. Josh peered at Mitch's hand and shook his head in dismay. What did he think, that I was going to keep barrelling forward despite the noise? 'Thanks dad, you can put your arm down now,' Josh whispered caustically, *hating* being treated like a child or an idiot.

'*Jesus Christ,*' Mitch whispered back, exasperated, as he peered nervously at the source of the sound. It could have been anything but it was unlikely to be natural because it kept happening, slightly different each time. Josh stopped next to Mitch, he gazed down, seeing another skeleton, but this time it was different. It was just over feet tall with two arms and two legs, not unlike the other, but it had a skull that was distinctly different to the first one they saw. It had a bony structure that started on its forehead and wound itself up to a distinct point. The rear of its head was elongated and similarly ended in a shallower point. Whatever it was, it probably represented a different species to the one they had already seen.

That didn't answer the noise though, it wasn't made by a skeleton, it was likely one of those dog-things, scratching at something, Mitch reckoned, the *next* time, he'd get a better look at it, try and define it properly. The one they had seen earlier ran too fast to photograph it, but he knew what to do if it was going slower. Mitch bent down and walked carefully through and mostly over the rubbish, followed by a wary Josh who tried to be as quiet as possible by using a careful toes-first step on the rubbish. They were both cautious and tried like hell to be silent by using the toes-first approach. Mitch was doing his best to home in on the noise without being seen.

Ahead of him were the remnants of a crushed building. Everything from inside was forced to the outside, through the windows, doors and any other opening. In some cases, it made its own hole. They'd seen a lot of paper with writing on it. But it meant nothing to them. It looked mostly processed but there was the occasional handwritten note.

Mainly, the writing, whether processed by a computer or handwritten, consisted of glyphs, symbols, lines and presumably letters that were entirely dissimilar to anything they'd ever seen. There were loopy and strangely shaped symbols that were the epitome of foreign. Maybe the reason for them being here would never be answered.

Josh could still hear an odd noise - it was low but pretty constant. He stopped and stared at Mitch who was also listening. Then the noise cut out and it stayed silent. It sounded like the noise was caused by something close, a bit like an abrasive or cutting tool of some sort. Mitch crept forward very cautiously and found a big white plastic-looking, or at least soft, white bag full of open and mainly empty cans. It looked like the plastic you might find at the local supermarket. Some of the residual food in the cans looked fairly fresh, and the cans themselves looked like they were made from a softish metal and had just been opened. They were soft to the touch but super-hard underneath Josh's boot when he tried to crush it. 'Go *figure*,' he said. Mitch was fairly sure the dog critter didn't open the cans. It had the appearance of a "dumb" scavenger.

'Follow right behind me,' Mitch whispered, scanning the area ahead of him, closely, prepared for anything, but knowing they had no hope against something big and hungry. They were totally unarmed and completely open to most anything that wanted an easy meal.

'Yes sir,' Josh replied, shaking his head at Mitch, and edging slowly forward behind his dad. He felt like saluting or goose-stepping, but that would have made noise so he stopped himself short. He simply walked where it hopefully wouldn't make any noise. He'd given up trying to prove anything too his dad – it was a waste of time.

Mitch peered above the rubbish but couldn't see a thing bar more destruction. Everything that was upright, was now under them where they walked, as destroyed and shattered pieces. The source of the noise remained unknown. Mitch kept thinking that *something* must have made that noise, although it seemed to be gone now. It did repeat and sounded like a cutting tool, so it ticked all the boxes.

Everything was still and silent now. He looked at what was once possibly a kitchen. He thought he could see machinery for heating and cooking food. There, near the corner of the room, draped over what looked like a set of cupboards, was *something*.

It was alive, a humanoid and had, he thought, just opened a can. He could make out two eyes and an odd head and face, but that's about it. The obscurity of distance was too much for him. The thing compared favourably with what he assumed was the common species on this planet, based on the few skeletons he'd seen. It had large, sharply diagonal eyes and a bald head, with, what looked like long and thin arms. There was an unusual circumference of what was probably cartilaginous flesh between the nose and mouth. It was

hard to tell the finer details because of distance and his piss-poor eyesight. Mitch swallowed heavily and did his best to visualise the creature.
It was definitely humanoid, comparable to the creatures they'd seen on Jarith, but it was very different from humans and different from Jathithians. He couldn't help wondering what this thing had evolved from.

Mitch stood on top of the rubbish to make himself seen. The creature saw him and immediately hid behind the cabinet, grunting and whistling as he went, scared stiff. The thing looked anxiously at Mitch from his hidey-hole. Mitch held both hands up in a sign of submission. Thankfully, the creature seemed to understand and came out of his hiding place.

The creature spoke to them in what appeared to be an excited state, whistles and beeps and other spoken noises summing to nothing that had any meaning to them at all. It was even completely different to that heard on Jarith. He immediately thought of Zamindar – he would definitely understand him. His ability to decode language was nothing short of stunning.

Now he was confronted by not being able to communicate. There was no time to use math or any of that crap. Basically, they were entirely incommunicado. Body language - shoulder shrugs, arm movement and finger pointing was all they had.

*   *   *

'I think we need to *show* him,' Mitch said, peering curiously at this emaciated creature that appeared so aggressive yet barely had the strength to stand up.

'Show him...*what*?' Josh asked, scratching at his cheek, not knowing what the fool was talking about. Josh focussed on his dad. He should use longer and whole sentences, Josh reckoned. *Use your words*, he felt like saying to Mitch, don't point and gesture to *me* so much. *Afterall, I did understand language*. Josh reckoned his dad was a real tool. He seemed to be using body language on me too, when he should be saving that for the alien.

Mitch peered at Josh and sighed, 'you know what I mean,' he said with exaggeration. He looked directly at the creature and pointed several times toward his mouth and shrugged his shoulders. The action was mirrored by the creature. It clearly wanted food. It was hungry. *Downcast*, but definitely hungry.

'*There you go*,' Mitch said eagerly, glaring at Josh, happy he could communicate with the creature, even if it was on the most basic of levels. Mitch walked over to a stack of cans and grabbed the top one. Grasping what looked vaguely like a manual can opener, he hacked it open and handed the open can to him to eat.

Mitch watched it up-end the can in its mouth, taking it all in, then throwing the empty can on the floor, wiping its lipless mouth with the back of its wrist and looking hungrily at Mitch again. He or she wanted more - it was obvious, he was still pointing to his mouth. He appeared to be ravenous, poor sod. God knows how long it had gone without food.

Then he remembered his cat at home that seemingly got hungry through the sheer act of eating, and he wasn't quite so sure. Perhaps this creature was always hungry despite the amount it ate. Like his cat, he thought. You couldn't feed the cat enough to make him full. The cat would eat the entire can – and there he'd be, begging for food at your feet. It was never-ending.

Mitch shook his head and stuck a finger sideways at the creature and yelled sharply and succinctly, '*no more.*' He repeated it several times and hacked his hand downward. There was no more food for him...yet.

Mitch pointed outside and made hand movements approximating bombs exploding and followed it with shoulder shrugs and exaggerated raised eyebrows. Mitch thought he'd queried what had happened to this place pretty well. He thought his performance was spot on, and it showed in his face. Mitch, chest out, gave a crisp nod to Josh.

'An actor you ain't, Josh said, grinning at his dad. Mitch's face fell.

'Well at least I'm giving it a shot,' Mitch said, peering at the creature, not grinning one iota anymore. He was deadly serious.

The creature was invested in what Mitch was trying to do, still thinking about the food he had been shown. The creature moved his hands and arms to show he got it and continued to move them. Mitch and Josh took its gestures to mean a lot of wind had hit the area.

Mitch shrugged again, coupled with the same raised eyebrows he held his arms out and flourished his hands just above his head and pointed at the sky, signifying, he thought, that he was querying who did it...*who* did it to them?

The creature pointed upward, suggesting they figured, that the source was beyond the planet. Of course, it could have meant that that the "wind" came from the sky. For ballistic weapons, that's exactly where it'd come from. But Josh and Mitch didn't think so. But they weren't entirely sure. They had to remember, there was virtually no radiation, but the devastation clearly came from some manner of very powerful weaponry. They needed to interpret them from other things like the pantomimes Mitch and the creature did.

Whatever the creature happened to be, it was damned ugly and smelt bad, but it was certainly humanoid. Whatever species it was, it needed a good shower or a wash or something, with plenty of soap.

could just see the outline of humanity boiling somewhere beneath its carbuncled skin. But he was repelled by the head and face...mainly the face, which was like eyeballing a monstrosity. It looked hyper-aggressive with their eyes close-set and downwards slanting.It seemed to understand basic body language, suggesting very elementary parallel development.

Why would another species rain down a series of what Mitch could only assume were bombs, or something similar, on this civilization and pretty much eradicate it, if this was repeated across the planet?

It was probably a large-scale war, this being an early battle maybe. Mitch was sure it was probably the same as most wars on Earth. Reasons for the conflict rapidly blurred to nothing or proved to be horribly inconsequential after a little time has elapsed.

The creature kept saying, with various clicks and squeaks in between, *Yobi arnan katoomb aparec.* God only knew what it meant. He and Josh certainly didn't know. Maybe it was nothing, but perhaps it was something important - to him at least. Who the hell knew? He would definitely ask the Virijians when he saw them. They'd know. Somehow, they'd know.

'What about fallout,' Josh wondered, the scan we did before showed very little. Ionising radiation wasn't much more than Earth.

'Perhaps they used low yield nukes, which means...I don't know what it means,' Mitch said, drawing his eyebrows together. How low is "low yield", he wondered? Maybe they were just bombs - regular munitions. For some reason, he thought they were an Earth only thing - which they weren't obviously. Any humanoid species that was sentient would have them.

'It all sounds like a load of bullshit to me,' Josh said, staring back at Mitch, breathing noisily. 'You and I both know what it means. They're coming *back*, whoever the *fuck* they are, they're coming back to this planet as soon as the radiation has dropped to the right level – which it has.' Josh looked at the sky then back at Mitch with owl-like eyes. Josh knew that a pure fusion weapon, one that didn't rely on a fission start up, would be intrinsically low yield. That means they're coming back now...or at least soon. Josh could feel his pulse thumping in his arm as he looked up at the furiously alien purple sky. He heard what Mitch said and tended to agree. If "they" were off-planet, which they probably were, they would soon be back to take advantage of an "empty" planet. If they were on-planet, they'd already be here.

Mitch stared at Josh. 'They'll come back to take this rock as theirs.'

What do you reckon, come back to have a tea party? Josh thought, peering at the sky, *seriously*, what a knob. *'Oh, for fuck's sake dad,'* Josh whined, 'it could be for any reason, to use it as a base, repopulate it with their own, or to use its resources, who knows.' Use your imagination for Christ's sake,' Josh thought angrily. 'Maybe they just wanted to subdue this species and aren't coming back at all, because they don't need to. Not everything is empirical. Sometimes a guess is the best option.' Poor old Mitch didn't see it like that, it was clear. He wanted everything to be a fact before he gave it any oxygen at all.

'Yeah, who knows,' Mitch whispered. 'You're right, it could be for any one of a number of reasons. Maybe they aren't coming back at all. The only one who might know, speaks a language we can't understand.

*   *   *

If we want to go, then we go now,' Josh said, ready for just about anything, flexing his fingers and drawing them into fists. This place sucked anyway. He looked around and saw a rubbish tip everywhere. '*What a Goddamn shit-hole*,' Josh said hatefully.

'We'll have to take "old clicker" with us,' Mitch said, peering and briefly pointing at the creature, trying to work out whether he was a he, a she or an it. Maybe what they assumed was a male, was a female, who knew? Maybe the creature was both or none. *Whatever*, Mitch reckoned, if they, that is whomever or whatever devastated this place, found him and we're right, well, it'd be goodnight for him. His home was also cactus. They could hardly leave the poor bugger like this, and in this place where there wasn't much food. The final decision would be his.

They walked back to the spot where they were when they heard the noise that led to finding the creature. *It*, followed Mitch and Josh, carrying his version of an environment suit and helmet, after Mitch beckoned to him to follow them, with a protection suit. He didn't resist. The creature followed close behind, making all sorts of beeping and clicking sounds which was his version of language. It was like walking with R2D2 behind you. At least it was humanoid. It could've been something a lot stranger than that, he felt sure. Thankfully, this planet favoured a humanoid species.

It could have been like a snail or a spider or even a dry-land squid, or a *lot crazier* even than that. It might have been impossible to communicate with. They could be particles or something almost metaphysical, like *One*. Or be some form of non-carbon life. Imagine, tangling with phosphorus or arsenic beings that walked on one appendage and looked pretty much like crabs. *No thank you*. This being was strange looking without being totally ridiculous. Mitch imagined trying to communicate with a land octopus. What in God's name would *they* use for an environment-suit? Nothing...something?

So much for the alternative life design, he thought. He'd always seen the logic in non-carbon-based life. The Universe was such a massive place, it gave opportunity to everything. *One* aside, what happens to worlds that are devoid of carbon or just don't favour our type of life? There's trillions and trillions of them. Trillions and trillions and trillions. Were these worlds dead and fated to be so forever? Mitch didn't think so.

What type of life do natural processes create if carbon life is not favoured? Nothing? More likely, *something*, he thought. But what? Geochemistry still eventually, over a lot of time perhaps, cedes to biochemistry, but what form does it take? It needs a solvent like we do with water, but it can be any liquid.

The life itself might be based on hydrogen, nitrogen, or oxygen and silicon. Forget the weakness of the bonds or the instability of the molecules, or even its corrosiveness. Life will find a way, right? But, so far, life was all like humans were – made of water and carbon. Mitch couldn't work out if that was good or bad, and whether *One* played any role in it. It was good for us, but probably not good for the Universe itself. On the face of it, that was just how it was. Afterall, the planets they'd encountered, all had carbon and were relatively warm with liquid water.

All of them started back toward the statue they'd seen when they first arrived on the planet. About halfway back, they heard a noise and with blinding speed, the indigenous creature that had been quietly following them, making a heap of strange sounds, dropped his suit and helmet, and raced and picked up a dog-thing and ate it, fur and all. Its mouth somehow unhinged and opened really wide. None of them had seen that coming. Clearly, it was very hungry.

'*Good God almighty*,' Mitch blurted, '*I wasn't expecting that.*' He stumbled backward, shocked to the core, wondering who and what they'd brought with them.

'*Fucking hell,*' Josh whispered, totally flabbergasted. 'He's a fucking predator. I thought he was something quite tame and, uh...intelligent. Although I suppose you can be intelligent *and* a ravenous predator.' Josh thought about it and nodded, agreeing with himself.

'Not something anyone would have expected though, but he is a new species, to us, I suppose, *anything is possible right?*' Mitch was watching the creature closely. It walked back stiff-leggedly and was part of the group again, still chewing on the recent kill. They wondered why he had very sharp and prominent front teeth, and now they knew why.

Mitch glanced at him, he was very hard to watch or be remotely near as he spat out the indigestibles, straight onto the ground in front of him. Some of what he ate was obviously bone and hair which he couldn't process. That ended up on the ground and he wasn't the least bit self-conscious.

All of them ambled carefully back to the statue, both Mitch and Josh prayed they'd have no more encounters with the things that looked like six-legged dogs – poodle-sized, that this creature had downed in *one swallow*. It was quite incredible. When "unhinged" he had a gigantic mouth. And by gigantic he meant fucking humungous. His body essentially became all mouth.

Mitch saw the statue in the distance and silently thanked God. It meant they were back "home". They were quickly upon it, so Mitch pointed to the statue and back to him, to hopefully show that they were one and the same person. To instil some trust hopefully.

The creature got excited and started clicking and whirring with a bit of "language" thrown in for good measure, staring at Mitch and intermittently glancing at the statue and raising his arm and pointing with a finger. Clearly, he'd made the connection between it and Mitch.

'Well, he's impressed,' Josh said, peering at the creature and hearing the strange clicking and other noises he made.

'Apparently,' Mitch replied, with a firm nod of the head. He looked around and remembered when he first arrived on this planet for the first time. Hopefully, it might give him a clue how to get off it again. Mitch pressurised his suit, and made sure the fan was working on his backpack, and the helmet mic was near his mouth before he closed his visor.

'Where were we when you and I first appeared Josh?' Mitch asked his son, eyes fixed on him nervously.

'We were about there, right?' Mitch was pointing to the spot he reckoned was about right.

'Yep, that's about right,' Josh said, pointing to a spot behind the statue, which Mitch was now right on.

'So...it's Josh, then him, followed lastly by me, all of us in our suits, ready for the worst. Expect vacuum, but hopefully we'll end up on something hard. Nothing might happen...let's just see. We can't fucking stay here, there's nothing for us here.'

Mitch pushed the audio feed down and forward and then fitted his helmet to the tracks properly. If he was going to go, he was ready. He checked the oxygen flow and fan and all was good. Josh's state of readiness was similarly as good as it got. His helmet was on, the mic good and the O_2 flowing. They were both fully self-sufficient.

Josh trod on the spot adjacent to the statue again and promptly disintegrated, quicker than the shifts before had initiated. Josh was here one second, gone the next. Disappearance was almost instantaneous. Mitch grabbed the creature by the shoulder, checked his suit as far as he could, and pushed him over to where Josh had been standing, and he stayed there. Mitch had his hands up in front of the creature and when he withdrew his hands, the creature vanished, as he thought, leaving his hands unaffected. Mitch did the same and disappeared. All of them were gone from the planet and the Antlia 2 galaxy. Welcome to the quantum world of entanglement, De sitter space and the Heisenberg compensator.

*   *   *

They emerged onto the Moon into a helium-rich vacuum. One after another, all of them came into view, having shifted successfully from the ruined planet. They saw the Virijians, Jessy and the Jarithians in the distance and watched Jessy pointing at them. She waved to them as only Jessy could do. She was excited to finally see them reappear, but she saw immediately there was an extra one.

She glanced at the creature with wide eyes, and almost did a double-take, wondering how in God's name his pink spacesuit worked – it looked more like a kid's night time outfit. The helmet was an odd shape, with a strange "bump" right on top.

Mitch waved back and Josh followed suit, frantically. The creature had no idea what to do but watched Mitch curiously. Jessy hesitated as she saw the creature come with them - she watched it slowly stand to its full height in the Moon's low gravity and start forward in its unusual spacesuit. '*Shit*,' she said, inside her suit, as she watched the odd alien unfold into its full being inside its pink suit.

He could almost see her eyes bulge. Mitch could hear her saying "*who the fuck is that*" and "what" and "how" through the suits comms system. Mitch wasn't sure how he'd explain him, or how they had such a circuitous route to get here, and then there was the small matter of his statue. He still wondered what the hell was going on with that. He had no explanations but a few decent guesses as to why he appeared on that planet as a statue. Of all things – and places. He was dumbfounded to see it, and still was.

Jessy and the rest of them bounded up to Mitch in single file. Mitch gaped at Jessy in full sunlight and saw that she still had the audio mic near her mouth. She looked amazing in the full sunlight of the Moon.

'I thought we'd lost you,' she rasped, 'we've been here for at least five minutes,' Jessy said, wrinkling her brow and glaring straight at Mitch.

Mitch chewed on what she'd said and found her statement confounding to say the least. '*Five bloody minutes*,' he yelled, 'we spent at least four hours on that planet didn't we Josh?' There was nothing but silence from his son as Josh thought about it.

'*Hello?*' Mitch said. '*Josh, you there*? He slapped his helmet, thinking the suit comms system had shit itself again.

'I'm here dad, *Jesus*, relax...um, *at least* four hours, *yes*,' Josh said, widening his eyes. '*Yeah, I'm here alright*', he said irately. 'Talk about fucking impatient,' he said, raising his eyebrows at his dad. *'Jesus...chill.'*

Some things never changed. He also found it hard to believe they were away for only five minutes, but then he remembered time-dilation, but this was the other way around. A long time out there had become a shorter time down here, which is "abnormal" in areas of high gravity and speed. *C'est la vie*, he reckoned. Murphy rears its head once again.

'It came from that planet?' Jessy asked,

'Yep,' Mitch said, before Josh could even take a breath. 'Found him on that planet. Hopefully Zamindar and Char can work out his language and find out more about him.' He was looking directly at Zamindar and glancing nonchalantly at the creature. They knew next to nothing about him. Zamindar appeared very disinterested indeed. But that was situation-normal for him and Char. Nothing they'd found or seen so far seemed to animate them. For all intents and purposes, they were like Virijian robots. Emotions were clearly a bridge too far for Virijians. Maybe they were in evidence a long time ago – but not now.

Mitch could hear the static, inter-cranial noise, the precursor to toning, always. 'I have been scanning him since I saw him. His name is Gaznoy and they are a technical species, a few thousand years ahead of humanity and are truly intelligent and self-aware beings. They are bipedal and bimanual animals descended from an animal similar to your feral camel, and they no longer exist as a civilisation, they were a non-fossil-fuel race. They had recently started to replace burning fossil fuels with energy from fusion reactors, but their actions weren't quick enough, apparently. According to Gaznoy, they were almost entirely a fusion energy civilisation when they were destroyed.

'What the hell does that mean? *"Not quick enough"*?' Josh said, swallowing heavily. He was pretty sure he knew what he meant. If what he was suggesting was right, it was absolutely ludicrous and criminal.

'I mean, they were devastated by a technologically superior civilisation,' Zamindar said. 'It seems they were attacked from space, which is somewhat ironic. The reason for the attack, which he thinks he knows, is almost certainly atmospheric change. They were given a deadline by this species, some time ago. But, despite their advances and huge investments in non-carbon producing technologies, it was deemed that they were progressing too slowly and had not met the target that was set. So, they destroyed this civilisation, to save the planet. It is clear to me they acted prematurely.'

'*...Oh, you think?*' Josh said incredulously. '*Of course*, they acted prematurely, they were in the process of making the change demanded and from what you said, they'd almost stopped greenhouse gas production. *What a load of bollocks.* Who is this fucking race - *who do they think they are?*' Josh was almost frothing at the mouth – he'd seen the horrible aftermath of their work and didn't think it was fair or right at all.

Mitch gave a heavy sigh and thought about it. '*Shit,* do they know about Earth?' Given how they behaved with this planet, he was worried that their influence might extend to Earth. He asked Zamindar and ignored Josh's blathering. He watched the Virijian, holding his breath. He hoped like hell they'd never heard of it. The last thing our planet needed was a demand from a third-party to rectify or die. We were having a lot of trouble controlling it as it was.

'Yes, they are aware of it, Earth is a known complication.'

'*Oh fuck...shit...damn it,*' Mitch spewed.

Zamindar had said it matter-of-factly, talking over the top of Mitch's exhalation of breath and swearing. 'You are on their list and based on their conduct, you can expect contact to come in some form and a deadline set for transition to a non-fossil-fuel burning base. Your atmosphere is suffering badly and it will be very difficult for humans to comply with such a demand, given the huge need for power and energy on your world and the fact that it is broken up into so many countries, each of which is very self-serving and heavily devoted to its own economy. This society treasures your world greatly as a home to a civilisation and a long-term provider of evolution.'

Mitch just stared at him and felt like screaming in frustration. It was the last thing the planet needed. A deadline for cessation of carbon production. We were having massive problems with that and so many other things. And he was talking about a *fucking deadline – or* destruction from above. It wouldn't, couldn't and didn't get much worse than that. Earth had wars, pandemics and famine to worry about, together with worsening weather. Seriously, Mitch wondered if a worse time could be chosen.

'*Fuck me* - You can't help us, in developing fusion power?' Josh asked Zamindar directly, more in hope than anything else because he knew about the NDA and didn't expect much assistance. He stared closely at the Virijian, not moving a muscle. He knew the answer but he felt like making him say it.

'I am unable to assist Earth with our technology but I can help with translation and understanding of other's technology,' Zamindar said, 'because of our agreement with the leaders on Virija. You know that.'

'*Okay...okay, I get it, "the agreement"...thanks for nothing, right?*' Josh said with a raised voice, glaring at Zamindar. They both understood completely, but it still rankled. It was the answer he expected and Josh got it, right between the eyes. The Virijians wouldn't help humans with their know-how. Big surprise. At least the Jarithians would. *Fuck 'em,* he thought, glaring at Zamindar.

'*Josh, please be quiet and relax,*' Mitch whispered forcefully. He stared at him with a vein twitching in his neck. By the look on his face, Mitch could tell he was about to "start". Zamindar was a friend and Mitch wanted to keep it that way.   Zamindar was simply complying with the NDA, in place to bring peace to Virijian worlds. Otherwise, it would be chaos. They had history with their opposition. It was critical Virija kept the truce strong and healthy.

Josh glanced every now and again at the Virijian and kept quiet. He preferred not to poke that bear but he wasn't happy. When it all came down to it, Zamindar was a gigantic being with huge capabilities. Josh imagined having him for an enemy. He didn't want that and really couldn't imagine it. It'd be a horrific ordeal and probably life-ending.

Josh strongly believed *that the enemy of my enemy is a friend.* He supposed that made Zamindar a really good friend. He hardly wanted that to change by demanding he make a decision between "friendship" with humanity and the NDA. Because he knew what would win.

'We can offer no more if we are to remain compliant with the document,' Zamindar toned with determination. He acted like he didn't give a crap about humanity. Josh took solace in the fact the Virijians were held back by a legal document which tested the Virijians devotion to their own species.

'Does he know the reason we took him along with us?' Mitch asked, gawking at Zamindar then glancing briefly at the creature named Gaznoy.

'He does,' Zamindar said. 'He understands perfectly and he is thankful, but he had a companion for whom he is responsible back on his planet which is called Geraldt.' Mitch forgot the Virijian could read the creature's mind. Gaznoy may as well have just told him. Mitch tended to treat Zamindar like a human, which was selling him way short. He could do things we couldn't, *period.* Zamindar also knew things which were way beyond us.

*   *   *

Finally, they were one group again. Mitch was with Jessy, and Josh was there with the two Virijians. Also, there were the two Jarithian fusion specialists and the creature called Gaznoy about whom they knew almost nothing, except when he's hungry, look out.

They were all on the Moon, adjacent to an oxidised body of ore that, according to most on Earth, shouldn't be there. So, their situation was very unusual. Their holiday to the Moon had yielded several surprises.

'Zamindar – can you find out if Gaznoy wants to stay with us, or go back to his companion on Geraldt, knowing the civilisation has gone and his future sustainability was deeply in question.' Mitch gawked at the Virijian, then glanced at Gaznoy, feeling a bit sorry for him. Ultimately, it was up to him whether he stayed...or went.

Zamindar made a series of squeaks and chirps, mixed with some meaningless language, even banging on his arm like a drum. Eventually he stopped and looked squarely at Gaznoy, who responded with what sounded like very similar noises.

'He wants to return to his partner, and he is unconcerned about the sustainability issue. Dying for them is a lot different than for you. He is far more concerned with discharging his duty to his companion.

'Oookay then...back to the planet it is,' Mitch said, looking straight at Gaznoy and pointing at the object. Mitch glanced at Zamindar and wondered, scratching his head. 'Will that shift return him to his planet?'

'Yes,' Zamindar toned. 'It is appropriately tuned.'

Gaznoy walked back to the object and disappeared before their eyes. Now he was gone – back to his devastated planet.

'He shouldn't have come with us if he didn't want to. It's not like we forced him to go,' Josh said, eyeing Mitch and shrugging his shoulders. He knew, in a sense, they did make him come with. It's not like the poor sod could speak to them. Saying he didn't resist or protest didn't really work because maybe his species didn't do that. Once more, it invoked xeno-psychology. Live and learn, he supposed.

'He felt forced,' Zamindar said, 'but you thought it was a favour to him, so he went with it.

'Different species – different mind-sets and ways of thinking,' Mitch said. 'Clearly, they mate for life, come what may, living per se is individually not that important. *Very strange.*'

The next step was for all of them to go back to Earth. Get back to the blue marble and start the process of replacing thermally-derived energy with clean, pure and sustainable "non-greenhouse-gas" fusion energy.

All of them realised that solar energy, green hydrogen and wind energy just weren't up to the job. But they had no time, and they realised, little hope of producing and installing fusion reactors in every country. They'd have to try though. The penalty for *not* doing it was steep indeed.

The last thing the planet needed at the moment was a deadline hard to attain. Mitch knew the world needed an extra push with energy. Having seen what this "police race" did to the planet called Geraldt - Mitch was shit scared, humanity was on the thinnest ice - one wrong move would see them crack it and fall through. Hopefully, they wouldn't get around to Earth for a long time.

Like it or not though, humans would have to smarten up their act, and quickly. He had to remember that humans had no weapons that worked beyond the Earth. In space, they were as good as defenceless. So, it was either stop belching carbon and other greenhouse gasses into the atmosphere, or it would be destruction on two fronts – environmental ruin from climate change, or race ending, via a superior civilisation who possessed space-enabled weapons, and they weren't afraid to use them, to save a rare, habitable, right-sized and pro-evolution planet.

Sounded easy. But when you lacked the technology and needed to build the knowledge from scratch...it was anything but easy. There was no "standing-on-shoulders" here, the development of fusion reactors was very much in its infancy on Earth. And tech and know-how, *engineering*, were only part of the jigsaw, albeit a very important part. Employment and economy were something entirely different, but also very, *very* important.

He wondered, *hoped* - could Dav and Cran help with those things, as well as tech? Mitch sure as hell hoped so. Because it was something humans really struggled with. It was probably more problematic than the tech which was extremely difficult in itself.

8

Change

**"The most hopelessly stupid man is he who is not aware he is wise."
—Isaac Asimov**

Mitch took the phone from his pocket which he'd had on permanent charge since they were on the devastated planet, they'd found Gaznoy inhabiting. Mitch called AASSA and told them what he wanted and when he wanted it, which was *yesterday*. He was Mitch Taylor. That made people jump to it, apparently. Mitch was so hungry and sore he pulled no punches.

Mitch refused to enter into discussions about where he'd been or why he wanted it. He just did, *period*. AASSA would send a Lunar spacecraft as soon as they could get a rocket on the launchpad, endowed with a lunar-capable craft, Mitch was assured. AASSA was virtually *his*. It certainly used to be his, now the entire place was named after him, for obvious reasons, one of them because he died ... supposedly. *Not so!*

Mitch was trying to decide who they should speak to on Earth to convey the urgency of the situation. And provide the technical aspects via the two Jarithians to ensure fusion actually provided the energy it *theoretically* could deliver. It needed to start very soon, and not in thirty years as was so often touted. Or, from what we now knew as truth, humanity would be gone. Earth itself was of far greater import than a mere civilisation, apparently.

If humans didn't get it right and do it quickly, all was lost, and "all" in this case meant most or all the people on Earth. The whole species would be wiped out, because if the worst case prevailed, humanity had absolutely zero capability in space. It couldn't be in space, and fire even a popgun in anger. So, if we failed to meet such a demand, if it is made, we had zero defence. The fact that we hadn't weaponised space, previously a source of great pride, was now the downfall of humanity.

'Who the hell do we speak with?' Jessy asked, thinking through the incredible enormity of the task. Everyone knew climate-change was a problem, but now it was much more than that.

'I'm thinking it through,' Mitch said, loudly tapping his foot, about to speak more, but closing his mouth instead. Mitch's mind was blank. The list was potentially insanely long.

'I feel better already,' Josh whispered sarcastically, adding unnecessary angst to it all. He was grinning ghostily, knowing they probably didn't have a chance in hell of pulling it off. They might as well roll the footpaths up now, Josh thought. We *have* to give it a decent go though, was his final, lasting thought. Mitch was of the same mind. They had to at least try. He really didn't want to contemplate the other option. Mitch looked at Josh and nodded, then grinned. He remembered when he was that age, and smiled widely.

'Between us and Zamindar, we'll have to decide,' he said, pulling hard at his ear, becoming very serious, doing his best to think deeply. The first thought was the UN, but he was unsure. They'd proven to be toothless and useless in the past.

Deciding who on Earth to speak to wasn't easy, but it was up to him and the boy, he reckoned. So, he better get on with doing it. So far, it was only them that knew what was coming. The rest of humanity were concerned with other things. That had to change, because soon enough, it would be front and centre in everybody's minds. *Everybody* meant the world over.

'By "us" deciding, you mean *you*, right?' Josh said. 'You'll decide?' He gazed at his dad accusingly.

'Well, yeah, I suppose that's right.' Mitch mused. He hadn't really thought about it in detail, but he was right. Josh and his wife would have to agree though. He was boss, though no one had installed him as such. But that's how he felt – he was "the one". The decision-maker. This was a democracy though, so he sought buy-in from everybody available.

'You don't think I'm an adult, dad...do you? You still think I'm a child...right? Josh was getting slowly worked up, his eyes tight and critical, staring tightly at his dad. He cracked his knuckles, a decent tell-sign for those that knew him. He looked directly at his dad, who avoided his angry eyes. Mitch could tell he was on friable ground with his son.

'It's hard you know, not that long ago, you were so little...a kid...I guess I'm influenced a bit by it subconsciously. It's hard to treat you like a fully grown man because I haven't seen you grow up. I didn't witness it.' Mitch had his head in his hands. 'It's fucking hard Josh.' He looked like he might cry.

'It's okay dad, thanks for being honest,' Josh touched his dad on the shoulder, smiling pensively. It *was* how it *was*. It would take time for Mitch to change, there was no quick fix to any of this. Time travel or time dilation required a lot of behavioural fine-tuning. He reviled "time" with a passion. Gravity had a lot to answer for. If only because of its dramatic effect on time.

*   *   *

They'd all fronted the United Nations with Paul Black at their side. Zamindar and Charijiok, Cranreb and Davtep and all the humans spoke with

Secretary-General Paul Blanchet and convinced him that urgent action was required to avoid catastrophe.

The United Nations General Assembly had made three proposals that were accepted by all members. They concurred that the list of countries, numbering about ninety, could speak for the entirety of Earth, because they represented 75% of the population of the world and 75% of the energy production, they would make decisions that would bind the entire world, a decision that would be ratified by the member nations of the UN. They also agreed that NASA and AASSA be the administrator of this decision. Further, they agreed this matter would come under the domicile of the UN Security Council in future which meant the result would be ratified by Russia, America, France, England and China. It was their purview according to the UN. The UN's stance was that fusion energy be adopted planet wide – and they had no issue with their opinion being widely communicated. They were aware of Cranreb and Davtep's assistance in bringing fusion energy to the world. The UN realised how important it was to the Earth. And what manner of threat the Bantha posed.

So, they needed to extract a determination from those who the UN decreed *could* in fact do it, legally. A positive result from them would bind the entire planet. Thus, an urgent discussion/meeting was organised with all the relevant individuals from agencies worldwide. Space Services, in AASSA and NASA were the arbiters and administrators of the meeting and were legally in control of the "Great Decision" as it would come to be known.

The AASSA and NASA No. 2 boardrooms were linked to discuss "A Solution to Global Warming and a Clear and Present Threat to Humanity" There was the threat from both climate-change itself and an existential threat from an interstellar species who desperately wanted to save the planet because it was so precious. Humans, and whatever else happened to occupy the planet with them, were apparently expendable. They were of far less importance than an evolution-encouraging, habitable-zone planet with *our* Moon and *our* Sun. In short, the planet was way more important than a civilisation.

Senior scholars, diplomats or heads from the USPA nations were waiting nervously to ferry details back to their respective Governments. As were numerous Heads from the Agency's network facilities at Stennis, JPL, Toulouse, Capetown, Toyama, Ningpo and Gorki.

The director of the Astrophysical Council was there as were four members from the SSEC and Heads or seniors from the Army, Navy, Airforce and Spaceforce. The heads or Number twos from NASA, ESA, CSA, ESA, Roscosmos, CNSA, USPA, DoD, and heads or Ministers from China, India, Australia, the US, Europe and Africa were there. The Department of Energy, the State Department, Department of the Interior, Department of Commerce and

Labor and US Homeland Security were also there. Paul Black, part of the Secretariat, was the UN's representative. From a government perspective, everyone was in attendance that was needed. And the meeting itself was ratified by the United Nations Security Council.

All of them were waiting to be told what to do by this Australian dude, Mitch Taylor, who was a legend, apparently. Most couldn't remember hearing about him since he went to Mars, many years previously. Some knew of his achievements intimately. They had all been updated and some had read the internet. They now realised why the man was venerated, and just what sort of extraterrestrial cargo he brought to the meeting.

Mitch walked to the head of the AASSA table and fingered the 120-inch TV to the ON position. A massive boardroom table came into view as did at least forty suits, the image graciously provided by AASSA, NASA and by Zoom. The people at the back of the mighty table were largely a blur. Of course, that was probably Mitch's eyesight. His ability to see distances sucked.

'Paul, can you hear me, okay?' Mitch walked toward the podium and made sure all his notes were where they supposed to be. He briefly flicked though the cards he'd made, all with handwritten bullet points on them which he'd done late at night. Mitch nodded to himself. He was nervous but ready. Prepared and ready for what though? He supposed he'd find out soon enough. Hopefully, the suits were friendly. Mitch doubted it. They all looked ready to kill. He knew what they'd be like – he'd dealt with them before, not the same people, but they may as well be, they were all very similar. Aggressive assholes, all of 'em. Most of them looked ready for a fist fight. The fact that he was an "outsider" didn't help at all.

'Yep, all good,' came the voice, piping up from somewhere at the back. Paul Shanahan, the Administrator of NASA was a good friend of his. At least his face was familiar, a contrast to everyone else who looked grim and bored.

'Okay then,' Mitch said to the crowded and mumbling \NASA No 2 Boardroom. *Jesus Christ*, he thought, peering firmly at the TV in front of him, these fuckers are just waiting for me to fall flat on my face. He surveyed their forbidding faces, and there was only Paul who offered a possible reprieve. The rest, *forget it*, they all looked annoyed and disinterested.

'We have been told by *One*, and it was fatally confirmed by the devastation of planet three in fuck knows what solar system. There is a race of beings that don't take kindly to climatic change caused by civilizations like us, pumping carbon and other poisons into the air. They don't like worlds like Earth being polluted and the atmosphere ruined with carbon and other atmospherically hazy chemicals. We believe they come from a different Galaxy.' Mitch looked at the NASA boardroom and they were all zeroed in on the camera, watching him intently. He guessed that was good. A few were doodling but mostly they were concentrating on what he was saying. Apart from Yuri Partington who hailed from Gorki in Russia, and was doing something on his phone and not making the slightest effort to hide it.

The big-toothed goon was smiling like a horse and not paying an iota of focus to anything, except whatever was on his stupid phone. Mitch didn't give a toss if he didn't listen. If he took shit back to Putin, that was his problem. And a *problem* it would be – for him. For him *not* to know what we're doing would invite the Kremlin to do their worst to him. It would be goodnight, Yuri.

Mitch wiped his face and continued, 'that sounds okay on the face of it. A socially responsible race flying around, interacting where it had to, to ensure precious planets are looked after, but it's not good, *not good at all*. For us, *for humanity, especially*.' Mitch's voice went up in volume and tone.

'Ladies and gentleman...we have been found out...seriously found wanting in our behaviours toward our planet.' Mitch swallowed and said nothing. Silence descended on the two rooms. Everyone looked at everyone else wondering what the hell was happening.

No one was doodling now. Everyone was laser focussed on Mitch, it sounded like a warning, even to his ears, when spoken aloud in rooms such as these. Mitch walked in a small circle wondering what he was going to say as a follow up. He knew what he was going to say but didn't really know how to put it. Mitch knew he had to speak. The small-talk was getting louder.

How in God's name would he put it to them...how would he frame it? Mitch tried to start but his throat was locked. He looked around and gawked at the TV screen...all he could see were hostile faces, both at NASA and even here at AASSA. Jessy looked super apprehensive, with eyes that seemed to bulge from her head. She was extremely concerned about their likely reaction to what Mitch had to say. *Fuck it*, he thought angrily. They all looked anything but happy and were talking in small, irate groups - exchanging Mitch Taylor insults, he assumed. He really didn't feel like talking to this mob. They looked really pissed. Most looked like they were all grinding their teeth. There were fake smiles everywhere, reddened flesh and no one was making eye contact with him, or anyone else in the room. Was he making it all up, reading too much into it maybe? He doubted it. Mitch coughed and then started speaking, nervously and quietly. He rarely spoke to a crowd this aggressive, especially one in this palpably poor state-of-mind and jam-packed with so many heavyweights. Here we go, he thought. Now or never, he supposed.

'This race to which I refer was apparently born outside of the Milky Way Galaxy.' Way, *way* out, he thought. Mitch searched for a more imposing, authoritative voice and cleared his throat with another piercing cough, 'and if a civilization doesn't comply with their demand to stop polluting the planetary atmosphere, they are, *removed*. We've seen the aftermath of this destruction with our own eyes. *It's not pretty...and it is potentially promised for Earth.*

Around them and everywhere he looked, eyes widened and mouths slackened. Everyone gawked at Mitch and realising what he was saying, was actually what he meant, they all looked like frightened children, turning away and covering their mouths, looking down and going white *en masse*. Their worst nightmare was coming true - the world might end in *their* lifetime.

'*Shit*,' Paul Shanahan, of NASA, uttered. 'You mean nukes planet-wide?

'Pure fusion probably...whatever, it is – it's goodbye civilisation,' Mitch said. 'There's no beg-pardons here, either compliance is total or life is removed. There are only two options. And total means *total*. The civilisation is gone Paul, eradicated by them for the benefit of the planet we are told.'

Jonah Phillips from the SSEC stood up, 'The Universe is a big place Mitch, perhaps they don't and won't know about us,' he said, gently biting his lip. 'Maybe they've never heard of us.' Jonah peered grimly at Mitch, holding his breath. 'And never will.' He desperately hoped. He knew better though.

Mitch cleared his throat again, loudly. 'They *know* about Earth,' he said dramatically. 'Zamindar confirmed it. Sorry Jonah.'

There was a huge amount of noise after his last statement, mainly blended voices that summed to nothing much at all, apart from panic, coming through Zoom. *"What do we do"* seemed to be the overriding theme of the noise? The rest was just enormous amounts of jarring clatter. No one was happy to be found out. That's what it came down to. The *Earth*, had been found out. by Earth, they meant *humans*. The entire room was scared and confused, a good insight into how any similar extraterrestrial news would go down with Joe public. Confusion and total bewilderment hit both sides of the Pacific. Mitch waited for the chatter to subside then continued

"What do we do you ask? Well, we can do it, with the help of the Jarithians here." Seated next to Zamindar were Cranreb and Davtep. Mitch flourished his arm and hand at them as he introduced them and described how they would help. They were key to the humans' success on Earth. We're familiar with fusion energy, but with their knowledge and experience, we'll be shown how to produce new high temperature alloys and miniaturise reactors, making them far more efficient.

'They have been brought to Earth to act as fusion *specialists* for us and will move from site to site to assist. Fusion reactors, the size of suitcases power their total energy needs on Jarith. They will show humans how they're constructed and how to create new alloys and hyper-strong gravitation. They will firstly prepare blueprints and then assist hands-on. 'Sorry to say that solar, green hydrogen and wind will not do it for us. Fission energy is too dangerous and too prone to environmental issues, no matter how careful we are. Humanity and fission don't mix. In other words, we need all cars to be electric and all energy for electricity including motor vehicles, to be fusion based or, the energy, at the very least, be fusion derived. Greenhouse gasses from these sources will be totally banned. New legislation will be drafted outlawing all greenhouse gasses from these sources. Anything humanity uses for heating, cooling, lighting...*anything* that uses electricity or moves people must do so free of these gasses so energy for *everything* must be derived from the strong nuclear force. Nothing is burned – *ever*. That's all we need to do to survive,' Mitch said, widening his stance behind the podium and grinning at the NASA boardroom.

Mitch reckoned the use of "all" would fire 'em up. Especially the red dragons. They would hate the very idea – their reliance on coal and oil was a national fucking addiction.

'So...it's simple,' Valery Yalkov said, the Minister of Energy for Russia, 'we *just* ban mining of fossil fuels. Good luck with that,' he rolled his eyes. You must be *fucking* kidding, he thought. 'You're fucking joking,' he finished on, said loudly and angrily with a hefty Slavic accent. By the nodding around the table, there was a lot of the suits in agreement with Valery. What they'd heard sounded like pure insanity. Targets were one thing, but this sounded like pure madness. How could we possibly expect the general public to understand?

'The economy of ninety or so countries would literally be gone overnight,' Peter Jennings of Toulouse said, sitting up straight at the table. Everyone nodded and agreed. In fact, everyone was nodding at fucking everything. It was driving Mitch nuts. They came across like a bunch of politicians, although presumably they were listening carefully to what was being said. Mitch really hoped so. This stuff was ultra-important. Actually, heeding and understanding the words and the message was key to all this.

Mitch was reddening in the face, his eyes narrowed and teeth bared. Do these arseholes *get it*, he wondered glaring at the screen, The Sword of Damocle's was literally wobbling above humanity, and all he could hear through Zoom was bickering and second-guessing. *Dumb fucks,* he thought.

This, *right here*, and right now, was life and death, and all they thought about was economy and money. Yes, economy was super-important, but when the species was at stake, surely that took precedence. It was simple logic.

Maybe the UN had brought the wrong people in, he thought. Mitch acknowledged that economy and "the budget" were important to any Government, that's mostly why they were elected...but surely, simply *surviving* trumped everything.

Mitch clenched his jaw and tried not to grit his teeth, 'are you all...serious? He shouted, looking around the table, and at the camera. '*Christ Almighty*, you people...seriously don't understand. We are at the crossroads...the fine line between life and death as a species. If we continue as we are, we will be exterminated. *Understand that please.*' He could feel himself spitting, he was so enraged and supercharged. What a bunch of dumb-fucks he thought, his eyes were almost hanging out of his head, *seriously*, there were few words in the dictionary to describe how he felt about them.

There were thirty of the best minds in the world, and at NASA, sitting around the table, but the reality of it all was that they were all a bunch of yes-men, willing to go along with the company-line of economy and budget before anything else. NASA was willing to make concessions to favour the environment, but when it came down to it, they had to side with the Federal Government. Their funding was very precious indeed to them. These people were torn between doing the right thing by the planet and the right thing by the US government. Most of the people here had no idea what to do. Ideally, the decision between the company and the planet should be the same. The thing was, people would listen to NASA more than any government including the United Nations. And they were hellbent on treading a fine line, even though logic would favour the environment substantially.

NASA had been empowered by every world government, after a lot of negotiation, to be the arbiter. Afterall, this was a decision about a space issue. Well, they came from space, anyway. Mitch was ambivalent about the decision to empower space services to be the global arbiter on this decision. But it was what it was, so they had to get on with it and hopefully get the decision ratified.

'We know roughly when they're coming.' General Stevenson said, US Secretary of Defense. 'So why don't we wipe them out, on first encounter? Before they have a chance to attack.'

Mitch peered at him as he would a naughty child, '*Jesus Christ General*...you're serious, aren't you?' Mitch asked incredulously, clenching his jaw so tight he could feel some of his teeth wobble under the strain. He'd expected such a statement from the old fool, but that didn't lessen the impact of the words being spoken by the General. We don't have a clue when they're coming, you fucker. And that's just to start with, he thought. 'We really don't know a thing...when, where, what? *Nothing.*' He glared at the General and stood very still. The silence was deafening.

Jesus Christ, who are these people? He screamed to himself. Mitch scrunched his toes tight and pulled his fists into claws as he tried to stay calm and speak with a modicum of coolness. He was the moderator, but he felt more like a cage-fighter, confronted by a cage full of fuck-wits. Mitch took a couple of deep breaths to right himself and prepare an answer.

'*General*, we have *NO*, capability in space whatsoever. It is most likely that they would release a phalanx of pure fusion weapons from a distance.' Mitch stared aggressively at the General who volleyed the same glare back at him, as if to say, "why not"? He was not one to take a backward step or be intimidated. The General adjusted his peaked cap and continued staring aggressively. Mitch knew he was an ignoramus, but still respected his station.

Mitch continued to glare at him, the anger nearing boiling point. 'We would likely not even know they were there, let alone mount a counter-offensive. What would we use against them...a fucking Raptor? Remember, this is in space.' Mitch felt like spelling it out in capital letters for him and then hitting him over the head with the whiteboard. 'It's the pinnacle of our air-force, but it needs an atmosphere to work in. In space it's just...junk.'

It was clear the General had never heard of space. It was somewhere above the clouds, but that's clearly all the idiot knew. 'Well...we can try, by God,' the General spewed. Seemingly, nothing would shut this guy up.

'If we try, we die – all of us. Be sure of that General if nothing else.' Mitch said, glaring at him. 'They are very used to killing on a large scale – that's their thing. That's what they do to save planets from harmful species.

'Earth should not be dictated to,' General Stevenson said, looking daggers at Mitch. It sounded like the poor old fellow had been gargling gravel while he wasn't listening to a word he said. Listening to him talk, it sounded like nothing had gotten through his thick skull. Mitch glanced back at him and started to feel sorry for the poor old sod. The General really had no idea.

'We need to do things differently with energy so...why don't we just do it?' He said, walking back a few steps, giving them all time to absorb the main thrust of what had been spoken about. Mitch looked at all of them and almost grinned. What a bunch of goddamned dinosaurs, he thought. If this is who makes most of the big decisions, God help us all, he thought. No wonder we don't have fusion, a bit unfair, he knew, since we simply didn't have the technology to produce a decent sized reactor that actually produced more energy than was fed into the damned thing. We didn't have a hope up there – we hadn't weaponised our space tech at all. No wonder we were still in the dark ages, burning fossil fuels and extracting oil like fucking Neanderthals. Mitch walked forward, toward the podium and continued.

'Earth has one chance to change gentlemen, you all have two clear days to come back to me here at AASSA and give me a yes or a no. There is no time for an election speech on these issues.' Mitch hoped a few had cottoned on to the seriousness of all this. As Government and corporate leaders and apparently men of repute, you have been carefully selected to relay the information back to your leaders and peers, and come back to me with your decision. It's either yes, you want to live and want fusion energy, or it's no, you want everything to stay the same until we have to confront the Bantha' Mitch wanted that little pearl to be heard by all...and hopefully for it to seep into their consciousness then continued, 'Obviously, it's necessary to immediately stop carbon products or like products – a list of which will soon be on AASSA's and NASA's website. If you want to live and continue the human species of course.'

He looked at all of them squarely, around the table at AASSA and in the camera at NASA. He'd tell them again about Gaznoy's run-in with the Bantha and then they could make up their own minds.

'The species we saw with our own eyes, were dead and gone, and they already had a mix of dirty and clean energy - in other words, Gaznoy's civilization were already *transitioning* to clean energy, *but it wasn't quick enough*.' He stared at them in silence and allowed it to hopefully filter into their primitive brains. What Mitch meant was any deadline set by the Bantha had to be met completely. You were guilty until proven innocent by the Bantha.

"We need to learn from experience. Gaznoy and his kind were within a stone's throw of pure, clean, sustainable energy and they were destroyed. Made extinct forever. Make no mistake, there is no negotiation with this lot. Comply or die gentlemen. That's what it amounts to. We *need* to start decarbonising right now. The UN agree that tackling climate-change direct, *and for good*, is the way to go. They believe that with Cranreb and Davtep's help, this can be done along with help from central banks. I await your final answer...within two days. My mobile awaits final calls or messages from all of you. There is no time for anything else.' Mitch had now finished speaking.

He slowly shook his head as he re-took his seat. *Christ*, he thought, nothing was positive or hopeful - not with this lot. They were very government and economy oriented. Mitch put both hands clumsily into his pockets, contemplating the end of everything that had been so very hard to build.

The Zoom camera was turned off and the link between AASSA and NASA was severed. '*Jesus fucking Christ,*' Mitch spat, reliving the nightmare of dealing with those knuckle-heads...who held the future of humanity firmly in their own hands. More than an hour of pure hell, Mitch reckoned, glancing at the digital clock on the wall, wiping sweat off his brow.

'We need twelve of them to say yes,' Josh said clearly, for the entire world to transform - that includes Russia and evirons, India, China, the US, Africa and Canada, Australia, Japan and Europe. There are other heavily populated areas but as far as energy and economy are concerned, the entire planet is fairly much covered.'

Mitch watched Josh with a knowing grin. He was proud to have him so closely onboard, knowing the emotion was severely misplaced, because of the shit they were in, but what the hell? He wasn't sure what did and didn't matter right now. All he knew was the answer from all those that attended needed to sum to twelve yes votes. Anything else was just a distraction and probably a lot more work.

Mitch couldn't get it out of his head – the worst outcome always gravitates to the front of his brain. 'What if the answer is *no*?' Mitch said, more to himself than anyone else. He cleared his throat noisily and repeated the sentiment. *Jesus holy Christ*, he thought to himself, if the answer is no, we are all in huge trouble. Especially since "they" know about "us".

It won't be long, he thought, screwing up his face. We're on their fucking list – in bold probably. Mitch couldn't believe it had come to this. From trying to solve the Fermi Paradox and the source of FRB's to attempting to survive the very aggressive threats from an interstellar species. He felt very unclean, and he knew why. Things had somehow turned 180 degrees up there. From searching for ET's, it was now hoping they weren't destroyed by them.

The Bantha will soon enough be on our fucking doorstep. Making all types of threats. Do this, don't do that - it'll be like conversing with an overbearing parent. Then, presumably, based on what we'd heard - they would make *"the demand"*.

Mitch was certain it wouldn't go down well with the world generally. Globally, humanity wouldn't accept it, either the demand itself or the power problems that would be associated with the change, which probably meant one thing. Many would be on the streets. Being at home simply wouldn't work for them. It would leave way too much time to think and ponder the likelihoods. They would be up against an impalpable enemy light-years distant that would essentially be immune from anything Earth might do – which they all knew was nil. The feelings of sheer impotence would lead much of the population to all manner of horrific emotions. And the only place to let off steam was the streets. Yet, there was no talk of keeping anything secret...yet.

Most would no doubt like to tell the Bantha to *fuck off*. But maybe that was the problem – we'd have to be forced into it – otherwise *change* would happen way too slowly. Once the atmosphere and planet were dead, or, the tipping point came and went, it was obviously way too late to do anything. All humanity could do then was countdown to the end to come or find another planet like Mars.

*   *   *

167

They mostly waited until the last few minutes to respond. *Mostly.* The final answer was close, and until the votes were tallied, it was anyone's guess what the answer would be. Their assumptions were useless. The NASA and AASSA group had the final say, if it happened to be a draw, but they hoped like hell it didn't come to that. But they knew it would be close. Those representing Earth had no real idea what to do. They were reacting to a demand that hadn't even been made – but was expected. They had to vote yes to live, didn't they? The votes were all in, and, as expected, it was close...in fact it *was* a draw, ten votes for yes, including Russia and the US, and ten votes for no, it was too hard, or their constituents demanded stable power, so it was up to negotiation with the Bantha to avoid their wrath.

The thick-headed countries who'd said that, and there were several, hadn't been paying attention to Mitch at all. He'd gone to pains to tell the entire audience that this race didn't negotiate with anyone. They simply made a demand and then, if needed, took action. That was it - the process was as simple as it gets. They could try and negotiate with them, but while they did it, Earth would be destroyed. He'd said it over and over again to all of them – and here we were with half the world hanging their hat on negotiation. '*Fuck.*' Mitch mumbled obscenities under his breath. So, it was up to the space consortium, which acted under the auspices of the UN. Back to Zoom it was, to again plead their case.

NASA and AASSA had already decided that it would be a totally democratic process, despite them holding the balance of power. There had to be an imbalance of impacted countries before they moved forward. It was too important for there not to be. The parent, NASA, wouldn't step in to break the draw...quite yet.

Mitch stood at the head of the table once again and pressed the image activate button. He was on *again*. The same thirty people were there, and they looked to be in exactly the same seats as they had occupied before, and they appeared even more unhappy to be there. They all looked as unfriendly as before as they waited for Mitch. But this time, many of them looked scared and nervous as well. Apparently, all of them knew better than Mitch, they already knew how this was going to play out. But no one had told Mitch. He, Jessy and Josh and all of AASSA were none the wiser.

Mitch cleared his throat, again, before he spoke to AASSA and the NASA room in North America for the second time. To try and talk some of them around, and God forbid, make them see some sense collectively. Mitch was also more nervous than the first time. This time, the decision *had* to be made, before they disconnected. There was no option – it had to be done. Mitch looked at the group of men and was amazed how familiar they all looked.

Unfriendly they may have appeared, but there was something familiar with the way they looked and moved, and positioned themselves around the table. He'd been here before. Mitch knew he had to be professional. Calling China, a bunch of wankers wouldn't do. Mitch started talking as he addressed the mic.

'As half the planet voted *no* to the proposition to halt greenhouse gas production immediately, we have been asked to again decide for the world.' He glared at them as if he failed to comprehend or remotely fathom their decision. Mitch had dark rings beneath his eyes but he stared piercingly at his AASSA comrades and into the camera for those turkeys at NASA.

Mitch slowly shook his head. 'Last time, the decision was split, half no and half yes. We need a majority before proceeding.' Mitch stopped talking, taking a huge breath, with an obvious swallow and scratched his cheek. He continued to stare at his own people and those at NASA. Mitch struggled to believe a majority hadn't already been reached. His glare was narrow and angry. This was the fate of the world at stake. Mitch wondered if they realised that. They were supposed to be a smart lot, not a bunch of naughty children. That made him feel a bit better as he smiled to himself and addressed the mic.

'I understand how difficult it is to ask your people to endure power outages and power instability, spanning days and in some cases weeks, while the transition occurs. Unemployment and other physical and state-of-mind difficulties...it is either that *or* it's civilisation death.' *Please understand that.'* None of them were talking or looking at their phones, *thank God,* he thought. This, *right here*, is something they needed to concentrate and focus on.

'Remember,' Mitch said loudly and clearly. 'There is no negotiating with the Bantha...*at all*. Once a demand is made, there are only two options. Change energy bases completely or destruction. There is no negotiation. *Period.'*

There was a collective 'AAARRGH' from both rooms when he finished talking. They all knew how horrendously hard this would all be. Their people would come to hate them - a great proportion of them. If the people found out they helped formulate the decision, they realised assassination was well and truly on the cards. Some would see them as heroes but a lot would hate them outright. Mitch focussed on the microphone which he reckoned was better than looking at any of them.

'Complications with the size of the reactors, their lifetime and the cost of things *can and will be* overcome, with the assistance of these two,' Mitch turned and gestured toward Davtep and Cranreb. 'They've literally done it all before,' he said, moving closer to the camera. 'And it was a success...they worked and provided the required energy to the network. We will get additional tungsten and rare-Earth elements from Chile and Russia. Niobium will come from Canada and Brazil. Steel supplies are in place, so, resources won't be an issue at any time. The main issues will be unemployment of those in coal or coal-related industries, re-training of some of the unemployed and salary-continuance for the remainder.'

*   *   *

'The units shoot pellets of Deuterium, obtained from seawater, at similar sized micro-pellets of Helium 3, obtained mainly from lunar mining, with powerful magnets. The temperature in the centre of the units is 100 million degrees centigrade. Along with another isotope, Helium 4, comes a lot of energy - *fusion energy which is ours to use.* We convert that to electricity instead of burning coal to do the same.'

Paul Shanahan, the top dog of NASA stood up and directed himself toward the camera. 'So, those two will assist construction of the reactors...we need new high temperature, long lasting alloys, and magnets,' he peered around, 'they can assist with that?'

'Like I said the first time, they can do it all Paul, they are proven fusion specialists. They will show you how to build small reactors down to the finest level of detail and that will include using brand-new alloys of tungsten which will be produced by ITER and the new global consortium, IFGT.

Paul sat down, seemingly satisfied with the answer from Mitch but completely confused and horrified at the responsibility and risk of severe injury or death to employees and technicians who used them or tried to construct them. Hopefully, engineering and construction of the new units was within the human capability. It was fine to demonstrate and blueprint the process, but it had to be do-able by humans, once the Jarithians left. The strong belief was that it was. Afterall, fusion reactors were produced on Earth, high temperature alloys and strong, durable gravitational fields were part of the game. The Jarithians seemed to take it all in their stride which was good. It showed the faith they had in their own abilities...and their ability to convey that to humans.

The Head of NASA had no idea how it would all fit together, especially the people involved in the coal industry and the car industry. What the fuck happens to them? His face was ruddy red and looked ready to explode in a detonation of warm blood.

Like a cork in the ocean, up jumped General Witte, Minister of Defense for Russia and he spoke loudly with a hefty Slavic accent. 'Technical aspects are fine, but what about *fucking* economics and unemployment. We employ almost *60,000 people* in the coal industry – what the hell do they do? Simply hang around...? Perhaps they could all, what do you call it, go down the pub for a drink?' He uttered more negative Russian expletives under his breath and

170

sat down harshly. He didn't believe a word of what he'd heard. To him, the whole lot sounded like a huge load of American spin. NASA and America were there simply to taunt Russia, just ask General Witte. He reviled all of 'em.

Cheng Zhigang, Chinese Ministry of Science and Technology, looked ill. He was red in the face and bent over the table. '*China has five fucking million in coal.*' He was a short, rotund man in a tight suit and was ruby red in the face, sweating profusely. '*Fuck*, this is a nightmare. five million...and *then* there's oil, petrol...*Jesus*. Maybe it'd be easier if they just did us in, he whined,' cogitating the logistical horror story they were dangling above. 'Stop coal mining, *yeah sure*,' he whispered, thinking it was all a horrible joke. It was impossible, he knew that much. The government and the general public would demand energy *en masse.* Where it came from was mostly irrelevant, he knew, the country would just want its lights on. China wasn't like other countries. They quite simply wouldn't understand, especially in the rural areas.

Chen imagined trying to sell the insanity to the Chairman. Might as well inject himself first, before they got to him, he reckoned. Do the job properly. He gawked at the Russian Defence Minister as he re-took his seat, blinking at him uncomprehendingly. He was stunned, confused and horrified and almost missed his chair, his ample behind hitting the hand-rest on the way down. He hit the chair with a thump that would have been humorous under regular circumstances. But there was nothing remotely funny here. The Chinese were between a rock and a hard place and Chen knew it.

Chen spoke again when he was finally seated and had re-taken his voice. 'Gradually okay...but *immediately*, no, it's impossible, surely, it's impossible.' Chen said out loud to himself, grimacing and sweating, with shaking hands and darting eyes that flicked over almost everyone in the room. He was spitting something rapidly in Chinese that was unintelligible.

'For something that's not magnetic, coal is so fucking polarising,' Mitch said, deadly serious, staring directly at the Chinese Minister. Director Chen nodded at him, having given up all hope of living through this.

'The power stations will remain the same, but the electricity will be created by nuclear fusion, not thermal coal. You've closed more than a thousand mines Director, demand for coal hasn't been lower since the 1960's. You know the air quality in your major cities is nigh on Venusian.' Mitch cleared his throat. 'It's coming Chen, best to deal with it now,' Mitch said, planting his legs wide. Mitch was confident, but expected anything, especially from Chen and China. These guys had never been put under pressure like this – *ever*.
Mitch realised he was asking them to make decisions that would seriously impact their entire country's way of life. He also knew there was no other way. The continuation of human life probably depended on it.

Chen had the insane sense that the air in Beijing was as clear as a mountain stream. *God*, he was infuriating. He should take a stroll out of his Beijing penthouse occasionally. The idiot would find out pretty quickly what it was like on the streets of the city. It was smoggy and it stunk. Mitch had been to Beijing recently and could speak first-hand.

Mitch stared at all those wanting eye-contact, 'what we need is a decision, to avoid what's gonna come from above, to substitute fossil-fuel electricity with electricity generated by fusion techniques. In short ladies and gentlemen,' Mitch cleared his throat and squared his shoulders, 'we need to stop *everything* that produces greenhouse gasses as a by-product - electricity, cars and aviation. Cost to the consumer will initially stay exactly the same. The rest, most of it, will be borne by Governments, the UN and the World Bank in the short and probably the medium term.'

'*Holy sweet fuck*,' Jack Chapman from US Homeland Security blustered. 'May as well ask us to hiss and yawn at the same time - that's gonna be near impossible.' The guy was a moron, but he just about got it right. It was difficult almost to the point of being impossible – but they needed to try.

'Not quite impossible Jack, but there will be huge problems, you'll work them out though. Fusion energy can't be perennially thirty years away...maybe they're doing us a favour by forcing our hand. Governments and the UN will assist with finance.'

There were moans and groans and the odd grunt and lots of whispered, murmured conversation from around the table, suggesting that they didn't necessarily all agree with the sentiment. *Fuck 'em,* Mitch thought. This was how it had to be. For the continuation of life as we know it.
Overall, the feeling was that it was do-able, but doing it gradually would be far preferable. That was a complete no-brainer. Mitch realised that it would never happen if it was gradual. He knew that for it to happen, the world had to be forced into it. Clearly, this wasn't only known to humans.

There were reasons for the Fermi Paradox and the great silence, and climate change might be one of the stand-out road-blocks for civilisations. Possessing intelligence meant industrialisation, which meant burning fossil fuels or similar for energy in the first instance. Unless a non-greenhouse gas alternative is developed, like fusion, to cater for total energy needs, the planet's atmosphere is doomed. Otherwise, it's irrevocable extinction.

'We have a media conference straight after updating the UN, to ensure people are aware of the situation and come on the journey with us,' Mitch said, taking a sharp intake of breath. 'Each major country will have their own TV crew to ferry it back to its people and break into programming where required. Hopefully, those that want to know, *will know*.'

Chen didn't know where to look. He looked down, up and to the side, essentially wherever people *weren't*. 'So, we just implement the change and wherever the chips fall...so, be it?.' The Chinese Minister of Commerce and Labour looked horrified, wobbly and like one small push would send him crashing to the ground, poor bastard. He was as white as a sheet and was visibly sweating. His entire face was covered with moisture. His hair was now flat to his head, wet through with perspiration. 'What do we do with the millions of unemployed?'

Chen was so right, there would be millions of unemployed – from coal mining to ancillary businesses. A lot of companies would simply close. House and business foreclosures would sky-rocket, as would bankruptcies, and everything else negative would go through the roof, except the housing market, which would collapse in a heap. Stock markets the world over would suffer badly. The Shanghai Stock Market would implode and Chen knew it.

'What the hell do we do with them all,' he whined. Chen swivelled around in his chair and stared at the floor. 'They'll all be protesting on the streets with the ACFTU right behind them, goading and pushing,' he groaned, his mouth opening and closing way quicker than he needed just for the words.

'No-one said it would be easy Chen, retraining and redeployment can come later. You and whoever Mr Jinping choose, are charged with powering your country with fusion energy *only*. The human element will come later.' Maybe much later, Mitch conceded to himself. 'The unemployed need to have their old wage maintained, so they are able to service their debts and maintain their normal life-style. The World Bank using IDA and the UN will help with that.'

'But there will be massive protests and unrest, Chen groaned, pressing his fists against the sides of his head. He could only imagine the terror and the awfulness coming at him in the near-future if this happened. 'The people on farms won't understand any of it – and they'll be anything but cooperative. The prisons will be full,' Chen said, still whining and sweating. He could only imagine Shanghai, Beijing and Chongqing. How the hell will they look? He was mortified with the way forward. His family were finished if this happened, he said loudly to his colleagues. Poor old Chen was white as snow and sweating like he'd just run a marathon.

'China would be a disaster area, the Stock Exchange will be no more and it will be a land full of the unemployed,' he continued to groan, making all sorts of odd noises. He was jumpy with bloated, staring eyes and raspy breathing. The mental image that made him sweat was of the Chairman's noose for Committee Members like him.

'It will not be like that, if it's framed right, Chen. If a clear distinction is made between choice - and death of the species, then it should work. Yes, it will be tough, uncomfortable, hard, probably the most confronting thing, you've, *they've…all your people, have ever done*, but you will all be alive to do it and unfortunately, to feel it. Chen glanced at Mitch with bolting eyes that flicked nervously to everyone in the room.

'The other option is to go slow or what is way worse, *do nothing and rely on negotiation*. Death waits there…for everyone. Earth will end up like Jarith's planet.' Mitch's jaw was set and his brow furrowed as he stared compassionately at Chen who looked shorter than he was, as he hunched over the table. You had to feel sorry for him, Chen had so much to confront. China was clearly in the worst position of any country on Earth. And it dealt with disappointment and distress so much tougher than other countries.

General Stevenson stood and sighed heavily, glaring at the AASSA group. 'So, you mean just get it done, *fuck the consequences*, right Mitch?'

'Well, yeah…I suppose I do, yes, it needs to be done, so, *yes*, just get it done. The human element will come later. Governments will go massively or further into debt to support the population. The newly unemployed will be looked after financially, of that you can be sure, we will ensure redundancy will not mean a reduction in pay.' Mitch gazed at the room in North America, chock-a-block full of world dignitaries, and he could see their eyebrows draw together as they considered the weeks ahead and who they'd need to rely on to get the impossible job done. They were all thinking about what had to happen. That was a good thing, he supposed.

All of them agreed that the whole thing was a surreal nightmare and they weren't even sure it was possible, but deep down knew it probably was. But given the situation if it *didn't* happen, well, they'd have to give it a decent go. Everyone present realised that future generations of humans depended entirely on what was happening here.

*   *   *

The votes came in and not surprisingly, the countries of Earth or at least their representatives had voted *yes*. They wanted to live as a species…as a planetary community. Fighting a battle in space, they knew, would go only one way. Saying "yes" was the avenue to life.

Now to front the world media and update the UN. Mitch was not looking forward to it, telling the media about Davtep and Cranreb, and *the warning*, which was coming apparently. And the change to the world which was so essential. It would affect everyone, countless would be impacted fundamentally. Many, to the core. But if we didn't do it, or converted too slowly, it was game over. The entire human race would be destroyed.

Some of the population would never recover from the change. Many would go bankrupt - many houses would be lost to repossessions and many businesses would fail and close. That was the price of life on Earth continuing. Future generations depended on what humanity did right now.

Planet Earth needed a lot of energy to feed cities, homes and technology, but its source would be something completely different. Earth would use the energy locked up in the strong nuclear force to power everything they used with sustainable electricity – homes, cars, planes, trains, buses and agricultural equipment.

Gone would be anything that held carbon in its list of constituents. Burning for consumers and commercially would be banned. That nothing be burned – by anyone, *ever*.

9

Enemy

"When stupidity is considered patriotism, it is unsafe to be intelligent.
— *Isaac Asimov*

Destination was a beautiful, blue planet that orbited a solitary yellow star on the third arm of the galaxy they were now in. The intelligent inhabitants called it Earth, but it was in its death throes as a stable, fertile world.

Its atmosphere was in the final stages of turbulent failure. It was even worse than the intelligence that lived on the planet thought. They still spoke of targets and goals as though there was no rush to fix it. The governments of Earth were the planet's biggest problem. This rare blue rock was in the deepest shit possible. The atmosphere was not sustainable as a life-giver to its highest intelligence and by extension, it would be unbreathable by everything else that drew breath on the planet.

The plasma-cloaked spacecraft had located it, but circumstances had worsened quickly. The planet was now at a critical tipping point. They had to move quickly and the Bantha knew it. Ocean levels and temperatures were rising, glaciers were melting, animals were becoming extinct at escalating rates, weather was wilder – droughts, bushfires and floods were becoming way too common – yet humanity kept pumping carbon into the air.

Floods and extreme weather events were happening with increasing regularity in China, the Sichuan and Guangxi provinces were underwater. In America, it was the same, Arizona, New Mexico and Utah were reeling from flash floods and evacuations. Flooding in the US was now nation-wide. Eastern Australia was a complete write-off. Waves of rainfall had left vast areas of farmland, houses and towns underwater. 180 countries had reported flooding around the globe. The only continent that didn't have floods was Antarctica. Yet, humanity kept relying on "targets" to get the job done, and meanwhile, they pumped tonnes of carbon into the atmosphere.

*   *   *

Approaching Earth, the craft was invisible to the eyes that looked permanently spaceward, and the episodic humans and machines that watched from the ground and used data from 'scopes in orbit. Even Webb saw nothing. The craft gave off no EMAR or anything else for that matter, it was all stopped by their excited housing of plasma extending over the ship. So, no one knew it was there doing its thing. It was invisible in infra-red and ultra-violet too.

The vessel was actually there in all its grandeur though, watching and analysing the planet, orbiting, but remaining unidentified by anyone who resided on or near the planet.

Zamindar had told Mitch the skeleton he'd seen, matched the race that currently threatened them. What Josh thought of as a new species was exactly that –brand-new to the planet and was one of '*them. A Bantha.* with pointy and long head, large, downward slanting eyes and short stocky bodies. Three fingers on two arms with a thumb. They were older than humans and started their days as a squirrel-like creature, a nervous, fearful animal with short fur and a broad tail. So Zamindar told them. And now they were all grown up and intelligent and wanted contact with the colorful planet below them. To convey a blunt warning...oh, and also to say hello. Unfortunately, Earth didn't have the luxury of saying "no". It was a demand with a rather harsh penalty if not obeyed.

Mitch, Jessy, Josh and the two Virijians stood on Helipad 2, the very spot where Earth met Zamindar and Char for the first time all those short years ago. The two borrowed fusion specialists were milling around in the background, not far from AASSA itself.

A shining white pod sliced away from the bigger craft and made its way through some scattered cumulus clouds and broke into clean air at a few thousand feet, almost directly above the AASSA base. The craft was essentially the shape of a whistle and emerged from the belly of the larger craft as though it were a dropped egg. As soon as the small craft passed the Karman line, it oriented itself downward and was visible to all remote watchers, electronic and biological. It was not cloaked.

Emeneepienene and his co-pilot in the opposite seat flew the craft to the helipad at precisely 11AM as agreed with Mitch Taylor. Mitch realised there was little profit in being evasive, let alone aggressive, so they agreed to meet the Bantha, with a select group of humans and Virijians and a few others.

There was a huge cruiser in LEO, so being overtly hostile to the Bantha would yield no positive dividend whatsoever. It might encourage them to do something unpleasant. No one knew about their mother ship but they were being logical. They were doing the exact opposite of what General Stevenson wanted – being welcoming to the newcomers.

The General was on drugs it seemed. He was a left over from a very dangerous world and had no business being here. Mitch and Jessy understood the sentiment, but in space, such a stance was perilously misplaced.

Mitch watched the craft drop from high above him to end up dominating his horizons as it set down close in front of him – soft as a baby's kiss. It made little noise as it landed, almost right in front of him. The colour of the vehicle was most unusual, he couldn't work out if it was blue or green, maybe a combination of both. He couldn't tell, and just when he'd settled on green, he thought maybe it was blue then went back to green again. What it was made of presumably led to the colour?. Zamindar said it wasn't made from a true metal – it was made mainly of carbon.

Mitch could hear the thump of rotors and looked skyward to see three choppers and a squadron of F21's higher up. They must have scrambled from the nearby military base at Alice Springs after a small craft was detected near the Karman line. Mitch showed a thumbs up to the choppers to say we're okay.

Only one of the occupants came out of the whistle-shaped alien vessel. Emneneepienene walked slowly out of what would be the air inlet or mouthpiece for a typical whistle, and stood near Mitch who was at the head of the group with Josh. Emneneepienene spoke clear English, and he also knew how to speak Mandarin and Hindi, and nearly all of Spanish it turned out.The Bantha knew a lot about Earth and Mitch. He turned his head and looked carefully and stiffly at everyone. How he knew to speak English or who had authority on Earth, no one knew.

The choppers had mainly left the area, although two had set down near the base of Anzac Hill. The rest thudded and chopped their rotors quietly in the distance on the way back to base. Similarly, the jets had all gone although coming back for another fly-over was possible.

The creature before them was clearly a humanoid of some kind, like a human cross-bred with a rodent maybe, but there were no whiskers and no tail. It had a short stocky body, with two arms and two thick legs. Black shoes without laces hid the toes. Eyes were tear-drop in shape and downcast, making the being look aggressive from the get-go. Its eyes were blinking like mad and it was scratching its neck like a cat. With an arm and fingers thankfully.

The creature looked extremely nervous and had a rather pendulous nose that was twitching. It wore clothes like a wharfie, light blue tracksuit-like pants and a plain black top of some sort with scuffed black shoes. No effort had seemingly been made to "dress-up" which Mitch thought was a worrying sign, although he didn't exactly know why. This individual hadn't even bothered to *clean* his shoes. That really irked Mitch. Maybe it was trying to blend in, but who dressed like that around here? Mitch decided he shouldn't judge so much.

Mitch wanted to collect a tiny piece of its skin to see if it had DNA at its base, or if its scaffold was RNA or one of the other million or so acids that could hold hereditary information. The way his skin moved, didn't differentiate him from humans at all. Looking at him in far greater detail would be required to define him fully. At the moment, he moved like a human. That's all they knew.

Behind them in building 11 L 2 were twenty or so heavyweights from NASA and Washington. Behind, and to the sides of the building, the media and public were corralled between two roads. They were scheduled to be briefed by someone after the meeting had occurred. Not by those at AASSA, thankfully, it was someone from NASA media who stood behind the group from AASSA. Mitch peered at the newly arrived vessel and at the alien and he shook his head. Like the other humans, he firstly questioned evolution, and secondly, questioned the intelligence of something that looked like *that*. He was deeply off-put by the head and the face. It looked like its cranial veins were on the outside of its face. It truly looked very odd indeed ...even ghastly

Of course, the Bantha probably had the same thoughts about humanity. Mitch was sure its thoughts, no doubt, painted us for what we were. A very juvenile race who had a hell of a lot of growing up to do.

My name is Emnene,' he said, looking deeply into Mitch's eyes, twitching his long nose, swallowing heavily. 'I know who *you* are.' He walked around Mitch and peered at Josh. 'I know you too,' he gazed deeply into Josh's eyes. 'I see you are with friends,' he gawked at the Virijians then at everyone else, twitching his nose at double speed and rubbing his hair covered throat.

'I know your planet well,' Emnene said in stilted English, suggesting he didn't use it very often, 'we come from a-different, relatively close-galaxy. Planets like your Earth, that can sustain life are rare, planets that can sustain long-lived, multi-cellular life, *intelligent* life are the very rarest of cosmic resources, he said, stroking his arm, seemingly drilling his thoughts into all that could hear him. It was clear from his voice he truly believed what he was saying. He'd said it God knows how many times before, to God knows who. Everything Emnene had said so far, they knew anyway. Mitch desperately hoped it got more interesting. Less on the obvious and the cliché, and more on the detail. Without any threats of death would be nice.

Emnene wasn't finished on the issue of exceptional Earth yet, 'Earth is not only special, it is blessed, because a very low percentage of worlds have an effective feedback mechanism like ice and generally, just by fortuity, it was able to absorb most external and internal events, and remain habitable and encourage evolution over billions of years. Most of these planets are habitable for a period, but quickly cover over with ice, or become too hot like a greenhouse, or are a dry, desert world and the atmosphere is lost to space.'

Okay already, Mitch reckoned, we get it, exceptional Earth. *Jesus*...next. *Fuck,* he thought, worried about what their *next* might be. He'd heard enough about how great their home was. It was pure superlatives overload.

Sean was standing with his NASA companions in the building and he could tell the initial inanities were well underway. '*Oh...get on with it,*' he whispered to himself.. George Teeler of NASA heard him and grinned. They didn't know it, but the serious stuff was about to begin. Sean looked at the panorama laid out before him and thought of Enrico and his famous Paradox. If only he could be here and see it. Everything would be answered. Meaning he wouldn't ask the question because there was no paradox.

Sean gazed at the gathering. He was looking at several different celestial species. Emnene stared at Mitch, his large, ovular eyes boring into him like twin lasers. Mitch knew the time had come. All the welcome bullshit was done - it was *time*, he could tell.

Emnene said to a very quiet crowd who were waiting for the ugly part. 'You are all aware that Earth's climate is changing. It is a natural change, but humanity is making it a lot worse, and a lot faster than it otherwise would be. Your planet will be unable to sustain life above bacteria in seventy years.

Mitch looked straight at Emnene, and shook his head. 'Not-that quick,' Mitch stuttered. He said it more in optimism than anything else. Mitch was sure the timings were wrong, but then he thought, why would Emnene be wrong? He'd hardly be on our doorstep if he was wrong. Just looking at Emnene, Mitch was a believer. Maybe it was because he looked like he did, or perhaps it was because Mitch knew he wouldn't be here unless it was way worse than he and humanity generally, thought.

'Seventy years,' Emnene said firmly. Based on the carbon and oxides you are releasing into the atmosphere - the planet will be in freefall in three years. Which means nothing terrestrial can save it, the planet will have its own ruinous inertia. Doesn't matter what humans do, the planet's atmosphere will be terminal for your type of life.

Mitch and Josh, and the rest of the humans were entirely speechless, it was hard to question someone who was so sure of his facts. Not to mention how he looked, which no doubt added to it. Zamindar and Char were silent and looked downward. That in itself was enough.

'Your world is dying – and quickly. You have to fix the atmosphere expeditiously.' Emnene looked deeply and seriously at each of them again, intensely, one by one. 'The planet will not continue to be habitable if humanity continues with these *targets*.' He might as well have spat that word at them. Emnene was severely unimpressed. The feeling among the group on the ground was that he was a being to be respected. And kept at a reasonable distance. He and his kind were dangerous, no doubt about it.

'To deal with the damage you have caused,' he said, 'it is critical to your planet, that you adjust your energy production, from greenhouse-gas producing to *non*-greenhouse-gas producing.' Total silence ensued. All the humans in the crowd looked at each other as though this was brand new to them. 'You must become free of gasses which requires a major structural and technological change.' Emnene stopped talking to allow them to digest his words. Then he continued to talk, still not issuing any demands.

'Zamindar has advised me you now have the technology and the ability to do this, so it is mainly the human component that still eludes you. We are frankly, a little disappointed that you have not implemented the tech already.' The creature eyed them with a questioning gaze that made them all feel rather guilty. The humans still looked from one to the other, wondering who was responsible, grimacing and lip biting. Mitch gazed around and saw nearly everyone with an accusatory face mingled with fear and trepidation. Mouths were pulled and pinched but eyes were wide and some shut. Mitch was sweating and rocking slightly on his heels.

'*Jesus Christ,*' Mitch whispered to Jessy. Where does the fool get "mainly" from, for *fuck's sake?*' The human element was probably, *no* it was definitely, the most problematic part, way harder to get right than the technical part. Having a contented population made technical work so very much easier. All of them realised that most of humanity would fall way short of "contented".

And then there was the use of "disappointed". Who the hell did this lot think they were? They weren't *One,* they hadn't been around since day dot and we didn't owe them a damn thing. Mitch was pretty sure they didn't create shit. They did claim to have saved numerous worlds from civilisations that, they maintain, *they said,* would have died because their planet would have reared up and killed them. So, according to them, the Bantha incredibly, were *savers of worlds.* Very ironic indeed.

They provided a service to the Universe, the opposite of Oppenheimer as it were, at least, that's how they saw it. That's how they justified it anyway. It didn't matter what they said, Mitch thought they were murderers of the highest, *worst* order. The Bantha could spin it anyway they liked, the simple fact of them being genocidal murderers was never far away from his thinking. He reckoned they acted far too quickly. But he wasn't *entirely* sure.

They quite clearly knew more than humans did. Saving Goldilocks planets was important, no doubt about it, but surely, there was a better, nicer way to go about it – so planet *and* civilisation survived intact. The Bantha clearly had a massive bias toward the planet.

Emnene continued, taking time to centre himself to address them all. *Here it comes,* everyone thought. 'So...you have to replace your current system of energy production, to a system that produces no carbon and no nitrous oxide, in short one that adds no greenhouse gasses to the atmosphere *at all.* And with that, would come zero-carbon electricity to run batteries in electric cars and aeroplanes. Burning fossil fuels has to cease. Pumping carbon dioxide and other poisons into the atmosphere *must stop*.'

Emnene looked closely and intently at each of them, making certain they understood the warning and its meaning. His face, ugly though it was, conveyed a picture of soberness and intimidation.

'*Oh der*,' Jessy said, quietly, opening her mouth to say more but sure it wouldn't help, so she closed it again. She felt like she was back in High School. being lectured to by a superior race. *C'est la vie*. It was very expected.

Mitch pinched her above the waist to encourage her to shut it. The explicit warning was coming, he knew. Mitch could see it in Emnene's eyes. The Bantha was breathing in deeper spurts. Mitch braced himself.

Josh had similar sentiments to Jessy. "Stop burning fossil fuels". 'Really? You don't *say*? That's what we've been trying to do. Doesn't chuckles over there know that? Surely, he does.' Josh stared at him with deadly concentration. If he didn't know it, *fuck him* and the rest of his race, he thought, who gives them the right to be judge, jury and executioner?

Jessy was well aware that humans needed to try harder to make it easier for their planet. It was great to have rovers running around on Mars and air ships on Venus, even probes well beyond Neptune, but what about good old Earth? It needed to be prioritised. She guessed that's why the Bantha were here. To do it for us – because we couldn't or wouldn't.

Emnene ignored them all. 'There is always an excuse *not* to do it. It is always sometime in the future, but the time for excuses and justifications has passed. *It is time to do*.' Emnene glared at them all in turn. He was definitely a humanoid, but he was very different from humans indeed. Josh looked at him and gulped heavily. *Ugly fucker*, he thought.

Surely, evolution wouldn't come up with those ugly outer cranial veins. Perhaps they were the result of an artificial add-on? *Yikes*, despite being humanoid, he was still the stuff of nightmares. Or maybe there was something wrong with this particular alien. He realised Zamindar would know the answer. Josh as a human could only guess.

Having gawked long and hard at each of the humans and the rest of them, the alien was satisfied they were all with him and understood what he was saying. 'Your world will be dead within one century. 'It will be entirely irredeemable in twenty years. Sea-levels will engulf your cities and the air and weather itself will turn on you.' He stared straight at Josh, walking broadly in a circle, moving stiffly. 'Weather will be totally unpredictable and wild, seasons will be gone, humanity will die, as will Earth's atmosphere in the short term, from fires, floods and disease. No animal life will remain. Planets like your Earth are incredibly rare and must be preserved. Life is quite common, but planets that can sustain long-term evolution and rear an intelligent species, like I said, *not so. Earth must be saved,* there is still time for the planet to bring another species to intelligence before the Sun expires. Maybe the new intelligence will be ape-derived and be like humans, or maybe they'll come from cows or possums or something,' he said. 'It's impossible to predict. Perhaps, although unlikely, nothing would eventuate. Time will tell,' Emnene said, giving a curt nod to everyone. In other words, if nothing new arose, that would be fine.

To Mitch, that made no sense at all. He wondered where the logic was to that? Mitch was confused, nothing odd there, but if we're gone, so will all the animals be gone. So, where does evolution come from? He guessed that was their problem. That means this is the penalty for fucking the atmosphere up – it is nothing to do with a precious world or bringing another species to intelligence via evolution. It is vengeance – pure and simple. That was Mitch's take, anyway. That put this whole thing in a different light.

Emnene looked around himself, at the sky and the landscape beyond AASSA. Josh twisted his neck and moved his head up. 'So, we're just taking up room, polluting the planet, and will soon be dead because of it,' he said, pressing his lips together, feeling deeply offended. 'What about all our achievements? The scientific, medical, artistic, all the exploration. Everything we've accomplished. Surely, it wasn't all for nought - *Surely*?' Josh's voice was breaking on the last few words.

'*No...no, it won't be, definitely not,*' Mitch said, looking at Josh full in the eye, to instill confidence.

'Sure dad, *whatever.*' Josh was less than positive about their chances. 'Ain't gonna happen,' he said, throwing an arm in the air aggressively. Josh knew that if we got passed this nightmare, we and everyone else should spend the rest of eternity doing hail-marys.

Emnene hadn't made an explicit threat yet. Seemed it was about to happen though. For a long moment, Emnene stared at Mitch and said nothing.

'Humanity has one year to stop sending carbon and other greenhouse gasses into the atmosphere, so the planet can start to replenish itself. Or...we will take control of the planet, away from humans. One year – if it hasn't happened by then, humanity will be eradicated from this planet.'

Mitch watched and listened. They were unsurprised by the words, but still surprised. '*Holy shit...one fucking year*...then...removed like a common virus,' Jessy screeched, feeling Mitch's nudge, telling her to be quiet. She knew it was coming but that didn't reduce the impact of the words being so boldly and unashamedly spoken. Mitch closed his mouth and put a finger over it, making his eyes almost fall out with the pressure.

The words were spoken by the Bantha as expected, but to hear them spoken out loud, in anger as it were, was truly dreadful. The Bantha had made their demand. Earth was now on formal notice. A situation they'd never, ever foreseen. The worst had happened, right there in front of them...*live.*

Jessy swallowed hard, lifted her chin, and met Mitch's gaze squarely. 'You know were done, right?'

'Doesn't have to be like that,' he said, meeting her gaze. 'With those two helping,' Mitch pointed to the two Jarithians, 'who knows what's possible? It's the human element that will be the hardest. In the short-term we need to build a brand-new fusion economy.'

'*Holy Jesus fuck,*' she could only imagine the torture and the torment. '...we have to try, I guess,' Jessy said, giving Mitch a tentative smile. 'It's not like we can say "no" or even defend ourselves. Like you said, we can't do jack in space. We just have to try and make the deadline.. What else we can do?'

'Fusion energy has been promised since the 60's and it's no bloody closer. We sort of have the technology Jessy, but the reactors are huge and massively expensive and let's be honest, don't really work as they're supposed to. They use more energy than they create, *for Christ's sake,* we haven't even reached breakeven yet or anything approaching it.' Mitch was shaking his head as he spoke. 'The Jarithians will assist with all that. It's doable, but it will be very difficult indeed. Humanity needs a push, and this is it. It's a gargantuan push...do it, or *all die. Jesus*...who would've thought. A threat by an extraterrestrial species. It's the colossal stimulus we needed. First, it was Fermi's Paradox and the great silence, where we couldn't find anyone in the Great Wide Open to now, where we are being threatened with extinction by an extra-terrestrial species. A new paradox has been born. And this one has sharp teeth. Out with the old in with the new, as it were.'

Josh was listening to the to's and fro's between Mitch and Jessy only a few feet in front of him. 'Comply or die.' He liked the phrase, it summed things up nicely. Be part of the solution, not part of the problem, *never* had more meaning, Josh reckoned. It was unquestionably time to act.

*   *   *

Construction and development, and infrastructure upgrades were all halted, capital and where appropriate, labour, would be diverted to the gargantuan fusion project. China had done it - they knew the only way was to go early and go hard. The US had followed. There were thirty-nine other countries with bills or amendments ready to go. On Earth, it was finally happening albeit a little forced.

10

The Sphere

"People think of education as something that they can finish."
— Isaac Asimov

From Moscow to Melbourne, Vancouver to Beijing and Rome, Earth seemed to be burning. Most didn't believe the threat was real. Even despite what was said and what the media said and how many times they said it. It was now two months since the announcement, and millions were sick and tired of not working, relying on government money, power breakdowns, scheduled turnoffs and evictions by banks, lenders and landlords. Boredom was a major problem with the world generally, and in China in particular.

For many, mainly the unemployed, made so as a result of the coal industry ceasing to be, it was a nightmare, especially for China where lines of the unemployed who were "unsuited to redeployment" snaked along streets from social-security offices. It was a day-to-day battle for a large part of the population just to eat. Money was available to the masses, but it required a lot of paperwork, and waiting. The demand for social security was enormous. Frustration in the community was growing. They needed something to fill in the time, and unfortunately, they found it.

Some of the former coal industry workers were re-employed in the fusion industry or state-sector, but many were totally unskilled and unsuitable for either. There was precious little time for upskilling. Even though the unemployed still received similar money to their paid employment, they were a big problem, worldwide. They had too much time on their hands.

Those that had been forced out of the coal industry or mines and were considered unsuitable for redeployment numbered in the millions. China and Russia had most of them and there especially, they were a problem. Every unskilled job had a thousand applications. A new population of long term unemployed were born. They felt marginalised and hadn't had jobs in yonks.
A lot of them were on the streets – and they weren't happy. They were told to get a job in another industry, but most couldn't due to a lack of skills and the sheer demand for jobs. Many were prepared to start at the bottom and hopefully, work their way upward but most times, that wasn't enough.

But the jobs, even if they got them, didn't pay enough to support their families. They were still reliant on some government money. The problem wasn't solved. Everywhere you cared to look there were problems. Most of them didn't want money for nothing from some third party, especially a government. But without it, they couldn't pay their debts – their house and car would be gone, and probably their spouse with it. Most of the people had to accept social-security payments.

Gangs were protesting in ways the world had never seen before. Water cannons and even live rounds were no match for these uprisings, they made the recent Hong Kong Government uprisings look like a neighborhood squabble. Beijing and Shanghai, Guangzhou and Wuhan, and fifty other regional towns were ablaze, and that was just in China. Government and UN security forces and the police had killed many people, making the unrest in China uglier, and the conflict tougher, and the people angrier, if that was possible, and the riots last way longer.

Many were happy with the changes across the globe, they wanted fusion and *definitely* no carbon, they'd tired of dirty air and wild weather. They wanted electric cars, electric planes and everything that came with it. They wanted a clean planet with clean atmosphere but at what cost? Most of the people though, just wanted stable power that they could rely on, be it fusion, coal sourced or whatever. They honestly didn't care.

Most people thought clean energy was a great idea, and they were even prepared to undergo some hardship for it, but they didn't fully understand why it was so rushed and why humanity was being treated like this. At the moment, the entire globe was covered by a sea of negativity, unrest, anger and unemployment.

The horrors all over the world, seemingly centred in China. Many smaller countries had simply imploded – Dominica, Bahrain, Grenada and the entirety of the Marshall Islands, went from churches-full to churches-empty, and the government and nearly all its people emigrating to Europe, the UK or the US. Churches were now ghostly empty - and not just in small countries.
The population of most countries, big or small, were bewildered and recent revelations took people out of churches the world over. People questioned who they were praying to. The Fermi Paradox was dead, erased by *One*, an advanced species that engineered the entire Universe, and the Bantha didn't like how humans were treating the Earth. It really had been quite the week for people on this beautiful blue planet that not long ago, was isolated in space.

If you were lucky and saw the nightly news, (it had closed down on several channels) it seemed everything on Earth was winding down. Civilisation was breaking down. China was a mess, civil war and wild fires had broken out and no-one was winning. The rest of the country was flooded. Huge and horrendous death counts were everywhere to be seen. People were shot or otherwise slaughtered on the streets, and sometimes in their homes.

That brought Jessy back to '*them...the Bantha*'. They were at the root of all this. Who the fuck did they think they were? Making such dire demands on us. She knew the answers to that but refused to concede it.

She thought deeply about the Bantha and their possible mind-set. That they'd think of the population on Earth as *weeds*. That's how they'd see us – as something noxious that needed to be exterminated - that took up unnecessary room, added nothing, and poisoned the environment. Once removed, something useful and planned, could grow in its place. Jessy was aghast at how accurate that analogy actually appeared to be.

Although a younger race, the Bantha were much more advanced than humanity technically, and were able to wage species-killing war from space. Humans and Earth would be totally unable to match them. So, they had to go for broke and try to make the deadline. But it was way more complex than it seemed. Apparently, this planet was only loaned to us – and we hadn't been looking after it, to the Bantha's standard.

`The Bantha were from a barred spiral galaxy slightly bigger than the Milky Way Galaxy, but had little trouble getting to Earth-space with their "shortening" technology which essentially made space disappear in front of them and appear behind them. It allowed them to go a lot faster than light by shortening space between two objects rather than travelling through geodesic space which had a rather annoying speed limit.

Humanity was slightly behind the deadline's "carbon schedule" in converting all their energy stocks to fusion. Davtep and Cranreb were currently in Shidongkou along with ex-employees of Sparc, and fifteen from Lockheed Martin, now employees of the new global consortium. Small, self-sustainable fusion reactors were being produced which produced a constant 300 megawatts of power, and when all this was sorted, aeroplanes and ultimately cars would carry a specialised version.

The plasma controller for the new units was very different from the old ones, as was their entire internal and external structure. Instead of the normal torus, the isotopic fuel, deuterium and helium-3, still in magnetic confinement, was thrust together and in conditions of ultra-high temperature, atoms fused into regular Helium and lots of energy. Then, the reactor created steam which turned a turbine and *wallah*, electricity. No carbon whatsoever – just steam.

What Earth didn't know was its ability to duplicate it everywhere, the whole lot was needed inside a year. There was so much to do. Engineering, technicality and economy. They had tonnes of helium-3 from lunar mining and deuterium was plentiful in seawater, so fuel wasn't a problem.

If it was five years until the reactors were needed, they would all be reasonably confident they could do it. But one year – it would be line-ball for all countries to be on-line. If they weren't dealing with the Bantha, they'd ask for more time. Their response, and Mitch and all of them knew it, would be to refer humans to the demand and. the answer would be a fat "no".

They could only make sure that everyone working on the project directly knew in detail about the deadline, what would occur if it wasn't observed, and then have everyone work as fast as they humanly could. The rest would take care of itself. If they were slightly short, would the Bantha allow them some wriggle-room? Or would they make good on their promise, and still exterminate all humans? Mitch supposed that we would work as fast as we could, and what would be, would be. We couldn't do it any other way.

It was a horribly qualitative future for the planet. Mitch doubted *close* would be good enough for the Bantha. One hundred percent would do it and it would be the only number acceptable to them. Jessy reviled the word "deadline". What should they do if they couldn't make it?. Earth didn't have the ability to do squat in space, so a pre-emptive strike was out of the question. She wished they could crush the Bantha, but humanity had no way to do it.

Jessy wondered if the Bantha had received a Sphere? She knew not everyone did. Maybe we should give them ours so they could see how we got to be what we are. They could see how much work was put into creating us. Zamindar could go with it, if they needed an explanation, which they probably wouldn't. Humanity, they knew, were really grabbing at straws here – but it sounded logical enough. Jessy reckoned they had to try everything.

He'd have to *want* to go though, Jessy knew, none of them could demand it. Zamindar would have to self-compel. They could only ask. He would want to go though, she felt sure.

Jessy ambled over to Zamindar and Char. 'What if we gave them the Sphere,' she said, shooting him a questioning gaze. Jessy stared at him but faltered part way through. Now, she was staring at the floor. Jessy was anything but a good actor. She was shaking and overwhelmed by the whole scenario.

'I had already thought of that Jessy,' Zamindar said. 'In any event, the Sphere may help you directly but it is unlikely to be successful.'

'*Jesus*, thanks for the vote of confidence,' Jessy said, 'but we need to at least try – I can't think of much else.' Expecting a nod from Zamindar was way too much. She gazed at Zamindar who didn't change his blank expression.

Emnene got back in the fat end of the whistle by stepping straight through and into it from ground level. Moments later, it shot straight up, then went at 45 degrees to the ship then invisible...and *gone*. The vessel made the noise of an electric vehicle, and moved as if gravity was entirely absent.

Jessy and Mitch both looked at Zamindar, then glanced at each other, pondering what the Virijian had just said and looking mildly surprised. 'What did he mean, "the Sphere may help you"? What in God's name was he talking about?' Jessy said quietly. Zamindar glanced at her, then stared at her. Hadn't it already given up everything, now it was just so much metal...right?

'How can it help us then?' Mitch asked, looking quizzically at Zamindar. 'You mean it has more information to offer?'

'No.' Zamindar toned. 'There is nothing more on offer regarding time on Earth. But it may be to humanity's benefit if they read it.'

Mitch glanced at Jessy and tried again to smile. They could both tell that the Virijian wouldn't say any more unless he was directly asked. Zamindar was talking rapidly to Char. He was silent and stayed silent to everyone but Char. Without him spelling it out for them, they had no hope of working it out. He assumed he was referring to the work put in by One to render humans ripe for evolution to kick-in. Was there anything else in the Sphere? If it benefitted humanity, it needed to happen.

'How do we get the Sphere to them?' Mitch asked of Zamindar. Mitch had no idea whatsoever. It sounded totally impossible in the human world. He couldn't even guess what the answer might be to that one. Mitch thought there probably wasn't an answer. The planet Bantha was so fucking far away. It would take years and decades in the human world. Their home galaxy was slightly more than fifty million light years away. Space was hard and getting *harder* for humans. Everything was so far away, Mitch groaned. How in God's name do we span those distances, he wondered?

'We do not have to take it to them, we ask them, using "QR", Quantum Reasoning, to pick it up,' Zamindar said, 'using brain to brain communication. We are all born with it - it transcends distance and the speed of light, and your Relativity. It involves entanglement and nonlocality in a process you are not familiar with. It will be simple because the message is straightforward. We will retrieve the Sphere and place it in orbit around Earth. Then the Bantha can collect it from there using their shortening,' Zamindar toned.

'Why didn't we just put it in Emnene's ship and do it that way?' Mitch asked, looking quizzically at Zamindar who looked non-plussed. 'It would've been so bloody easy.'

Zamindar glanced at Mitch and toned. 'Their craft uses "shortening" technology and their ship needs to be of very specific mass. The Sphere, although light by human standards, needs to be counted. Otherwise "shortening" can't be used, so the trip home would be a very long one indeed.'

Also, the Virijian admitted to having thoughts about Emnene that were..., that was all he was prepared to say, *nothing*. Zamindar continued. 'We will contact a Bantha we have dealt with before, that we know will do as we ask - not personally, but he will properly oversee the venture.

Josh peered at the Virijian and said, 'let's go then.' He really meant, c'mon *let's get it over with*. Josh hated flying, in the atmosphere, or in space. Josh sort of wanted to do more of it to get used to it, so he didn't hate it so much – mainly for his dad. Flying in whatever medium was second nature for Mitch. How anyone could love flying so much was a mystery to him.

Zamindar glanced at Mitch who shrugged his shoulders. The Sphere had been retrieved so they were essentially ready, they just needed to get it aboard the ship. *One* had already come and gone so they didn't really need it.

It was okay by Mitch. Josh could go, he was an adult and could make his own decisions. So, if he wanted to go, so be it. The Sphere was loaded into the Satellite Dock of a Lunar Express aircraft. After making the requisite pre-flight checks, it winged away, destination, high geocentric orbit around Earth.

'I will place the craft on auto-pilot once we reach orbit and 27,000 kilometres per hour velocity. Then I will push the Sphere into space from the air lock,' Zamindar said.

'*Jesus, why am I here then*? As ballast?' Josh asked, feeling useless as he gawked around the craft to see if anything else was aboard. If he couldn't actually help, why was he here? He was tired of seeing plenty but doing nothing.

Zamindar eyed him without interest. 'What do you suggest Josh?' He asked, seeing that Josh was seething. He drew his lips into a tight scowl, eyeing the Virijian as he organised the controls. Josh knew what had to be done.

'You stay at the controls, *I'll* push the Sphere into space,' Josh said, shaking his head and bugging his eyes out.

'Okay,' Zamindar toned. 'But I promised Mitch I'd look after you. I was undertaking a minimum risk manoeuvre. You are quite valuable, apparently.'

'*Well, don't.*' Josh yelled, 'it's not necessary ...I am *not* a kid or require special treatment. Mitch treats me like a baby if I let him - *and I don't like it.*'

'Noted,' Zamindar said. He looked back at the control panel and quite deliberately, not at Josh, or anywhere near him. He left him to himself.

Josh started with the cooling garment, then proceeded to fit the suit and skull cap and then helmet. He was now ready for hot and cold vacuum. A few steps took him to the airlock and he was ready. So was the Sphere.

Zamindar took the craft to high orbit by leaning on the MPS, hit the required speed and Josh evacuated the atmosphere in the airlock until he was languishing in total vacuum.

'Here goes nothing,' Josh whispered to no one but himself. Even in the weight-reduced conditions of space, the Sphere was hard to move, mainly because of its size and shape, not its mass. It was light as a feather but quite large.

The space-plane was for passengers, not commercial apps like satellite catching. In those circumstances, they would have used the payload release system to put the Sphere into orbit. Of course, they'd have to wait for availability - which they couldn't do. This had to happen right now. With a lot of jimmying and pushing, Josh moved the Sphere into space where it took up its correct HEO. It was now orbiting Earth much like its original orbit around Titan. It would stay stable for a long time in that position. Josh watched the Sphere move away from the craft through the small windows of the airlock, which were now closed and locked. Pressurisation was occurring and Josh flipped open the lock on his helmet when he saw the green light come on.

Punching back through the atmosphere at 400 degrees and nearly 30,000 kilometres per hour Josh watched Zamindar closely who had both paws on the directional controls. 'When will they pick it up?' Josh said tentatively. How long will they take, he wondered? Josh knew the question was very likely to be unanswerable, but he asked it anyway. It made him feel better.

Very soon,' Zamindar said, 'I do not exactly know when, but it should not be long.' He stared at Josh uncomprehendingly, like a human looking at an abstract painting on a blank wall somewhere. Josh strapped in for landing. Zamindar pulled up the nose of the craft and finally deployed the wheels for landing. As usual, he locked the wheels in really late, almost leading Josh to believe they'd be landing belly first. He hated *normal* flying, let alone flying in and from space. Both were bone chilling.

*   *   *

'How will we know if they have it...and how do we know if they can read the damn thing?' Josh asked, peering at Zamindar fixedly. This really seemed like a waste of time, but he conceded, there was little else they could do. Josh noticed his heart was drumming at a huge rate, so he tried to think of something else to cool himself down.

'Yes, on both counts, I will know when they have read it,' Zamindar said.

How do you know?' *For fuck's sake,* Josh whispered to himself, finally having his heart under control. He repeated the question and stared at Zamindar then glanced at his mum. 'Does he know everything?' The query rattling around in his head was steeply rhetorical. He really did want to know though, but *just* the answer, not all the leadup and the justification crap. *Just the fucking answer.* He felt like screaming that to the Virijian.

Zamindar looked squarely at Mitch, completely ignoring Josh, and toned. 'There is something in the Sphere which was there when we first read it, but we decided not to divulge it to you, but it may now prove useful to you.'

He looked remarkably nervous, making short, jerky movements. Did he feel emotion afterall? Maybe on the inside - who fucking knew?

'What the hell is it ? Josh gawked at the Virijian, blinking, then focussed his gaze. He already disliked the Sphere, it had way too much to say.

'When we get the Sphere back from the Bantha, I will tell you,' Zamindar toned, sounding oddly reticent.

'In other words, just shut up and wait,' Josh gawked at Zamindar and realised quickly that indeed that was exactly what be.

*   *   *

'It's time Josh, the Sphere has been read and digested by the Bantha, all that remains is for us to pick it back up,' Zamindar toned while unfolding his legs. 'They understand it was originally found orbiting Titan and they have read your story as it laid it out. The Bantha found it interesting but it failed to have the desired effect. Nothing will exceed the value of the planet. The Bantha are entirely tunnel-visioned when it comes to habitable planets that promote evolution – like Earth.

The space-plane was fairly much ready to take off and regain ownership of the Sphere. It had been fully refuelled and it took off for high Earth orbit that was needed - to re-capture the Sphere.

They essentially did in reverse what they did before. Josh, tethered to the spacecraft, breathing almost pure oxygen in his fan-driven suit, pushed the Sphere into the airlock of *Lunar 4* easily. Landing quickly, its cargo was on Earth, and ready to be inspected, in need.

Zamindar grabbed the Sphere with a minimum of effort and placed it on the concrete at AASSA, much like a weightlifter. It must have weighed 100 kg here on Earth, much lighter than if we built it. To look so new and be so old, despite extremely harsh conditions, it must be made of something incredibly exotic. An alloy presumably. Mitch couldn't help wondering what he'd see if a piece was stuck under an SEM. Even Zamindar couldn't assist on composition. The Virijian placed his pendulous digits in the slits that sat within the casing of the Sphere. A bit like a gargantuan bowling ball.

Why he was doing it, none of the humans had any idea, but it opened along a line that divided the east and west hemispheres which was accompanied by a blast of really smelly gas. 'Ammonium polyphosphate, a fire retardant,' Zamindar said. The humans assumed he wyould seek out the part that might help the humans. It might melt or detonate, Mitch supposed, but catch fire? Not bloody likely. There was nothing to catch fire, *was there*? Not in what they saw – it was all metal. Mitch waited for Zamindar to contradict him, but be didn't. There was only silence, which was odd. He normally loved to correct errors – which probably meant he was right.

Zamindar made them all jump by toning, without the normal static warning. He just started, completely out of the blue. '*It seems* that *One* has made sure you were always in a position to defend yourselves. Having got your species going from an evolutionary standpoint, they wanted you to be able to guard yourself in need. They knew only too well it had already grown to be a dangerous, hazard-filled universe.' Zamindar stood coolly, looking down on everybody as he toned. He knew all this was brand new to the humans, but apparently it was critical to our long-term survival.

'There were quasars, supernovae, gamma ray busts, rogue black holes, but mainly there were hyper-aggressive civilizations that could potentially represent a rather inglorious end to all their work with humans. They understood your capacity for curiosity, which meant, venturing into space but not building any basis for protection for a long time. There is an extensive dialogue which comes with the weapon, around it not being used as an implement of war.' He paused and stared quite deliberately at Mitch. Zamindar was satisfied, everyone who might touch the weapon, would pass the test. 'This is never to be used on Earth, or against humans...*ever*.' Zamindar stared firstly at Mitch, then the rest of them. Mitch and in fact everyone wondered what it could be. Something very unpleasant and powerful obviously.

The Virijian hadn't finished yet. 'It is never to be used by an aggressor, or used offensively in any way. It may never be reverse engineered or copied and will always remain the property of the Sphere finder.'

'*Christ,*' Mitch thought. 'What the *fuck* is it? Zamindar raised his chin with a cool stare in Mitch's direction. 'These were *One's* specific directions,' He toned. The Virijian had clearly finished now. Zamindar folded himself up and sat on the ground. He'd conveyed what he wished to.

Josh gazed at his dad. Everyone joined him. All eyes were on Mitch, waiting for Zamindar to say it.

'Ooo-kay, lay it on me,' Mitch said loudly, his face becoming a mix of sincerity and "oh fuck". *What the hell is it?*' He asked. 'Is it a bomb and how does that help us...a missile perhaps.' Now he was getting warmer.

'Come closer Mitch,' Zamindar said, flourishing an arm. 'I am only able to show you.' He was confronted by a diagram that made little sense, narrated with strange figures and strokes that looked like hieroglyphics. It was a bunch of meaningless bullshit as far as Mitch was concerned. That Zamindar could make any sense from it was quite incredible. Zamindar said, "Knot physics" was the right approach, apparently.

'I need to show these plans to an engineer.' They'd understand it more, but it probably still won't mean a lot,' Mitch said, peering closely at Zamindar, for what he didn't know. He got exactly what he expected - *nothing. Zilch*. Then Mitch realised there were no engineers familiar with this stuff, but some engineers, a very few, were used to some pretty exotic stuff. Perhaps they could help. Thankfully, Zamindar would help with un-encryption.

'I can show your people how to build it from these directions and how to extract it from your LHC - you will need sixty grams of anti-matter, in this case anti-iron, to fill it, using the processes detailed in the Sphere. They can be produced and trapped at the LHC in the LHCb detector and fed directly into the weapon's magnetic confinement tube using a second mag field.' Zamindar gazed at Mitch from a foot away. 'It must be done carefully,' he finished on.

It was clear to Mitch that it was a rifle of sorts and Zamindar understood its destructive potential well. 'It delivers ten blasts, each of which is equivalent to a two-megaton explosion, more than enough to destroy an alien vessel, Zamindar said. 'I am able to assist if my only role is decryption or showing you how to use information *One* have supplied to you Mitch.'

The humans were lucky because the construction of all the elements of the gun did not involve developing any new technologies. They already had a full knowledge and use of quantum mechanics. Had a new technology been required, like 4D or something based on super-symmetry or unified field theory, building the weapon would either have been impossible, or taken a lot longer.

Zamindar toned 'But the rest is up to you. I am unable to help you further if we are to remain compliant with the Document of Peace. The information provided should be enough, to build a working machine,' he finished on, 'and you currently have the technology to build it. The explosive blast if properly directed, will be more than sufficient.'

Mitch gazed restlessly at Jessy. 'So...no pressure to the schmuck behind the gun,' Mitch piped, now gazing straight at Zamindar, assuming it would be him, *Mitch*, who would be doing the shooting. Josh also peered at the Virijian and was wondering where his responsibilities lay. Would he be prepared to break the NDA if it truly meant life and death for humanity? Josh blew out his cheeks and exhaled loudly, gawking at Mitch who shook his head. None of them knew the answer to that one.

It was obvious that Mitch knew what Zamindar was thinking and didn't want the Virijian pushed. Zamindar read what they were thinking. He paid close attention to both of them. There was nowhere to hide with the Virijian.

'I will not break the agreement,' Zamindar stated, appearing very serious indeed. He knew very well was at stake. He wouldn't break it for anyone, no matter what the circumstances.

'*Oo-kaaaay...there you go then, case closed,*' Josh said grinning at Mitch, 'case closed,' he repeated quietly, turning on his heels and walking off.

'*Whatever...*I think we will need to use this machine to defend ourselves,' Mitch said. 'Because I know we will not make the deadline.' Mitch's face darkened with emotional pain and he stepped back and looked down. He was contemplating the deadline, it always bordered on the ridiculous and it was proving to be exactly that. A lot of the world was still without its new form of "greenhouse-free" energy. It was on the way but wouldn't be where it had to be by the deadline. Humans had left it too late. The deadline was too tight.

China still had several coal-fired power stations running in Xi'an as did Russia in the Ural's and some of the smaller countries around the world. Their energy starved populations demanded energy and they really didn't care from what source it came, as long as the fucking lights went on when the switch was pressed. They wanted power, *period*. China produced as much carbon as the rest of the countries combined and its appetite for coal was voracious, so this was a wise starting point to transition. They'd gotten about half-way so far. Everything above or near Tibet hadn't been touched. Coal-based electricity still dominated their farms. The area was largely rural and predominantly flat but consumed a lot of power. The Chinese "rust-belt" was next on the list to be "fusionised". China's rapid development as a country would be affected by installing fusion energy, but only in the short term.

Hong Kong and the Middle East were complete write-offs. Rioting was everywhere and they were still burning mostly coal. China thought it could control its democratic off-shoot. It was wrong. Their people were as strong and heavily armed as the military. So, it was a stalemate on the streets.

North Korea simply refused to let inspectors or the transition-team enter, under threats of death. The transition team was stopped at the border and threatened with machine-gunning if they proceeded any further. Brazil was half coal as was Iceland and most of the Slavic countries around Russia were all coal. Even West Virginia, Kentucky and Wyoming in the US were still mostly coal. Africa was a real problem, South Africa, Tanzania, Mozambique, it seemed the poorer the country, the harder it was, and it was *nothing* at all to do with economy. The world had a *long* way to go before it could claim anything.

They all had plans to transition, but most planes were still gas-guzzlers, even though over 3,000 airlines had converted. Most used new batteries in existing planes and only changed over aircraft gradually which was fine. The new planes were made-to-order fusion aircraft that had their own reactors in the nose-cone and underneath the pilots.

Agricultural machinery was a problem. They were previously scheduled to transition to fusion-based batteries but many in the rural sector actively resisted it, despite several old harvesters being crushed with the guarantee of consequences for all if the change wasn't immediate. If farmers couldn't pay for new electrical equipment, all they needed to do was provide a few details and it would be delivered to them. Still, uptake was slow. Despite demands and threats, harvesting food would still deliver carbon into the atmosphere for a time yet.

There were still massive riots worldwide – violent protests by thousands of people who were unemployed - been made redundant, continuing to suffer frequent blackouts, brownouts and general interruptions to the local power grid.

Governments were hoping that most of the riots would have run their course by now. But they were still going strong. Getting stronger even. Petrol driven cars weren't allowed on roads and if found, were crushed, adding to the angst of the general population because there were plenty of crushings, some televised, showing the owner crying. Earth had done a lot to conform to the demand, but there was still a hell of a lot more left to do. And the deadline loomed. Now, it wasn't long.

Earth would come close, but there was no way it would be in the demanded state when the deadline ticked over. Mitch could see that and acknowledged it. No way China and Africa would be ready. Or even Australia and New Zealand. Most of the developed world would be close, but not quite there. That likely wouldn't satisfy the Bantha, given their previous behaviour, which Mitch and Josh were unfortunately intimately acquainted with.

Mitch looked at Zamindar, then at Josh, lastly, he glanced at Jessy. 'Please take us, you as well,' he pointed to Zamindar, 'to Geneva, to the, Large Hadron Collider. Mitch gazed at Josh and smiled, shrugging his shoulders. It's time to get this thing really going.

Josh understood, he was smiling back, and was happy not to go. Anti-matter was a terrifying substance. Zamindar carried the cartridge that was to have its magnetic coils filled with the required antimatter. The cartridge was held tight inside a red suitcase. Customs had already been alerted to the substance by Washington. What it would look like under X-rays was anyone's guess. Customs had been ordered by a higher authority to let it go through.

For the weapon, they needed what the LHCb could produce, to make the damned thing operative. To give humanity some defence against the Bantha. They wouldn't make the deadline, that was clear, and they wouldn't just sit idly by while the Bantha destroyed humanity. They saw it as their duty to defend the planet and humanity from extreme threats such as the Bantha posed. "The duty" as it were, all emanated from Mitch. He steadfastly refused to concede to this race of murderers.

Jessy was initially sure that if we explained our position to the Bantha, they'd understand. Mitch had repeatedly told her what they were like, which was clearly very tunnel-visioned and determined, and explained what they did to Gaznoy's planet, even though they were very close to a complete energy-base change - a lot closer than humans would be. Jessy now reviled the Bantha. She believed strongly that they represented the devil incarnate.

*   *   *

Landing at Geneva Airport in their own private plane, they had about an hour before they were due to meet at the LHC. Zamindar walked through the airport with a very large, full hijab covering his head and face which, apart from the laughter of a couple of small children, did the job well. He was virtually invisible from the outside – it was just his two pale arms at the side, which he kept permanently pocketed. The third was hidden behind his shoal. It seemed that no one knew what or who he really was. If they did, he'd be like Moses, parting the masses or at the least having them running in the opposite direction. He looked awfully like a rather large zombie. If his real identity became known, they'd be running in all directions, away from him. Thankfully, his identity remained a secret. He was just another large, covered person.

They had an appointment with the Director-General of the LHC in a few minutes, to talk through what they needed to build the machine. One of POTUS' minions had rung him and told them what he wanted and when he wanted it, and provided the approval, which was actually a demand, to just do it. POTUS was backed by Germany and the UK, both Rishi and Frank-Walter had previously been on the phone about future funding. CERN had wisely said "yes sir" to every one of their requests. Their on-going funding, they were told explicitly, depended on them bending-over backward and doing everything asked, no matter how odd. This was going to try and save the world.

The LHC had the people with the engineering skills and the ability to make the antimatter they required. By producing heaps of very high energy collisions between iron particles, it could be completed. And the engineering and fabrication of the weapon could be completed - but they'd have to put their research on hold for a while. The rest was just a formality, they hoped, peering at the milling crowd. The so-called "Geneve Aeroport" was full to bursting with people from every part of the world.

Zamindar and Mitch met with the Director-General of the LHC, who confirmed they could and would build the device for NASA and AASSA. They'd been given the word to "just do it" by CERN. The LHC was strictly a benign and independent research group, so building such a machine was in contravention of their strictly non-aggression charter. The Head of CERN, and the Director-General of the LHC knew exactly what the machine was going to be used for.

The Operations area of LHC initially said "no" to their advances. This started Zamindar on a rant about saving humanity. It was LHC's charter versus the future of humanity because no one else could make it, so it was them or they were genuinely fucked. The Virijian toned it in a much nicer fashion but the sentiment was the same. He said they must listen to their people at the White House and the governments of Germany and Britain and do what we and they say, unconditionally. No questions asked. Otherwise, the world was destined to be gone. That was enough to get them moving. The approvals were there. *Check with the boss for Christ's sake.*

Mitch and Zamindar were right, it didn't matter how you said it, they were trying to save humanity from obliteration. Apparently, the LHC and CERN still had to make a few calls to make sure they could do it. They already had verbal instructions to do it, they just wanted to make entirely sure, given that it was so very unusual.

11

Weapon

"A pawn is the most important piece on the chessboard—to a pawn."
— Isaac Asimov

'What about the ISS?' Mitch asked, pondering its role in all this and thinking about where they would house the weapon. Afterall, it was already in space. He reckoned they could put it in an Orion craft, but it would be easily visible and how do they explain it being up there? It would look extremely out of place. The Bantha would expect the ISS to be there. Essentially, it was part of Earth's furniture.

'What *about* the ISS?' Josh said, rubbing his chin. 'They've or rather, *it's,* already been agreed that the ISS will house the weapon.' He already knew that – it had been discussed. The device had to be used in a vacuum, so the choice came down to the ISS only. Anything else would stick out like a sore thumb, and probably be taken out first.

They quickly decided, including Jean-Pierre, the head from LHC, that ISS would be the one. He was right next to him. Mitch had to remember that. Hopefully, he wasn't listening and was thinking about something else. Getting something else up there to house the weapon was unwise. Everything about the ISS had to look the same as before, when and if they come close enough to see the enemy.

The weapon had to be pretty much invisible. Nothing was being taken for granted. The eyesight of the Bantha and their tech in this regard was unknown. All we could do was proceed using our own abilities. Guessing theirs was a genuine impossibility.

'Okay Josh, okay - I tend to agree. But what if they decide to take the ISS out before they turn to the surface of Earth. It's a possibility, right?' Mitch said, cocking his head to the side. He knew, everything and anything was a possibility up there. But he asked anyway. Who knows how the Bantha thought.

Zamindar joined Mitch and Josh and said, 'we do not believe they will harm the ISS, remember it will probably be protected by orbital distance.'

'That's a big "probably" Zamindar. It might also be right on top of them, when and if they approach,' Mitch said, his expression growing harder as he spoke. 'Depends solely where it is on its orbit around Earth. Remember, it only takes ninety something minutes to go all the way around the planet.' He may have disagreed with big Virijian, but he knew how amazing he really was.

Zamindar acted as engineer, technician and flight controller on the space platform, having already figured out how to move it adroitly. He was never idle.

'That is true, but unlikely,' Zamindar said. 'Based on probability, it will be hundreds or thousands of kilometres away. It may be on the other side of the Earth and far away. Guessing is fruitless.'

'*Whatever*,' Josh said grimly, 'pigs might fly too,' he mused quietly, 'the first step is building the weapon, the second is transporting it and installing it in the ISS. Let's do that before we consider other possibilities.'

'Said like that, it sounds easy,' Mitch said, looking serious, 'but all of it, every step, is incredibly hard. Outside is a vacuum, remember.'

'The best part is the anti-matter,' Josh said, 'any mixing with matter and I mean *any*, including any hadrons between us and the target, and *poof*.' Josh made an explosive action with his hands. He knew they couldn't use nukes as they would pose a risk to Earth because if they were exploded close to the planet there would be fallout that would affect Earth. So, no nukes. Even pure fusion weapons. They were entirely off the table, in favour of a very dangerous alternative that only produced cosmic rays that would be stopped by the atmosphere. There was no ionizing radiation at all. For the anti-matter they were using, and its method of discharge, cosmic rays would be maintained at a minimum. There would be no fallout that should be a concern to the planet. There should only be a huge anti-matter annihilation, a flux that would destroy any vessel. Earth and its inhabitants would remain fine and life would continue.

The Bantha would not send a second vessel, that's what Zamindar believed quite firmly. They didn't have time to fight an interplanetary war. They'd go to the next on their list. That was good enough for humanity. The Virijian had never been wrong so far.

*   *   *

The weapon was before them and it was amazing and very big, *too big* surely. To Mitch, it looked like a massive rifle, he was assured that the engineers had gotten the scale right. Ames said it was an *exact* replica of the plans - size and everything else included.

It would be up to Mitch and his group, to direct the installation of the weapon into the ISS. It would go into a window opposite the nadir window in the *Destiny* US Laboratory.

Installing a gun on an orbiting body in a vacuum was a very tricky proposal. Correcting the optics of Hubble was a piece of cake by comparison. The anti-matter gun could only be deployed in a fixed direction relative to the vessel which meant the ISS had to tilt to ensure the gun was properly directed.

Russian supply ships, *Soyuz*, were already attached to ISS and with eight of their engines, would provide a quasi-nimble station as long as ISS was turned or yawed along its centre of gravity. If that happened, all was good. If it didn't happen as it was supposed to, ISS might plunge into the atmosphere, break up and burn up.

There were also massive gyroscopes that maintained the orientation of the platform. They could be shifted to tweak the ISS. So, the fact that the weapon was very limited in movement, hopefully wouldn't affect them too much in targeting an object.

Josh peered at the weapon grimly, knowing what its potential for horrible destruction was. *Where the hell* was the anti-matter, he wondered, he couldn't see it? Josh knew it was magnetically confined in there somewhere, but all he could see was the trigger and the gigantic breach. The rest was just a black *something*. It was anti-iron held in a magnetic field, he knew that much, so essentially, they were firing anti-bullets, which sounded crazy, but he knew they carried a *real* punch. They just had to direct them correctly. That small detail would test their technology and their abilities on ISS to the fullest. Of course, it wasn't *their* technology, but that wasn't the point, they'd made it and put it together. Therefore, it was ours.

They would use the same transport, six of the AASSA engineers got the machine in, squeezed between the seats. It wasn't in the airlock this time, it wouldn't fit, now it was in the middle of the space-plane, with some seats removed to get the damn thing in.

On Earth, it took six men to carry it gently, but in space, because everything was so much lighter, two men could do the same job, but they still needed to be very careful indeed. It was locked "off" and the anti-matter was sturdily held in gravitational suspension, but the men and in fact everyone treated it like the gun was on a hair trigger. This type of weaponry did that to people. Doesn't matter how secure it was, it was akin to holding pellets of nitro-glycerine in your hands, except this stuff was way worse.

The four engineers who would mount the weapon in the *Destiny* node on the space-station were already in the ISS. SpaceX had assisted with that from Florida free of charge. Zamindar would pilot the craft carrying the weapon to dock with ISS. Mitch would be his co-pilot. Josh would, in his words, be the grunt. Jessy would stay on Earth with the others.

*   *   *

Several small spurts of gas escaped the craft, initiated by Zamindar, small orbital corrections to align the vessel with the chosen ISS airlock, in this case *Pirs*. The craft started behind the ISS and through a series of burns and U-turns in space, their craft ended up in front of the ISS and burnt away distance and direction to line it up exactly with ISS. Zamindar did it like a twenty-year veteran of space. He seemingly had an innate skill but it was probably just the fact that he was Virijian.

Josh looked behind himself and trembled when he saw the Earth, so fucking far away. Outside was an inky black abyss with stars deep in the background. Sheer emptiness and heights were a problem for Josh. He disliked anything but a firm footing under his feet. Heights and space – *forget it*. He felt it in the pit of his stomach. This was no place for someone with a fear of near everything that wasn't a hard planet under him. Perhaps that was why becoming an astronaut had never seriously crossed his mind, he'd had the interest because of his dad, but lacked the desire. Even commercial flying made him bilious. Being in the air or in space generally, was unnerving indeed.

After several minutes of noiseless shutdown, Zamindar exited the vehicle through the *Pirs* airlock and stood tall next to Mitch and Josh, and seemed impatient to get on with it.

Once they'd stopped, Mitch slapped his knee enthusiastically and exclaimed, '*well...that was a good flight*,' gazing directly at the Virijian. Expecting a pleasantry from Zamindar was a bridge too far, he mused. The Virijian was as stiff and unyielding as ever. Stupidly, he thought it was worth a try. And yet again, he got the result he expected. *Nothing.*

'Always the comic,' Josh said, grinning and staring at the Virijian and glancing at his dad . God, he was so inflexible and stark, he reckoned. They both reckoned. He needed to relax - *a lot*. Josh idly wondered if he'd ever enjoyed a beer, or *anything* alcoholic. Imagining Zamindar as a giggling wreck brought a huge smile to Josh's face. He almost laughed out loud.

The Virijian was watching him with a focus he'd never seen, tilting his head like a dog. Josh's final thought on the subject was to wonder if any of the Virijian worlds possessed alcohol – clouds of it had been found floating freely in the universe, so it was clearly not just an Earth thing. It was naturally occurring and could be used by anyone. Josh stared back at Zamindar, bugging his eyes out and then resuming a more modest stare at the window, almost laughing at the mental image of the Virijian holding a Jacks n' Coke. Zamindar maintained his expressionless stare at Josh, very unimpressed.

Three ESA engineers who had come to the ISS previously, floated past them, using hand grips to great effect, and stopped, gazing only at the weapon, barely looking at Zamindar, who they knew a lot about. They very cautiously picked up the gun with their fingers and took it to the US Lab, *Destiny* and placed it on the floor between the foot grips and mats.

The gun was treated with the greatest respect. It had the potential to kill them all and in fact completely destroy the ISS, potentially sending broken remnants of the space station to burn up in the Earth's atmosphere. Everyone was very careful when moving it, even though with only its magnetic coil active, it was quite safe. So, the engineers said anyway.

There was a large hole in the hull, a brand-new window created opposite to the nadir port. The new cut in the superstructure of *Destiny* was covered by thick space-rated plastic and fastened with hyper-adhesive, thick plastic tape to keep the vacuum at bay and keep it attached to ISS and the weapon. The tape was as strong as steel.

One astronaut, fully suited for vacuum EVA, with a pressure gun, took out twenty-four rivets and popped a window in the depressurised node that was locked at both ends, then enlarged it with an electric vacuum saw, in an EVA that went for seven long hours. It should have taken even longer, except the astronaut who did the cutting and fastening was extremely good and quick. When he'd finished, he said it was worse than running a marathon, he was so tired he almost needed to be scooped out of his suit. Removal of his spacesuit took a full thirty minutes with "oohs" and "aahs" and "fucks" aplenty.

Now "all" the engineers had to do was mount the gun so it pointed near the window. A further EVA and a depressurised *Destiny* truss would allow the final mounting of the gun flush with the outer hull of the ISS, with its own metal moulding that would also provide the required pressurisation and movement of the unit. There was also some expanding foam used that stayed elastic and was rated for space use. And none of it was to be seen, either from far away or relatively close up. It was the humans' *secret* weapon. If it worked that is.

If it didn't work, humanity was gone, that's all Mitch could think about. He assumed it was simply a matter of aiming it, but what if the fucker didn't work? It'd been tested with non-lethal ammunition but never, for obvious reasons, with anti-matter. Surely, they'd do that before the weapon was used in anger. It seemed to Mitch, anything new had to be tried first.

The gun sat in its semi-static mount that was soft-riveted on both the bottom and roof of the ISS. Josh bent down and peered at its contours closely. It sure looked lethal enough. Knowing its potential for destruction, the gun was as scary as hell. Hopefully its bite was as good as the way it looked.

'I guess all that's left is to try it.' Josh said hopefully, wiping both palms on his pants, which were already wet from rubbing sweat on each side. This stuff was way beyond his comfort zone. The thing was designed to be humans' saviour, he knew that. Would it be though, would it even work, he wondered and worried. Blowing up the ISS would be horrid. Would it end up being humanity's nemesis? It could be either. Nemesis or saviour. And, if they happened to be successful, would it prompt the Bantha to send more craft? Zamindar said no, but it could be the start of something very unpleasant indeed. Potentially, a war, which would likely be brief and likely wouldn't go in Mankind's favour.

'It must be tested with the anti-matter,' Zamindar toned seriously. He appeared highly alert and ready. 'It is time,' he toned.

Mitch glanced at Josh, 'but tested where, Zamindar...the Moon? Away from habitation obviously.' He gazed at the Virijian who looked...just like Zamindar - totally and utterly blank.

'The Moon,' Zamindar eventually toned in confirmation.

'Who will be the shooter?' As if he didn't know. They both looked back at him, confirming what he already knew. He fully expected to be the one and he was right. Mitch was the shooter.

'*But I've never shot anything,*' he spluttered, ' ...let alone anything like this thing. *Fuck,*' he yelled at himself, knowing how much of a novice he was.

'You think *we* have?' Josh said, trying desperately not to grin. 'You love firsts, you'll be fine. Just aim and shoot.'

'Ooo-kay, as I thought,' Mitch mused. He looked through the sight, and all he had to do was lock and fire. He did his best to play the seriousness down. It was hard though - he'd fought with the Fermi Paradox and the great silence all his adult life and now he was expected to kill a ship full of extra-terrestrials. The fact that the Moon was travelling at nearly 4,000 miles an hour was immaterial, Zamindar said. The anti-matter would move at half the speed of light. They decided on the middle of Mare Nubium, a thousand kilometres south of Copernicus Crater. Hopefully, he'd hit it somewhere around its centre.

Nubium was well away from any habitation and the Gateway orbiter. The Moon was occupied only with those that refused to move. The majority left soon after the threat was made. The Moon was essentially empty. Where they were shooting, it was empty even in the Moon's best times.

Mitch sat in the chair. He'd already couched the trigger, it was at a good height and distance from the rear wall, he thought, giving a tentative thumbs-up to Josh who himself was hellishly nervous. It was easy when you weren't doing the shooting. It was nerve-wracking in a different way when you *were* doing the shooting. All Mitch needed to do now was hit the red button and it would go green, and then he was ready to go, apparently. He hadn't shot at anything since he was twelve years old, when, after considerable egging by mates, he took a shot at a rabbit with a wonky air-rifle, and missed by a large margin. It was pretty hard to hit anything with both eyes closed though. This time he would be really aiming, even though it was "just a test." Both eyes would be well and truly open, although aiming would only need one.

Mitch sighted the Moon and it looked beautiful, even so far from the shine of Earth. He had a pair of binoculars with the strap around his neck, and looked at Aristarchus and the chain of mountains headed by Eratosthenes. He zeroed in on Mare Nubium and pressed the red button. The light hummed a bit and turned deep green meaning, he hoped, it was ready to use.

Zamindar had tweaked two of the Station's gyroscopes so the Moon was almost entirely front and centre. The weapon's ability to move a small ten degrees in any direction, did the rest. He was ready to shoot.

'*Here* we *go*,' Mitch said, his face reddening, and his eyes bouncing from Zamindar to Josh. Mitch looked through the sight and made a few corrections until Nubium was front and centre. "3...2...1",' he looked through the sight and, making sure the centre of the Mare was still targeted, he hit the trigger, and it was as he thought, stiff and stubborn. Mitch pulled it harder and it shot with almost no recoil. A firm, serious pull did the job.

Ten grams of shielded anti-matter was sent at incredible speed by a field change in the magnetic trap, and it exploded moments later on the Moon. Fast didn't do this thing justice.

'*Jesus Christ,*' Josh whispered, studying the storm-cloud of dust and dirt and rocks that sprang from the detonation site in the weak gravity. They were glued to the window, watching what happened, imagining how it would be if it hit a craft. Total and utter devastation, he was sure. '*Holy shit,*' he exclaimed. He was sure with this weapon they could defeat the Bantha ship.

All that, from a few grams of anti-matter, shit, the explosion was massive and -so bright, like a fucking star. It formed a mushroom cloud on the Moon, millions of tonnes of dust and rock and a hole at least fifty metres deep, Much of the dirt and the dust left orbit and formed a torus behind the Moon. The detonation was akin to a nuke, the damage, the cloud and although it generated plenty of gamma rays and some high energy photons, there was almost no residual radiation, as would result from a nuclear bomb with fallout. The atmosphere of Earth would stop all the nasty's created by the anti-matter.

'Well, it works,' Josh said. '*My God does it work.*' His expression was like someone had thumped him in the face with a shovel. His eyes were huge and he was gasping, his whole body shivering, staring straight ahead at the newest crater on the Moon, mostly shrouded by a cloud of dust and dirt.

'We're-ready...I guess,' Mitch said, widening his eyes, looking from the Moon to Zamindar to the gun, smiling widely. 'As long as we can aim, and do it fast enough, we can win.' Mitch's smile was huge. '*This thing is amazing.*' He gazed at the weapon and smiled again. This thing could save us, he reckoned, still smiling. Suddenly, he was feeling optimistic.

It seemed like the planet was ready. When the Bantha arrived on "B-Day", those on the ISS would destroy them with the anti-matter gun. That was the plan anyway. Most of the population of Earth thought they were up here to try and negotiate with the Bantha. We'd come clean after the event. If the worst happened, it wouldn't matter much what we did or didn't do, Mitch assumed. If we succeeded, the world would know what we'd been up to.

They'd all seen what the weapon could do, it had been tested, and the damn thing actually worked, perhaps better than they expected. They would continue to work toward fusion energy at home, quicker than we'd ever thought was possible. While each of them truly believed in what they were doing, it seemed that Earth as a whole, didn't. The population was torn – it obviously wanted to live...but it didn't want to go without power either. As a planet, and as a people, it wanted its cake and to eat it as well.

*   *   *

The greater population felt that doom was only as far away as the Bantha. The world's media were the problem. It seemed that only a few of those corporations actually *believed*. Being negative apparently sold good copy, whether online, TV, or hardcopy. The world's media had a whole lot to answer for. They maintained that they were only telling the truth. Telling it "Like it was". Bully for them.

The stance taken by most the world's media had a severe downside though, and it only took a glance at the world's major thoroughfares to realise what that downside was. It seemed that the likes of CNN, Fox, MTV and ESPN didn't care about the fate of the world. They wanted a healthy balance sheet.

Deadline

"Anyone can hunt a bear fearlessly when the bear is absent."
— Isaac Asimov

Earth's mindset had slipped a bit. In fact, it had slipped and been ripped in half, torn up and shredded. And more than half the world believed they were going to die. Destroyed by an extraterrestrial civilisation bent on ridding the universe of races that were negatively impacting their planet's biosphere, and refused to comply with demands to rectify the situation.

Any civilisation that progresses to become a technical race goes through an "industrial revolution". Not one civilisation has bypassed it. A race tends to burn what it can to obtain energy...frequently it turns out to be the dead relics of past vegetation – coal – which is used. Natural gas and oil are formed from similar sources. Carbon and nitrous oxide are pumped into the atmosphere. Most races progress to "clean" energy, mainly fusion-sourced, in the right time-frame for the planet. Some civilisations don't, and it's those that end up on the Bantha's list.

The other half of the world believed they would somehow prevail. None of them thought they would make the deadline to rectify. And because of it, a growing part of the population wanted their old stable power back again. Fusion power wasn't going to be introduced and replace fossil fuels within a year, they thought. They had no faith in what humanity was trying to do.

The world had seen the reports. The counter-measure was well publicised now, but most believed that was doomed to failure. We just didn't have the ability to effectively deal or negotiate with the Bantha. The shocking history of the Bantha had been well publicised.

What the world didn't know about, was anti-matter. Mitch and the entire group on the ISS hoped that would be the difference. We couldn't negotiate with the Bantha, but we could kill them. That was the plan. Anti-matter was a deeply guarded secret, one that Mitch and the others didn't agree with. As far as they were concerned, "full-disclosure" was the right way forward, Mitch was sure of it. Using it, he thought, was fully justified, keeping it hidden from the population, was not.

Protests and marches continued in most major cities but generally, they weren't trying to influence or encourage anyone, they just wanted desperately to be heard over the blare of the Bantha. There was looting and robbery which drew a heavy reaction from the police. Many of the population had been killed and injured the world over. Civil groups had grown into dissent and full-on opposition as the groups grew in numbers of protestors and numbers of groups on the streets. The US and China were burning. Good news or bad didn't matter, the world, it seemed, was beyond that, and ready to meet its fate – good or bad.

Sean rang Jack at NASA in Washington. 'It's a bloody nightmare Jack, a complete and utter madhouse. If you're on the streets it's bedlam...a Goddamn nuthouse,' he said, his voice husky with despair and lack of sleep. 'It's full of people with a violent agenda. If you go out there, be prepared to fight and probably to shoot. Stay inside, it's the only safe way.'

Jack knew his city was on fire, he'd seen the long lines of fire-trucks. 'Some of our people are fine,' he said, 'and just waiting to see what happens up there, poor sods, but the population generally are out of their minds, they don't believe we will prevail, and a lot want their due before they go, whatever the hell that means.'

'A lot of them are on the streets. L.A., Houston, San Francisco, Memphis, Vancouver, Sydney, all over China, Beijing, Guangzhou, New York, name a city and it's on fire or out of control with large-scale riots. Our ability to keep up with fusion-change is currently unaffected but that won't continue for long. Eventually, it will all grind to a halt. *Everything will just stop.*'

'Similar here,' Sean said quietly. His heart froze, and then pounded – it was a very strange feeling. A long silence ensued where Sean tried to get himself under control. He didn't like the mental images that crawled into his mind and roosted. He honestly didn't know what to do or to think – he just hoped their mission up in space went well and the Bantha left without creating too much trouble.

Everybody on Earth was relying on what they did, although they had no idea about the anti-matter, their hope was that negotiation and showing how far they'd gotten, was successful. Unrest on Earth was entrenched now, whether you were in China, the U.S. or Mali – it would take a long time to normalise – now that it had gained its own unfortunate momentum.

You still there Sean?' Silence persisted. *'Hello?'*

"Yeah. I'm still here.' Sean huskily answered.

'You can be thankful that you live on site there at AASSA. You're protected from all the shit going on across the globe,' Jack said, feeling like he was drowning in all the violence that was now endemic around the world.

'Yeah, I suppose, but I've had plenty of time out of this place. I've seen what it's like out there...its absolute chaos. I've never seen the planet like this.

Maybe we should have shared "anti-matter" with the world. We thought it would be badly received...couldn't get much worse than this though, right?'

'It would only give the people something else to get riled up about. I just hope the Bantha turn up when they're supposed to, and we can take 'em out with this goddamn weapon of ours.' Jack said forlornly. He didn't feel very confident. If they managed to actually hit the craft, he'd be amazed. *Stunned.*

'Um,' he wasn't quite sure how to say it, or even if he should bring it up... 'what...if a flotilla...of craft turns up. Not just the *one* we are-expecting,' Sean said nervously, rubbing the back of his head hard, as he eventually gave way to his worst innermost fear. Sean had unnerving mental images of multiple craft coming at Earth. They could kill one, maybe two or three, but we'd have no hope against twenty or fifty if they were all packing the same weapons.

'Is that, er, likely?' Jack said, hoping it wouldn't be true.

'No, it's not likely, but...*anything's possible,'* Sean said nervously, scratching his head. 'Maybe nothing will turn up, who knows, right? If numerous ships arrive, we try to fire on all of them. We must defend ourselves,' Sean said, holding his breath, almost passing out, with horrible thoughts still consuming his brain. Feeling dizzy, he continued to hold the phone to his ear. *Shit*, he thought, glad it wasn't him aiming and pressing the trigger of that thing. The gun scared the shit out of him. He would prefer to have nothing to do with it. He was happy to watch from a distance. He didn't envy them at all.

'What if they actually want to negotiate?' Jack asked quite seriously.

Sean gazed at the phone like a sideshow clown. 'You're kidding, tell me you're kidding Jack. Bit late for that, they've threatened the entire population with death. Any "negotiation" should have come well and truly before the ultimatum. If you threaten someone, expect the worst, right?'

'You're right, of course you're right,' Jack said,

Both of them wished the other good luck and disconnected. '*Jesus, shit*,' Sean said to no one after he hung up. The future looked grim. Earth was okay right now, and it was AASSA and NASA's job to ensure it stayed that way. It was getting harder for Earth, with unrest spreading like a rampant cancer. It was multiplying *and* getting more intense. Looters and gangs were now more common than regular people. No-one ventured out at night – not even emergency services. For everyone, it was simply a waiting game.

*   *   *

If he missed the Bantha craft, they were done, as would be on Earth. He looked at his shooting hand for a long time, *no pressure*, he thought. '*Jesus*,' he whispered to himself. Maybe, that's why he was chosen, because of his ability to perform under pressure. That's what he took from it anyway. He realised how much crap that probably was, he was chosen because no one else wanted to do it or would do it. He was left at the front of the group when everyone else took a step backward. It was incorrectly assumed that he *wanted* to do it. They were wrong - he didn't want to do it. But it was way too late to back out now. Mitch needed to at least appear confident, even if he wasn't.

Mitch, Zamindar and Josh were due back from the ISS in the morning after overseeing the installation and testing of the gun. It seemed to work nicely so they were "happy" that it went well. It could have ended in catastrophe.

*   *   *

Sean was sitting on the outside balcony of his home at AASSA on the seventh-floor of the fifteen floored accommodation, a building called *Zenith*. Light-brown bricks and an elevator that shuddered on its way up and the way down. He was offered executive lodging as head of the space-centre but he declined, telling NASA and AASSA he was happy with what he had. He realised he would blend in more there. As Mitch's replacement, Sean had no desire for more. He wanted to be one of the Joe's and somehow unite with everyone. He knew it was a pipe-dream, but he had to try. He didn't want to lead by fear.

Sean was relaxing on his balcony with Josh, sitting with his legs hanging into the air, watching the last sliver of the Sun disappear behind Anzac Hill which plunged the whole area into deep twilight.

'This place is so gorgeous,' Josh said, giving Sean a slow nod, turning and fixing his eyes on the small silvered Moon, and the dark landscape. It would take a while to get used to the newly positioned Moon.

'It's-beautiful, no doubt about it, but they are spot on. If we kept on like we were, the planet was dead...and gone.' Sean glared at Josh but softened slightly when he saw the look on his face. Josh looked mortified. Too much thinking about the future.

Still, he continued, 'pumping all that carbon into the atmosphere from coal and the burning of oil by cars and planes...seriously, that was only going in one direction, right?' Sean looked at Josh again, scrutinizing his face as closely as he could. Josh had more colour but was clearly still very concerned. 'Even with the carbon-dioxide rich atmosphere, the wild, unseasonal weather and rising sea-levels, we still didn't truly get it. We thought it would keep worsening at the same rate or perhaps stay the same and only gradually get worse. Some still don't believe in climate change, despite the haunting visuals around the world. Pick a spot really. The entire globe is suffering. Floods, fires, rising sea-levels, melting ice, evacuations – it's not normal you know.'

'We talked about mid-range targets and behavioural changes needed to avoid the worst. Leaders just don't and won't ever get it, climate-change was still fundamentally about the Goddamn economy,' Sean was almost frothing at the mouth,

Josh could see he was working himself into a frenzy. 'It is too late for window-dressing to work', Josh said, with his eyes still closed. 'We need major structural change...such as is occurring now, to turn it all around.'

Sean's eyes flicked open and they looked flinty and hard and deadly serious. 'To make the planet liveable long-term...to render us, and Earth sustainable.' Sean whined, now looking a little tired as he stretched his arms up. 'Anyway... I'm going to bed.' He finished on that comment and stood up.

'Zamindar and Mitch are returning early in the morning so, yeah, bed time,' Josh said. He also got up and headed for the door with Sean and then moved toward the elevator. Josh stopped before he reached the door. 'So, maybe they did us a favour,' he was thinking as he was speaking, scratching his head. 'Perhaps they've given us the push we needed,' Josh said. 'Assuming the plan with the gun works of course. If it doesn't – it probably doesn't much matter.' He glanced at Sean grimly. No one knew the answer to that one.

Sean didn't have any answer as he breathed sharply. They were certainly busy enough up there trying, he reckoned. They could only go as fast as they could down here, maintaining errors close to zero. With high temperatures, and odd, new alloys and structures, the last thing we needed were mistakes. Errors and blunders meant fatalities.

Risk mitigation and oversight always had to be high. If they proceeded as quickly as they could under this framework, Mitch was confident they would succeed in bringing the right product to bear for Earth. It was the timeline that was the real problem. He knew they wouldn't fully implement all fusion and related products in that time.

That's why they were out there, in space, ready to blast the Bantha out of existence. That was the only way to be sure. The only way to protect Earth. Negotiation wasn't an option that could be explored. The Bantha would destroy humanity if they didn't act first. Complying with their ill-timed demand wasn't an option. It was way too tight. *Period.*

Josh thought, it'd be what it would be. But Mitch disagreed. Many had said, put anything in place, go at your own pace, just stop belching gasses into the atmosphere. But *what* if they checked on sustainability, which they surely would. We'd be found out and humanity would be obliterated.

The only way was to get rid of them before they vented on Earth. Mitch couldn't believe he had used the word "only". It had no right being there. It was a horrendously difficult task, no matter which way you looked at it. We were talking about destroying a starship. What if we destroyed one craft and they sent another? The Virijians said they wouldn't, that such a show of force by us would in essence scare them off. But what if it didn't? They couldn't know for sure, could they? Zamindar had never been wrong before, but there was always a first time. And this would *not* be a good time for it.

What if they arrived in solar space and shot at the planet from a long way away? So far away, that they couldn't even see them in the ISS? Again, Zamindar said no, they'd shoot from just beyond the Karman line. Risks and unknowns were everywhere they looked. Unless they accepted what the Virijians said as absolute truth. So, they did. The entire human defence or offense was predicated on what the Virijians had told them. Zamindar was very firm about it and had never been wrong, so far.

*   *   *

It started as a silver dot in the distance, shining like a mirror in the sunlight, *Lunar 7* was a shimmering bubble getting visibly bigger as they watched. Soon, the craft was large in front of them, coming in for a landing on the No. 2 runway, earsplittingly loud from use of its MPS. Returning from ISS, the light blue vessel stopped in front of them, using its RCS engines to reposition itself. Zamindar was visible through the side porthole window.

'We're-back,' Josh said nervously, stating the obvious, walking along the tarmac, glancing sideways at Zamindar. The Virijian looked grim as, Josh heard him grinding his teeth. God knows what that meant where he came from but it didn't sound great.

Jessy saw Josh and immediately felt like running up to him, but wisely tried to act casual. 'We noticed, Josh,' she said, smiling warmly at her son. Zamindar was quiet. No surprise there.

'All went well mum,' Josh said, the weapon works as planned. We shot it at the Moon and it made a Godawful mess. It does what it's supposed to. It's pretty much ready to go.'

Mitch broke in, mainly to avoid more motherly drivel which he could tell by her face, was coming, and said, 'next step is to take you to the ISS,' he glanced at Jessy, 'and destroy their vessel when and if the opportunity presents.' He admitted to himself how easy it sounded when put like that.

'If it's only one craft, and if the gun works as well as it did during testing, it is theoretically okay,' Mitch said. 'But in practice it is very fucking difficult, mainly because we have no idea what the Bantha craft might do...for a start...it is totally unpredictable.' He gazed at Jessy, blinking rapidly, thinking deeply, getting nowhere, 'very...difficult... indeed.' Mitch finished on, feeling extremely anxious and unsure. 'We need to make certain we don't panic…slow and deliberate is the only way to go.' Mitch gazed at Jessy again, locking onto her huge brown eyes. She understood how hard it would be.

'It is *anything* but easy,' Josh said aggressively, with bulging eyes. We're talking about killing a starship full of beings, it doesn't matter how you do it, it's *never* easy. He almost slapped his brow with exasperation but stopped himself short. 'Killing anything is hard,' Josh trailed off.

'I did say *theoretically*,' Mitch whispered. '*Jesus*, relax Josh…please.'

'*Whatever*, dad,' Josh replied petulantly. He coughed to clear his throat and his mind. 'Tomorrow is one-year since they gave us their twelve-month demand to stop belching greenhouse gasses into the atmosphere. We haven't fully complied with their demand, and if they return to make good on what they said, we will be waiting for them.' Josh had a comical, yellowing image of Mr Burns from The Simpsons, saying "excellent" and he almost laughed out loud. But he knew this was as serious as it got.

'But what if no-one comes when we think they will – what if they come later…maybe much later. I mean, we can't stay up there forever,' Mitch said.

'If you leave, which you'll have to eventually do if they don't arrive, you will fully brief whoever is the new Commander of the ISS which NASA will select to use the weapon – in your absence.' Zamindar toned. 'You will be happy to know that you are not expected to stay here forever. I do not believe that situation will arise however.'

Mitch eyed Zamindar for a long moment and then nodded. At least that question was answered. Only a million to go…

*   *   *

Executing a number of small RCS bursts, Zamindar lined up the *Lunar* with the ISS's PMA-2 docking port near the *Harmony* node, the same one used by the new Orion's, Soviet TMA-M and SpaceX. Zamindar tapped the front touch-screen a few times and then the flight computer took over. The capsule's docking mechanism woke up its counterpart on the ISS. Soft dock was quickly followed by hard dock. Within a minute, the *Lunar 7* capsule was pulled in and locked in place by twelve motorised latches. There was now a fully pressurised means of safely entering the ISS. Zamindar did the job of the most experienced NASA astronaut easily. Apparently, it was as easy as pie if you knew how.

'*Lunar 7* arriving,' Zamindar toned and spoke seriously, pressing the touch and talk, the main comms system for the Lunar series vehicles.

They entered into the now reasonably familiar, untidy confines of the ISS. They wouldn't leave again, hopefully, until they'd successfully dealt with

213

the Bantha. All of them realised that. Wires, cameras and laptops and science experiments were everywhere. This place looked scarily old but was actually quite new. It was just untidy to the eye. One look at the place equalled mess and clutter. Hardly surprising given where it was, how long it had been there and how many people wanted to use it.

To think that the civilisation on the planet below was banking their entire future on what they did here, *that* was drop-dead terrifying. It was truly the few in charge of the many. If they fucked it up, all of them were gone.

Jessy didn't like the idea one little bit. It was too much responsibility for too few. But still, they were there to try. No one on Earth had a clue what was going on. They thought we were going to try and negotiate with the Bantha. Somehow board their ship and reach a conclusion that didn't involve violence and the Bantha acting on their demand. What a joke.

Anti-matter and particle annihilation was a complete secret from the general population of Earth. They'd all agreed it should be kept secret to preserve the mind-set of the population. That was another fucking joke.

The entire group decided pretty much at the last minute that Zamindar should and would be the one to engage with the weapon, which Mitch was more than happy about. In fact, Mitch was ecstatic that it was someone else's responsibility. He didn't want to do it, despite what they thought.

Apparently, with this sort of technology, everyone trusted Zamindar more. Fair enough, he reckoned – Mitch agreed that it was the right decision. Once the decision was made, Mitch second-guessed himself, hoping like hell that Zamindar did a good job. He did the testing and *now* the Virijian is doing the job. It was odd, having a Virijian in charge of saving Earth, but he was fairly sure the decision was the right one.

Zamindar was walking quite well if not a little slowly, but the rest of them were struggling even to move in the weightless environment of the ISS. Floating off the ground was a constant problem for the humans. They walked and floated and generally struggled through the main Truss Segment and Unity Nodes, and they could all see the gun sitting in the main US Lab. It looked ready for something. The digital clock said 5am UTC. One year clicked over at 8am UTC as far as they were able to define it.

Zamindar fully understood his role in all this, and sat behind the weapon, entering a state of regeneration for two-and a-bit hours, or until he was needed in a wakeful and fully alert state behind the gun in the US Lab.

The rest of them went on another tour of the facility and then tried to relax, in a sleeping bag if they desired, firmly attached at both ends so they didn't roll or float away. The sleep habs complete with mounted laptops and other personal extras offered pretty comfortable surrounds in a confined compartment.

Unfortunately, they had a fair bit on their minds, so resting was very difficult. It was mainly a fear of failure, but failure at this point carried a horrible extra dimension. Death for them was probably death for everyone on the planet. Josh felt the blackness and did his best not to let it overwhelm him. He was only partly successful - it was with him all the time, like additional weight around his middle. When he looked inside himself, he saw a darkness that he reviled. He tried not think about anything but the saving of humanity.

Zamindar came back to full consciousness with a few minutes to go. Mitch, and the rest of them joined the Virijian in the US Lab and looked at Earth through the *Destiny* nadir window which gave a good coverage of the sky. All eyes were then on Zamindar. They all hoped like hell he was paying very close attention to what was happening outside. Despite the way he looked, they all trusted him to get the job done. They all had implicit faith in the big Virijian.

It was 8:02AM and they were still alone in space. Zamindar relaxed slightly, as did they all. Jessy relaxed slightly. They all had to remain on guard, but it was difficult to stay vigilant when the expected doesn't eventuate.

'Who knows when they'll arrive...maybe tomorrow, end of the year, next week...maybe never,' Mitch said, with flighty hand movements. He was sure the Bantha would come, he just didn't know exactly when. 'Don't worry,' he said, raising both thumbs and patting the weapon like it was a fucking dog. 'They'll come,' he said anxiously.

'*Brilliant*,' Josh said, grinning sourly at Mitch and rolled his eyes. 'He means they'll be coming and don't worry,' Josh whispered. 'Yeah, *right*, he thought, stroking his throat and grimacing. *Don't worry*...he must be *fucking joking*. Josh fairly spat it at his mum.

'Oh...they're coming,' Jessy said quickly and firmly, backing up her son. '*And soon,*' her voice unnaturally shrill. Her eyes were enormous with terror. Then it was *there*, not emerging slowly from a disruption in space like they expected it to arrive, it was just there. *Bang,* its huge length and girth appeared from nowhere. The whole thing was abruptly before them. And it was huge and appeared immensely dangerous. Whatever way their "shortening" tech worked, they'd just emerged from it.

The Bantha were at their destination. Rising from space, one of its turrets, whether by design or coincidence, was already aiming at them and it shot before Zamindar had the time to move or to think. It just appeared and fired. Like picking up a ball and throwing it in one action, like all decent first-grade baseballers and cricketers do. It seemed to be ready for us somehow. It had to be coincidence, he reckoned, the Bantha didn't have time to aim.

'*Oh fuck*,' Mitch howled, both at the sudden appearance of the gargantuan craft and the fact that it had clearly fired first. The plasma loped from the vessel and hit ISS square on the SPDM arm, around mid-ships. Also known as *Dextre*, the "arm" took the full brunt of the first attack from the huge ship. The "goo" covered the entire ship fast. The stuff, whatever it was, seemed to rapidly grow all over the ship, like a wildfire, that quickly consumed the skin of ISS. It looked like a thick layer of loosely packed snow.

Zamindar had destroyed the large craft, pretty much as soon as it arrived. But not before it had got a shot off at them from a turret that happened to be pointing directly at ISS. The vessel didn't have to move the weapon at all. It just appeared, seen our rifle, and *bang*.

Everything the enemy craft was, now passed them as fiery remnants including a few strange body parts, or at least that's what they thought they were. Whatever they were, they were oddly shaped. That didn't help though, because the Bantha somehow got the first shot off, be it luck or good planning.

They all looked horrified, even Zamindar appeared resigned to a rather ghastly death. They all stared at each other, dumbfounded as to why they were here and still alive to debate it. They were struck pretty much in the middle of the structure and they were waiting for what, they didn't know. If it was pure destruction, they assumed they'd already be dead. Maybe, it was delayed destruction or something biological...like Anthrax - none of them knew, but *whatever* – they'd been shot. And the Bantha weren't known for benevolence.

Mitch's mouth was open and moving but no words were coming out. He coughed piercingly to clear his throat, "We shouldn't b-be here, right? Did it miss us?' He knew it hadn't. His eyes were bulging with terror. '*What the hell did t-they shoot us with then*?' Mitch knew the ISS had sustained a hit. The question blurted out automatically, he already realised that it had to be something very odd. He also wondered if it was somehow delayed. If it was similar to what we used, it would have ended in a tremendous explosion, and we'd no longer be here. But we *were* still here, so it couldn't be that.

Zamindar peered beyond the window and then back at Mitch. His huge eyes were mirrors of the cosmos. 'It wasn't that sort of weapon, he said, 'not explosive,' Zamindar pointed straight forward with his middle arm, 'Earth?' It was a rhetorical statement clearly. Earth no longer filled the nadir. They couldn't see it anywhere. They were alone in space on the ISS. Earth and in fact all the familiar stars and structures had disappeared from view. In its place was blackness and a very odd sky.

Jessy gazed below the ISS where normally blue Earth was resplendent from horizon to horizon - a beautiful blue marble punctuated by puffy white cyclonic clouds. Now through the nadir window it was just black with unfamiliar stars in the far distance. And nothing in the foreground. And the stars and constellations were all totally foreign.

Jessy's heart beating rapidly in her neck. She turned her head and gawked in every direction but she and they couldn't see familiarity anywhere. The stars they could see were entirely unfamiliar. There were no recognisable constellations at all.

'Earth has gone', she said, with a gaping mouth. How, she wondered ominously? It's...impossible...surely, it's not possible, Jessy thought. There was definitely only one explosion. She was so confused. The poor girl was close to losing it entirely. She clutched both arms tight to her body. Everyone was just staring at where Earth used to be, mumbling part-sentences.

Nothing made any sense. Zamindar looked out of the observation window in *Destiny* and saw the green plasma coating all the surfaces of ISS he could see, although interestingly, it didn't cover any of the windows, although it coated the closed portholes. It looked similar to a thick coating of blue-green algae – all courtesy of the Bantha.

'*Gone,*' Josh said distantly, still staring through the nadir like he was half-asleep. Perspiration shone on his brow. He was seriously confused, *bewildered*, rubbing his chin and his neck. None of this made any sense at all. '*What-happened?*' Josh gazed disbelievingly at his father. His eyes were so wide they were at splitting point. Mitch wondered himself, Earth was there and then not, in a split second.

'You are correct,' Zamindar toned loudly. 'We are no longer part of the Earthly system.' He walked and floated to the zenith facing window and looked at the odd star formations, which to Jessy appeared totally unfamiliar. Sirius and Canopus were no more. Arcturus was similarly gone from the sky. The sky was full of seemingly small stars, but none were familiar. Clearly, they weren't where they used to be. Their own Constellations were only memories. The Virijian had virtual star-maps printed on his brain, so he knew where they were.

Mitch glanced, and then stared at Zamindar. What the *fuck* was he saying ..., if they weren't part of the Earthly system any longer, where the hell were they? His eyes were restless and flickering as he looked out of the nadir window and hunted for anything vaguely familiar. Mitch found nothing but dim stars with no suggestion of the Milky Way Galaxy.

Mitch's head and eyes moved quickly, glancing and dancing everywhere but finding nothing that was recognisable. At the moment, they knew they were truly lost in space. They could only rely on Zamindar's knowledge of the Universe, to help them.

Zamindar toned, 'Earth has not been destroyed, nor has it gone anywhere...we have,' Zamindar toned. There were multiple and long gasps of disbelief, but Zamindar simply toned over the top of them. 'The ISS has been struck by some sort of spatial weapon, X-Rays, entanglement, De sitter space and non-location and such, we have been moved about as far as we can go. ISS is now moving away from Earth, on the expanding cosmic tide.' Everyone wondered how they would get back – which they soon realised was impossible.

'That's all fine,' Mitch said, '...but *why* didn't they just destroy us? Do the job properly. Get rid of us permanently. It makes no sense to transport us...and not kill the station that housed the weapon, especially given the Bantha's history of dealing with dangerous civilisations.

Zamindar looked at him. 'I believe we surprised them with our appearance, despite us trying to conceal it, they saw our weapon and acted quickly. They knew humanity had no weapons they could use in space, so, they were surprised to see us there. One of their weapons happened to be fortuitously aimed directly toward us when they appeared from shortened space. So, they fired that weapon, which thankfully for us, wasn't a killer. It did remove us from the area though, so from their perspective, it was job done. They removed the problem. They were aware of our weapon as soon as they exited their bubble, whether it was optical or electronic, I do not know. It is likely that the anti-matter was detected by the ship.'

'Gee...well, thanks for the heads-up on that. We could've been destroyed outright I suppose,' Mitch said, puffing and rubbing his ear, grinning weakly at Josh. He supposed they'd been lucky to an extent. Mitch cast a veiled look at Jessy, who shook her head ruefully. 'Lucky us, I guess.'

'*Oh God, seriously? Is that what you took from us being here...geez, we're lucky?*' Josh peered at his mum and dad incredulously, and really couldn't believe it. They were both truly knobs if that's what they both believed. He snarled at his dad, shaking his head. Josh felt like laughing in his smug face. 'I agree with the sentiment, but surely that's something you keep to yourself.' He stretched out his arms, '*Look where we are for fuck's sake.*'

I don't need winding up Josh – that I *do* know,' Mitch said, his eyes fixed on Josh, glaring, and leading into extended silence.

Josh held his tongue, he didn't want to start a heated argument here, and that's exactly where it was heading, wherever the hell they were. Outside looked black as hell. Josh made a mental note - *don't* look through the windows or the portholes. Nothing good will come of it.

Glancing at Zamindar, Mitch could see the Virijian had something else to say, as he stared at them, quietly observing, and then gawking through the nadir window. There was a slight static buzz between his ears.

'I do not think they meant to hit us with that weapon,' Zamindar toned, 'but as far as they were concerned, it removed the problem. Their choice would have been the same one we made – kill, which they would have done if they had the time. Whatever happened to us – we should be thankful – ISS should have been destroyed like the Bantha craft was.'

Mitch, Josh and Jessy all gazed questioningly at the Virijian. 'So, okay, but how far away from Earth are we?' Mitch asked, gawking at all of them, waiting for the answer he knew Zamindar would have. He also knew the answer would probably blow his mind.

'Ninety-two billion light years...approximately.' Zamindar toned to all of them. As expected, unlike the humans, he didn't look at all surprised or confused or upset. It just *was*, apparently.

Mitch blinked slowly and his mouth fell open of its own accord. His tongue would've rolled out too if it wasn't stuck to the roof of his mouth. None of them spoke, although Jessy was making a noise and then tried to speak, but none of it made any sense. She coughed and spluttered, eventually clearing her throat with a piercing cough, *'Wha...what?'* Jessy eventually managed, screwing her face up, flaring her nostrils and staring at the Virijian like he'd suddenly grown a second head. She was completely flummoxed and gave up trying to speak, staring at the floor with eyes like an Owl, struggling to process Zamindar's statement. She finally got something out that sort of made sense. Mitch and Josh looked like they'd both swallowed something they couldn't get down.

Mitch swallowed hard and shook his head, also coughing to clear his throat. *'No, it can't be...that's further than the size of the Universe,* for God's sake,' Mitch boomed, seemingly glued to the spot, arms limp at his side. 'It's only fourteen billion years old, nearly everyone knows that. How can it be'? Mitch's eyes were wide open, and he swung his head around sharply to look out the window.

Of course, Zamindar was right. Jessy was breathing in hissing gasps, listening and staring at Zamindar, assuming he'd say more. She also assumed that somehow, they were now at the very edge of the Universe. The idea of being so far from Earth was bone-chilling. Jessy looked around herself but everything seemed the same.

Josh hadn't moved a muscle since the Virijian had made the pronouncement. He, too, found it hard to believe, impossible to conceive. He was doing what he could to digest Zamindar's declaration. His ears and brain simply rejected it as fantasy – it was in the realm of *couldn't be true.*

They weren't outside the Universe, so *where the hell were they?* On the edge presumably, but there wasn't one, was there? Another Universe perhaps? He preferred not to ask Zamindar for fear of being bombarded with indecipherable goggledegook. He'd heard quite enough from him. That far from home indeed, it sounded like a fucking fairy story. Being in the ISS was bad enough...but *here*, it defied all things.

Jessy eventually opened the outer porthole cover and they all gazed into space from the nadir side. Knowing they were so far from home added real unfamiliarity to this space, it looked way blacker than usual...way scarier.

Ninety billion light years, none of them could forget or imagine it with any substantive meaning. That distance didn't mean much to any of them - only that it was an illogically long way away. Getting their head around it was nigh on impossible - It simply didn't compute.

It turns out that the Universe had been expanding faster than light for some time. Mitch had heard that but had never really thought about it too deeply. Afterall, he'd never be going far enough in space for it to matter.

Zamindar gave them a crash-course in the evolution of the Universe and he told them that space itself is not bound by the speed of light, it's only what travels through it that is bound by it. Space itself can expand at any rate...so being full to bursting with dark energy, it did. That's why they were in a part of space they couldn't image from home, even if they had a big enough telescope. It was and always would be, *beyond* the envelope Earth was part of.

Apparently, Zamindar was a little surprised the Bantha had the technology to send us there. They weren't *highly* evolved - they were still a relatively young society. That was one of two things that were difficult to estimate, the rate of evolution and the rate of technical acquisition.

It differed a lot between species and wasn't based on anything identifiable apart from eating a lot of meat and their mind-set. *Xeno-psychology again*. Having the desire and the *want* to improve and problem-solve helped. So, it was all rather qualitative. Depends exclusively on the nature of the species, Mitch supposed.

'So, we're, um...*stuck* here,' Jessy said breathlessly, shaking her head, hoping it wasn't true but knowing better. 'I mean with the thrusters we have, and the amount of fuel...we just can't...' Jessy's voice had risen alarmingly, to a cry of anguish. She stopped talking and gazed at Mitch with her chin quivering, clenching her jaw to kill the scream and the panic in her throat and mind that threatened to overwhelm her. She knew they could never get home under their own power.

'*Fuck*,' she screamed. Mitch grabbed her, but he looked as panicked and confused as she did. They were beyond the most senile star, all the quasars, beyond even those galaxies in Webb's extreme deep field photograph by its NIRCam. They were just *beyond*. Jessy took a long breath and looked out the window, shaking. *Holy shit,* she thought. She didn't like this one bit. They were way beyond the observable Universe. Part of the expanding Universe.

Zamindar gazed at Jessy. 'Yes, we will remain here until something changes.'

Mitch felt like screaming *WTF*, but thought better of it. They all looked at each other, wondering what the Virijian meant. They knew he understood more but wasn't telling them. Josh mouthed the last part of Zamindar's sentence, without making any sound. He looked like an Owl...an open mouth stare at the nadir window. Terror crossed Josh's face. He closed his bloated eyes tightly - panic was close. He was so far from his AASSA workstation it wasn't funny. Josh felt dizzy and weak and struggled even to sit down, taking ages in the weightless environment to entwine his toes around the foot-grips.

Mitch stared fixedly at Zamindar, speaking very uncertainly, 'what do you mean, 'until something changes?''

Josh was even more fearful than before. His breathing was shallow and quick, and his face was noticeably red and wet with moisture. He was struggling with being so isolated. He'd heard of these indigenous Indians whose tribesman were dubbed the "most isolated". Well...they had nothing on us. He really hoped Zamindar would answer the question.

Zamindar gazed blankly at Jessy who was biting her lip and swallowing a sob. He glanced at Josh, who was staring back anxiously, then said, 'The ISS will be shifting by will of the "goo" that coats the station, in line with the dictates of the Bantha.'

'Moving to where?' Josh asked timidly, pondering their next stop. The Virijian was a first-class detective, he thought. If you committed something or did something, or were responsible, he'd know.

Yeah...where are we going?' Mitch asked Zamindar more directly.

'We will literally have to wait and see,' Zamindar said, moving his grasper up and down which apparently held some meaning for Char whose cranial knot suddenly sprang to life. That was Virijian for "I don't know" apparently – over to you.

The need to scream loudly and never stop was coming fast and hard. Josh reckoned everything around him seemed way too bright and tilted somehow, yet Zamindar appeared like he was out for a Sunday drive. The word *nonchalance* didn't do this guy justice, even under these circumstances. Josh felt trapped by the ISS, imprisoned by the station that surrounded him, knowing its behaviour was beholden to the mysterious whim of an alien third party. Any move made by the structure was nothing to do with the people inside or what they might want to do. They gave up on trying to move it with its own thrusters ages ago. It simply wasn't theirs to use.

And then there was Zamindar, totally and utterly calm, as though nothing had changed. For him, it seemed - it was what it was. The difference in the emotional states of the species was wider than the sky. That was evolution for you. Totally unpredictable and influenced by so many biological and environmental factors - that it was literally anathema. It was a law unto itself.

Jessy and Josh gazed out of the round window in one of the Truss segments near the middle of ISS. Space was as black as they could remember. But there were distant stars and galaxies and a bit of dust, and some structures they could see in the background. Now, post-shift it was a horrifically alien cosmos, no Earth, and all the rest of the familiarity was just gone.

By pulling out the winder and winding it closed, Mitch shut the external white window covering - walking and floating, and grappling using the wall and floor mounted grab rails back to the US Lab, waiting for something, *anything* to happen. All of them just waited – they knew they could do nothing to affect their position in space...so they just waited for something to happen, and watched space outside, like a hawk.

The first thing they had to do was rid themselves of expecting the Bantha to think or act like humans. Again, that was xeno-psychology which no human knew anything about. They wouldn't have the same logic or thought processes. *No way.* The likelihood was that they would think totally differently.

That was obvious because instead of killing us, they sent us on some difficult-to-fathom journey. So, they would murder an entire civilisation, but send a few of us on a journey across space? Zamindar said it was fortuitous that we were shot with such a weapon – and Jessy agreed. The Bantha would have preferred to kill us. *No doubt at all.*

So, it was a big fat "I dunno" for everything involved with the spatial shift. At worst, they supposed, it would be an insight into the Bantha's thought process and state-of-mind.

Mitch and Jessy returned from their window on the cosmos, and all of them sat together as a group - on the white rubberized mat, stabilising themselves by pushing their feet between the small silver rails that were there just for that purpose. They'd seen quite enough of this distant space.

After twenty or so minutes of silence, ISS shook like something had it in its mouth and was shaking the shit out of it. Bits-and-pieces were coming away from the walls and drifting aimlessly into the ether. Untethered wires were everywhere. Everything shuddered violently until Jessy was sure the space station would simply fall apart and decompress in a ruined wreck. The structure abruptly became still, with the ISS thankfully still in one piece and its atmosphere secure.

If they were touching any part of the ISS, they shook too, quickly learning to stay in the air if they wanted to avoid shaking along with the Station.

Zamindar got further from the ground and floated gracefully to the window. He was followed there by everyone else, almost in single file. They all gazed hopefully out of the window. Surely, *something* had happened, the quake must have meant something – it was *so* unusual out here. It was too dramatic and climactic to mean nothing.

Below them now, peering tentatively through the nadir window, was a bluish, greenish world, slightly bigger than Earth, with huge chunks of bluey-violet forested land visible from where they were. The world had smaller and much greener oceans than Earth. Life on a vegetative level was clearly everywhere, but it looked unpopulated and untouched by intelligence or technology as far as they could see, to the horizon. They didn't know it yet, but it was the same on the other side.

The planet looked pristine and untouched by the hand of intelligence, or anything for that matter. But then, so did parts of Earth, Jessy thought, but not such gargantuan, continental tracts as these huge land areas virtually entirely covered by something bluey-violet – that looked like forests, much different from Earth. There were no icy poles. High, snow-covered mountains outcropped in a few places but the forest or bluey-green growth or whatever it was, even intruded on that, and reached quite high altitudes. But nowhere were three signs of intelligence. Of course, there was always underground. Thoughts of sustainability and liveability were thick in his mind.

'This is a planet that held as many beings as your world,' Zamindar said seriously, glancing at Mitch. 'It was on the precipice of falling to climate change, until the Bantha stepped in and removed the planet's problem.' They all caught on immediately. This was what was on offer to Earth. *Gee, thanks for the insight*, Mitch thought.

Zap, civilisation removed – planet lives. The planet may be warm and habitable but what was there now – vegetation certainly – but what about mobile life capable of evolution? *Yes...no*, the philosophy of the Bantha was severely in question because if there was no longer anything to evolve, then how was the planet better off? Their status as the space patrol was just wrong from the human perspective. It needed a hell of a lot of adjustment to get it right. Their philosophy was way too black and white. Their whole way of thinking showed the gulf between humans and the Bantha. What they were doing on these planets made no sense. Remove a hard-fought civilisation just to leave the planet empty of mobile life?

A blue pearl with a pristine atmosphere might be the result...but at what ungodly cost? And why? If the planet is empty of mobile life to *evolve*, what is the fucking point? Was it a problem with human logic, or understanding? If it wasn't, then the Bantha were just wrong.

This was at least some insight into the Bantha's mind-set. This is what they wanted. An empty, but healthy, habitable planet. Incredibly, this is what their behaviour suggested. Of course, *we assume*, they'd prefer an evolved species that lives in tune with their planet. But the jury was out on the correct answer. Like any police force though, there was no doubt, a harder-core element involved.

Mitch was going to ask Zamindar how he knew all that, but didn't bother. The Virijian knew things they could never know and could read most species. Zamindar could also predict, forecast, foresee, analyse, calculate and a whole lot more beside.

'So...that planet down there held as many beings as Earth?' Jessy said nervously, taking raspy breaths and staring at it with widened eyes. '*Shit.*' She exclaimed, finding it hard to believe. There was no sign of them, not a relic, *nothing*. 'The Bantha killed them a-all?' '*Jesus,*' she said under her breath. '*Holy shit,*' she finished on feeling ice-cold moisture dot her forehead.

'Removed the problem apparently,' Josh said loudly.' That's a pleasant way to say it, but you know what it really means...population genocide...*right*?' He looked directly at Zamindar but received nothing in return as though no-one had even spoken – he didn't know why he bothered to speak at all.

Jessy stumbled back a bit and her mouth fell open. '*Fuck me* - isn't a civilisation more important than a damn planet...even if it's a habitable, warm, oxygen bearing one?' Jessy glared at the passive Virijian. Mitch was nodding and about to speak.

'*No,*' Zamindar toned loudly. 'The Bantha consider those planets to be the very highest priority. Considerably higher than intelligent life-forms.'

When questions arose or he was contradicted, Zamindar rarely proffered a thing. He obviously didn't think he needed to. The Virijian was never wrong. Just ask him, Josh thought, grinning wistfully. Maybe that was the problem with humans, Josh pondered, too many emotions to cloud the brain, which evolution would eventually rid us of. We'd be just like Zamindar. That terrified Josh. He didn't like the thought of an emotion-less human. Sounded too much like a computer - too much like a Virijian.

'*Yikes,*' Josh found the concept hideous. We were only "human" because of who we were and emotions were an integral part of the package.

Mitch, Jessy and Josh moved carefully and slowly to the observation hub in *Destiny*. Zamindar by himself, watched through the port window of the Japanese JEMS node which wasn't far away.

Mitch gazed at Zamindar, 'We *just left*. It's not like we wanted to leave, but we *left Earth space*. Fuck knows what Earth thinks happened to us.'

'Nothing good,' Josh whispered. None on Earth would have thought that *this* was the result. They'd think we were dead, *no doubt about it.*

Mitch tried not to think about it, but knew an empty Earth was possible. That invoked another craft, or numerous craft, coming from Bantha, behind the one they killed. Zamindar said it was unlikely, but was a possibility. The Virijian was never wrong and Mitch hoped against hope that this wasn't the first time.

'They want you to look and absorb I assume,' Zamindar toned, 'this is what will happen to your world..."bounce back". This is what Earth will eventually do. 'I don't believe you were meant to be hit by that geographical weapon, but still, here you are.

Mitch was still thinking about Zamindar's comment about "bounce-back". 'After we're removed, you mean?' Mitch stared wordlessly at him, his heart pounding, ready for an emotion-less reply.

'Once your atmosphere has renormalised,' Zamindar confirmed, 'with or without you.' There was no empathy in his voice or face at all.

Jessy watched the planet below them. 'So, this is what Earth will eventually look like, apart from the colour of course.'

*   *   *

All of them took the swirling water in the bottle on the table behind Zamindar as a sign that they were about to shift again. Experience had taught them that swirling water and a shaking structure equalled shifting.

ISS was coated with the weapon's green snow-like goo. Having seen what Earth *could be,* would they now travel home? It had to be a possibility - it would be very welcome indeed. They all wanted to stand on something large and firm and see people they knew. Different people to the ones on the craft. The idea of seeing Earth again made Jessy's heart skip a beat. She didn't realise how much she loved it. But returning to Earth was unlikely because this was the Bantha's IT that coated the spacecraft. So, returning to Earth was nigh on ridiculous. Still, it was a hope.

Jessy watched the water like a hawk. It was her guide as to when it was safe to touch-down on the ISS. The water stopped swirling. Jessy sat down and stabilised herself. Everyone did the same. She followed everyone's gaze and turned her head, looking down, she saw they were orbiting a beautiful orange disk that was deeply incised with long gone fluvial systems, and a deeply weathered iron-oxide surface, with a very narrow and anaemic atmosphere.

'Mars,' Josh said abruptly, 'has to be, surely. Orange, weathered, dry.' He said, eyes cast downward, staring fixedly at the planet, laid out below them.

'It sure as hell looks like Mars, Mitch said, taking a good gander at what was below. It was truly beautiful. He could see the whitish poles of the planet and the heavily cratered highland, meaning the plain below them had to be Acidalia Planitia, 'but Mars was destroyed, wasn't it?' Mitch said, trailing off a bit. He was even more confused than before. '*WTF*?' He said loudly to himself.

They all knew the "red planet" was no more and hadn't been for yonks. In the re-design of the solar system, Neptune or at least its rocky core, was put into ex-Mars orbit along with Titan, for future human and Virijian co-colinisation. Now there was probably no Neptune or Titan, and Mars was back. If it indeed was Mars, which it appeared to be.

'Well...if it was destroyed, it's back,' Josh said, thinking his father had totally lost it. Mitch said it was destroyed in front of his eyes, yet, here it was. He was *tripping*, surely. Olympus Mons, the mighty volcano, the size of Missouri, went by slowly underneath. He could see the massive cliffs careening to the dusty orange plains below. Everything was orange with flecks of brown and black. And long-gone fluvial systems. He truly *knew* it was his Mars.

Mitch pulled his hands through his hair and stared at the red planet. He was totally and utterly bereft. Where the hell had it come from? Even Phobos and Deimos were there, shining in the light from the Sun. Either he was completely nuts or this planet and its moons had re-formed. Mitch gave up trying to explain it, he just accepted it. He scratched his chin and tried to speak but there was nothing there. All he could do was move his mouth but not an iota of sound escaped his lips. So, Mitch just waited for it to pass.

He'd seen Mars die, but now, for whatever reason, it was back. Back, presumably with all the old stuff but it made no sense. The rebels from Virija had destroyed it, hadn't they? Zamindar remained quiet – he knew.

Everyone was quiet as they gawked at the planet. The whole thing made no sense whatsoever. Zamindar made reference to time shifting, but that was no more than goggledegook. It meant nothing to the humans aboard.

'I reckon, probably the same as you...but that doesn't mean we have to state the obvious,' Josh whispered, staring at his dad and grimacing when Mitch looked at him. To think *he* ran AASSA, Josh thought sourly. He was more confused than people go to Washington state and ending up in DC.

Jessy watched the two interact, sighing deeply and massaging the bridge of her nose, saying, 'if you two have finished,' she glanced at both of them, standing-floating in the *Harmony* node, eyeing them like two bantams who had squared up for a fight.

Jessy had to let it out. '*Why the fuck...*' Her wide eyes gawked at Zamindar and she wiped moisture from her eyes. 'I mean, like the planet before, there must be a reason we're here, right?' Jessy eyed Zamindar closely, waiting for his toning, crossing fingers on both hands. She knew there had to be a half-arsed reason.

'There is a reason,' Zamindar toned loudly, scrutinising Mars and then going quiet. Everyone was looking at the Virijian now, studying him closely, *waiting* for the toning they knew was coming, from the loud mid-ear static.

'Mars had an intelligent community more than a billion years ago that hadn't long before commenced an industrial revolution. Their atmosphere was nowhere near as forgiving as yours. They almost killed their planet by burning coal and oil, hastened by a huge meteor that heated the upper atmosphere and blew the dying troposphere and stratosphere into space.' Zamindar drew in a huge breath and showed a torso like a bear.

'The most important thing here is that the planet was mostly killed by their own people.' Zamindar toned clearly and distinctly. Well before the *Bantha* evolved into what they are today.'

*   *   *

Shaking and quaking soon enough gave way to stillness and tranquillity aboard the ISS. They all believed they had shifted again. Josh didn't want to, but gazed through Cupola and saw a new planet below which they were orbiting dangerously close. ISS was going in and out of this planet's exosphere. No doubt, this planet had a significant atmosphere.

It wasn't Earth, was everyone's first depressing take. This planet seemed a little larger than Earth, but something else made it look very different indeed. The entire place looked like a fantastical candy-cane wonderland - but it was clearly very real indeed. The colours were in response to the EMAR from its tiny red star. It was maybe 5% of the Sun's mass.

Overall, the world looked purple with patches of bright colours intruding here and there, it had oceans, but they too, appeared purple. Everywhere they looked, the planet and everything around it was *purple* but in places it was red, yellow, green and pink. Space outside the window of the craft, continued to look, very unfamiliar til you saw the planet which was like a colourful lolly in a storefront window. Alpha Centauri and Arcturus were nowhere to be seen. Zamindar would know where we were though. He knew everything. The huge Virijian had star-maps printed on his brain. Josh wondered if all Virijians were as smart as Zamindar – he doubted it. He was probably similar to Stephen Hawking in relative intelligence on Virija. In other words, he was a genius although his insight from a human perspective went way further than that.

Mitch peered at the planet beyond the window and then at the Virijian and shrugged his shoulders.

Zamindar picked it up. 'We are near an old M-Class star smaller than your Sun. I will not give you the name of the galaxy but it is not yours.'

Mitch held back saying "*der*" but he was thinking it. He knew it wasn't their Galaxy. 'This is the same as the other planet?' Mitch said. 'It is all sorts of purple and other colours but it is essentially the same, isn't it?' He peered at the planet...'bounce-back, right? Seen it before. They don't need to hammer home the point...we *get it* for Christ's sake. The Bantha must think the recipient of their spatial weapon, in this case *us,* are idiots.'
He had to remember that they were almost certainly shot with the weapon fortuitously. Potentially, this voyage could be for any reason. It didn't have to be for edification, which was worrying. ISS could be here for any reason and it didn't have to be for learning. Mitch gulped and wished he hadn't thought of it.

Josh said, 'we're outside our Galaxy, so trying to estimate where we are is hopeless right? It's chilling to think we're so far from Earth, sent here by our *enemies.*' Josh felt himself shaking with fear. 'This is truly a *fucking* nightmare.' He gazed out the window, something he promised himself he wouldn't do. For Josh, all bets were off. He had little doubt they'd all eventually die. Shot by anything, including a spatial weapon.

*   *   *

'I want to see this planet more closely. They can't be showing this to us because they want to show us a rock restored, it can't be, not again. *Surely not again.*' Mitch didn't think the Bantha would repeat anything. It was a strong feeling that pervaded him. 'There's got to be something else going on with this planet...*we've missed something,*' Mitch whispered forcefully, gazing passionately through the nadir window, assessing all he could about the planet which, from where he was, was its colour, approximate size and not much else.

'You complete twat,' Josh said roughly, shaking his head. He couldn't believe his dad sometimes. 'What if this thing leaves while you're gone? The ISS I mean, and don't say it won't happen, because it damn well might. Then you're gone, because I doubt, we'll be back to pick you up,' Josh said firmly, continuing to shake his head in utter dismay at Mitch and his selfishness.

Jessy was horrified. She was used to his self-indulgence but this was something else. This was bordering on insanity.

Mitch ran a hand through his hair while he kept both eyes on Josh, focussing closely. His son could see that Mitch had made his mind up. Mitch had his arms firmly crossed – he'd made the decision and wouldn't be swayed.

Mitch spoke quickly, without blinking. 'But I doubt it will break us up. I don't know why I feel like that, but I do. It wants us together.' Mitch's stupidly and obsession with exploration had put a gleam in his eye and a smile on his face.

'*Fair enough,* Josh said caustically, risk your life based on a hunch...I'd expect nothing less. I'll remind you of that when we shift or move or *whatever* we do, *without you.*' Josh had a bemused, annoyed smile, scrutinising Mitch's annoyingly steadfast face. What an irresponsible clown, he thought, quite seriously. This guy would endanger his life based on nothing more substantial than a tenuous "guess". Enough said.

'Who wants to come with?' Mitch asked, deliberately upbeat, looking from Josh to Jessy, eyes peeled open - but all eyes were fixed on the floor. 'We have a fuelled-up *Lunar* that'll easily make the voyage.' Mitch looked at both of them hopefully. All eyes were fixed downward, saying no without saying no.

Mitch was eyeing the solar panels of Soyuz which were attached to the ISS, as he spoke. '*I won't stay here, doing nothing.*' Mitch's pupils were flinty. No one dared to argue with him, not even Josh. He was an explosion on a hair trigger, ready to go off. Mitch meant business. He glared at everyone in turn, to make the point. 'I'll go by myself if I have to,' he said bitterly, as he roughly grabbed his helmet and environment suit.

'*Oh Jesus...*' He knew what his dad was doing, and also realised what had to be done, not because he wanted to. 'I'll come with you dad,' Josh said, wrinkling his nose and narrowing his eyes. Josh stood up and joined Mitch, near the nadir window. 'The things we do for family,' Josh said to his dad, feeling hot in the face. He genuinely reviled space, and when people talked about its "incredible potential", it just made it worse.

Jessy tilted her head and made eye contact with Josh, looking as though she was going to plead with her son not to go. In the end, she said nothing at all. Jessy just held her breath. She hated what Mitch was doing, but she was anything but surprised.

Josh wanted to be with his father – she understood that. Jessy understood him going but hated it all the same. She blamed it all on her husband. Self-indulgence, narcissism, greed, egocentrism – call it what you like. He was all of them. Jessy felt like jabbing a finger in Mitch's face, calling him all of it, because that's what he deserved, but she didn't. She scrubbed a hand across her face and remained quiet. Space and investigation always came first for Mitch. She was less than pleased to have both of them off the station at the same time. Nothing good would come from it.

'What if ISS is gone when you get back?' Jessy stuttered, glaring at Mitch and flicking her eyes to Josh, daring either of them to say something.

'I...uh...' Josh started to say.

'Josh, don't encourage him.' If he wants to go, fine, but not you Joshy.'

Josh turned to his mum. 'I tend to agree with dad though,' Josh offered a placating face to his mum, saying *it's okay*, over and over again. Jessy was distraught about him going. Josh knew Mitch would go by himself if he needed to. And God knows what would happen then. He'd take unnecessary risks and kill himself for sure. At least this way, he could watch over him.

Mitch was the first to admit he was obsessed with discovery, afterall, he was a former test-pilot who pushed everything to the limit, Jessy reckoned he had a death-wish, but that wasn't true at all, according to Mitch. He just wanted to get things done and find out about things first. If he didn't do it, someone else would. If that was a death-wish, then he certainly had it. He was the first to admit it was an obsession – he reckoned it was a good passion to have. His loved-one's weren't so sure. In fact, they disagreed completely.

*   *   *

Mitch and Josh sat in the *Lunar* and were ensconced in pre-flight checks getting ready to break away from the ISS. Thankfully, the green-goo didn't extend to the connected pods. Comms check was okay and electrical and environment were fine. Propulsion was good, and there was plenty of fuel. Astrogation and control systems were operating okay and were correctly programmed. Final confirmation came with the hatch closure, which was checked by Josh on their side and Jessy on the ISS. They were now good to go for release from the ISS. The *Lunar* itself was properly locked off from ISS and they were on their own – ready to detach.

Jessy peered through the porthole windows of the space-dock and waved a teary goodbye to her husband and son. They were going and that was that. She knew it might be the final goodbye. Mitch was such a *fucker.* Jessy wasn't happy at all. She loved Mitch but hated him too.

Mitch was smiling widely and Josh was shaking his head and muttering under his breath, *situation normal*, Jessy thought as she backed away from the *Lunar* and the Progress 76 airlock. There goes the exploration freak and his patient son, she reckoned to herself as she watched them fade away.

The ship first got a mechanical push that separated it from the latches on the ISS. *Lunar* then took a programmed burn lasting about five minutes. The burn slowed them down and the computer aligned them with the atmosphere of the new world at 50 degrees. All they could see were fire and flames until it cleared and below the clouds, which were grey and tepid like Earth, the planet bared itself.

'*Holy shit,*' Mitch barked, overcome by the colours, which were so different from their own planet. '*Check it out,*' he said, his eyes lighting up after they got used to the light. The colours were very different from Cranreb's planet. This one was seemingly a world of its own – rich with unusually bright colour that simply had to be rare. Mitch and Josh stared fixedly below, their eyes wide open, pupils dilated, Josh initially giving a gasping cry.

Is this why ISS was brought here? *Because it was pretty?* Seemed unlikely in the extreme, Mitch reckoned. But in the next breath he realised it didn't matter because it didn't diminish its sheer vibrancy. Mitch imagined imaging it on Webb. Even small and out-of-focus, Earth would go nuts.

Josh was struggling to believe what they were flying over. Even from twenty thousand feet, he could tell that the plants and trees were huge, the forest or jungle was extremely dense and colorful, and from here, he could also see there was no place to land.

There was a huge amount of life on this world, *boy, was there life* – purple, red, orange and yellow vegetation was thick, by the look, impenetrable and everywhere down there, intergrowing like mad. Hopefully over the horizon, there would be a place to set down and take a ground perspective of this place. As they descended Mitch saw a reddish star, low on the horizon.

The wavelength of the star's light and maybe its seasonal variations clearly influenced photosynthesis, which was chiefly responsible for the multiple colours of the chlorophyll that pigmented and powered the vegetation. Mitch and Josh could see it everywhere. In its search for the most efficient energy, the trees reflected a yellowish colour, and most everything else they could see was sort of crimson and violet intergrown like the meeting of two mighty multi-coloured oceans. The trees had bright yellow leaves and yellow-grey trunks, entwined with violet and in places crimson ivy and large purple flowers – and they grew everywhere. From a distance it looked amazing, like a massive pinwheel of rainbow of nearly every colour on display. All the l vegetation was intergrown, essentially a solid wall, and was denser than dense.

They kept flying within the atmosphere and flew through swathes of floaty things, thousands or maybe millions of them, floating in the air in groups, each only about fifty centimetres across, all partially translucent, like polymeric jelly-fish. They left oily marks on the windows as they flew through them, like a boat moving through huge schools of forage-fish. They were organic, balloon-like creatures with a stomach blown up tight with a gas of some sort, helium perhaps, that allowed them to float in the air, with two small eyes and one anomalous hole on its face. And a large funnel-like mouth that was always open, as far as they could see. The floaty-things seemed to be feeding on something but whatever it was invisible. Micro-organisms presumably. Their craft ran into a lot of them and the Aerojet engines no doubt munched up a few swarms of them. Just as well the engines were bird-rated, Mitch supposed, but even so, he tried to avoid them by flying lower.

All they saw was virgin, untouched forest, albeit an odd color, broken by huge lakes of green fluid that lapped against the vegetation on its edges. There were also oceans but they too were better described as large, inter-connected lakes, Mitch counted six on the half of the planet they flew over. There was more land here than Earth, although the planet appeared about the same overall size. The water was very green, perhaps tinted by algae. One lake perhaps three hundred kays across, had water that was bright red and quite stunning to the eye, possibly affected by the local rock type. The forest bordered the water very closely, almost as though there'd been a recent flood.

Having circumnavigated the globe, it was beautiful and very odd, no argument there, but there were zero places to land. No place to set down and get more acquainted with this colorful world and see what, if anything, ran around on its surface.

Mitch reckoned he needed to land to find out why this planet was part of the strange excursion. And see if any mobile life lived in the forest. Surely, there was multi-cellular life somewhere in there. The forest was so thick and vibrant. He was sweating with the need to know.

'So...what the *hell* do we do now?' Mitch said, looking into the distance while the computer flew the plane.

'You're the Goddamn pilot, aren't you?' Josh whispered, peering at his father bug eyed. He felt like screaming, *you fucking tell me!*

'Well...we can't land and we've orbited the planet...so I guess we go back to ISS, there is no third option, right? It's either land in the water, or back on the ISS.'

'Unless you want to land in the trees...let's do it then, back to the ISS,' Josh said, thinking *thank God*, waiting desperately to feel the glorious inertia of the craft turning, then thrusting back into space.

He pushed his feet hard against the floor until his calves ached. Josh didn't realise how happy he was not to land. He knew his mum would be stoked. Josh hated flying at the best of times. And this certainly wasn't one of those.

Mitch keyed in the end point and made sure the computer knew where they wanted to go. Main engines fired and their acceleration using liquid oxygen and hydrogen propellant increased as did their incline to space.

'I saw animal life among the trees,' Josh said nervously, looking at Mitch. 'Something unusual. Not like Earth.' Josh tried to speak more but nothing came out. He had no specifics on what he saw. He was still trying to process it. Josh first coughed piercingly to get the air flowing in his throat.

'They looked a bit like monkeys, but they had *three legs*.' He looked aghast, then excited, 'they moved fast too...like lightning through the trees. Using the Celestron telescope, I couldn't keep up, they were fast. They also had a very strange, pointed head and long, long tail which they seemed to use to grab branches, trunks and vines. Josh's cheeks burned with awe and anxiety. He still wanted back on the ISS.

Piloting the craft, Mitch headed slowly for the Progress 76 air-lock and undertook a further burn, slowed the *Lunar* to walking pace and clicked the craft's imaging crosshairs on the centre of the Dock, engaging the computer to take the craft in and dock. Soft-dock was followed by the craft being pulled into hard-dock and a pressurised gateway to the space station.

Onboard, they knew something was up when Mitch and Josh returned so quickly. Jessy was ecstatic to have both of them back on board. Although Mitch remained silent at the news of the monkey-things, internally he was doing somersaults. This was exactly why he wanted to land. If there were monkey-things - there was likely an entire alien ecosystem they were missing out on. Mitch could feel it. *Opportunity lost* boiling in his stomach.

Zamindar toned quite clearly to Mitch that, *had* he landed on the planet, the probability was that he would have been killed by the indigenous life. On the land beneath the trees somewhere, lived the apex of the local ecosystem, a rather aggressive arsenic-based life form, where arsenic formed the backbone of DNA, not phosphorus.

Now his frustration turned to thanks. This world was rich in arsenic and correspondingly poor, maybe free of phosphorous. Mobile life was still overwhelmingly oxygen breathing even though the backbone of the DNA was slightly different.

The animals on this world were mainly carbon and water – the same foundation but very different from life on Earth. The one at the top of the byzantine food-chain had a dark exoskeleton and large pointed teeth. It killed and ate indiscriminately, and anything that landed on the planet would be at great risk of being eaten and dispatched in a very ghastly fashion indeed. Zamindar didn't know anything about them and, until he sighted it through the 'scope, didn't know it existed here.

It was a healthy passion to have – discovery, and finding it first – but if it gets you killed, it's anything but healthy. Mitch shook his head and saw stars, and then had his hands interlaced on his head – he'd try and remember that. The monkey-things spent most of their time on the top-tier of the forest, safely out of reach of the predators and only came down when it was "safe". The humans, being relatively slow-moving creatures, and essentially meat-bags, would form ideal candidates for food, assuming the creatures liked their taste.

It was due to the vibrancy of this planet, *sheer luck*, that they didn't land and end up on the menu. Mitch sorely wanted to thank Zamindar for the warning but knew he wouldn't understand the inference, so he didn't bother. Once they were out of their suits, Jessy hugged her son tight, and ignored Mitch. She was certain both would die – she'd convinced herself. The poor kid, she thought, taken from AASSA and dragged literally across the Universe, after all the chaos he'd endured with his dad and her.

Jessy then thought *fuck it,* and hugged Mitch tight. Crossing herself, she thanked God - *they were both still alive.* She was quite sure the lack of somewhere to land saved Mitch and Josh from not coming back at all.

'We definitely couldn't land.' Mitch kept his hands in his unvelcro'd waist pockets. 'No...no, couldn't do it.' Mitch hated being defeated even though, this time, it seemed to be to his and Josh's benefit.

Josh felt the movement and the lurching because he was sitting on the matting floor of the ISS with one foot wrapped around the long metal grips that were all over the station. It was either that or float away. He was swaying and vibrating along with the station and looked anything but happy.

'*Not fucking yet,*' he screamed, none of them were ready to shift yet. Mitch and Josh especially, were still trying to come to terms with the insane purple planet. Josh was so tired. Shaking continued until it saw the entire structure flexing and bending around them. It wouldn't wait for anybody, least of all him. When it was ready, *it was ready.*

'*Fuuuuck,*' Josh roared, as the ISS continued to bend and contort around them. He half-stood and half-floated gripping the rails as everything moving around him, made a horrible high-pitched *screeching* sound.

The ISS hadn't moved under its own power since they'd used the anti-matter weapon. None of the Russian thrusters had been turned on and none of the gyroscopes had been tweaked. All movement was induced by others...beyond the station itself. All those aboard the ISS assumed the Bantha via the spatial "goo" induced all their movement. It was without doubt, they thought, "*intelligent*". It seemed to know exactly what it was doing.

*   *   *

Would "they", whoever they were, have shifted the ISS if he and Josh weren't *in* the station? He doubted it, but if that indeed was the reason, that probably meant they were watching, perhaps monitoring remotely, or something? He moved his head in every direction, looking everywhere in the ISS. Unless it was done remotely, he decided it wasn't possible. No way they were being watched locally...*no way.* If it was remote, Mitch knew there wasn't a damn thing they could do about it.

ISS kept bucking and rolling around them, but they still hadn't shifted. Mitch was gazing at the planet below, not sure if that was good news or bad. Mitch eyed space through the side Cupola window and ISS had *definitely* shifted. What was near them had gone from beautiful and benign to violent and extremely hazardous. Below them, thankfully further away this time, was a gigantic, active and clearly spinning black hole, feeding off a rotating ring of bright, roiling gas that slowed down when it reached the event horizon itself and fell into oblivion. This thing was spinning *fast* and it dragged spacetime around with it in an effect described by Einstein's Theory of Relativity.

Mass, so crushed that all free space and in fact everything inside the atomic configuration was gone, digging a hole so deep in Euclidean space that nothing escaped, ever. Of course, Josh wondered why the fuck this was part of the voyage. Was it to kill them? Cue negativity.

The whole thing looked super violent. A narrow jet of magnetic, superheated particles spewed backward and forward into space from the monster. Mitch saw it, coming from above the event horizon, the last spot where anything could escape. God knows how far the jet went, probably light years. Below it, everything was gone, escape requiring the breaking of physics.

Humans didn't understand the quantum workings of black holes, but above the event horizon, we were all over them. Humanity loved black holes for obvious reasons. They seemed to be at odds with everything else in the Universe. In essence they were dead and crushed stellar cores, but their remaining quality was very much alive. Their gravity was an absolute killer - space was absent entirely. All light was almost without energy - brutally reddened by gravity.

Below the event horizon it was goodbye to everything, including light, the time carrier, not only was it reddened and trapped forever, it now acted as space itself. Roles were reversed. Spacetime became *timespace*. Whatever was ahead of you was, like it or not, was in your future. Shwarzschild and his metric told them that. That meant instead of the singularity being ahead of you in space, it was in your future and irrevocable.

Mitch peered at Josh. He watched him turn away and could almost hear him saying "*And?*"

'Yep, it's a very large black hole,' Josh said casually – 'It's stunning to be sure, but a little underwhelming at this point.' Mitch could see the thing guzzling hot gas and dust, and spewing a beam of supercharged particles straight out and up from its event horizon. It looked pretty frigging amazing, Mitch thought. *Underwhelming, my arse,* he thought. Josh refused to be overwhelmed by it. He stared at the floor and scrunched his toes in his shoes and squeezed his eyes shut. He'd had quite enough of this place.

They and he especially, wanted back to Earth. The question of *why they were here* was forgotten for the moment as the visual became clearer. He could see it was rotating very rapidly. 'ISS is also moving,' Josh said. And by moving, he meant to a lower orbit around that thing.

ISS was now travelling toward the black sphere and was almost on it. The black hole was gigantic, way too large to estimate and totally flat from where they were now, but from a long way away it was clearly spherical. It had to be a super-massive black hole, Mitch thought, totally awed by the scale of things, the brightness, and what he knew was around him. New physical laws were within spitting distance of where the station orbited.

This thing they were almost inside was gargantuan...a monster among monsters. Its outline or at least the inner part was made obvious by the bright material falling into it. Jessy was amazed – she could actually see *inside* the event horizon. She could see lights.

Then they were inside the black sphere, and it was black for as far as they could see. It presented like normal, regulation space although it was totally, and not surprisingly, starless. But there was light in the extreme distance, four anomalous points of white light that went from sharp to diffuse in a rapid pattern. Mitch tried to name the pattern but couldn't.

Jessy's head was pushed hard back into her head-rest and she had eyes like an owl, breathing in quick spurts - she hadn't expected to travel *into* the damn thing. If they continued their path, they'd be spaghettified by pressure waves from the singularity itself.

But onward into the blackness they went, below the Event Horizon, the continuation of the pinch in space. Presumably, they were heading toward the zone of maximum distortion, where gravity crushed matter until atomic bonds yielded completely. But given the size of this thing, it could be a long way away.

Jessy thought about it and wondered how the fuck they were supposed to survive all that – and with a thump in her stomach, thought they probably weren't. So far, they saw no singularity, but it was out there somewhere, in their future no doubt.

Behind them Mitch could see that the outside had shrunk to a tiny red dot. Now it was a blue dot. Around the tiny coins of colour was blackness...nothingness. There weren't even any stars.

How far would they have moved in time, when and *if* they exited. Jessy felt sick and was ready to vomit – it felt like motion sickness or something similar...how you feel just before death, she reckoned. Jessy kept her eyes closed and counted to keep her mind active. She willed it all to be over.

Ahead of them, far in the distance, but approaching quickly was a particle-spewing, splayed tubescence that was mirrored on the side she could see and probably on the other side as well and also behind them. All engines and gyros were off and untouched. The ISS was not just being pulled in the direction of the objects ahead, it was being accelerated forward by the intense compressed mass. They were moving *fast*.

ISS creaked and groaned like it was being exposed to drag, Jessy watched through the Cupola window and the strange objects were everywhere and changing shapes , like a distortion-mirror at an amusement park. She was sure it was above and behind her as well.

Suddenly, she was outside the craft, looking in at all of them, and she watched herself for a time as she looked down, noting how terrified and machine-like she looked and then was back inside the ship gawking outside at the guts and gristle of the black hole itself. This thing was messing with her mind severely. Then she was suddenly back home, in the forest behind her first home. Jessy was eleven years old when she moved to her new house, but she remembered this day very well. The memory was still strong.

Ed and she were playing hide and seek in the forest until they came across a dead, half eaten horse. Jessy would always remember the flies...and the smell. Ed, her future husband, had found it, killed it, and then she saw it, partly eaten by a bear apparently. Then, she was violently thrust back into her own time, staring outside like a bird following a worm.

She gawked at everyone else, they were moving in rapid motion, talking to each other as though a fast-forward button had been pressed, but they each looked blurry and covered with an odd reddish hue. Jessy found herself outside again. Even Zamindar and Char were similarly covered by odd light, but were still and staring outside, then seemingly moving in fast motion as well when they left their seats and clambered over to the window. Jessy looked down at herself and saw the same red hue covering her body like a sleeve. Thankfully, she was still moving at regular speed when she walked.

Zamindar loped to the airlock and incredibly, came outside, totally unprotected and left the airlock door open. He floated over to her and he toned, 'do you know where we are?' The Virijian abruptly disappeared and she peered inside the craft, which was well-lit. The cosmos outside reflected in Mitch's eyes which looked way bigger than they should have for a normal human. His and in fact all their eyes took up half of their heads, which was nuts. It felt like this place was a crazy asylum or mock-up or circus of crazy mirrors. Mitch was looking straight at her and smiling broadly.

Mitch had his eyes closed now - this thing was playing havoc with everyone's mind. He was remembering experiences from his younger years that he hadn't thought of in yonks. So, his eyes were plastered shut and he was singing and concentrating on inane songs and thoughts, and trying to ignore this thing entirely. And disregard the horrible creaking and screaming from ISS. Eventually, he stopped singing and opened his eyes, re-joining the insanity.

'Einstein-Rosen bridge,' Mitch bellowed, he *hoped,* peering at it and nodding his head sharply. Josh's mind was still spinning. He'd heard about these things, but believed like most others that they were impossibly unstable.

ISS was swallowed by one of the mouths and was immediately caked with a thin swathe of seemingly wet or very shiny particles on top of the remaining bluey-green "goo". It was so extreme in the interior that laws in here danced to a totally different beat from the remainder of the Universe. There were two sets of rules in the Universe – inside a black hole or outside. That was it. But the ISS stayed intact, despite the incredibly high-pressure environment. It groaned and creaked and continued its forward journey.

Mitch couldn't work anything out and really didn't want to. The tunnel-thing was twisting and meandering, yet ISS seemed to follow it perfectly. Perhaps it was gravity or maybe it was the coating of particles – or both. When ISS approached the "end of the line", there was no white light or even a feeling of exiting. ISS was simply spat out, not into space, but into what seemed like another black hole. It was very black, entirely starless, not to mention spooky.

Was it the same black hole? They were all wondering the same thing. No, they didn't think so. This one looked different, at least where they were. Maybe it was just perspective or parallax, but it was like...this one was smaller. This one only had two red lights ahead, which wasn't definitive, but the strong likelihood was this one was different and distinct from the first one and they'd gone straight from one to another. Mitch was holding his breath and released it in a huge phalanx of breath but didn't break his stare from this thing.

They saw the Universe enlarge from a point-like something, to be everything around them, as they emerged from its event horizon. They were back into Euclidean geodesic space, the normal, regulation Universe. The fact that they *emerged* from an event horizon hadn't escaped them, but they put it aside. There was a shit-load of other things to think about. They were out. Somehow, they'd broken several physical laws which seemed impossible. But he didn't care – at least they were out. *How,* didn't matter...yet. There was too much going on. Mitch immediately saw dozens, probably more, very old large, red stars, and one that had clearly been ripped apart by tidal forces and existed now as a huge lenticular cloud of dust and plasma that didn't quite make it to the black hole. It still shone like a star even though it had been torn asunder. Mitch's eyes became wide open as he took a look through the window.

'We've shifted to the middle of the Milky Way Galaxy I think,' Mitch said, staring fixedly through the window at the new vista that unveiled itself. He put his raised hand slowly down.

Char peered at Zamindar, who thankfully put it to bed, 'you are correct Mitch, we are indeed in the centre of the Milky Way Galaxy. We have shifted from Messier 104 galaxy to yours. As to why this black hole is part of the voyage, there are probably two reasons.' Zamindar paused and seemed to be winding up. After a huge whistling breath, he continued, 'apart from general edification about the laws of the Universe this species favours. 'The first reason is that super-massive black holes are a transit system for the Universe, one leads to another and so on, and secondly, these black holes are the power and the energy that needs to be used for interstellar travel. Of course, you have to be in a position to take advantage of them, meaning a certain level of technology is necessary to extract the required benefit from them. Black holes like these are at the root of all substantive transport in the Universe. It is the only way – the speed of light is too slow to get where we and everyone else wants to go. We believe that *One* designed these wormholes to form part of the Universe. They created civilisations so they could eventually meet and hopefully, mix. Hence, a Universe was made that could and would sustain black holes with artificial Einstein-Rosen bridges.'

Mitch knew NASA was working on a laser supported system that would work by sling-shotting light around a spinning black hole to "kinergise" light sails that could potentially move a large starship at relativistic speeds by sending a powerful laser toward the black hole and around it, back to its source. The ship wouldn't even need to carry fuel to accelerate or decelerate. Kinetic energy would be transferred from the black hole to the starship. But that approach didn't assist in firstly *getting* to the spinning black holes.

Zamindar turned his head and looked at Mitch knowingly, 'Gravity and curved space are quite possibly the nexus for all complex life.' Zamindar toned dramatically. 'This was the Bantha's message from their spatial weapon. What that race didn't know, was that you, *humans,* would be a recipient of this insight. It's certainly not something the Bantha planned, I can assure you.'

ISS clawed its way from Sagittarius A, the rotational centre of the entire Milky Way Galaxy. Stars were literally *everywhere*, especially those near the end of their lives...huge bloated red ones not far from supernova, were scarily close to them. The stars around them were so numerous they almost looked like they were touching...almost.

'So, what now?' Josh said nervously, gawking at everyone. All eyes went to him. 'I mean, we've got fourteen months of food, unlimited water and oxygen...but if something goes wrong that we can't fix, which *will* eventually happen, what the *fuck* do we do then?' Josh gasped 'Something will eventually go horribly wrong without servicing by NASA. And probably soon.' Josh took a hissing breath that ended with a gusty sigh of resignation. He was certain of eventual disaster and was a nervous wreck because of it. Stuck in one place with zero resources didn't appeal to him at all.

Josh looked distraught; his splayed hands were against his chest...he was pleading almost. Close to panic. Josh was massaging his collarbone now, stressed to the max. He peered directly at his dad with eyes like saucers, holding his breath. 'Seriously...what do we do then? Is-there anything we can do?' Josh was breathing quickly - almost hyperventilating with terror.

Mitch gazed deadpan at his son not really sure what to say or do. 'Well, then we're in...trouble Josh,' Mitch said, stating the obvious, whispered through a slack jaw knowing he had to be honest and remain calm and set the example. Mitch glanced at the Virijian for directions, hoping against hope that he had some ideas. Because Mitch was all out.

Zamindar unfurled his feet and left hand from the foothold and handhold - float-walking back to the Zvezda Module and Window 12. He preferred silent time to think, rather than entertain wasted discourse about obtuse possibilities. Quantitatives and facts were all he was interested in. The rest was just a waste of energy. What was happening among the humans was a total mis-use of good oxygen.

*   *   *

"Up" had little meaning. Sleeping bags were fixed to walls and curtains ensured some privacy. Some of the individual pods had laptops connected to the structure and books or I-pads to read, so entertainment or work was taken care of. Just long days and similarly long nights. *Waiting.* They all dreamed of Earth, and longed to return. But on this journey, ISS had a mind of its own. The station was guided by a different hand with its own wants and wishes. The occupants could do nought except observe. Josh looked through the top of the Svezda porthole and saw the gooey plasma had retreated from the roof of the ISS. He had no idea what it meant but hoped it was a good sign.

Using the chemical engines, that were attached to ISS made no difference to its heading and speed. ISS still plodded-on at the same speed and on the same heading as before. Something external, or some third party, was guiding the space station. All of them knew the goo was involved in their movement and navigation. After six weeks, all of them were restless and fed up perhaps with the exception of the Virijians. They could simply turn off. If the Virijians wanted to, they could hibernate for years.

The humans were sick of the food and sick of the sight of each other. It had descended into a surrealistic nightmare just to clap eyes on each other. *Same-old* was becoming a real problem aboard the ISS.

It was a daily ritual that all the vessels saw on deck were the two Virijians who seemed to have changed little since they'd started the long wait to shift. The rest of them on deck together, was fairly much a memory. Eating even occurred by themselves, *everything*, became a solitary task. It had now been twelve weeks since they'd been belched from the black hole the humans knew as *Sagittarius A,* the rotational axis of the entire Milky Way Galaxy.

One thing Jessy couldn't understand was how the gravitational titan let them escape, what was a physics-proven *one-way trip*. And that one-way was opposite of their direction of travel when they exited Sagittarius A. They had come out, of what was supposed to be a white hole, but clearly to them, wasn't. They were pretty sure it wasn't white at all. But somehow it let them out. They came out of a black hole – which on paper was *impossible.*

The absence of white holes had always frustrated physicists. It should be that anything allowed by math and physics occurs *somewhere* in the Universe. Yet, white holes seemed to break that theory. Math said they should occur as an opposing analogue of black holes. But they hadn't been found anywhere. Maybe, Mitch thought, they had just experienced a white hole. He held his head in his hands – Mitch really had no idea what had happened   all he knew for sure was that his brain hurt.

Yet, it had happened. It made no sense, the only object to escape black holes was supposed to be Hawking radiation. And they were simply virtual particles – which surely gave them as human beings - octillions of particles, no hope? Jessy wondered about impossibility and counter-intuity and ended up tying herself in knots and feeling once again, bilious and ready to throw-up. She'd never been more confused and thoroughly bewildered in her life. Jessy guessed that's how it felt when you'd done something that on paper was entirely, one-hundred percent, *impossible.*

Char looked at Zamindar and they shared something if their writhing neck-flesh was any guide. No one was any-the-wiser about their conversation. It was strictly between the Virijians. Char sat down, entwining his feet in the rails, letting his upper body float free and gazed directly at Mitch silently.

This one joins with Messier 104,' Char said, pointing with his right hand, knowing what Mitch was going to ask.

Jessy thought about what he'd told them, rubbed her eyes and said what was running through her head, and probably Mitch's as well. 'Of course, we've got to *get* to a super-massive first, before we can use them. The nearest is our own, Sagittarius A, which is still *twenty-five thousand* light years distant,'

Jessy said, rolling her eyes and shaking her head. 'We'll never, *ever* get there. Maybe fusion energy will help.' She gawked at Mitch and grinned lopsidedly, as if to say *like hell.* 'Well, it's something I suppose.' She rolled her eyes and gave Mitch a small, tight smile. To Jessy, it seemed hopeless.

Char wanted to be positive, but realised how Mitch must be feeling. 'It's a natural timer,' Char said. 'When you get there, you'll be ready to use it. It will not be far away.' Like Jessy said, you now have complete knowledge of fusion technology on Earth. Small reactors can be built that could power a space vehicle at almost the speed of light.

Mitch shook his head and looked to the sky. 'I'll say it again, for those *not listening…it's t-o-o far away.*' Mitch boomed, staring at his own dark refection in Zamindar's huge eyes.

'Dad is right - it's still a bloody long trip, even if we factor in time dilation,' Josh said, feeling a shudder that shook his core. '*A long, long way.* Multi-generational. *Jesus* - no one will want to go, no one will fund it. I hate being negative, but that's all there is. We'll never get there. I agree with dad. It's a dream, and it always will be.'

Zamindar toned, 'from Earth, in flat space, you're right Josh, it will be a generational voyage or you could use "nap traps", or choose to send your AI initially. There are other means of getting there too Josh.' Zamindar stared emptily at him, leaving Josh wondering if the Virijian was going to continue. Eventually, he spoke.

"'Perhaps like the Bantha or us,' Zamindar said firmly, 'you will uncover the tech for "shortening", which I am confident you will do.' He stared at Josh again, glancing spiritlessly at Mitch and Jessy.

He was actually right. A young Mexican lad had worked out the physics for "shortening" many years before. The best thing about it was it theoretically worked. It allowed warp drive or faster-than-light travel by surfing on a bubble of space rather than travelling "through" space. The only problem humanity had with it was that we had no idea how to source negative pressure or the huge amounts of energy needed to use it. It is hoped that the discovery of dark matter would assist its feasibility. Whatever though, Zamindar was right, we would *eventually* solve the problems.

Jessy gazed at Mitch with tired but determined eyes. 'We will probably start by getting energy remotely,' she said. 'Sending a laser to close orbit the spinning black hole will energise it by adding kinetic energy which in turn will impel a ship forward. Being close to it will make the exercise more effective.'

Then it suddenly happened. ISS finally did something - shaking and rolling, vibrating and pulsing like a tremendous heartbeat. Anyone who was touching a surface, started jigging and shaking, vibrating, preparatory, they believed, *hoped*, to shifting.

Mitch didn't want to go somewhere impossibly distant, or to a new black hole, he'd had enough of that shit. He, like all of them, wanted to go home. *Period*. It was *time*. They'd been away far too long. He knew it was odds against, but he really wanted to know what was happening on Earth. So, Mitch closed his eyes and crossed fingers on both hands and hoped like hell. He hadn't broached the "why" question yet. Why the hell would the Bantha's spatial weapon take them back to Earth of all places? If they were indeed shot fortuitously the end of the trip would *not* be Earth. *No way.* It was simple logic.

'*Thank God,*' Jessy shrilled, seeing the water boiling in the plastic cup. She wanted to go home more than anything else, but she was glad just to see quaking and shuddering. Anything but more of the same. Anything but *nothing*. Isolation was great for a few days, but not for months...*it sucked* and it was deeply depressing. Having something to talk about brought humans together.

Mitch wondered if there was even a home or people left. Maybe another Bantha craft had set a new deadline, after seeing the progress we'd made toward becoming fully sustainable. *And pigs might fly*, Mitch thought, knowing their ghastly history too well. But possibly, they had dispatched all of humanity because the demand date had passed and as a result had done as they promised for non-compliance. The mind-set of the Bantha was totally unknown...and highly concerning. To gauge them or forecast based on "what humans would do" was useless and stupid.

Their reaction to our offensive act was also totally unknown. From our viewpoint what we did was justified, but from theirs...probably not. They undoubtedly assumed that we had been obliterated. Again, that was an assumption...and we didn't know the real story. The Bantha probably didn't have a clue where we went. Or maybe they did, down to the finest level of detail. In other words, everything was a guess. *Xeno-psychology* was a total unknown.

Not far away in space was something small and bright. Whatever it was, looked *wrong*. It didn't equate with anything any human had ever seen before. It was sort of like red but it wasn't red, or any other primary, secondary or tertiary colour either. No one had a name for it, which was very strange, straight off the bat. It was light like yellow or white maybe...but that's it. Its real colour didn't have a name in any human language. It looked truly bizarre.

In any event, Jessy and for that matter, all the humans were bemused by the small object itself. It wasn't a new shade or mix of colours because that would be called out and named. *WTF* was high in their minds. As was odd, strange, bizarre, unique, weird and so on. Zamindar unfolded himself from the floor and prepared to tone, appearing as intrigued as they'd ever seen him, as intrigued as he was during the episode with *One*. Jessy and probably the others, could hear the static and cranial noise. He'd gone from total indifference to mildly interested, which, for him was nigh on amazing.

I am surprised you haven't worked it out yourselves,' The Virijian said. Mitch peered out the window again, the colour still meant nothing to him.

'We are near the centre of your star's L3 Lagrange point,' Zamindar toned, 'where the Sun's and the Earth's gravity are fairly much in synch. Gravity is cancelled out so, the ISS is stable, but given what has happened previously, anything is possible. L3 is stable for a stationery craft, but if force is applied, we move.' The Virijian stopped toning and looked out the window. 'That object, on the starboard side of the station is something very unusual indeed. Firstly, it is producing light of a color and energy which is not seen on Earth or anywhere near it. Secondly, what is it?' It looked super strange, the size of an asteroid, but clearly not an asteroid. Mitch tried to assign a name to it but couldn't. None of the humans had a clue what it was.

Mitch opened his mouth to have a guess but closed it again when he decided he didn't have one he wanted to share. Zamindar continued, believing the humans would have little idea.

'It is a naked singularity, a black hole where there is no cosmic censorship and the insides of the black hole are visible. This is probably the rarest of cosmic objects. One was recently found near Trijicyon which Sean can attest to,' the Virijian said, appearing very serious indeed. 'This one holds a shift which we should investigate,' Zamindar toned, his words suggesting excitement, but his face and the way he delivered the words, suggesting severe disinterest. *Go figure.* Emotion might cause blood pressure hikes and probably health problems, but being without them would make humankind way less human...similar to computers. Being an emotion-less bag of data like the Virijians was very unappealing.

'I'd say I didn't want to go on such a voyage, but I probably don't have much choice...right?' Josh said, holding his stomach, feeling the gurgling. The writing was on the wall. *Again*, he thought.

Mitch peered grimly at the thing in front of them and wondered what the hell it was connected to...*something* according to Zamindar. He said there was a wormhole buried within. The information conveyed by the Virijian was hardly embracing. Their choice was to ignore it and stay here...or go on the voyage. The previous shifts had gone to plan, and he trusted Zamindar, so he looked at Jessy and Josh and nodded crisply.

'I suppose we enter and see what's what, we can't stay here and Zamindar seems happy enough to go,' Jessy said, looking directly back at Mitch who again nodded. Jessy knew very well they couldn't stay here. Zamindar said that we should enter and that was good enough for her. They were doomed to expire if they stayed here. That made the choice easy.

Josh wasn't making eye contact with anyone, looking down and swallowing and blinking rapidly. The poor kid was as pale as a ghost, and clearly not looking forward to the next stage of the voyage. '*Christ* Joshy...are you okay?' Jessy asked tenderly.

Josh opened his mouth to speak but nothing came out. He coughed loudly and then said he was fine in a muffled, trembling voice, noise that just managed to escape his mouth.

The Virijian knew that the spatial "goo" had receded sufficiently for the onboard engines to work, and he had the remote controls sorted, and ignited two Progress engines on the Svezda Service which sent the ISS forward. This was the first time the ISS had moved under the strength of its own power since it was hijacked by the Bantha. The object ahead was banded and had what looked a bit like Jupiter's atmosphere whipping around its torso. It was a mighty odd-looking object, colour unknown.

According to Zamindar, it was a naked singularity. As soon as they got within twenty or so kilometres of it, things changed. They all started to feel a bit groggy. Presumably, pressure waves started to deeply effect space...or should that be *time*. The object was abruptly bright yellow in colour and clearly cubic...then it changed to triangles and then octagons and then hexagons, trapeziums, rhombohedra...dodecahedra, and back to spherical. It was intense and vigorous, effecting the human brain by releasing dopamine everywhere.

It then changed shape again, going through the different forms again. With each shape change, came a different colour, from yellow, through red, green, pink, blue etc. back to the indescribable colour - its default condition.

Inside the ISS, the walls of the station disappeared and reappeared, blinking on and off rapidly, causing Jessy to hold her head in her hands and stop watching. Everything out there wasn't really happening, she said to herself over and over. It was all a mirage...an illusion, imposed on them by very high gravity. That was her firm belief. She refused to think any of it was real.

They were travelling slowly through an area of highly distorted space that did very strange things to the human mind. Jessy glanced at the object. It compelled her with some sort of inertia – now it was a sphere and covered with numerous mouths full of saliva or moisture that seemed to drip from it. .The object vanished entirely then returned, not as the pinch in space but as the house she lived in when she was young. The dopamine in her brain was doing its job. It materialised in front of her. She shook her head in dismay, trying to clear her mind, but the house remained. There were three windows and a brown door that was visibly banging – open and then closed. *Bang, bang, bang.*

When it opened, there was a skeletal figure observable, standing in the doorway, peering out. Jessy shut her eyes and stopped looking, massaging the middle of her forehead, singing a song to herself, under her loud hissing breath to avoid panicking and running around the ship screaming out loud.

Keeping the structures open, according to Zamindar, was dark energy - the substance that provided the inflationary inertia to keep them and it turgid. Zamindar had told them all that, and confirmed that all the information came courtesy of *One* through the *sphere*. Dark energy that kept the wormholes open was *not* natural they were told. The implications were clear. Jessy was right.

Then they were upon it, and the pounding abruptly ceased. It was another bridge to another place, and all the humans had the same question embedded in their brains. Where in space and when in time would they come out? Perhaps a different Universe, another of *One's* creations, or the same spot, but a million years in the future? The possibilities were boundless.

One thing Jessy and probably the rest of them noticed, were the hexagonal patterns on the wormhole when they first entered it. It was still there and seemed, to their eyes, to mark the structure as synthetic. None of them knew if that was the case, and it probably didn't matter either. If the wormhole worked, it worked. If it pinched closed...well...

They weren't inside long. ISS popped out into painted space packed full of old and huge bloated red stars. ISS was coursing through space near the galactic centre, and like before, they all saw the majestic glow from Sagittarius A, surrounded by starloads of bright material that was slowly being consumed. The entrails of stars formed ribbons of gas that were gravitationally bound to the hole, forming a huge multicoloured pinwheel that lost momentum near its inner surface and spiralled into the darkness.

Looking out at the Galaxy, he saw millions of stars studding the north polar spur, shining between enormous clouds of colorful dust. Mitch hoped like hell the boron, nitrogen and oxygen nanotubes woven into his suit would protect him and them from the X and gamma rays they simply had to be dosing up on. And same for the Virijians, he thought hopefully. He felt pretty good, so he took that as a clear "okay" on his health.

Then, they were back inside yet again. Mitch saw the hexagonal pattern on the surface flash passed the window to the side. Zamindar took manual control of the GNC, felt the heaviness of the controls and made changes to Progress, Svezda and the gyroscopes, where necessary, although it followed its path and got momentum automatically. Mitch watched pieces of the wormhole wobble off and quickly re-join, as ISS smashed into the seemingly delicate surface. If what Zamindar said was true, they were coursing through an Einstein-Rosen bridge full to the brim with Dark Matter.

The ISS was spat out at L3 and Mitch and Jessy reckoned they were being shown the "flexibility" that existed within the transport network. Who knew really – they were given a lot of think-time, so that's what they did. They spent a lot of time trying to decode reasoning for each object or location, and probably got it all horribly wrong on all of them. The humans thought they knew what each one meant – *but did they really?*

*   *   *

Zamindar began the relatively short journey from L3 back to Earth. Jessy watched the object through the Cupola window, as the naked singularity receded in space, rotating maniacally, still unable to identify its colour.

As they travelled away from it, the mouths became singular and it closed like a sutured wound. The glowing particles slowed in their rotation and completely stopped. Mitch tried to avoid asking himself "how" and "why", but the object gave the strong impression of being unnatural. He guessed he'd never know the real story. The "goo" had completely gone now, according to Zamindar. They were free of it for the first time since they left Earth.

Jessy watched through the rear of the Cupola window at the goings on with the object and couldn't help thinking "machine". It looked anything but a natural part of the Universe. *Why* had it shed its apron of darkness? It carried a strong mark of intelligence. If unnatural had any meaning left in this Universe, then it had to be tagged to that object.

*   *   *

Mitch spoke to Zamindar at length, and he actually responded, trying his hardest, it seemed, to work the Bantha out. Their journey in the ISS made little sense to Mitch and he wanted to know *why* they were sent on this incongruous voyage. I mean, he knew where they went but not *why* they visited these things? Guesses just weren't sufficient for Mitch.

Zamindar gave them "fortuitous" as a reason, but it wasn't enough. Why did the Bantha want to send *anyone* on a spatial journey? That was the answer he sought. He understood getting rid of an enemy to another location, but again, what they had endured was a lot more than that – it was "educating". Mitch put it down to xeno-psychology again – the Bantha had very different neuro-wiring to humans. Any expectation of consistent thinking was quite simply wrong.

Apparently for humans, the want, the desire, the *obsession* to truly decode the Universe and learn its mathematics, was shared by perhaps a few

247

thousand, maybe a few million individuals. On Bantha, that obsession ran *far* deeper and hit many, many millions and quite probably billions of individuals.

The Bantha apparently had a hundred "Einsteins" and numerous "Hawkings". Their species was far better equipped to decode the operation of the Universe than humans, even though they were a significantly younger species. It was *mind*-set that was important. That's why, as a civilisation, they evolved so quickly, and how they had tech almost as advanced as the Virijians. The Bantha were less than half as old. In space, *learning and understanding* remained at the core of what they tried to achieve as a species.

The Bantha expected every interstellar traveller they encountered to be the same. To be hungry for knowledge, with a strongly developed desire to learn. Hence, the spatial weapon they were hit with, probably by chance, mind you. It turned out, this was not a weapon of "aggression" per se. *Go figure*. It was a weapon of translocation and re-education.

*   *   *

They'd returned from L3 and below them finally was beautiful blue Earth around which they were in a low orbit, moving just above the planet's exosphere, occasionally moving in and out of the atmosphere. This was very close to their starting point.

Earth had grown a torus, a tail of gas or dust or both, that extended behind the planet into space. From further away it was very prominent as it caught the rays from the Sun. To Mitch and everybody on-board, it was highly concerning. Because it wasn't there before. The Karman line seemed intact though and he could see the iconic solar panels of the Galaxy satellite, which among other things, sent digital TV signals to the east coast of America.

All seemed to be in order thus far. Maybe the torus was natural, he thought, although, it was a hell of a coincidence. Mitch wondered if Earth knew they were here via their numerous ground telescopes, the Hubble and other remote orbiters. He refused to entertain less desirable outcomes.

They and the ISS had shifted back close to its starting point, and had returned from L3, without the intergalactic horror from Bantha being in front of them. Everything seemed okay, so far. Looking away from Earth though, space seemed unfriendlier and more hostile than it had before. Thank you Bantha.

The Bantha craft which had offered so much aggression and devastation was now nowhere to be seen because they had destroyed it. The question was - had a new one done what the destroyed craft had promised, or did the Bantha proffer a new deadline? Maybe they just left Earth alone? Mitch admitted to himself that it sounded like a feeble pipe dream. But he'd keep believing in it until he knew different.

They couldn't tell from here, but radio waves and EMAR generally would tell the story. All the satellites seemed to be there. If the planet was loud with radio waves, that would tell them all was probably okay. If it was silent, it would tell an altogether different and probably extremely unpalatable story.

Mitch floated over to the nearest radio and pressed the button to tune it manually. After a minute of fiddling, he looked up with sorrowful eyes, huge with terror and fear. '*Shit* ... there is *nothing* on AM radio.' He'd gone from end to end on the band and found nothing but static, 'nothing is being broadcast, er...at all,' he said, '*empty...totally fucking empty,*' he was still moving the frequency band but found only static. 'Earth is not broadcasting anything in AM or FM.' Mitch turned it off with a fist. '*Fuck,*' he boomed, pressing his hand flat against his forehead. He knew what it meant.

Mitch darted his gaze over all of them, muttering expletives to himself. He knew what it meant in the first nanosecond. 'Nearly every country should be producing AM signals,' Mitch said, looking downcast and sighing sadly. He turned his seat as far as it would go away from the group, and bit his lip with his eyes closed tightly to keep in the tears. *He knew.* The tears came anyway, in a torrent of anguish.

'*Fuck, fuck, shit,*' Josh vented loudly. All of them knew exactly what it meant. It meant no one was broadcasting. It was very, *very* bad for the planet, it had to be. Normally, the atmosphere was literally alive with radio signals. Jessy held her head with both hands, sniffing and wiping at her nose, clutching at her neck. She found it impossible to believe. '*Shit...it can't be...can it?*' She shrilled, piercing Mitch with her words. She put her head back in her hands and moaned to herself. Jessy was almost hysterical, thinking of all those lost – an entire planetary population. The Bantha had a lot to answer for. She honestly didn't think they'd do it...threaten it, *sure*, but never, ever go through with it.

Josh refused to believe it, wanting to try the radio, again. Mitch said *no* forcefully. 'Use that pound or so of mush between your ears Josh, what do you think it means?' Mitch snapped, glaring at him, and then peering off into the distance and closing his eyes again. What the hell should they do now? He wondered. No radio meant no people, right? *Fuck*, he thought. The very worst had manifested before his eyes. He too, didn't think it'd ever happen. There wasn't even a government broadcast.

Mitch looked at the globe below and felt like screaming, or yelling until he ran out of breath, which might be...well, who knows when that might be. Hitting something was definitely an option, but *what though*? In this situation, a show of temper was bad because it could snowball into something difficult to stop. He had to calm his emotions...his heart was beating out of control in his neck. Him having a heart attack and dying ingloriously would be the final ignominious act for all of this. Mitch would prefer that it didn't happen even though things weren't looking good for anybody.

As an astronaut with NASA, he'd been to psychologists to learn how to deal with bad news and poor outcome scenarios. He was supposed to breathe thoracically, wipe the news from his mind, and not get concerned over new responsibilities or make impulsive decisions – follow the agreed rules whatever they might be. He hadn't had the need to think about it since it was laid out for him, but now it sounded like a load of under-reaction bullshit. *We were talking about everyone from our entire planet.* That had to be enough to get upset about, even using NASAs stupid standards. Mitch knew that was the typical first reaction – to deny a painful truth. He tried his best to breathe normally.

Jessy was staring at her hands, mind totally enraged. All those people and the human babies and those just born, she thought, feeling like curling up on the ground and never getting up again.

Mitch knew that withdrawing was no way to deal with "the probability", but there it was. It was hard not to react that way. He watched Jessy and Josh, they both looked terrified and totally overwhelmed. Their dull, empty stares said everything. They were probably the last few of a very endangered species. He wondered how many humans were still alive on the planet below them.

Zamindar had said if the first craft was destroyed, the Bantha wouldn't follow up with a further craft. They would go to the next name on the list. He was wrong – for the first time it had happened. Mitch shouldn't have been surprised...our logic would say a second craft was always going to come. But the fact that Zamindar was wrong, *was* surprising. Of course, that begs the question of how serious he was with the answer. Did he just want all the concentration to be on the first craft? Or did he just want us not to worry about things that were beyond our control. Again, it came down to *xeno-psychology.*

Training had equipped Mitch to some extent so it was up to him to set the tone, he realised that and swallowed hard, squaring his shoulders. *What a fucking nightmare*, he thought, shaking his head and looking at the planet that used to hold an entire civilization. The globe was a huge ugly cloud that covered most of the Atlantic and Africa – and it wasn't a regular cloud either. Mitch felt like screaming – no amount of psych training could prepare you for this. They always knew it was a possibility, but to see it was heartbreaking in the extreme.

'What the hell do we do now?' Jessy said quietly, darting her gaze over everyone. She too looked completely devastated.

Zamindar toned, 'we will go to Earth to look it over, the *Lunar* vehicle has enough fuel to get there and back and do what is required.'

'Okay,' Mitch felt like saluting him or calling him "sir", 'that's the plan, assemble with gear in *Destiny* by 1200. We go to Earth to see how bad it is.'

Josh was ready to kill, he felt hatred for the murderous bastards that had probably done this. If only we'd destroyed their craft a little sooner. That would have sent a stronger message to their home planet. Do not fuck with Earth. If you do, you die. Also, we wouldn't have been hit by the spatial weapon. Clearly, another craft or crafts had followed the first one and done the job.

*   *   *

Mitch eyed them. 'Onto the *Lunar*,' he said, showing the way with his arm to the IDA-2 airlock where the ship was docked. Zamindar was in the pilot's seat with Mitch beside him. The Virijian understood Earth tech as well as his own. The Virijian gave separation instructions to the *Lunar* which released hooks and latches. Once mechanically released into free space, a short burn was followed by a larger burn which had them in the atmosphere and enjoying molecular friction in short order.

'Where do we land?' Josh asked, while the ship was still fighting with re-entry, thinking somewhere in North America. At NASA maybe, afterall their first priority apart from checking out Earth was probably fuel.

'We will land at AASSA, we are all familiar with this airfield.' Zamindar said, looking at each of the humans quite deliberately then flicked open the manual RCS cover as a huge sonic boom enveloped the craft.

They quickly broke through the lower cloud cover and the answer to their first question became obvious. The buildings that formed AASSA were virtually gone, only broken, shattered and crushed remnants remained. The large block of apartments that housed many of those who worked at AASSA was gone. There were no plants or even substantial remnants of the twisted, thin trees in the landscape, anywhere. There were no bodies or skeletons anywhere, although, ground truthing would give a better more detailed picture.

It was a bit like someone had sandpapered the landscape clean of anything, living or not. Thankfully, the runways remained pretty much intact. They were a bit potholed and covered with sand, but they were still there, and he believed, on preliminary inspection, they were still serviceable.

Seeing such devastation and annihilation was the worst visual possible, he reckoned, looking around and feeling the hopelessness and loneliness kick in. And a lot of guilt. Had they destroyed the Bantha craft earlier, might things have been different? Or maybe a second craft would have come, irrespective of when or if we destroyed the first ship. Perhaps they would have sent a second ship to determine the outcome – *period*. In other words, our position was worse than we thought from the outset. That would mean Zamindar was wrong though, which was very odd - he was so adamant. He'd never been wrong or even off before, so it was a bit strange.

The annihilation of humankind, which seemed likely, was impossibly hard to deal with. It was insane even to think about it. Mitch in particular was struggling with it; he was wondering what would have happened if he was in charge of taking the shot. He would never, ever know whether it would have made a difference, which made his mind-set even more grim. Second and third guessing was a strong Taylor trait.

They landed at AASSA on Runway No 2 which terminated near the spot where the main building and accommodation wing used to be. Not surprisingly, there wasn't a person to be seen. Ordinarily, Sean would meet them near the tarmac, but that didn't happen. He, along with everybody else, was gone...annihilated in an unknown but clearly violent manner by the Bantha. All were gone. The building Sean lived in completely pulverised and destroyed. There was only dust and tiny remnants of a once grand structure in the desert.

And incredibly, Anzac Hill was no longer there - *levelled*. They all wondered, *what sort of weapon did that?* A geomorphic weapon perhaps.
All of them stood in a group, unsure what to do, unsure where to go. Josh and Jessy and Mitch were probably amongst the last members of Homo Sapiens, and now stood on Earth with "beings" from other worlds. It was surreal. Mitch sort of knew what the next step had to be. He refuelled the space plane using the only unexploded fuel-truck he could find at AASSA.

They needed to go to Norway. Mitch had discussed it with Zamindar and Char, and they concurred with what he was saying. Apparently, it was an excellent idea, probably the only thing they could do. Who would've thought that going to Norway was *ever* a good idea? Right now, it was a great idea...probably the only decent option. Hopefully, the seed vault on Spitsbergen Island was still intact. It was several hundred metres underground, and built into the mountain built to survive nuclear strikes and be able to ride out an apocalypse –The only worry was that it may be under-water.

If they could, they would gather certain seeds and scatter them from the air. Some would germinate, most wouldn't, but eventually, some would grow into rice, corn, trees and plants of all kinds. Hopefully, they would, in part, re-green Earth. And supply food to them and any survivors. That was the plan, longish term as it may have been. Mitch and Zamindar agreed, at least some would germinate and grow. Earth would slowly become vegetated again, over many, many years. They needed a plan – and this was it. They had no idea if the soil was any good post-Bantha, but they would keep their fingers crossed on that one. Nothing ventured, nothing gained, Mitch supposed - some of them would grow. It couldn't be known if the remnants of vegetation would be any good, so, Earth had to be forcibly brought back to life. So, the atmosphere could recover...he guessed but still, wondered. And any trace of humanity?

Underground was the obvious answer, those that didn't die in rock-falls, would probably be alive, Josh thought, mostly Chinese males, he reckoned. Thousands of them. *Here come the reds* - Josh knew they'd get us in the end, he thought, grinning wickedly, keeping his thoughts to himself.

'Pockets of humans *must* be there,' Josh said to himself. If you were underground, you were fairly safe. That's about it, even those in Antarctica would have been killed if they were outside, or in a building above ground. So, if you were below ground, you probably survived. Above ground, you died. Hence, very little life remained on Earth. That answered the lack of radio.

Those aboard the space-plane had plotted their course. They would travel over Indonesia, Iran, Ukraine and finally Finland and then Norway. Then, if they could, Zamindar would bring the craft down on Spitsbergen Island in Norway, assuming the runway was intact. Mitch knew stretched across a tiny peninsula. Good luck, he said to himself. The landing strip was tiny.

It begged the question again – what weapon did the Bantha use against Earth? Using nukes seemed like a complete anathema – senseless beyond reason. Those weapons would fuck with the atmosphere like no other. Mitch thought of the planet they found Gaznoy on. Earth was similar in that bodies of the dead were fairly much absent. Zamindar told them, based on results, it was probably a high intensity extra-aural ultrasonic weapon that disintegrated all flesh and bone it touches, if the frequency is right.

So, he reckoned it was death by disintegration for billions of souls. It sounded impossible and immediately made Mitch think of the Martian "death ray" championed some time ago. As ridiculous as it seemed, it was probably as close to the truth as they were gonna get. The fine layer of smelly dust they found everywhere was probably just that – *people particles*. And the effect on the atmosphere was nil. All it created was an amount of dust that settled to the ground in short order. Bantha 10/humans 0.

*   *   *

'What do we do if there's no a-airfield,' Josh said shakily, 'or even island?' His words dried up mid-sentence. Josh was going through the options in his mind, none of which he particularly liked. Just maybe, the island was non-existent and only cold ocean remained in its place. *Fuck*, Josh thought. Pitching into the freezing sea didn't appeal to him one bit.

In fact, flying itself didn't thrill him much – give him a couch and a pair of Ugg-boots any day. Josh hated heights. For his family – he was an odd specimen indeed.

Mitch just glared at his son. No words were needed. If that happened, they were likely all *fucked*, because if the airfield was gone, it's highly likely they all were. Pock marked or potholed, to a degree would be okay, but if the runway was gone or too badly damaged, or worse, the ocean had risen, they would eventually have to pitch in the sea. And then it was probably goodnight. Survival gear was only useful if a rescue was a possibility.

Josh felt sure they'd fall from the sky well before they made it to Norway. Positive thinking had never been a strong point with him.

13

Perpetual Repercussion

"Almost-right is no better than wrong." —*Isaac Asimov*

Zamindar was speedily getting through the pre-flight checks. 'Altimeter and directional gyros set, fuel gauges and trim checked, flight controls checked, ready to go,' Zamindar said. Inwardly, he was a little surprised that so many systems needed checking every time the *Lunar* took to the skies. He could tell how each system was, just by looking at its monitor and "greying", whatever that was. If he did that, Zamindar would immediately know if the craft was good to go or not. And if it wasn't, he'd know why.

Mitch nodded at the Virijian, so he gunned the Rolls Royce engines and at 135 knots pulled back the flight stick and the space plane thundered into the sky. Zamindar always gave Mitch the feeling of being in full control of the craft. Off they went and the sky was theirs...apart from insects and a few lost birds, they were the only remaining denizens of the blue. No flight clearance needed now.

Indonesia and southern India were a wasteland of nothing, no people and no structures. Tamil Nadu and the Lotus Temple were erased like they were never there. These countries were normally teeming with people and life, so many and too much - people were nearly standing on top of each other in urban settings. Incredibly and depressingly, Mt Bromo was gone from Java, he remembered climbing the damn thing not long ago, now it was totally gone. The volcano was now just a featureless plain in the Semeru National Park. No doubt, if given the chance, it would rise gain.

A tapestry of confusion and food had been erased like it was never there. The second and fourth most populous nations on the planet were no more, sandpapered clean, all the temples, places, and memorials were gone. Whatever they used to be, was crushed and annihilated. People just weren't there.

Zamindar reduced height to 5,000 metres over southern India and it was truly horrible. The Meenakshi temple, and the Chola monuments weren't there at all, just mounds of broken rubbish like the others. They flew over Iran, the southern tip of Russia, what used to be Ukraine and into Sweden and the story was the same. All human infrastructure was gone and all humanity disappeared.

Approaching Norway from the south-east above the icy ocean and coming up on the island, it was still there, thank God. There was even a bunch of polar bears on the ice flows they flew over, so that was a good sign. There was *life*. The bears no doubt had been underwater when the weapon or whatever it was, hit.

The island itself, from here, looked like a series of parallel snow-covered mountains, the landforms themselves looking untouched by anything, The mountains lacked snow and ice though – which was odd. From what he'd read, the island had a covering of snow and ice all year. But now, the hills and mountains had nothing – no snow or ice. On the plains though, it looked normal, there was snow everywhere down there.

Jessy said that she spied the entry area to the seed vault through her binoculars and said that it looked *acceptable*, whatever that meant. She offered a small smile. At least it was positive...she meant it was still there presumably and she appeared happy enough.

It was unlike Longyearbyen, which was squashed and gone. The old proud Soviet settlement of Pyramiden was the same – crushed beyond recognition and gone.

The seed vault was a bit like a massive computer hard drive peeking out of the snow. She and everyone else on-board were now looking for the airport. They desperately needed somewhere to put down. Josh disliked exercise intensely, but he needed to stretch his legs and walk around a bit. He'd had quite enough of this cramped craft that only promised death and sore legs. Always the negatives.

'*Over there,*' Josh, looking rather pale, snapped, tapping on the window - on a short outcropping piece of land, was an airstrip which still looked intact, apart from a few holes and cracks, but there was definitely no airport. It had been flattened by their friends from Bantha. It looked pushed over, and squashed, otherwise obliterated and mostly gone, like the other towns on this island.

Zamindar already knew the airstrip was there, and reduced airspeed for a landing. He angled the plane toward the head of the airstrip and increased the rate of descent. '*Whooooah,*' Josh barked, feeling like the craft had stopped in mid-air, and was about to fall out of the sky. He felt dizzy and woozy – flying definitely wasn't his thing.

'Do not worry,' Zamindar said, piloting the craft. 'We are aligning ourselves with the runway and will be landing soon. The landing strip itself is icy and wet, Be prepared for a rough landing. It is the only way.'

Josh looked out of his window and was nauseous and queasy as he gawked at the snow and ice that was everywhere. He felt better when he focussed on the seat in front of him, even better when he held his head in his hands – looking out the window at the snow and the mountains was a really bad idea.

There were occasional outcrops of rock and darkish strata below them. 'Er...uh, righto,' he whispered, feeling like a dick at his behaviour in front of his mum, who was watching him closely. He tightened his seat-belt so it was skin tight. He'd never flown in such a small aircraft. In his mind's-eye, Josh could see his dad react to his phobia. It wasn't pretty.

A thump hitting the landing strip followed. All of them waited for directions from the Virijian pilot then Zamindar led them into a small group, standing next to their transport. It was freezing cold outside and there was ice and snow everywhere around them.

De-boarded from the small, warm spaceplane, they stood on the icy, windy, runway and peered at the dreadful kilometre of walking they needed to put up with through a freezing snowfield, which lay between them and the seed vault. Josh had his cap pulled down as far as it would go. Clouds of cold breath escaped equally cold lungs and throats, enveloping them before quickly vanishing into the ether.

It wouldn't be easy, Jessy thought, looking at the back packs that were empty now, but would be full and no doubt heavy as on the way back. Some of them ran on the spot to feel less cold, which didn't work. It was really fucking cold. Mitch looked out to the ocean and saw a walrus dive into the water from an iceberg, to get away from a polar bear. *More life*. But not human.

Hopefully, on leaving this place, their backpacks would be full of seed packs, they would open them with their teeth and be ready to throw seeds from the yawning airlock door at the appropriate time. Josh looked at the walk ahead and took the first few steps and disappeared up to his thigh in heavy snow. 'Best you er, follow us,' Mitch said, seeing Josh sink in the loose snow, as they walked up an ice-covered road. 'Don't go near the off-road parts, they're deep and unpacked and possibly dangerous,' Mitch said.

'You might have been more specific earlier,' Josh replied, pulling himself roughly from the deep snow and walking delicately onto the road with the others, puffing hard and filling his own horizon with white clouds.

*   *   *

'We're...*relatively* warm, but it won't last,' Jessy said, rubbing her hands together. 'If you want to get warmer, we need to get inside that damn thing, and away from this wind which is more than formidable. Then there's more walking to do, I'm afraid. Walking, walking and then more walking. *Fucking great.*

Groans and moans about more of the walking stuff were abruptly terminated by Josh who was ahead of them, working hard on the entry to the vault, and getting frustrated by something.

'*Fuck it,*' he yelled, kicking the wall. Everyone turned to look at him. '*Damn it,*' he snapped, poking and prodding something on the wall of the vault. 'We need a keycard and passcode to enter this thing. He tried his best to get in, but the steel door was locked by heavy cylinders and pins. They were indeed stuck outside - there seemed no way they were getting passed this heavy password-protected door without the correct code and a pin-card.

Char walked up to Josh and turned the handle and pulled the front door open with nothing short of brute Virijian force. They were inside, but it still felt like being in a meatlocker. It was as freezing inside as it was outside. The difference was, there was no wind in the vault. '*Thank you, thank you,* Josh whispered, blowing into his cupped hands, the lack of wind made it at least ten degrees warmer. Now it went from bloody freezing to just freezing.

'So, there's five doors between us and the seeds, right?' Josh asked anyone that was listening, hearing his own echoing voice. A statement more than a question, he'd thankfully read up on the place, previously. He found it quite interesting. Doing a refresher unfortunately wasn't possible. The internet was only a memory.

was so incredibly quiet in here - you could hear your own heart pump. Or any other part of your anatomy that made a noise.

No one heard a thing though, everyone was focussed on getting past the first door, which was covered in a fine sheen of ice, the crystals shining in the light that came from above. The door was frozen shut. It was locked without being locked. Totally different to the outer door to this facility, but shut and stuck all the same.

It looks unlocked,' Mitch knelt down looking closely at it. The door was encrusted with ice crystals but not locked - the handle still turned. Josh eyed the back of Mitch's head, running on the spot, with his hands in his pockets to try and keep warm. Nothing seemed to help. It was *so fucking* cold in this stupid place. Walking didn't help at all. He felt like running back to the craft and shutting the outer hatch, or putting a spacesuit on or maybe turning on the thrusters and standing inside one. It was *that* cold.

Mitch turned the handle and opened the door, once the ice was broken - it wasn't locked, which to him seemed odd, but with the front door of the facility locked, perhaps it was okay. Security was still pretty good, but security from what though, he wasn't sure?

*   *   *

'Here it is...*thank Christ*, the last door. *Hallelujah*. Mitch was almost walking on his knees, but he'd finally made it. He felt so tired and cold he almost couldn't go another step, but everyone else looked bright-eyed and reasonably fresh, albeit cold, so ego drove him on.

Mitch was essentially the leader of the group, or at least that's how he felt. And he was more or less responsible for what was left of humanity. The future of the goddamn species – no biggie. There were probably isolated pockets of humans that survived, but he didn't need to worry about them right now. He was responsible for the future of the species with these seeds firstly. To make sure there was a future, of some sort. No wonder he felt tired.

He'd walked so far into the mountain, Mitch and the rest of them were almost at the actual seed repository. It was still cold, but with the exercise and lack of wind, it felt slightly warmer. Several of them had undone the top buttons on their coats.

The concrete and steel structure, Josh explained, could survive just about anything, including major climate change and massive sea level rise. Not to mention nukes or anything similar you might care to throw at it. It had survived the best an aggressive alien race could throw at it. That looked pretty damn impressive on its CV.

There was enough room for several billion seed species in the three strongrooms. They were only interested in the second room, the only one used so far, that stored more than a million seed species. It sounded like there was a lot of species here, but it only sounded that way - there was a *lot* of spare room.

The fifth door was sparkling with crystallized ice, and opened easily once the ice was removed with a foldable knife, by Mitch who managed to cut his finger in the process, so there was blood amongst the ice on the floor.

Jessy applied a plaster to his finger, calling him "an uncoordinated goose". He was genuinely hopeless with small tasks. Getting to and walking on Mars, no problem, but take the man shopping and he was useless...he couldn't even add up with a calculator. *Go figure*, Jessy thought. He could make NASA happy...cock-a-hoop even, but give him an everyday task...*forget it/*

All of them jumped a bit at a sudden noise behind them. It sounded like a door shutting. They looked behind them to see where the noise came from and they saw an elderly woman approaching them, holding something long in one hand, stepping aggressively toward them.

They all stood to attention, already cold but now frozen in shock, waiting for her to attack them with her unknown weapon. Who the *fuck* was this individual and why was she coming for them? She continued to move forward and didn't look happy. In fact, she looked ready to kill.

'*Who in God's name are you lot?*' She said angrily, tromping straight up the walkway, apparently not afraid in the least, weighing them all up with a critical squint. Whoever the hell it was, she looked like she'd been waiting for them. Hiding and waiting.

'*Who the hell are you?*' Mitch said back to her, without answering. He was going to use an expletive but decided not to. She looked irritated enough already. He shot her a cold look, rubbing the back of his neck.

'I'm Rosie Jones,' she said...almost immediately starting to scream, then wobbling and fainting in a disorganised heap beside Mitch on the floor. She'd seen Zamindar and Char and probably thought they were here to kill her, or do some serious damage to her and the facility.

Mitch initially thought she'd dropped dead, but checked her vitals, and the old bugger was still breathing and her heart still beating. He peered up at the Virijians in the half-light, and the picture became clearer as Mitch spoke to her.

Mitch glanced at the Virijians again and really didn't blame her, they looked rather macabre in the gloomy twilight offered by this place. Rosie looked so old, even her wrinkles had wrinkles - she must have been over a hundred years old. Maybe she'd just had a hard life, it might have been the job around here, who knew? She made the old lady from Titanic look positively nubile.

The thing she was carrying was a broom so Rosie was probably a cleaner and had lived through the attack, protected by the facility and the mountain, and the snow. It was possible she may be able to tell them what happened around here or more likely, she wouldn't be able to tell them a thing. Time would tell, Mitch assumed.

Rosie showed signs of coming around and was now almost fully awake. Mitch saw her eyes gravitate toward Zamindar, seeing them widen and then bulge as she gawked at Zamindar and Char.
'You...you're one of them Virijians I've been reading about. God knows what *he* is,' she said, looking at Char, whose features were different. '*Jesus*,' she said, rubbing her eyes and continuing to peer up at him, swallowing rapidly. '*Shit*,' Rosie kept saying, ping-ponging her eyes between Zamindar and Char. '*Shit*,' she continued to whisper. Mitch grinned at the old bugger - he couldn't help it. Her reaction to the Virijians was nothing short of classic.

Mitch and Jessy studied Rosie closely. She was a pretty good representation of people on Earth...the average, archetypal person. The job was well and truly in front of them they knew.

'I'm a cleaner...as much good as it's doing.' Rosie said, sitting up while on the ground. 'I haven't seen anyone for yonks, apart from you lot.' She was around seventy-five years-old, and probably Australian or Canadian. It was hard to tell. Rosie was okay once she was convinced that everyone was friendly and she wouldn't be hurt by anyone here.

'So...what did you hear of the event?' Mitch asked of the small, dark-haired woman who seemed barely awake. Apparently, she would rather sleep than answer any of our questions. He felt like clapping loudly to bring her to full consciousness and attention but abstained...just. *Christ*, he thought, looking and listening to her. She was old...but seemed together enough and appeared to be quite intelligent although she sounded a bit like a sloth.

'It, er,' she scratched her head and by the look on her face, it was as though she were retrieving a very painful memory, which of course, it probably was. '...sounded like distant thunder which went on for a long time, went on for yonks actually, then it got closer until it was, uh...right over me and then slowly moved away...really slowly. It sounded a bit like thunder and an earthquake combined, everything shook and rattled. Guess it was lucky I was inside at the time...' Rosie ping ponged her gaze at all of them and wondered if they even believed her.

By the looks on their faces, they did, and were waiting on the edge of their seats for more. It was probably the first narration of the event they'd heard, their initial first-person recollection that is. Rosie took a deep rattling breath before proceeding. They all reckoned she was sick or dying...or maybe just old.

'Then it got further away and it sounded like it did before – distant thunder, then more of the same, it went on for yonks. I was too scared to go outside for days. I thought for sure I'd be killed or injured...or *something*. It was like someone was blasting their way in here, so I hid. Obviously, I now know that I was wrong.'

'I blamed it on the Ruskies...I thought they'd attacked.' Rosie gawked at them all, looking for confirmation. When she didn't get it, she looked down, and Jessy thought she was going to cry. Rosie didn't and still kept talking. 'That's about all I can tell you. It sounded like the end of the world.' Little did she know, Mitch and his family thought, Rosie would die with a leg in the air if she knew she was pretty much spot on. They decided she was too old to know the truth. If they told her who was responsible, Mitch doubted she'd believe him. Mitch just told her that the Russians had initiated an attack, it was easier, but she'd catch on to the real story soon enough. They all locked eyes for a few seconds.

Rosie ran a shaking hand through her wild grey hair and continued. 'After that, seed deliveries stopped, in fact everything stopped, including people...er, regulars and the like. I've been down to the airport in my snowmobile and to my old home and town in

Longyearbyen, *nothing is left*, everything is crushed and destroyed. *Goddamn Ruskies*,' she exclaimed. She didn't realise how wrong she really was. The Russians were as affected as everybody else.

'*Radioactivity*...I've, uh, got no idea,' Rosie said, wiping away a tear. I keep waiting for the diarrhea and hair loss to kick in, but it never has, well...not really. I live on base now. All the time, in the room near the outside door. It used to be the gift shop...now it's mine, been mine for a coupla months.'

'What the hell do you eat, not the seeds I assume,' Josh asked.

'Well, what do I eat? I got a shotgun and plenty of ammo, you do the math sonny.' Rosie glared at Josh and dared him to say something. 'Lucky, I've got a hankering for bear and reindeer. Seal ain't bad either, and of course there's the occasional washed-up whale. Gotta be quick though,' Rosie said with a smile and flourish of her hands. 'Lots of birds and big fish like 'em too.' Rosie laughed wheezing at the same time. 'Don't go looking around the side of this place though - full of fish-guts and other rubbish,' she said. 'Soooo, what the shit happened to everything?' Rosie asked with a pleading note, peering up at Mitch who was looking elsewhere and he stayed that way. Rosie wanted to know, even though she didn't really want any details. 'It was a war or something, right?

Mitch gazed back at her sombrely and said nothing. *'Fuck it*, he thought. She'd hear about it sometime, probably in less than satisfactory circumstances.

'We w-were attacked by a totally different civilization that thought Earth itself would be better off without us.' Mitch said to Rosie. She looked directly back at him, without changing expression, trying desperately to process the words which she was struggling with. 'Apparently, we were killing the planet by adding harmful chemicals to the atmosphere. Most would agree with them. We tried our hardest to improve, but we weren't quick enough. So...they did what they promised to do. They wiped humanity out,' Mitch said dramatically to Rosie, darting his gaze to everyone.

Mitch heard a clunk and it was Rosie once again, hitting the turf. This time, she got herself up without any help. '-*Holy fuck*, ETs did all this? I can't...It's hard to imagine...are you sure?' Rosie looked squarely at Mitch who widened his eyes to confirm it. 'Well *fuck* me, didn't see that coming.' She gazed at the floor and pulled the zipper up on her sweater as far as it would go and shook her head. Rosie was really struggling to believe it. 'So much for contact,' she said.

'So far, we haven't seen any skeletons or bodies at all, just a lot of empty space because of the type of weapons deployed.' Mitch then stared wordlessly at Jessy, feeling his heart pounding. Where was everybody – the dead should be piled up, millions of them...at least fucking skeletons, but there was *nothing*.

Zamindar stood up and planted his feet wide. He'd clearly heard quite enough of this human drivel and saw Mitch's frustrated face which demanded the Virijian speak. 'The Bantha deployed pressure weapons at a certain frequency,' he said. 'It has crushed everything, pushed over structures and disintegrated nearly all biochemical material on land, including humans, animals and vegetation.'

'I know that...it was obvious that it was no "regulation" weapon,' Mitch said. 'It looks so wrong though, there should be skeletons, or bodies everywhere...and *yes,* I know it's because some tuned aural weapon was deployed, but it looks wrong. Is it to make it easier on the Bantha? Our civilisation has just vanished – it's *horrible*. It'd be horrific with bodies and skeletons, but somehow it was worse without them,' Mitch said with a breaking voice. He wiped at his nose. He wasn't made of *stone*. The loss of their society was eating away at all of them.

'You yourself have been saved,' Zamindar turned his ponderous head to eye Rosie direct, 'because you stayed inside this sarcophagus. We are here to collect some seeds that will, to a small extent, help re-green this world. They have denuded this planet to a point where very few species of plant will recover and re-grow. There should be underground pockets of surviving humanity. They deserve this re-greening attempt as do Mitch...I mean, and *us*.' Zamindar folded himself up and sat back down, reckoning he'd said enough. That would at least stop Mitch from wondering where all the skeletons were, as if he didn't already know. They were shattered and pulverised, case closed.

Shit, Shit, fuck,' Rosie said. There was a long silence. 'Who would've thought...killed by an alien race. I always thought global warming would get us ...and it did, well...sort of, it did I suppose, get us.

'Never thought of it like that,' Josh said, 'but yeah, you're right...it has well and truly bitten the whole lot of us on the arse. Even if it didn't get us directly, it still got us. Got us good,' Josh said, eyeing Rosie intensely. She grinned faintly at Josh in agreement and rolled her eyes.

'Well put...well put indeed.' Mitch said, keeping his eyes fixed on Rosie and then Josh.

'Stay with us Rosie,' Mitch said, as they started walking slowly toward the strongroom, not far in the distance – where the seeds lay. We need to locate all the living humans we can,' Mitch said. 'We are very rare indeed – even on our own planet.' He finished on. 'Never thought I'd be saying that but there you are.'

'Please come with, Rosie, we have the room. If you stay here, you'll eventually die,' Mitch said, lowering his head slightly. She didn't want to hear it, but he was right. Rosie would, sooner or later, die if she stayed put.

'We all eventually die son. But yes, I will come with you, I'd already decided on that if it was possible. Thanks though, means a lot to an old girl like me...there's no choice is there? Stay...die, leave...who knows, right? I have to roll the dice and see what happens. I just might surprise myself I suppose. There's still life yet, right?'

Steel doors were freed of ice by Mitch and the unlocked doors, were opened. Ahead of them was a black and gold wire fence, that too, was hanging open – the gate was already pulled fully back. Someone or something had opened it for them. The first thing they saw were small Canadian flags adorning cardboard boxes, maple leaves, lined up, on metal racks, full of seeds. They were *definitely* in the right place.
There were racks, full of cardboard boxes, all full to the brim with seeds. Some of the flags were unidentifiable, but nearly the entire world was represented somewhere in the Vault. That meant that seeds from nearly every country were here.

'Get the packs out...as many as you can, and fill them using your list,' Mitch said loudly. They were searching for trees and plants and certain food crops. A broad covering was decided on. It was the best approach...apparently. The seeds were heat-sealed, mostly in silver aluminium packs, clearly marked with what was inside. If they weren't clearly marked, they were discarded. This was no time for guessing games. It would be only the second time seeds had been taken from Svalbard, after a country in the middle-east where all cultivation plants were lost due to warfare and the like. Fingers and everything else were crossed, hoping against hope that this mission turned out okay. They could only do so much though. There wasn't anything they could do about the missing civilisation. "Okay" was very relative, Mitch supposed.

Rosie could hear scratching and tearing sounds as they grabbed the seeds from their plastic containers, and ripped open some of the silver sachets. American redwoods, pine trees, oak trees, rubber trees, Orchids, Bromeliads, Baobab trees, Acacia trees, Whistling Thorns, Kapok trees, Oranges, Apples, Rice, Wheat, Bananas, Walnuts...the list seemed endless but eventually they filled all four large backpacks with packets of seeds.

Jessy, Mitch, Josh and the two Virijians, once fitted with the bulging backpacks, headed off, back to the airport, with Rosie coming with. They looked like a bunch of strange homeless people, carrying their lives on their back, which he supposed, was pretty much who and what they were, and what they were doing. There was one clear difference though, they were trying to save what was left of humanity and the Earth.

Approaching what used to be the airport, they could all see the remnants of the tower with the satellite dish and the hangar together with all the public facilities – had been pushed over and crushed. A toilet was a few hundred metres away, incredibly, still intact, sitting right way up on the snow. It looked severely out of place.

From what Zamindar said, all the biology including all the people had been pulverised to dust...and distributed on the ground where they stood. What looked like topsoil or dirty snow was actually animal and people particles, bone and flesh. Apart from that, all that was left, was the potholed and rubbish-filled runway that ran down the narrow isthmus. At least the sea level up here allowed Spitsbergen to still peak above the waves.

The backpacks were loaded in the *Lunar*, into the rear airlock, the contents of which would be distributed while in the air, to the Earth below. Some would germinate, most wouldn't. Luckily, there weren't many birds left to feast on the seeds. It should be enough to re-green the world, *eventually* if dropped in the right areas with the right rainfall. It would, in time, hopefully create food for the isolated collections of humans that were alive and struggling to exist. That was the plan anyway.

Those few, like Rosie, that were somehow protected from the pressure beams from above, lived to tell the tale. More than likely, those that happened to be underground at the time, like miners and potentially underground rail passengers.

Imagine, coming up to the surface after *that* trip. Either the city was ensconced in destruction, or it was over and nothing was left, people...or *anything*. Just dust. It'd be quite the morning trip. What in God's name would you think, walking up the stairs of the subway, a walk done thousands of times, to see...nothing but severe devastation and dust...*everywhere*.

*   *   *

Lunar took to the skies on its way to hopefully refuel its tanks with liquid oxygen and liquid hydrogen. They would travel west to Canada, south through the US, refuelling in Florida, if possible, east to South America and north to Russia, then on to Europe, Asia and Australia, distributing seeds to key sites along the way.

But what if they couldn't re-fuel, Mitch thought. He didn't bother answering the question, because there were no options apart from getting more fuel, otherwise they would drop from the sky like a lead weight, an inevitability, if they ran out of fuel to keep them aloft.

In Josh's mind's-eye he saw them dropping from the sky like a stone, the fuel tank completely dry. He was frozen stiff in his seat as he contemplated the dreadful vision.

They needed to find a fuel truck in the Florida spaceport that was unexploded, *and* had fuel in it, and importantly, had an intact coupling device. Thankfully, the *Lunar* used the same fuel as the new SLS Shuttles. The good news was that all NASA vehicles used the same stuff.

*   *   *

Lunar was at two-thousand metres and had dropped Redwood seeds in California and Pine Tree seeds in Texas, and a whole lot more besides. All they needed was for it to grow in a very meagre layer of soil; a big ask indeed. The Golden Gate Bridge was gone from California along with San Francisco itself and the Giant Cross from Texas. In their place were huge piles of rubble, rubbish and dust. Now, it was time to look to the Kennedy Space Centre for fuel. The entire space centre looked like Houston city...flattened, and mostly just gone. Cue the sanding machine.

They landed on Runway 5 and slowed to a stop, avoiding all the major potholes and squashed, broken and buried vehicles. From the air they could see no intact fuel trucks at all, hopefully, on the ground, their experience would be different. They really weren't sure what they'd find. Closer inspection is what they needed - from the ground. Their craft needed fuel, *period* - otherwise, they were stuck here. And in major trouble. There were worse places to spend eternity – but the way things were, anywhere on Earth was unpalatable.

Together, on the exit to the stairs and in a light breeze, and full Sun, the devastation was obvious. All that remained of the space centre were long, potholed runways. Jessy could see that the Visitor's Centre in the distance had suffered a similar fate to the rest of the place. All of them filed down the stairs of the *Lunar* and stood in a group on the potholed runway nearest them.

It was one thing checking out the devastation from the air, an entirely different one to seeing it at close range. *Jesus*, it was a horrible , smelly mess. All the old rockets used for display to the public were gone, replaced by mounds of dirt and rubbish and dust. It was like walking through an image of extreme WW2 destruction. There were unidentifiable *things* everywhere, covered by dust and ash, which continued to drop from the sky like snow. It wasn't raining water - it was still raining the pulverised remnants of what used to live at and around NASA.

There was a truck that looked fairly intact, buried under a roof and rubble. But how the fuck to get it out and check it? It was pretty deeply wedged in, in fact it was jammed into the ground, squeezed between what used to be two walls that existed elsewhere. Zamindar grabbed the truck with all three arms and pulled, bringing down the roof and rubble in a dusty, sooty mess that penetrated everything. Pulling out the truck was an impressive physical feat, but it was bone-dry in terms of fuel, the massive fuel tank was broken and twisted, with a huge, jagged hole in it. Whatever fuel that had remained in it, had evaporated some time ago.

'*Damn it,*' Josh rumbled. '*Not a goddamn drop,*' he gawked at Mitch, his eyes looking tired and his face dirty as though he'd up-ended a bucket of dirt. Josh offered his dad a partial smile. He got up slowly and dusted himself off. 'We have to find some fuel or we're done, gone...*cactus.*' He said, reconnecting with Mitch's gaze.

'Keep looking,' Mitch growled. '*Keep fucking looking,*' he repeated louder. Cactus, he silently concurred with Josh, although he'd never tell him that. They had to find fuel. Josh just stared at him. As did Jessy. They both realised how close to death they really were.

Mitch spied a dusty umbilical hanging out of the ground, the end covered by rubble and dirt and pieces of dusty rock. Mitch pointed to it and Zamindar grabbed it and eyed the coupling once it was off the ground.

Of course! NASA has an *underground fuel farm*, Mitch thought suddenly – like AASSA. The coupling appeared to be okay, but would it fit the *Lunar?* The coupling was designed to be universal. The damn thing *should* fit, but trying to get it on would be an ordeal, even if it did fit.

The *Lunar* was shifted by Char, using the fans only. With the vessel now close enough, Zamindar had one end of the umbilical and Mitch the other, as though they were wrestling a gigantic, ribbed snake. Mitch tried to attach it but couldn't quite do it. He tried again and failed again. It was frigging heavy, that's all he knew. It must be designed for at least two large men, Mitch reckoned, which made him try harder.

Mitch saw Zamindar on his way over to help and watched as he grabbed the coupling and this time it took, attaching it to *Lunar* with a shove and a turn. Zamindar was very, very able-bodied.

As it turned out, the fuel farm was almost full, and it transferred its lot until *Lunar* was entirely full, in fact the vessel leaked fuel even after the stop was fitted. Mitch reckoned they should feel lucky that the Farm was full of fuel, although that was probably how NASA kept it. Full as a boot at all times. Good old NASA. Gotta love 'em, Mitch thought.

The vessel took off and headed toward the Northern Territory in Australia where they saw Uluru or Ayers Rock with deep lacerations all over it and Bitter Springs and Kakadu shaved clean. Further drops were scheduled over Iran, China, India, Malaysia and New Guinea along the way. Once they finished their tour, their mission would be complete.

Then, they all wondered, what the hell then...what on Earth should they do then? The humans knew Earth was almost free of their own species. Nothing they did now would change that. Everything they did was only window-dressing for the few who remained.

Zamindar peered upward and clearly had something to say. He went out of his way to look at them which was a strong tell-sign. Static they could all hear, suggested toning was imminent. 'They will be here soon,' he toned.

'Who the hell is *"they"*?' Mitch asked Zamindar immediately, glancing at Josh and Jessy, who showed raised shoulders and furrowed brows. Rosie still looked drop-dead terrified, her eyes were huge and she wasn't blinking - the others were more impatient about Zamindar's latest offering. *WTF* was all that came to mind.

'*What are you talking about?* Mitch demanded.

Zamindar stepped forward and toned, 'I have requested assistance from the Morij, the panel of twelve who rule our planetary system. Assistance is due now.' He said, crossing all three arms in a way none of them had seen before. His arms were intertwined quite intricately.

Was this a sort of clandestine emotion, or show of respect, Mitch studied the Virijian's pose. There was more to these beings to be uncovered, he was sure of it. They had no overt emotions, but they had *something*. He stared at Zamindar and nodded his head, wondering what lay beneath the pale veneer of his carbuncled and partially see-through cellophane-like skin.

Zamindar explained that sending messages with their cortex, using entangled, specific frequency transmission, was something they were all born with, within their Parahippocampus, every Virijian had it. It transcended the speed of light. This was unlike the shadowy and tenuous ESP boasted by some humans, which they all thought was so much bullshit.

'We try not to use it, but sometimes we cannot avoid it.' Zamindar said, looking straight at Mitch and not wavering. 'Sometimes it is needed.'

Mitch was about to ask why they tried *not* to use it, when two small vesicular bubbles fell from the clouds and landed softly in front of them, their controls barely concealed by an almost transparent bubble, and the pilot and co-pilot's seat being completely empty. They came very quickly – as though they were waiting in orbit and ready to go. There was no noise at all. Silence was uninterrupted, yet before them were two just-arrived space vehicles.

"Ask and ye shall receive", I suppose,' Mitch eventually said, glancing at Jessy and Josh. Neither were amused. As far as they were concerned, this was all as serious as it got. No time for anything approaching levity.

Jessy would use '*the thing*' all the time if she had it. It'd be like being born with a mobile phone in your head, and your brain was solely in charge of who you linked up with. And it could be used for instantaneous conversations, no matter the distance. Sounded like an amazing idea to her. Yet, '*they*' preferred '*not*' to use it. Go *figure*, she thought, it didn't make any sense whatsoever but maybe it caused physical issues. Perhaps, psychological. Probably a lot more to it, *had* to be, if Zamindar didn't want to use it often.

Mitch couldn't work out why they hadn't called the Morij before, for assistance. It's not like we didn't need it. Was it something to do with not wanting to use brain to brain comms. Or did they prefer not to intrude on the Morij. Probably a bit of both, he reckoned.

Thank Christ, Josh thought, gazing at the pods, at least *something* was happening, even if it was just the arrival of two unoccupied alien space craft.

It made him feel better that someone knew about their plight – even aliens. He realized their time was very limited on Earth with little food and water.

Without food and water, they could only last so long. Jessy was wondering what they could possibly do about it. To survive here, long term, they needed sustenance, and there wasn't any. For the short-term they were fine. but long term...no. They had to leave Earth but the *lunar* didn't have the required fuel to get them safely to orbit. No doubt though, the Ajiron did.

Rosie refused to travel anywhere by transparent alien bubble, however. No one could blame her really, if you didn't like flying or had issues with heights, it was no-doubt a truly horrific exercise. One that Rosie couldn't contend with. Josh agreed with her sentiments completely. Travelling in them would be a shocker. Akin to flying in a totally transparent plane. *No thank you.*

She wouldn't budge, despite their efforts. Rosie said she'd take her chances on the ground. They would come back for her if they could, which Rosie replied, "not to bother", because she wasn't waiting around for them. She was off, to God knows where. She had her own ideas. They said their goodbyes and indeed she was off, tromping up the runway until she was a tiny figure amid the destruction, dirt and dust of the space-centre. They all hoped she had something firm in mind.

Zamindar got in the front seat nearest the controls of one craft, Char in the other one and they ferried them all to "empty" low Earth orbit. Mitch could see the Hubble and a few other satellites, and wondered what the Virijians had in mind? Neither of the Virijians would say anything.

*   *   *

Into the field of vision came the overwhelming hulk of a white Virijian starship. Whomever had said "smaller is better" forgot to tell the Virijians. The thing in front of them was huge, kilometres long and white as polished alabaster. It looked something like a huge sea anemone, long, but roughly round with skin covering spines and bilges that reached into space. It must have been built in line with its propulsion and its movement through gravity bridges and whatever else it was supposed to do, hence the numerous collapsible spikes and excrescences, Mitch knew these would deflate like snail's antenna before it entered. He'd seen it before. The craft would be slick as a polished bowling ball. When it came out, the spines would become tumescent as before.

Although they didn't hear anything that suggested thrust, they slowed, changed orbit and docked with the overwhelming vessel, not as they did with ISS, or like any other vessel really - they entered the huge ship through a wide entryway and set down within it. The humans' eyes were enormous as they watched their transparent cocoon enter the huge craft and land amid the whiteness. It was totally unlike the ISS. The difference in size boggled the human mind.

The entry-way behind them closed by reforming, molecules returning in their centillions. A nitrogen-oxygen atmosphere with a pressure of 1,000 Mb and gravity of about 9 metres per second^2 promulgated in the huge space almost immediately. A white light seemed to come on from the wall and roof everywhere, despite their being no obvious "lights". They were in conditions not unlike the surface of Earth during the daytime.

A huge crack of what looked like lightning, obviously without any sound suddenly propagated in space outside the massive craft, which was brief but very bright indeed. Everyone saw it and everyone goggled at it although no one had a clue what it was. Even Zamindar was flummoxed. Zamindar had detected its output but could not shed any light on it, which said volumes.

Doors to the pods popped open and the Virijians were the first out on the floor, looking around at the craft and the blandness, and doing their own version of smiling, which was not smiling as humans would define it. They looked disinterested at best, although their mouths sort of curved upward. Mainly, they just looked apoplectic.

Josh was overwhelmed with this place and the horrendous flight to get here, holding a shaky set of fingers to his forehead, trying to look in every direction at once. Where the hell would this all end, he wondered? He'd had enough a long time ago. Josh could barely stand for some reason. He was dazzled by the flash of light from space and the extraordinary size of the vessel. It was truly a humongous piece of space hardware.

Extra-terrestrials and humans stood together as a group at the foot of the two Ajiron, taking in the huge white space they now stood in. They could see Earth through the huge window – it was grey-brown on the continents and the oceans were bluey-green. But there was a slight grey tinge in them too.

The Atlantic Ocean was quite green. On the whole, the planet appeared less blue than it used to, although the Pacific region including America looked pretty good. Was this the planet's final attempt to live...an end-of-life rally of some description? The last time he saw Earth it seemed entirely greenish and a little listless. Right now, overall, it looked okay. Mitch was rather surprised. He half-expected it to look totally grey and dead from orbit.

It didn't matter how it looked from orbit though, Mitch had seen it and knew Earth was now very sad and forgotten, what was once a planet among planets was now very much a rock that was *ho-hum* at best. Now it was just a planet among the trillions more that teetered on the edge of a habitable zone.

Nothing made it special. Not its Sun, and certainly nothing of itself. Not anymore. Hawking was correct. It was a dangerous Universe.

Zamindar toned to them all. 'We'll be making a detour to visit the Bantha as soon as we exit the shift, to make sure they do not return to Earth.'

There was a long silence as the humans thought about and digested the words. Why on Earth would they bother going to visit the Bantha? There could only be one reason. Mitch peered at Zamindar and tried to read something, *anything* in that face. '*You must be kidding,*' he whispered under his breath. He wondered why he bothered to even look at him, force of habit, he knew. He might as well look at Zamindar's feet or his finger-nails, he reckoned, all would be as equally illuminating as his annoyingly passive face.

'So, you're going t-to *threaten them*?' Josh asked, well aware that his question was rhetorical. Of course, they were. Imagine being threatened by a race that had a vessel this big? It'd be terrifying, surely? He was sure the threat would involve some sort of chilling demonstration.

'Yes,' Zamindar toned. 'We will tell them that any further visits to Earth will stop, or we will destroy their planet.' The Virijian looked squarely at Josh. 'This is where you say, "thank you".'

'*What?*' Mitch uttered, his mouth literally falling open, staring at Zamindar dumbfounded. 'Thank you', Mitch said..."*thankyou*",' he repeated, not sure he'd heard him right. Was it an attempt by the Virijian at humour? Mimicking Josh because that's exactly the sort of thing he'd say.

'*Jesus Christ...*it's the first time,' he reckoned. Zamindar already had his back to him, so who knows, he thought. Humor, or Josh's influence, who really knew, Mitch mused. Either way, it didn't matter, it was still absolutely amazing. Chalk it up as the first time ever.

*   *   *

The black hole was directly in front of them and it had no pinwheel of colorful particles orbiting it. But they could see it. The black hole was rotating against the background of space, blocking out stars as it moved. The vessel was going to pierce it to take them back to the Virijian planets; then another shift to take them out of the galaxy, relatively close to the Bantha. Antimatter would do the rest. After the gravity shifts, they would travel to Bantha in purely geodesic space, and it wouldn't take long, using the power of antimatter.

Mitch mulled over the word "threaten", it was the Virijians doing it and they could back it up. Unlike humans, that could barely engineer a fart in space.

*   *   *

They had left Trijicyon behind them some time ago and travelled through the two shifts, and were now plying regulation space with Bantha swelling in size before them. It was a deeply blue and white planet, like old Earth or Virija. Bantha probably had similar gasses if looks were any guide. It had white clouds dotting the globe, and continents, blue oceans and, no doubt oxygen, vegetation and so on. It was populated with a humanoid intelligence with a strict code of veracity around preserving habitable planets and their atmospheres. They expected others to uphold similar values. Planets like Earth were rare in the Universe and the Bantha apparently knew it.

An intelligence only develops after thousands of centuries on a world with a nurturing atmosphere. There was a responsibility to ensure the atmosphere of such planets was maintained as they were *amazingly* scarce in the Universe. They *had* to be looked after by a third party to ensure they continued as nurturing, healthy atmospheres. Being the administrators of life and habitable planets in the Universe, the Bantha was certain that a "higher" authority needed to look after these worlds, because self-policing didn't seem to work. So, rightly or wrongly, that made it their decision to make. They had installed themselves as the final arbiter on which civilisations died or lived. The ones that died were solely the fault of the polluting civilisation – they would have died anyway. That was the philosophy of the Bantha. All of it had to with the degree to which a species lived in harmony with their world.

Those that didn't warrant a demand, or complied with the demand, lived. Habitable, evolution-assisting planets had to be saved, *period*. The perfectly positioned and richly oxygenated world's role in evolution in this Universe was too important to be ignored. It was more important than the "rights" of a polluting civilization. If life actually formed, natural selection, competition, interbreeding, variation and inheritance were guaranteed.

Zamindar took the colossal craft into a high orbit around Bantha. The colours of the planet were the same as old Earth, bright blue, brown and white.

'No doubt they know we're here,' Mitch said, nodding.

Josh listened to his father, shook his head in despair, but held his comments within. He was going to say something like, *"Der"* or *"thanks for the bleeding obvious dad"*, but swallowed all of them down. Josh felt totally out of his depth, and anxious, so he kept quiet. It'd be like something orbiting Earth in its hey-day, of course we'd know it was there. Similarly, the Bantha knew we were here. Unless the Virijians had used their cloaking device, but Mitch doubted it. The Bantha would know soon enough, anyway. It was no secret. Probably, in this craft, the more we were seen, the better. Josh remained silent and stared at the alien planet below them. It looked so much like Earth of old, it was beautiful and made him miserable and homesick, and extremely angry, knowing what had happened to his planet.

'The Bantha know we are here,' Zamindar confirmed. 'We need to move quickly. Just Charijiok and myself this time.' Small ships from the Bantha went whizzing past the Virijian vessel. Two of them were moving with the ship, effectively stationary, just off the bow of the huge craft, watching and monitoring for any signs of anything. The Virijian's had communicated their intentions to the Bantha. They accepted their stopover. They had no choice.

A larger ship was further away from the Virijian vessel. The Bantha were assessing their every move, as expected. The Virijian ship was huge and looked aggressive, even though in actuality, it wasn't. Its main purpose was simple transportation. The Virijians themselves were here to be aggressive though, although their comms to the Bantha didn't convey any such intent.

'I will take Ajiron and we will return soon,' Zamindar toned, looking at the other Virijian, both of them walking toward the small vessel which would take them to meet with the Bantha on their home planet.

Mitch saw Ajiron become a fiery meteor and disappear among the clouds. Jessy, with help from Josh, had the Celestron telescope set up to look out of the nadir window. She was watching the Virijians come into land on the Bantha's planet, *somewhere.*

After about ten minutes they reboarded the Ajiron and eventually took off. It became apparent they weren't returning to the larger Rou vessel, which begged the obvious question – where the hell were they going? Had he done the deed or no...and they didn't accept it, instead, sending the Virijians off for something more grievous? Mitch doubted that was the case. You'd hardly fly to your own execution...or was he was missing something? One thought from either of the Virijians would send the Morij screaming into the atmosphere to rescue them, although it was difficult to imagine them ever needing rescue.

Arcing upward to about ten thousand feet, the spaceplane with the two Virijians levelled off and flew some distance until once again it started in for a landing, on a large island with a prominent mountain. Apparently, the first landing hadn't been successful, the right people probably hadn't been located. Thus, the craft with the two Virijians was now moving on to this island. Being redirected, it seemed, to find the audience it sought. They all had theories but the "right audience" seemed most likely. It was all good, they thought...so far. Although, what the Bantha would do with a dead planet was unknown. Mitch was confident the Virijians would look after them.

Jessy watched through the telescope as Zamindar and Char alighted the vehicle. The last she saw was a group of about a dozen Bantha come to meet them and escort them away. They looked friendly enough with their long bodies and serious faces. It was difficult to tell from here, but the Bantha appeared official at least. Not particularly angry, not particularly happy – hopefully, it'd stay that way.

'Wonder how it's going down there?' Jessy said, gazing uneasily at Mitch, chewing the inside of her cheek. Jessy didn't realise how nervous she was, blinking rapidly and biting her lip. How would the Bantha react when *they* were threatened? The tables would be well and truly turned.

Maybe the Bantha were used to being confronted, given the odd business they were in. Perhaps they even had a protocol to deal with races wishing to negotiate or talk or whatever. Jessy guessed they'd find out pretty soon, assuming the Virijians returned unscathed. Mitch hadn't even considered what they'd do if the two didn't come back. He admitted that he had no idea how to contact the Morij.

'All they're gonna do is tell them,' Josh said, 'although I don't know why they bothered, Earth is already as dead as it's gonna get. We all agreed, there's probably pockets of people alive, but that's about it. Apart from them...well, there's probably no-one. Billions are dead,' he let out a harsh sigh and closed his eyes, curling his toes so hard, they hurt from repeatedly pulling them tight. If some were broken, he wouldn't be surprised. 'And God knows how many animals.' Josh felt like crying...all the people, the animals, the pets.

After almost an hour, the Virijians returned to Ajiron with only two Bantha there, seemingly guarding the ship. Zamindar and Char re-entered the Ajiron and prepared to come back to the mother craft presumably. There were no goodbyes or gesticulations to the Bantha, as far as Jessy could tell. By the look of it, the threat was conveyed, business over, and now it was time to return to the orbiting starship, both Virijians about to start the journey back.

*   *   *

'Welcome back,' Mitch said effusively, for a second time, both greetings totally unreciprocated by the Virijians. Not even a grunt. They had zero time for inanities or pleasantries. They both looked unhappy, at best miserable. High evolution such as the Virijians boasted, looked like a real hoot.

'We told them what would happen if they visited Earth again and eventually gained agreement on that,' Zamindar said, glancing at Char who was watching him closely. 'We told them to leave the planet to us and they are never to come within five light years without an explicit invitation. They were told, and it was agreed, the major part of their work had been done already.'

There was something unusual in Zamindar's toning, something more supplicating...unassuming. That worried him, although he didn't know why. It was outwardly positive but it meant he'd changed. Mitch was the first to admit he didn't have a clue how they operated or whether it was significant. The Bantha wouldn't return to Earth...that was *good*, he supposed.

"We also spoke about repopulating Earth,' Zamindar said, flexing the fingers of his grasper, repeatedly, over and over. All eyes were on the Virijian now, gawking at his pale, passive face, pondering what was going on in there. What the hell did he have in mind? Jessy wondered, sure as shit you couldn't tell from the expression on his face. He gave nothing away, but it was genetic rather than deliberate. It was just how evolution had worked on their world. *He* was the result of it all.

Josh and Mitch could only speculate on what he meant by *"repopulate"*. None of them liked any of the mental images it invoked. No plan had been discussed with anyone. Clearly, the Virijians had already thought about it in some detail. Mitch glared at Zamindar expectantly, waiting for some sort of statement...*anything* about Earth's future as *they* saw it. If they had some sort of plan, it was only fair that they, as humans, were involved. Afterall, it used to be our planet. Was still *our* planet, even though it was kind of dead and shaved of biology.

Zamindar stood tall and peered first at Josh and then at all of them, slowly, deliberately, one by one. The static Mitch could hear in his head and Zamindar's behaviour suggested the Virijian was going to tone to all of the humans about something serious.

'We intend to provide ten thousand Virijians drawn from our home planets of Virija and Trijicyon plus whatever humans we can find on Earth, to form the first town, to be known as New Jycyon, which Mitch has agreed to - the first settlement on New Earth, to be created in what used to be Nigeria in Africa. The land around it, we believe will sustain attempts at cultivation. It will be electrified and run by fusion power only, a detail promised to the Bantha. Metals or anything we need that cannot be garnered locally, will come from Virija and Trijicyon in the first instance. Only then would the Bantha agree to listen to us. In effect, they had little choice and no negotiating power, but still, we wanted to appear amicable and flexible, even if we were not.'

Zamindar looked directly at Mitch before he toned further. 'Char and I agreed that you three would join us at the new town. And that Mitch, you and I would be the joint CEOs of the town.' Zamindar stopped toning and eyed Mitch, waiting for his reaction.

'*Jesus Christ, you what*?' Mitch stopped talking, convinced he was deadly serious, and stared at him for a long moment. It was a whole lot to digest. Ten thousand Virijians, and me and Zamindar are *what*...joint *Sheriffs*? '*You're kidding, right?*' Mitch was struggling just to believe it. He continued to chew on what the Virijian had just said - laughing out loud was definitely an option. It was nuts...wasn't it? Zamindar was such a joker. Trouble was, he was as serious and severe as. '*Sheriff,*' The word brought up ridiculous visions of gunslingers and horses, and dust. And saloons corsets. Mitch couldn't help chuckling. It sounded insane. *Was insane,* but then, so was everything else.

Zamindar continued, 'you would be President Mitch, along with myself, to decide the direction of the town, at least during the period of start-up.'

'It'll be like the old west in America,' Mitch said quietly, grinning at Jessy and Josh. Again, it sounded batshit crazy.

'Betta get you a six shooter with a nice pearl grip dad,' Josh quipped, 'so you can start flashing it around to the civilians.' He couldn't help chortling at the ridiculous images evoked by the Virijian's unexpected statement. To Josh, it sounded plain ridiculous.

Mitch eyed Josh, half grinning, and couldn't help himself, he laughed at his own cognitive images. He was quickly silenced by the need to answer Zamindar, who was waiting, looking very serious and intense. Zamindar leaned in, waiting for a response from Mitch.

'Er...um,' Mitch scratched his chin, 'okay Zamindar, yes, and we'll see how it-goes,' Mitch said nervously, shrugging his shoulders and flicking his gaze over everyone. What choice did he have? He had to at least try, what would happen if he gave a big *no,* it would then fall to Jessy or Josh, so, he said "yes" to keep the wolves at bay.

Zamindar told them that the Virijians had prepared a plan for Earth. In ten years, they intended to have 20,000 people and in fifty years New Earth was scheduled to hold 100,000 people. They also included population and other details for 100 and 200 years, all with similar geometric population increases and for those future years, there was no distinction between Virijians and humans. It seemed, that was the case through interbreeding. They would become one species. Both species would be free to interact...and breed. That begged the question of fertility. The Virijians obviously believed there was mutual fertility – what did he know that we didn't? He obviously believed there was genetic compatibility between the two species, and he'd never been wrong before, well hardly. So, the humans were inclined to believe him. Mitch knew it would be way more than just an assumption. There were also specific plans for cultivation and self-sufficiency, including energy and quite detailed food needs.

Josh and Jessy were offered high ranking jobs within the New Jycyon Government. They eventually agreed, afterall, they wanted to be with Mitch, who was seemingly at the top of the triangle. Mitch, as Sherriff of New Earth? That'd do him it seemed. Nice title, Mitch thought. The job itself terrified him, especially having the Virijians as his "boss".

'We will be here for about six months, after that, Char and I will return to Virija, assuming all is going to plan on Earth. Zamindar glared at all of them. He didn't look happy at all. But that was probably human bias, Mitch was sure of it. He had no reason to be annoyed. He'd gotten what he wanted.

Josh could only imagine what it'd be like to have Zamindar as a senior. His mouth fell open and his upper lip curled back as he watched him walking impossibly quickly. *Oh fuck*, he said to himself, looking closer. The Virijian would be hopelessly demanding and there'd be no thankyou's or beg-pardons. Expectations of his close people would be incredibly high. *Fucking stratospheric*. Josh gulped heavily as he thought about the Virijian and his likely heavy-handed and micro-managing approach.

Josh glanced at Mitch and grinned weakly. Josh knew that the Virijian could pretty much read his mind anyway. Clearly, Zamindar was a massive, *maddening* perfectionist. Working under him would be a nightmare, he reckoned, but the chance to work with his dad, he couldn't give that up. Although he wouldn't be easy either. The whole thing would be a Godawful horror story *and* he'd be getting no money. Mind you, it had never been a motivating factor so that really didn't matter. He felt like they had to do something to get this planet moving. At the moment it was just sad and dead. The plan was for Mitch to eventually be solely in charge of New Earth, although a future democratic government was planned.

Gaia Solaris was to continue to remain untouched. The Virijians wouldn't consider taking any of that population that was still in its formative stages on a recently oxygenated world.

14

Rarity

"In life, unlike chess, the game continues after checkmate."
—*Isaac Asimov*

Char walked in and toned to Zamindar although Mitch couldn't hear him, but he could see both of the Virijians with their goitres squirming. They were also studying each other closely. Clearly, they were conversing and deliberately excluding Mitch. None of the humans could hear a thing. For some reason, the conversation was very private indeed - solely Virijian.

After a while, Zamindar turned to face them. 'We have received a communication to urgently provide assistance,' he toned. 'A race called the Pteron have asked someone, anyone, for immediate help,' Zamindar toned, making a fist with his middle arm, while the other two remained limp at his side - an action they'd never seen before. It must have been indicative of something special, though they had no idea what.

'We encountered them recently and we have offered to provide assistance,' Zamindar toned. 'They are a unique species and deserve to be helped. They asked for help by using their EMAR and also, significantly, gravity waves. Radio is straightforward but they possess the ability to mimic the tidal forces created by two very adjacent black holes, in a mobile device. They unfortunately, haven't weaponised their technology at all, because they haven't had to. That is good for a number of reasons, but it does leave them open to threats from others.'

Previously, the Pteron had been threatened by the Bantha and they made it clear that they would not come close to making the deadline they set. In fact, they told the Bantha that from the outset. By the sound of it, they were significantly further away from being carbon-free than Earth was. So, their destruction was a formality. The Pteron didn't have a snowball's chance in hell of making the deadline.

'And they're reaching out *now*?' Josh said. 'A tad late, isn't it?' He took a quick breath. Surely...*too* late...?

'It is very late, but perhaps they believed they could negotiate the dead-line,' Zamindar toned. 'Misplaced confidence, I believe. Whatever the reason, they are too rare to be exterminated.'

'So, where are they?' Mitch asked. Near, he hoped. Problem was, "near" in space, could still be a very, very long way away.

'In a nearby galaxy,' Zamindar toned, 'you call it Segue. It is about 75,000 light years from Earth. We will use the gravity shift beyond Neptune to get there.

'It's a long, *long* way away...*near*,' Josh huffed to Mitch. His heart was thumping in his chest as he contemplated it. So much for "near", it was as he thought. It was "near" in shifted space, but a long, *long* way in regulation geodesic space. Josh thanked gravity sincerely. Without its help, they'd have no hope of getting anywhere. The Universe was just *too big*.

Mitch peered at his son, grimacing. As he said, distance never seemed to be a problem for the Virijians. It appeared as though there was always an opportunity for gravity to provide help - shortcuts in space, it seemed, were common . They were generally hidden inside black holes, which were also more common than humanity thought. They were *everywhere* in space. Wormholes or "bridges" were similarly way more common. It was just as well gravity had such an effect on spacetime because distances were so incredibly vast there was no other way to span the distances in Euclidean space due to that pesky mass-related speed limit.

*   *   *

Zamindar had told Mitch and humanity as much several times, maintaining that they only met after a series of extraordinary circumstances that led to a very rare event indeed.

'Surely, there must be some flat-space travel, it doesn't go to their doorstep, right?' Josh asked the Virijian, already knowing the answer.

'Only a small amount of direct travel,' Zamindar toned quickly as though answering the question was a major inconvenience. There was a long break in transmission. Silence descended on them all as the humans waited impatiently for more. Mitch started making small noises with his tongue. but there was nothing else from the Virijian.

After a long pause, Zamindar finally proceeded. 'The Pteron are evolved from bees, they are large, intelligent, conscious, self-aware and have their own language and civilisation. They do, however, produce too much carbon, for similar reasons to humans, hence the deadline set by the Bantha. 'We cannot lose the Pteron. As a species, they are far too special, far too unusual to be destroyed because of carbon production,' Zamindar said. Mitch felt like screaming, *and us?* But didn't.

Zamindar was well aware of their rarity. 'Far too special to be lost to the Bantha irrespective of whatever negative planetary changes they have made.'

'How the hell do they make too much carbon,' Mitch asked, drawing his lips into a tight smile. Jessy glared at him.

'They're not like bees on Earth *Mitch*,' Jessy said, '*Christ,* listen to what Zamindar has toned, would you...*Jesus*,' she shook her head, 'this is not the time to act like a fool,' Jessy said annoyed. 'As to how they created too much carbon, same as us, like Zamindar said.'

Zamindar looked at Mitch and confirmed it. 'Very much like Earth did. I said, '*evolved*' from bees; they stand upright, are flightless and have opposable thumbs, arms and hands. They are quite intelligent,' the Virijian said, peering directly at Mitch. "Unlike you", he may as well have said. Mitch caught the drift. He looked out of the huge window and although he didn't feel a thing, he saw that they were skimming through non-Euclidean space. No doubt, soon enough, they would meet the Pteron. Evolved from bees, what did that exactly mean? Nothing good, he was sure.

*   *   *

All they had was their knowledge of bees on Earth, the fact that they were large and bipedal, with two arms, and their own minds to fill in the gaps. Like the Virijians. It took Jessy a long time to get used to the idea of the Pteron. No doubt, for her, the Pteron would be a frightful atrocity.

It had taken a full day to get there, which was literally nothing in space travel terms, but they could have swapped *universes* in that time, if they were appropriately gravity-assisted in non-geodesic space. Now they were in fairly close orbit, directly above the Pteron's planet and it looked as they expected, peculiar. They were above a world that was partly covered in bluey-green oceans but it looked blotchy, with profuse pinky-red "sores" floating in the atmosphere, dark red lakes on four large continents that were an unusual pink in colour and not quite as bright as Earth. The whole lot looked extremely odd from space. Coupled with the colour was the strange shapes of the continents, one was virtually pentagonal – it completed the picture of genuine *alienness*, especially since they knew what was running around on the surface of the planet. Still, the planet was a mix of ocean and dry land, like Earth.

Why did bees evolve to intelligence here, but remain insectual on Earth? That was the question, he reckoned. Mitch was mulling it over in his brain and had to admit he had no idea at all. Maybe because of *One's* intervention, or because we were lucky or bio-chemically ready to split off from Apes. He was no Palaeontologist. They would need an expert to comment. There were so many factors involved, you needed to be a scholar to get your head around them. Whatever the reason, the reality was that bees had been selected, perhaps by *One*, perhaps by luck or certain circumstances, to be the supreme leaders of their planet through intelligence and self-awareness.

Mitch could still not hear anything from the vessel which meant either it was very well shielded, or the propulsion made no noise, both perhaps.

'Josh, can you hear any noise?' He realised younger ears might pick something up.

Josh turned around and looked at his father, grimacing and shaking his head. What a knob, he reckoned, asking that now. '*Can't you hear it*?' Josh had fingers in his ears. '*Are you deaf?*' He said, looking straight at Mitch with a surprised stare.

Well, I can hear *you*,' Mitch said gruffly. 'Unfortunately.'

'No, it is completely silent dad,' Josh said genuinely. Both of them grinned and met each's eyes steadily.

Zamindar told them that the Bantha had agreed to talk with the Pteron once again, on the surface of this planet at 38.7799 N 77.6754 W, which was the centre of their main city on this planet. They were aware that the Virijians were also attending as facilitators. The Virijians had demanded the attendance of the Bantha. They were very serious in providing assistance to the Pteron.

They broke through the karman line into a violet sky which didn't look too unusual, given they'd already encountered the colour before. The clouds were a different story though. They were huge cumulus-type formations with significant vertical development and amazingly, were pink in colour. It was raining further away and they could see that the water being discharged was *red*. Clearly, the red water made the purple clouds appear pink in colour. Purple and red made pink here on this planet apparently.

Mitch could see rivers emptying into the sea, red water slowly giving way to the greeny-blue of the ocean. There were also lakes brim full of red water that looked uncomfortably like blood...square kilometres of it.

From up here, the houses looked like a series of hexagons, which had to reflect some type of genetic inertia. The humans certainly thought so. Zamindar wasn't so sure. On Earth, Mitch knew individual bees worked for a collective – their genes demanded it. Would he see that here? Did they take the calling they had as insects on Earth through to intelligence?

Hexagons were also associated with bees on Earth, but that was a human structure *imposed* on bees, wasn't it? Turns out Zamindar said, that honeybees make their beehives in a hexagonal shape – so hexagons were seemingly important to all bees, whether large and intelligent or tiny and insectual. Nothing to do with humans. Mitch found it all quite intriguing. He'd also heard from Zamindar that bees on Earth had a swarm mentality, and that the larger queen was the leader in every respect. The queen was the empress, and the rest of the bees did her bidding, *whatever* that might be. Did that mean anything here? The intrigue grew. Mitch was chomping-at-the-bit to see more of their planet. Their hold on those characteristics was possible...but totally unknown. For bees on Earth, it was relatively easy to determine, for these, not so much. A lot of the dwellings below them appeared to be modular and were hexagonal from lower down but rectangular and thin when you looked at them from the air. Some were single units placed together for what seemed like maximum integration.

Nearer to the city-proper were tall, very attractive honeycomb-style units stacked on top of each other, light blue in colour. 'Once a bee, always a bee,' Josh said to himself. He struggled to believe what he was seeing but, it seemed to make sense. There seemed to be a strong inertia for bees to build certain things, no matter what their stage of development was – or their size.

They came upon what was probably a city as we would define it, a place of notable size with structures composed of smallish hexagonal units stacked one-on-the other, reaching perhaps a thousand feet tall. They were all very closely connected. Around them were individual dwellings that went on for a long way. From the air, it was a huge multi-level gathering of abodes that all looked very similar and went half the way to the horizon.

Further away was vegetation, mainly trees, but nothing like ours at home. These were purple all over and had divided trunks that seemed to be in vertical sections – looking a bit like purple cricket stumps, although much bigger, longer and sturdier. They were a long way away, so it was a bit of a guess. To Mitch they were extremely blurred and indistinct. But they clearly had free space in between their three trunks that almost looked like legs. They were separated by fresh air as it were. We'd call them *triarbre* or something similar. The trees or whatever the hell they were, looked extremely odd indeed.

They hovered quite low in Ajiron, maybe three or four thousand metres and below them was an edifice of life, everything seemed to emanate from that destination, which was sharply hexagonal in plan, but as to why it was there, and what it did and meant, well...they didn't have any idea but clearly, it was popular with this society. Whatever was inside, was very attractive to them.

Further away was a large building that looked starkly different to all the others. It had steeply curved walls and was cube shaped. It was populated by many individuals in work-a-day clothes who were going in or coming out. Mitch wondered if it was similar to a monastery. He didn't even know if these bees had religion. A statement he never thought he'd say, *ever*.

Looking at the hexagonal building they were above gave away no clues as to its reason for being there, but it seemed to form a nexus of some sort, full to bursting with beings, highly inter-connected with the other buildings.

The Virijians knew what it was. It was connected to all the surrounding hexagons with straight, very narrow walkways that again, were full of beings. The walkways looked like they had room for only one being going one way. It didn't seem wide enough to allow two-way travel. *Go figure.* From the air, it looked like a diagram depicteding a process or algorithm. Everything stemmed from the central hexagon. This place was clearly very important to the whole.

The Ajiron landed near the large hexagon. That meant *they* were in there...waiting for them probably. Mitch knew the significant question was - how would his wife react, coming close to them? Jessy prayed she wouldn't embarrass herself. But they'd evolved from a fucking insect – from a *bee* no less. She remembered that she evolved from an Ape, which made her feel slightly better, but still terrified. Her heartbeat rose and she could now feel it thumping in her chest and her neck as she contemplated the meeting. Sweat broke out over her entire body, coating it in a fine sheen, and her cheeks were burning. Her physical reaction to meeting them was *not* what she'd hoped. Jessy was drop-dead terrified. She wondered seriously if this was a hot-flush...her reaction to the Pteron.

The creatures they'd all met so far had been quite steeply humanoid, and they'd scared the hell out of her, and then there was the Virijians, she remembered the first time she saw them, *Christ, they were horrible*. Jessy had gotten used to the Virijians simply by repetition. She forced herself to look at them and listen carefully, and gradually their other more personal qualities shone through. Would that happen with these bee-people, they were far *more* different than the Virijians. Jessy's jury was completely out on that one.

At least the Virijians were humanoid. And she would have no time to get used to the Pteron, they'd just be in her face. *Fuck*, she yelled at herself, shuddering and taking a sharp breath, gazing at the ground. It would truly be a nightmare. And there was no getting around it. *Not now.* This was one situation she'd have to somehow deal with, and *not* be totally freaked out by. First impressions were critical. Perhaps, they'd find *us* ugly and difficult to look at, she thought. It made her feel a bit better thinking of it that way.

They descended and landed near the central hexagon - a horde of bee-things were kept at bay a long way away, whether it was by bodily security-like restraint or something entirely non-visual, like a high-energy particle wall, they didn't know. They couldn't make out individual beings, just a bustling mob of very strange things. Lots of arms and legs and things that were unidentifiable or peculiar, Jessy was absolutely sure, or at least pretty certain some of the unidentifiables were antennae or something as mundane as thin, hairy legs.

No doubt, the same situation was playing out on the other side of the hexagon - they were being held back there, in a similar fashion.

Two of them approached the Ajiron, they were security for entering the structure apparently. They had two legs, walked upright, had two arms with three long hairy fingers and a thumb. Their chests were huge, the clothing probably hiding a thorax and abdomen or something very bee-like. Jessy struggled to look, but she also, very oddly, felt sympathy for this thing which stood before her. She reckoned it was because it was so ugly...she felt sorry for it, like she would a blobfish or the mole back home.

Jessy pushed her toes into her shoes and held her whole body rigid, determined not to faint or do anything to embarrass her species. She knew there'd be a lot to be concerned about in this get-together. But she also knew she'd just have to suck it up. Put her big girl pants on, as it were. She realised it was first contact with this mob, so initial appearances were important.

The creature in front of them was wearing something that looked like black, baggy activewear with a big badge-thing hanging off it. The arms were thick and looked more like legs but they had hairy hands and long finger-things on the end of them that were also dark and hairy. It was above, where the real nightmare began. Jessy took a sharp intake of breath and held it. She could feel her head spinning but was determined to stay upright.

They were covered with black bristly hair and it appeared to be peeking out of their shirts as well and probably growing on a dark-brown exoskeleton which may or may not have extended downward. They were likely covered by it, was their best guess, because it peeked out top and bottom. Their large roughly triangular heads had small bumps on the side, presumably where antennae used to be and all three sets of legs, wings, proboscis and mandibles were gone. They were replaced by a small mouth with chewing teeth.

It was their eyes that were the worst part by far. Instead of five eyes, including two large compound ones for a garden variety bee, this creature had two massive round eyes, reminiscent of a giant Barn Owl, with small ebony centres surrounded by a light green iris. Overall, this was a very odd and steeply unattractive creature...to humans anyway. Their sting and pollen basket were a mystery because they were hidden by clothes but they assumed they were gone. They probably wouldn't be needed by an intelligent being.

'*Holy shit*,' Jessy whimpered quietly to Mitch, gawking at them, and stiffening every muscle she had, and retreating unconsciously backward...very slowly. Jessy tried to stay still...but she couldn't. She retreated subconsciously. 'They looked like...' She couldn't find the right word. *"Hell"* would've been a good one. Ugly or ghastly just wouldn't do and the right tone for worthwhile interaction would hardly be set if she ran the other way. Jessy tried not to be put off, but was *profoundly*, repulsed, with the Pteron. She simply had to look away. These...*things* ... looked horrific. She had to remember – this was their world - they had built everything on it. They were intelligent and self-aware beings with full consciousness and with special talents.

Mitch was staring at the Pteron and was also mortified, but he kicked open the exit on Ajiron anyway. He tried to act calm and casual and urged himself on. Jessy could tell he was overwhelmed by how stiff he was. He gestured at her with his hand to stay still and be casual and cool.

He'd leave the greegints to Zamindar who had already toned as much to Mitch. He'd stay with Jessy - she wouldn't cope with a formal meeting with these beings right now. One look at her face and body was enough of a tell-sign, he reckoned. She was right on the edge.

Zamindar went with the Pterons to first have a discussion with them about energy and the Bantha. And then, most importantly, Zamindar would speak to the Bantha, to ensure they didn't follow through on their threat against these beings. Zamindar told them that the Pteron were a rare race and required protection no matter what the Bantha believed they'd done. In short, even if they produced a little carbon beyond the deadline, cut them a break. They were pretty much irreplaceable as a species. The threat was volleyed back at the Bantha and they did the right thing and took it very seriously indeed.

It wasn't that long since humans were the only civilization the Virijians knew of. By then, many of the Virijian race thought that the Universe was comprised of them and only microbial life. Multi-cellular life took so long to get going, they reckoned it was almost a miracle – restricted only to their planet. Incredibly, they were wrong. Now the Virijians knew of a handful of races that were truly intelligent, not as advanced as them, but intelligent and self-aware all the same. It was amazing how a few years can change things. From none for many thousands of years to many in a few years.

After about an hour, Zamindar returned and didn't tone or look in any direction apart from down. It was like he was trying to hide. It was an unusual countenance for him. Normally, he was right in your face.

'Well?' Mitch's breathing and heartbeat went faster. 'How did it go - did you speak to the Bantha? Mitch asked nervously and impatiently. He didn't like Zamindar's body language. Normally he didn't have any. Looking toward the ground, wasn't him at all.

Everything went to plan,' Zamindar said, very calmly. We spoke to the Pteron and then to the Bantha and explained the Pteron's rarity, and the new commitment they had to the non-proliferation of carbon and like products in the atmosphere. I told them that their deadline could not be observed, but that we would monitor their progress in the short-term elimination of artificially produced carbon and like products. I advised the Bantha that no deadline was set and no action would be taken.' He looked directly at Mitch and Jessy. 'Oh, and we promised planetary destruction should they not like it, to all three of their home planets. And we told them exactly how we'd do it. So, it was agreed that the Pteron would continue to live uninterrupted. The Bantha agreed with our plan. They had little choice.' Zamindar concluded with a long empty stare at Mitch, which said they had little choice. 'We can't read the Bantha, so it was their words that we sought.'

'No wonder they fell over themselves agreeing with the Virijians,' Mitch said. 'Sometimes, that's how it has to be, I guess. Use aggressive words, not aggressive actions.'

Zamindar stopped toning but restarted pretty quickly. Mitch thought he heard a sigh of exasperation from Char, but he must have heard that wrong. No way he'd do that. He was a Virijian afterall. Any display of emotion, like frustration, was simply not allowed. All this time he'd never heard or seen anything that suggested anything like emotion. It was all business - they were very focussed.

'That was a good result,' Zamindar said, next stop is Virija to land and pick up some of the souls destined for Earth,' he toned, as he sat down, looking at the controls. He was all business. No time for pleasantries, he looked and acted extremely seriously. Always focussed on a plan.

*   *   *

The enormous vessel turned 180 degrees and was now headed directly toward the shift anchored in spacetime not far from Pluto, in our solar system. The nitrogen-rich, icy dwarf lived its life nearly twenty degrees out of synch with the rest of the planets. That's roughly where the black hole was. Just beyond the gravity well of both the black hole was Pluto-Charon itself.

15

Revenge

"Today's science fiction is tomorrow's science fact." — *Isaac Asimov*

The craft was travelling fast in geodesic space using its positron reactor toward the shift and their arrival was imminent. All of a sudden, they were thrust upward toward the roof, then downward toward the floor, to be left sprawled on the floor of the vessel. All of them ended up like a bunch of kelp, left behind by a receding tide.

Mitch was vaguely aware of something blaring in his ears. He felt concussed or severely off-centre as he lifted his head, noticing the loss of pressure, and then dropped his head to the floor again, under super strong gravity. Something was very wrong with the craft. It shouldn't be like this. Not surprisingly, it sounded like nothing he'd ever heard before. A deep whooping sound that clearly meant *emergency*. A large hole had been dug in both sides of the craft and the receptors were damaged, so it had significant trouble healing itself. The holes healed from the inside to out but kept breaking open – and when sealed, the material was translucent and flickering.

'What the hell happened?' Mitch stammered He and everyone else fell down again as gravity increased again, and then something else struck the ship, making a God-awful noise and giving the ship a huge jolt. Mitch fought and struggled his way over to a window, and using the ledge, he pulled himself up to look in the strong gravity. He saw about thirty white vessels in an arrow formation. *Bantha*, Mitch reckoned, had to be. He couldn't think of anybody else who would have the required wherewithal to attack this craft. They clearly weren't happy with the decision-making process that had been "somewhat" forced on them. Said a lot about their mindset, he thought. His hatred for the Bantha increased a notch, although it was already very, very high.

The huge ship continued to roll underneath them, *up, down and yawing*. The craft that attacked them were small, each about the size of a Chevrolet sedan and God knows what they packed, they weren't nukes, or anything like that, if they were, they'd be dead. Whatever the things were that they shot, they were very clean, and very destructive to this ship.

Mitch knew they had to get away from the Virijian craft. It was being turned into Swiss cheese and slowly destroyed by this mob. The squadron of small craft kept shooting at the strangely quiet and unprotected Rou.

Josh was pointing toward an Ajiron and reckoned again, that they had to get off this now hopeless craft. It might have been big, but that was half its problem. For some reason the ship remained totally exposed. Normally, the Virijians would have shielded the craft with their energetic argon-nickel plasma field, but that didn't happen – which was very odd. There appeared to be no answer to it. The Virijians were still nowhere to be seen.

'Dad?' Josh yelled as the Virijian ship moved like it was struggling on a stormy sea. They simply *had* to get off this doomed vessel. It continued to take hits. *Where the hell were Zamindar and Char?* They hadn't seen them since the Virijians ran for their survival suits when this debacle first started. Since then – *nothing*. No evasion, counter-attack or protection. Mitch knew this vessel possessed a plasma-field which protected it – where the hell was it?

The atmosphere within the ship was almost gone. All three of them had to do something definitive right *now*. And they knew what "definitive" meant. They were all huffing and puffing, nearly hyperventilating, air and pressure were almost gone. The Virijians were on their own. The humans needed to act for themselves, otherwise they were all dead. The first thing was, to get off this *fucking craft*.

It was de-pressurising fast. He wondered if there was something the Virijians knew that we didn't. Mitch didn't have time to ponder their behaviour. Normally, the craft would handle such an event easily, but filled with so many holes, it couldn't keep up with the loss of atmosphere. He wondered again what happened to the Virijians, his mind kept returning to it. It seemed very strange behaviour indeed.

Mitch turned in a full circle, they were quite literally nowhere to be seen. Maybe they were further away. They had gone to the control room, and they hadn't seen them since. But if they had gone to the control room, why were we still here like this? He didn't like the probable answer. Occam's Razor said the ship was *fucked* and the Virijians were gone.

Mitch also reckoned Ajiron would give them the best chance of escaping effectively. He'd seen Zamindar use it enough times, so he was of the belief that he could fly it successfully. If he couldn't, well...they were done,

could see atmosphere whistling milkily into the vacuum from a hundred or so holes, and the mighty atmosphere processors weren't keeping up, or were wrecked. He could feel it now. Mitch knew that it would continue and probably get worse if they kept taking hits. The onslaught from the Bantha continued. It was unrelenting. They meant business.

All the humans moved quickly into Ajiron, Mitch in the pilot's seat, Jessy next to him and Josh behind him. He put his hand over the round piece of plasticky stuff and all the doors closed for flight and the onboard atmosphere-processors turned on. Ajiron automatically moved to the edge of the huge vessel and they could see the wall trying to disappear. Step one complete,

Mitch thought gratefully. The wall that separated them from outer space shimmered and disappeared for a second and then returned, it was a bit like a fluoro coming on in reverse. Depressurisation was automatic and already complete. Eventually, it stayed open and the craft automatically departed. They could see the wall re-form properly this time, behind them, and the Rou still being peppered with non-exploding munitions.

Mitch again questioned the plasma-field - *where the fuck was it?* That would surely have protected them. Normally, they would have used it. *Where the hell were Zamindar and Char?* The question was crushing him.

Fortunately, they exited on the portside of the huge vessel away from most of the marauding fleet of small vehicles that were fairly much restricted to the starboard side. None of them had any idea what happened to Char or Zamindar. *Thanks for nothing,* Mitch thought angrily.

Apparently, they'd done a runner. Gotten in an escape pod, or the like. The lack of any toning or talk to tell them what they were doing seemed odd and out of character. The Virijians didn't engage in pleasantries or repeat themselves, but they had always kept the humans abreast of significant happenings. The fact that they were silently conversing when they left, he saw both of their calluses rippling, made it even more intriguing and worrying.

Oh well, Mitch thought, "strange race" is all he could come up with. They didn't comply with Earthly standards...*big surprise*, he reckoned. They *were aliens*, Mitch told himself. He knew how many "anythings" were possible. Their mindset remained a total mystery. Xeno-psychology was a complete unknown to humans.

Mitch put his hand fully in the gooey protoplasmic stuff in the middle of the console. He squeezed it and could feel gravity increase slightly. Turning his hand caused an equivalent turn by the craft. It was pretty easy, Mitch thought, he was getting used to it already...sort of. He was in free space, though. Of course, it was easy...*here*. There was nothing to bash into.

Mitch could see the huge craft behind him become rapidly smaller, still taking hits. At least none of them were following the Ajiron, Mitch new it had protection, but actuating it was a whole other thing. Using the Ajiron was easy enough but navigating properly was another mystery.

Earth was where they wanted to go, even though it was dead - but how in God's name do we get there? The Virijians would've plugged the RA and Declination, or whatever they used for astrogation, into the craft recently...but how to find it? Mitch had tried just about every form of stimulation and caused Ajiron to execute many unnecessary manoeuvres. He'd finally tried a sort of one-finger tickle to the protoplasm and a number of recent trips lit up on the invisible dome. At least that's what he thought they were. The symbols could've been anything, but given where they were and by a process of elimination, they'd decided on that as their meaning.

Writing in the Virijian language, meant nothing at all to him and would take him a long time to master, if he had the time and the desire. Splashed over the dome, it meant less than zero to him. It wasn't based on anything definitive. Like Earth languages, Virijian was totally subjective...of course.

Mitch looked for destinations that were repeated and were recent. They *could* be Earth, but they also might be something in the Virijian system. If they were, they were in serious trouble indeed. Because this vessel was very fast and the destination would be set until they were able to change it. He found an entry that ticked all the boxes. Time would tell if he was correct, he supposed. If they ended up in a black hole in Bode's Galaxy, he would know he was very wrong indeed.

Mitch touched the dome and it appeared on the screen in front of him. He touched it once more to confirm their destination, and it was made so. They turned quite sharply. He wiped sweat away, hoping to God he'd chosen the correct destination. One-touch astrogation was great – *if* you knew what you were doing. Afterall, this was an alien craft and capable of many things. Some, no doubt, were totally unknown to them.

They travelled into a shift and he wondered where the hell they might exit. It could literally be anywhere. They might end up at the extremity of the Universe again. He remembered Murphy's law and then wished he hadn't.

Thankfully, *surprisingly*, they appeared back in regulation space not far from Neptune, the blue ice giant that marked the very edge of our solar system. It was cold, dark and whipped by supersonic winds. It took a while to recognise the planet, but the Sun lit the double rings and Mitch spied the white spot in the atmosphere. '*Thank fuck,*' he said, tapping a fist against his chest. They were where they wanted to be.

Earth was "not far ahead". They seemed to be on track. Jessy let out a bursting breath of air at the sight of Neptune, once Mitch had finally determined what it was. She was finally back in her own system, and Jessy felt like a pig in mud.

Mitch couldn't help wondering why the Virijian ship had been attacked? And where in God's name Char and Zamindar had ended up...were they okay? It must have been the Bantha, it had to be, Mitch reckoned, totally confused and bamboozled. Those two-faced bastards. To the Virijians, they said yes, but behind their backs it was all nos... '*Scheming bastards,*' he said vehemently under his breath. Well...we'll never know, he thought, their craft, *them*, the Bantha, they were now probably light-millennia away, in Euclidean space. It was clearly a smash and dash raid, and all of them had now gone, probably back to Bantha. Mitch was trying to figure out why the Bantha had chosen not to defend their position in the first place by speaking out? Or why the Virijians had seemingly fled and toned nothing to the humans. They gave no reason for their absence at all. And then there was the protective-field used by Rou. It all seemed extremely odd - the whole *fucking* lot of it.

'I reckon they were taking revenge, of sorts...the *Bantha* I mean, to show they're not intimidated by the Virijians, or certainly by us, by destroying their vessel slowly, with non-lethal impacts. That hopefully means Zamindar and Char are okay.' Mitch peered at Josh and Jessy and held his breath, thinking hard.

*   *   *

In close Earth orbit, they spied something totally unexpected. Around the side of the planet, they saw the ISS come forth on its typical low-Earth orbit, and a *Lunar* in the process of docking. *How could that possibly be?* Mitch's mind was swimming in the deep end.

That was the thunderous question they all asked themselves. It looked most unusual, *ridiculous and bizarre*, because how *the fuck* did ISS get there? The space station *should* have been a long way away in space – they'd left it there. They watched ISS closely, totally bemused and utterly bewildered, none of them had any idea how it could possibly get to its current locale. Mitch and Josh did a double-take when they saw it. Jessy just stared, blank-eyed at it. It shouldn't be there - *period*. It was literally impossible. But somehow there it was. Nothing made any sense anymore...Mars, the ISS, He had no explanation. How the hell did the ISS get all the way here? Answer - It couldn't. Not without breaking the laws of physics, so we can cross that one out. Mitch felt like he was going to implode, he took a deep breath and tried to steady himself by leaning hard on the backrest of Ajiron.

Mitch copied Zamindar and when he hit the exosphere, which wasn't far underneath the ISS, he ensured the main "gauge" read something that looked like a circle within a circle. It looked like forty degrees too, Mitch reckoned, nodding to himself. If he came in too steep, they would have to endure a bumpy ride but they would probably survive. If he came in too shallow, they would bounce off the atmosphere and back into space, but with plenty of thrust, they could and would try again. They would get into the atmosphere sometime - sooner or later.

If they burnt up, it was game over. Would the Ajiron burn up? Mitch doubted it, but he had no real idea, if he knew what it was made of, he would have a better idea, but currently, all he knew for certain was that it was made from some softish material that glowed when touched. What thermal qualities it had - he had no idea at all. Maybe it would burn up, maybe it wouldn't. Mitch had to assume the former until or if he ever knew definitively otherwise. For the record, knowing the Virijians, he didn't think it would burn up. Mitch didn't know it was made from mainly carbon.

Travelling through the clouds, they broke into clear air at six thousand metres and flew above southern Russia, above Georgia and onto Turkey and into Africa. There were people everywhere in Russia and all the various structures looked intact like the beautiful Zhiviopisny Bridge and St. Peter's Cathedral and tall buildings in Moscow like the incredible, "twisted" Evolution tower, with people and cars everywhere on city streets and in Red Square.

All of Moscow looked fairly much untouched. How could that possibly be, he wondered? Mitch's brain was whirling in circles as he gawked at the incredible view of a populated and civilised city and quite probably, Earth. Everything in this part of the world was back and looked "normal".

Before ... they were all destroyed and the people were killed - he saw it with his own eyes. All people were gone, all the human structures demolished and pulverised. And it wasn't very long ago either. Then he remembered what happened to him and Jessy, clearly there was an issue with time. Their travels and speed had created some disconnect with Earth. It had somehow caused them to re-trace time, but this was the reverse of time dilation. Instead of jumping forward, we'd gone backward in time, where nasty paradoxes lived. Like murdering your grandfather or meeting yourself. Entire timelines could be deleted. Mitch reckoned the jury was out on that one. Mitch knew it was *fuck knows* again, but clearly something very odd had happened to the world.

Moscow through Georgia and Turkey all had tall buildings and a *lot* of people and traffic and no catastrophic damage, so they hadn't gone back too far. Was it something to do with *One*, the "lightning strike" in space or their travels at high speed? Or a combination of all of them? He didn't have a clue. But below them was the Earth of old.

'Must have been the black hole,' Jessy said, scratching at her cheek and biting her lip. 'But black holes and gravity only dilate or stop time, right?' Jessy said frowning. Which means we go forward in Earth time, *not* backward.' she said, glancing at Josh, hopeful of Mitch proffering an authoritative opinion.

'Backward time travel invokes all sorts of nasty paradoxes which can't be accounted for, right?' Mitch peered directly at Jessy.

'Well, I'm no astrophysicist, you know better than me, Jessy said, taking a deep, shaky breath.

'You're right, and I say it's wrong.' Mitch said, tapping his lips with a fist, thinking hard. 'All of it is *wrong*,' he said. He thought of the phrase, "it is what it is" and nearly vomited. 'There *has* to be a decent reason for all this...unless One are involved. They clearly have the ability to muck around with time...remember the demo.'

'Yeah...I mean, how do you explain all those people down there? Look,' she said excitedly, pointing an arm and a stiff finger. 'There are thousands of them...*everywhere*. People, structures, vegetation...*everything*. The whole lot is back,' she said, unsure whether she should scream in elation or not. Jessy decided on "not". Not yet anyway. Jessy gazed below at the untouched Chouara Tannery in Morocco. Previously it was gone in its entirety. Scrubbed clean from the landscape. It had returned and looked great – especially all the people coming out of it and going in.

'I can't explain it.' Mitch said, scratching his chin, still deep in thought. 'It all makes no sense...at all.'

To avoid all the pointing fingers from the ground, they left North Africa and flew on to the AASSA airfield near the centre of Australia, keeping low to avoid commercial aircraft. Mitch was pretty sure they thought we were a UFO and they probably didn't know how right they were.

Sean was the first on the tarmac to greet them. Mitch was the first out of the craft. 'I thought you were going to the ISS?' Sean said, looking concerned. He was nodding and blinking at Mitch with the Sun in his eyes, waiting for the answer that would hopefully put everything to bed, because sure as hell, Sean was deeply bewildered. Sean was full to bursting with questions. The first one was why they were in an Ajiron?

'It's a-long story Sean...-what is the date?' Mitch stuttered and wiped his face. Sean just stared at Mitch in silence, wondering why in God's name he wanted to know the frigging date of all things. Sean wanted to know why they were here, in an *Ajiron* of all things. A long silence ensued between all of them while Sean stared at Mitch and then the group.

He'd been asked a lot of left field questions so he just went with it, 'July 25 and it's about 1500 hours.' Sean replied suspiciously, narrowing his eyes. He turned and gawked at Ajiron and then turned back to Mitch.

Mitch looked at Sean and could tell by his slitty eyes that he was still sceptical about him and what he was doing. 'We went to the ISS and decided to try and get more familiar with the Ajiron craft. So, we flew it here and it went surprisingly well.' Mitch smiled at Jessy who tried to act like it was the truth.

'Well, you better get back, right?' Sean said, with a flat voice. He squinted at Ajiron and looked sideways at Mitch. Sean was thinking how odd it was. Sean didn't really care what he did, as long as they were all there to "greet" the Bantha when they arrived.

Mitch immediately turned on his heels and got back into Ajiron, looking deliberately at Josh, then at Jessy. They had another trip to make, all of them, to the ISS to make sure, that this time, they destroyed the Bantha craft before they had a chance to do *anything*. For whatever reason, they had another chance to do it. And this time, it needed to happen successfully.

That sort of begged the question, what would happen if your older self physically met their younger self? Nothing good, he felt sure. Perhaps, for some reason, they physically couldn't meet. They somehow were unable to meet themselves. Like two positive ends of a magnet. Paradox solved. It probably wasn't that easy. Whatever happened wouldn't be nice. If they actually met, maybe it would invoke instant dissolution involving one, or all of them. Or a more horrible paradox maybe. An explosion like antimatter colliding with matter perhaps. Or perhaps nothing, he thought.

The Quest airlock was directly ahead of Ajiron. It was fairly close to the US Lab and it was time to dock and get this over with. This time he knew what to do. He'd practiced it and thankfully, it was pretty easy to use.

Mitch hadn't forgotten what *One* had done for humanity. What that meant for their current predicament though, he had no idea at all. He had ideas but that's all they were. They weren't backed up by anything definitive.

Mitch could have docked normally if he'd chosen to. Instead, the craft sensed docking was near and sent out a piece of the clear membrane to join with the ISS which carried atmosphere. It turned opaque in its fore-section and without ever opening itself to the vacuum outside, it formed an airtight seal and a means of entering the ISS, a much different sort of entry to the great structure than they were used to. Ajiron somehow knew it was docking with an atmosphere inside ISS.

Mitch knocked on the outer hatch of ISS, which was totally unlike their normal mode of entry. Moments later the cylinders, pins and latches unlocked, after Mitch was confirmed as the knocker and his mission. The hatch opened to allow all of them access to the station. They exited the vehicle and walk-floated past hundreds of mechanical devices and were directed to the right by a T-shirt clad NASA astronaut. Incredibly, they saw Zamindar and Char looking closely at the huge gun in the US Lab. For the Virijians, it was business as usual. The backward step in time was not even a talking point.

Neither showed any interest in them, despite them giving the Virijians an effusive *hello*. It was like they'd never left. *C'est La Vie*, he supposed. He needed to remember their lack of interest might be related to time as well. God only knows how it affected them. Mitch glanced at Jessy and rolled his eyes. '*Jesus*...they're none the wiser...it never happened...they never left this

Goddamn station – it was obvious by their attitude and demeanour, Jessy thought, nodding and smiling wistfully at Mitch.

'This is it,' Zamindar toned, looking squarely at Char, 'this is the gun that must kill the Bantha, and send a message to their planet,' he toned, glancing at Mitch and Josh.

'We need to be moving laterally when they arrive,' Mitch said, 'make it harder for them to properly target us.' He guessed being a stationery target made it way too easy. The Bantha could see our gun, and they probably would, but there was nothing they could do about that – it was too late to make changes. It was what it was.

He was sure he could still target the craft though, given that he knew what their probable behaviour would be. But what if they arrived in a different position? If they did then it changes everything – including the spatial weapon they were shot with. Time wouldn't repeat. Circumstances would just happen again – meaning *anything* could happen once they appear in solar space.

'If they arrive, like before, they will fire as soon as they hit our space.' Mitch knew they would come *again*, in just over an hour. Watching him was a NASA astronaut who would take over Mitch's duties on the gun, if and when he left the ISS. Pete Riordan was watching Mitch like a hawk, taking copious notes, ensuring he would be in a position to use the weapon against any further Bantha craft, assuming Mitch destroyed the first one. If he didn't, Pete was probably dead along with everyone else.

*   *   *

Two Russian Progress craft were still attached to the ends of the ISS. They would move the platform when the time came. There were also thrusters built into the Svezda module which could also be used. It would induce rolling, pitching and yawing, perhaps all of them might be required to evade and target the alien craft. They needed to be ready for everything. But all that aside, they would shoot as quickly as they could after the craft emerged into our space.

Mitch reckoned, all things considered, it would emerge from exactly the *same* spot. He believed it would be a repeat of what happened earlier. Mitch would be ready for anything though. They couldn't take their opportunity for granted. They needed to take maximum advantage.

Essentially, they would have another chance to kill the Bantha craft. That was the way time travel or time reversal or *whatever* you called it, *worked*, wasn't it? If events were any different, they were in major trouble. And if he was honest with himself, he had no idea what would happen. They would certainly have re-think everything – if they weren't killed.

The two NASA astronauts were due to move ISS to a higher orbit in four minutes. Similarly, Zamindar and Char would use the two Progress vessels to ensure everything moved in the direction of the centre of gravity of ISS.

This time, Mitch would be behind the anti-matter gun and would aim and shoot as quickly as he could. Hopefully, it'd be like picking up a ball and throwing it in one action. He knew, last time, Zamindar hesitated, he was too careful. Targeting was essential, no doubt about it, but there could be *no* hesitation. Mitch would be ready for it, waiting for it to appear from the same spot. Any advantage from all this time-stuff would be his.

Mitch, Jessy and Josh waited in the US Lab. Mitch was behind the gun and was comforted by the green glow of the light from the weapon. He heard the Progress engines fire up then both Soyuz did the same. It was incredibly loud inside and the whole place was shaking and quaking, but gradually it settled down as the thrusters worked in harmony with each other. They had about two minutes to go, and were ready to move on demand.

Mitch was frosty behind the green light and the trigger, and telescopic sight of the gun. This thing would make mincemeat of the Bantha craft, but they, *he*, had to aim it properly first. It was no mean feat, Mitch thought as he aimed through the sight. He had to fire on target as soon as it arrived. Otherwise, those on the ISS, and those on Earth were gone.

Mitch was humming some inane tune, which annoyed Jessy no end. Still, if it helped him, *hum away*, she supposed nervously, peering through the window in front of her, the same one Mitch would aim through. Being thrust into the vacuum from a broken station didn't appeal to her at all. Nor did going on another "trip" through the cosmos. So, it was critical that Mitch fired first. Not being annihilated would be nice. The spatial weapon – *forget it.*

'One minute,' Mitch said seriously, with his game-face on tight, readying himself to move at any time. He saw his little finger flinch. What if multiple craft turn up like had just happened with the Virijians. He would kill 'em all, he thought, if that was even possible. It probably wasn't, because by the time he'd done it, poor old ISS would be so much scrap and they'd be gone. He assumed the craft would turn up and shoot exactly as it had the first time – but seriously, what if it didn't? Predicting behaviour was probably a bad idea. Murphy's law said that, and Mitch knew it. Still, anything negative *had* to be excluded from his mind. He knew that too. *Christ...*get this over with already.

He concentrated on what was in front of him and tried to put any possible scenarios out of his mind. Mitch saw Sirius the Dog star shining in his field of view of the Cosmos. Then the ship that promised death to so many billions of humans appeared right in the crosshairs of the gun, where Mitch hoped it would appear. Mitch shot, and the vehicle from Bantha was no more.

It was destroyed in the same fireball of devastation which quickly became nothing, like before. Everything it had been, or most of it anyway, whipped past them on fire, and burnt up completely in the Earth's atmosphere. Mitch let out a huge breath and all he could think of was, *"no more sheriff"*.

He was ecstatic at the outcome of both events. '*Thank you, God,*' he said to himself loudly and breathlessly. Mitch deflated like a balloon '*thank fuck for that,*' he wheezed loudly. Mitch let out a huge breath of air and watched Earth being bombarded by fiery remnants of the Bantha vessel. None were likely to hit the ground – each piece had little mass.

Mitch felt like doing a jig but he restrained himself. He got out from behind the weapon and hugged Jessy with one arm and high-fived Josh with the other hand. It seemed like a dream. Somehow, humans had prevailed. Everything that used to be the Bantha craft, was now burning up as it thumped into the thick wall of molecules that was Earth's beautiful atmosphere.

A NASA astronaut, schooled in its usage, and having watched Mitch minutely, slid himself onto the weapon's seat to take care, hopefully, of any further Bantha craft that arrived. He would wait many hours and days, in shifts of several astronauts in need. Their brief was to prevent further Bantha vessels from arriving and surviving by using the new weapon.

Jessy looked at the spot in space where the Bantha craft arrived and expected to see more following it, but space was clear of...everything, except stars in the distance. Last time, Earth was destroyed by another craft that followed the first one. The first craft was destroyed last time, so the impact of later craft must have been why Earth was devastated. So keeping a vigilant watch for any further Bantha craft was crucial so if they arrived they could be destroyed immediately.

Zamindar had said if we destroyed the first Bantha craft outright, they wouldn't follow it with more. He was wrong. The Virijian was adamant about it – which was good enough for the humans. Because he'd never been wrong. *But he was wrong.* When directly confronted about it, he refused to respond and to date he still hadn't.

Mitch felt extremely satisfied, lucky definitely, to have killed the Bantha ship, but he couldn't help deep curiosity about *why* they were afforded a second chance? Why in God's name did we get to come back and have another go? The question was festering in his mind to the point where nothing else registered in his brain. Why...why...*why?*

If they had missed, would there have been a third opportunity? And maybe a fourth and fifth...and so on? Until they were successful? Was it a reasonable answer. "Reasonable" meant it didn't break any of the laws of physics – so the bar was extremely high. The humans of course felt like they were *meant to be*. Whether this was right or wrong – who knew?

Given that they had the power to do almost anything, there was little doubt that *One* were heavily involved. All of them realised that if it was natural *and* a coincidence, it was way too much to believe. Occam's Razor was never supposed to be stretched so thin. It had to be them, *One*. It just had to be.

The humans knew they were saved by "God". *One* who created our minds and then made sure we persisted in the Universe. In short, they or he or it, refused to let humans be snuffed out of existence. What if we had been taken out for a second time by the Bantha, would we miraculously return for another go? Maybe...maybe not. Probably. *One* would demand it.

Mitch took great solace from what he hoped was true. That humanity held a special place in *One's* "world". To be special to this God-like species would be a very good thing indeed. That would mean they were like a "back-stop" to humanity, should anything go really awry, like it did.

Whatever the answer was, it really didn't matter. Earth was alive with people and cities and landmarks. Everything was in place. Fusion energy would soon be the only energy source, from the smallest country to the largest – from countries like Vatican City, Grenada and Monaco to China and the U.S.A. The world would do it, *before* the tipping point.

, the Bantha had done humanity a favour. By being shot with the spatial weapon, they had learned that "bridges" existed between supermassive black holes, and there were massive amounts of energy they could harvest from them for interstellar movement. And of course, there was the "small" issue of two-way travel inside a black hole. Also, they forced us into a change that had to happen to avoid a catastrophic atmospheric event on Earth that would've killed everything alive, from humans to mice and to plants and trees.

The Bantha were the only reason Earth would be sustainable in the next few years. The only greenhouse gas that would reach the atmosphere would not be created by humanity. It was methane from cattle that would do no damage. Nothing else would be added to the atmosphere. All transport and energy needs would be supplied by fusion reactors which were, without a doubt - *our saviour*.

Cranreb and Davtep had returned to their planet, satisfied that humanity had learned the proper methodology for fusion reactors and that the reactors on Earth were the same as theirs on their own planet.

Mitch contemplated the awfulness of seeing Earth effectively destroyed by the Bantha and its population of humans killed. There was literally no one left on the surface. The Bantha had removed humankind almost entirely. Major landmarks were annihilated – what made Earth *Earth* was gone, sand blasted away by this bastard race. It was the sixth great extinction and this one was a beauty, there was no coming back from it *because everything was gone*. BUT all of it DID come back. All Mitch could think was to thank *One*.

What would *One's* analytical thinking be? Let 'em die, see what we can learn, or save them at all costs. Only *One* would know the answer to that conundrum. From this sequence of events, Mitch reckoned their position was clearly the second one - save the species at all costs.

All humans could do was guess, Mitch thought, and it turned out, he didn't think they did that too well. *Human logic,* which supported our guesses, was just that. *Very human*. Mitch was damn certain it couldn't be relied on in the wider Universe.

One or "God" not only created us as a species, but then saved us from annihilation. We owed *One everything* - creation and salvation. If it sounded familiar...that's because it should be. The Christian Bible says so.

Mitch tousled Josh's hair and tickled Jessy in the small of her back, he knew they had beaten the odds. Somehow, humanity still existed.

One had made sure of it.

<u>The End</u>

www.ingramcontent.com/pod-product-compliance
Lightning Source LLC
Chambersburg PA
CBHW071420200726
48294CB00002B/463